FAVORITE STORIES OLD AND NEW

Favorite Stories Old and New

Revised and Enlarged Edition

Selected by

Sidonie Matsner Gruenberg

Illustrated by Kurt Wiese

DOUBLEDAY & COMPANY, INC., GARDEN CITY, NEW YORK

FOR MY GRANDCHILDREN

Peter Barnard

Daniel Barnard

Nicholas Benjamin

Elizabeth Allée

Richard Joseph

Ann Matsner

Kathryn Mary

Jean Allée

Judith Sidonie

Joel William

Matthew Alan

Richard Matsner

AND MY GREAT-GRANDCHILDREN

Joshua David

David Mark

ACKNOWLEDGMENTS

The compiler wishes here to express her genuine gratitude to Josette Frank, Staff Advisor to The Children's Book Committee of The Child Study Association of America, for valuable counsel and suggestions at various stages in the course of this project;

To Margaret H. Lesser, for interest and help far exceeding the requirements of her position as head of the juvenile department of Doubleday & Company; and, in connection with this revision, for her warm cooperation and wise suggestions;

To Helen Ferris, Editor-in-Chief of the Junior Literary Guild, for her enthusiastic encouragement and help in enlarging this collection;

To Cornelia Zagat, for her earnest and enthusiastic assistance as an experienced children's librarian;

To my son, Ernest M. Gruenberg, M.D., who, while far removed from the days of his childhood stories, helped with many decisions and selections on the basis of his wide reading and his remembrances;

To my secretary and friend, Hettie Harris, who watches over all my undertakings;

To Benjamin C. Gruenberg, for the rewriting of the myths, Bible stories, and some of the legends and fables;

To my daughter Hilda Sidney Krech, for rewriting some of the fairy tales and folk tales;

To Bella Koral, whose knowledge of the literature for boys and girls was of invaluable assistance in revising and enlarging this collection; and

To my friend, Edna Jones, for competent and intelligent aid in preparing the manuscript.

I am grateful to the following publishers, agents, and authors for permission to use the material indicated:

D. Appleton-Century Company—for "The Turtle Who Couldn't Stop Talking" and "The Monkey and the Crocodile," from *Jataka Tales*, by Ellen C. Babbitt.

Artists and Writers Guild—for "Samson" from *The Golden Grab Bag*, by Peggy Du Laney, published by Simon & Schuster, copyright, 1951.

Bank Street Schools, 69 Bank St., N.Y.—for "The Red Gasoline Pump," from *Streets: Stories for Children under Seven*, by Lucy Sprague Mitchell.

Dorothy Walter Baruch, for "Big Fellow's First Job," from *Big Fellow at Work*, published by Harper & Brothers.

Walter R. Brooks—for "Henry and His Dog Henry," copyright, 1954, from *Story Parade Magazine*, June 1954; Brandt & Brandt, agents.

Margaret Wise Brown—for "The Little Cowboy," from *The Little Cowboy* by Margaret Wise Brown, copyright, 1948, and with the permission of Wm. R. Scott, Inc.

Coward-McCann, Inc.—for "Karoo, the Kangaroo," from *Karoo, the Kangaroo*, written and illustrated by Kurt Wiese, copyright, 1929.

Dodd, Mead & Co., Inc.—for "A Week of Sundays," from *Tell Them Again Tales*, by Margaret and Mary Baker, copyright, 1934; "Rhyming Ink," from *Fifteen Tales for Lively Children*, by Margaret and Mary Baker; "Five Nonsense Verses," from *The Complete Nonsense Book*, by Edward Lear.

Doubleday & Company, Inc.—for "Black Face," from *Black Face*, by Thelma Harrington Bell, copyright, 1931; "Mr. A and Mr. P," from *The Street of Little Shops*, by Margery Williams Bianco; "The Poppy Seed Cakes," from *The Poppy Seed Cakes*, by Margery Clark, copyright, 1924; "General Store," from *Taxis and Toadstools*, by Rachel Field, copyright, 1926; "Carrie-Barry-Annie," from *Tea Time Tales*, by Rose Fyleman, copyright, 1929, 1930; "The Shire Colt," from *The Shire Colt*, by Zhenya and Jan Gay, copyright, 1931; "The Elephant's Child," from *Just So Stories*, by Rudyard Kipling, copyright, 1900, 1912, with special permission from A. P. Watt & Son, The Macmillan Company of Canada, and Mrs. Bambridge; "The Blue-Eyed Pussy," by Egon Mathiesen, copyright, 1951; "He Is Our Guest, Let's Not See His Mistakes," from *Pinocchio in America*, by Angelo Patri, copyright, 1928; "The Vegetable Tree," from *Bright Feather and Other Mayan Tales*, by Dorothy Rhoads, copyright, 1932; *Airplane Andy* by Sanford Tousey, copyright, 1942; "The Silver Flower," from *Peppi the Duck*, by Rhea Wells, copyright, 1927; Doubleday

& Company, Inc. (Garden City Books)—for "Davy Crockett" from *The Real Book of American Tall Tales* by Michael Gorham, copyright, 1952, by Franklin Watts, Inc.

E. P. Dutton & Co., Inc.—for "The Fierce Yellow Pumpkin," "The Fish with the Deep Sea Smile" and "The Good Little Bad Little Pig," from *The Fish with the Deep Sea Smile*, by Margaret Wise Brown; "Ah Tcha the Sleeper," from *Shen of the Sea*, by Arthur Bowie Chrisman; and "The Merry-Go-Round and the Griggses," from *A Merry-Go-Round of Modern Tales*, by Caroline D. Emerson; "Winnie the Pooh Goes Visiting," from *Winnie the Pooh* by A. A. Milne, copyright, 1926, renewal 1954 by A. A. Milne; "How the Singing Water Got to the Tub," from *Here and Now Story Book*, by Lucy Sprague Mitchell.

Ginn & Company—for "Why the Baby Says 'Goo,' A Tale of the Penobscot Indians," from *Myths of the Red Children*, by Gilbert L. Wilson.

Harcourt, Brace & Co., Inc.—for "The Tiger's Tail," from *The Kantchil's Lime Pit* by Harold Courlander, copyright, 1950; "The Coyote and the Fox," from *Tay Tay's Tales*, by Elizabeth Willis DeHuff, copyright, 1922; "The Middle Bear," from *The Middle Moffat*, by Eleanor Estes, copyright, 1942; "The Terrible Olli," from *Mighty Mikko*, by Parker Fillmore, copyright, 1922; "How Little Pear Wanted Both a Top and a Tang-Hulur," from *Little Pear*, by Eleanor Frances Lattimore, copyright, 1931; "Blue Silver," from *Rootabaga Pigeons*, by Carl Sandburg, copyright, 1923; "The Coming of Max," from *Max: The Story of a Little Black Bear*, by Mabelle Halleck St. Clair, copyright, 1931.

Harper & Brothers—for "Pelle's New Suit," from *Pelle's New Suit*, by Elsa Beskow; "The Magic Glass," from *The Spider's Palace*, by Richard Hughes; "The Apple of Contentment," from *Pepper and Salt*, by Howard Pyle, copyright, 1885, 1913; "Indians in the House, from *The Little House on the Prairie*, by Laura Ingalls Wilder, copyright, 1935; the Harris Family—for "The Wonderful Tar-Baby Story," by Joel Chandler Harris.

Henry Holt & Co., Inc.—for "Talk" (The Talking Yam) from *The Cowtail Switch*, by Harold Courlander & George Herzog, copyright, 1947; "The Cupboard," from *Peacock Pie*, by Walter de la Mare.

Holiday House, Inc.—for "Ol' Paul and His Camp," from *Ol' Paul, The Mighty Logger*, by Glen Rounds.

Houghton Mifflin Co.—for "The Peterkins Try to Become Wise," from *The Peterkin Papers*, by Lucretia P. Hale; "The White Hare of Inabi," from *The Wonder Garden*, by Frances Jenkins Olcott; "Johnny Ping Wing," from *The Lively Adventures of Johnny Ping Wing*, by Ethel Calvert Phillips.

Alfred A. Knopf, Inc.—for "Ballet," from *Ballet for Mary*, by Emma L. Brock, copyright, 1954.

Kohler, Julilly House—for "The Little Boy Who Wasn't Lost," copyright, 1949, in *Story Parade Magazine*, August, 1949.

J. B. Lippincott Company—for "Animal Crackers," from *Poems*, by Christopher Morley.

Liveright Publishing Corp.—for "The Boy Who Drew Cats," from *Japanese Fairy Tales*, by Lafcadio Hearn.

Longmans, Green & Co.—for "Too Heavy," from *Once the Mullah*, by Alice Greer Kelsey, copyright, 1954.

Lothrop, Lee & Shepard Co.—for "P-Penny and His Little Red Cart," by Amy Wentworth Stone.

The Macmillan Company—for "The Lion-Hearted Kitten," from *The Lion-Hearted Kitten and Other Stories*, by Peggy Bacon; "Ask Mr. Bear," from *Ask Mr. Bear*, by Marjorie Flack; "Charlie Rides in the Engine of a Real Train," from *Charlie and His Puppy Bingo*, by Helen Hill and Violet Maxwell.

Macrae Smith Company—for "The Twins and Tabiffa," by Constance Heward.

Phyllis McGinley, "The Horse Who Had His Picture in the Paper," copyright, 1951, published by J. P. Lippincott Company, Curtis Brown, agent.

William Morrow & Co., Inc.—for "Little Eddie Goes to Town," from *Little Eddie* by Carolyn Haywood, copyright, 1947.

Thomas Nelson & Sons—for "Elizabeth—The Cow Ghost," from *Elizabeth—The Cow Ghost*, by William Pène Du Bois, copyright, 1936.

Oxford University Press—for "The Sandy Mound by the Thicket," from *The Little Black Ant*, by Alice Gall and Fleming Crew.

Picture Scripts—for "The Tugboat," by special permission of Picture Scripts Editorial Board at Lincoln School.

The Platt & Munk Co., Inc.—for "How Ice Cream Came," from *How Ice Cream Came*, by Carolyn Sherwin Bailey.

G. P. Putnam's Sons—for "William and Jane," from *William and Jane*, by Dorothy Aldis; "The Princess Whom Nobody Could Silence," from *Candle-Light Stories*, selected and edited by Veronica Hutchinson.

Rand McNally & Co.—for "Pony Penning Day," by Marguerite Henry, from *Misty Chincoteague*, by Marguerite Henry, copyright, 1947, as condensed from a book *24 Horses: A Treasury of Stories*, collected by Francis Cavanah and Ruth Cromer Weir, copyright, 1950; *Space Ship to the Moon*, by E. C. Reichert, copyright, 1952; "Puddle: The Real Story of a Baby Hippo," from *Puddle: The Real Story of a Baby Hippo*, by Ruth Ann Waring and Helen Wells, copyright, 1936.

Charles Scribner's Sons—for "His First Bronc," from *Young Cowboy*, by Will James.

Frederick A. Stokes Company—for "Little Boy Pie," from *Old Sailor's Yarn Box*, by Eleanor Farjeon, copyright, 1934; "Puddleby," from *The Story of Dr. Dolittle*, by Hugh Lofting, copyright, 1920.

Story Parade—for "The Wisdom of Solomon," by Elizabeth Coatsworth, June 1947; "Almost an Ambush," by LeGrand Henderson, October 1944; "Lisa's Song," by Ruth Kennell; "The Lazy Farmer," by Jane Prescott, October, 1952.

Vanguard Press, Inc.—for *And to Think That I Saw It on Mulberry Street* by Dr. Seuss, copyright, 1937.

The Viking Press—for "The Trading Post," from *Little Navajo Bluebird*, by Ann Nolan Clark, copyright, 1943 by Ann Nolan Clark and Paul Lantz; "New Folks Coming," from *Rabbit Hill* by Robert Lawson, copyright, 1944; "The Story of Ferdinand," from *The Story of Ferdinand*, by Munro Leaf and Robert Lawson, copyright, 1936; "The Little Rooster and the Turkish Sultan," from *The Good Master*, by Kate Seredy, copyright, 1935.

Whitman Publishing Company—for "Casey Joins the Circus," from *Casey Joins the Circus*, by Dorothea F. Dobias.

John C. Winston Company—for "The Rabbit Hunt," from *The Land of Little Rain*, by Muriel Fellows.

FOREWORD TO REVISED EDITION

To Boys and Girls:

I have had many satisfactions in my long life. Among these I cherish the thought that my first collection of stories has found its way during the past thirteen years to so many thousands of boys and girls. That book was dedicated to my two first grandsons; but now I am thinking of my other grandchildren and you other boys and girls who are growing up with them.

It has been a delightful task to work at the collection again, to enlarge it and revise it. I hope it will interest you and introduce you to many different kinds of stories—and of people, too.

I have added some newer stories that have become favorites since you were born, especially a few that would not have been written for children when I gathered my first collection, like those that have to do with airplanes or space ships or ballet dancing for little girls. And I have added a few older stories that are now favorites as more and more readers have become acquainted with them, like one fairy tale by Charles Dickens. I have also chosen some from authors who have become favorites during these years.

Among the Folk Tales, I have added some from older lands which we are hearing more today, such as Persia and Old Israel and Africa.

I can only repeat my hope that this book will help you find out which are your favorite stories. More important still, I hope that these sample stories will help you find your way into the fascinating world of adventure and fun and make-believe and dreams and struggles that men and women have been writing into *books* for hundreds and hundreds of years.

Sidonie Matsner Gruenberg

New York, 1955

FOREWORD TO FIRST EDITION

To Boys and Girls:

Here is a book that I have been thinking about for a long time and I am very happy that at last it is ready for you.

It contains stories of many different kinds. There are funny stories and sad stories and stories about animals. Some of the stories are about real boys and girls and the things that happen to them every day. Some are about things that happened a long time ago. And some are about things that never could happen—not even long ago or in faraway countries.

I have been interested in children's stories and books for many, many years—when my own four children were growing up, and in connection with my work, and as one of the editors of the Junior Literary Guild. But I have always tried to keep in mind what kinds of stories all boys and girls like you enjoy hearing or enjoy reading, for I believe that everyone has a right to like what he likes. There is no story that everybody has to like or enjoy. But of course you have to try out a large number before you can make up your mind which you like best.

And you may change your mind too. You may like one kind of story best when you're little and another kind of story when you're eight or nine. And we like different stories at different times. At one time you may feel like reading a sad story and at another time you may feel like hearing a silly one.

I think it is very interesting that some stories have been told over and over again in different countries all over the world. The story of *Cinderella*, for instance, is told in China, France, England, Germany, and probably in many other countries as well. All of us know how Cinderella felt when she was left at home while her sisters went to the ball. In fact, this story has become so well loved and so well known that when someone is always treated badly and is always left out of good times we say that she is a regular Cinderella.

Some of the older stories have been told over and over in many different ways. I have tried to pick out the ones that I think you will like best.

Of course I do not expect every story in this book to be your favorite story. But I do hope that every one of you will like most of the stories. I hope this book will help you find out which are your favorite stories. For every story in this book there are hundreds of others something like it. When you know what kinds of stories you like best, you can ask your mother or father, your teacher or librarian to help you get more of the same sort. More important still, I hope that these sample stories will help you find your way into the fascinating world of adventure and fun and make-believe and dreams and struggle that men and women have been writing into *books* for hundreds and hundreds of years.

Sidonie Matsner Gruenberg

New York, 1943

CONTENTS

I Real Children and Real Things

II Stories about Animals

III Stories of Make-Believe

IV Fairy Tales

V   Folk Tales

VI   Myths and Fables

VII   Bible Stories

VIII   Tales of Laughter

Real Children and Real Things

Some of these stories are true and some of them might be true. Even if some of these things didn't really happen, they are the kind of things that do happen every day.

The boys and girls in these stories are boys and girls like you. They live in cities or in towns or on farms very much like the ones you know. Their mothers and fathers and sisters and brothers are somewhat like yours. And when the stories are about things—like wagons and boats and airplanes and steam shovels and bathtubs—the things are real things. And the happenings in these stories are the kind that really do happen.

THE LITTLE COWBOY

by Margaret Wise Brown

Once upon a time in the far wild west, there were two cowboys.
Only one cowboy was a big cowboy (big as a man)
and the other cowboy was a very little cowboy (knee high to a grass-
hopper).

One had large boots . . .
One had little boots . . .
One had a big lasso . . .
One had a little lasso . . . And they both had BIG HATS.
One had a big low voice . . .
One had a high little voice . . . And they both sang cowboy songs.

They lived in two ranch houses right near each other (miles
away). One cowboy had a big black and white pinto pony who
ate sugar from his hand,
and the other cowboy had a little black and white pinto pony who ate
sugar from his hand.

Just as the sun came up on Tuesday there were two terrible
clouds of moving dust far out across the plains . . . The cows
were running away.

So the big cowboy threw his big lasso and caught his big
pinto pony and galloped away out over the western plains after
his big cows.

The little cowboy threw his lasso, got on his little pinto pony and
galloped away out over the western plains after his little cows.

And as he rode along, the big cowboy slapped his big thighs
and sang: "I've traveled up, I've traveled down, I've traveled this
wide world all around. I've lived in the city, I've lived in town,
and I've got this much to say . . ."

And the little cowboy slapped his little thighs and sang: "Give me a great big horse and a great big plain. I'll go punching cows today." And he shot his sixshooter in the air.

Take that bull by the horns!
Take that bull by the horns!

Then the big cowboy had a big round up with a Ki Yi Yippee Yippee Ae!

And the little cowboy had a little round up with a Ki Yi Yippee Yippee Ae!

And when the big cowboy's cows were all rounded up with a fence around them,
and the little cowboy's cows were all rounded up with a fence around them,

They headed for home, just as the sun went down. And the big cowboy sang in his great big voice: "I've traveled up, I've traveled down, I've traveled this wide world all around. I've lived in the city, I've lived in town, and I've this much to say . . ."

And the little cowboy sang in his little high voice: "Give me a great big horse and a great big plain, for I'm punching cows today."

And when they were almost home, and the big cowboy galloped up to his big ranch house, and threw his ten-gallon hat into the air, jumped off his horse and tied him to a post.

And the little cowboy galloped up to his little ranch house, and threw his one-gallon hat into the air, jumped off his horse and tied him to a post.

Then they rubbed down their horses, and bedded down their horses, and gave them an affectionate pat and a bucket of oats. Just as the stars came out they opened the doors into their ranch houses, jumped into their homes and closed the doors behind them. And the big cowboy reached for his frying pan and cooked himself a beef steak.

And the little cowboy reached for his frying pan and cooked a beef steak.

And they sang a song to the lonesome moon. The stars were shining and it was all so peaceful.

WILLIAM AND JANE

by Dorothy Aldis

William liked it standing still. When he was hoeing or raking or planting seeds or picking peas he stood just as still as he could. Even when he ran he looked as though almost any minute he'd be standing still again. That's the way William was.

Jane wasn't that way, though. She liked it hopping and skipping and jumping and climbing and crawling under and wriggling over and squirming through.

"William," Jane would say to him, "why do you like it so much standing still?"

"Well," William would say very slowly, "well, Jane, because I do. Why do you like it so much hopping and skipping about?"

"Oh, because I do," Jane would say, and go running off somewhere else to play.

One day Jane had an idea. "William," she said, "how would it be if for one whole day you went skipping and hopping about the way I do and I went around standing almost still the way you do? How would that be?"

"Well," said William, "why?"

"For fun," said Jane. "To surprise my mother and father, and the twins and the twins' nurse and cook."

"Well," said William, "all right." And he went on very slowly pulling up some beets. After he had finished pulling them he put them in his basket and very, very slowly stood up straight again.

"Well," he said, "when had we better start?"

"Tomorrow morning." Jane gave a little skip. "I'll begin the first thing I get up and you begin the first thing you get up."

"Well, all right," said William, "but I don't think I'll like it very much." And he went off toward the kitchen with his beets.

The next morning when Jane got up she didn't jump out of her bed the way she usually did. No. Instead she shoved one foot out very slowly from underneath the covers, and sat and looked at it.

"Jane," said her mother, who had come in to help her button her back waist buttons, "why aren't you getting up?"

"Well," said Jane slowly, the way William said things, "I . . . am . . ." And she poked her other foot very slowly from underneath the covers and sat and looked at *it*.

"What's the matter with Jane?" called Jane's father from the next room, where he was neatly lacing up his shoes. "I don't hear her getting up."

"I don't know," called back Jane's mother. "She's acting very queerly. I wish you'd come and see."

So Jane's father came and looked at Jane too. They both stood and looked at Jane looking at her feet.

"Get up, Jane," said her father.

"Get up, Jane," said her mother.

"I'm counting, Jane," said her father. "One, two, three, four, five . . ."

But suddenly Jane's father saw something out the window.

"Goodness," he said, instead of saying six.

What he saw was William washing off the furniture in the garden. But William wasn't doing it slowly and carefully, standing still in between washes the way he generally did. No. Instead he was hopping and skipping about waving his sponge and his pail.

"William," called Jane's father from the window, "whatever is the matter?"

"Oh, nothing," called back William. "I'm just hopping. Tra-la, tra-la-la-la."

"This is very queer," said Jane's father. And he and Jane's mother ran downstairs and out into the garden. They ran as fast as they could, but when they got there William had stopped washing furniture and was off skipping underneath the cherry trees.

"William," called Jane's mother, "whatever are you doing?"

"Oh, just skipping," cried William. "Tra-la, tra-la-la-la."

"Well!" said Jane's father and mother.

And they both went in to breakfast so surprised.

"Where's Jane?" asked cook when she brought in the cereal.

"She isn't dressed yet, cook," said Jane's mother. "I don't know what's the matter with her. When we came down she was just sitting and looking at her feet. Do you suppose she's still sitting and looking at her feet?"

"I hope not," said Jane's father, "but I'd better go and see."

"Jane," he called from the foot of the stairs, "are you still sitting and looking at your feet or are you putting shoes on them?"

"No . . . Father," said Jane very slowly, from a long way off. "No . . . Father . . . I'm . . . still . . . looking . . . at . . . them . . . but . . . I . . . have . . . a . . . stocking . . . in . . . my . . . hand . . . and . . . pretty soon . . . I'm . . . going . . . to . . . put . . . it . . . on."

"I can't imagine what's the matter with Jane," said Jane's father, coming back to his cereal. "She's never been this way before. I wonder if we shouldn't call the doctor."

"The doctor?" asked Jane's mother.

But just then William went by the window. He was going down toward the garden with his hose to water the flowers. But he wasn't going down to the garden with his hose the way he generally went down to the garden with his hose. No. Instead he was playing skip rope with it.

"William!" cried Jane's father, rushing to the door. And "William!" cried Jane's mother and cook, rushing to the door.

But William didn't even look at them. He went right on playing skip rope with his hose.

"Why, this is dreadful," said Jane's father, going back to his breakfast once more. "William acting the way he is and Jane acting the way *she* is. I don't know what to think of it, do you?"

"No," said Jane's mother, "I can't think *what* to think."

"Well," said Jane's father finally, "I'll tell you what. After I've gone to work you'd better telephone me at my office and tell me just what's happening."

"All right," said Jane's mother, "I will."

So then Jane's father went upstairs to kiss Jane good-by.

Jane was standing still in the middle of the room when he came in. She had one stocking on and was looking at her shoes.

"Why, Jane"—Jane's father stared at her—"we've finished breakfast and I'm all ready to go to my office, and here you still are."

"Well . . . yes . . . here . . . I . . . still . . . am . . ." Jane said.

"Why, Jane," said her father again.

Then he couldn't wait any longer to talk to her, because he was so late. So he kissed her good-by.

"Don't forget to telephone," he called to Jane's mother, and ran down the street.

After he'd been at his office about an hour the telephone rang. It was Jane's mother.

"Jane has both stockings on now," she said, "and she's started with her shirt."

"She's only as far as her *shirt?*" asked Jane's father.

"Yes," said Jane's mother, "and William's raked a pile of leaves and now he's rolling in them."

"*Rolling* in them?" asked Jane's father.

"Yes," said Jane's mother, "around and around."

"Oh," said Jane's father, "how awful!"

"Yes," said Jane's mother. "Good-by."

So then Jane's father went back to his work. He talked to some men, and wrote his name on papers, and opened letters with his knife. But all the time he was thinking about William and Jane.

About lunch time the telephone rang again.

"Jane has her shirt on," said Jane's mother, "and she's lacing up one shoe."

"Just her shirt and her shoe since you called me last time?" asked Jane's father.

Jane's mother sounded sad: "Just her shirt and her shoe."

"And what's William doing?" asked Jane's father.

"William's crawling under the porch," said Jane's mother.

"Why?" asked Jane's father.

"I don't know," said Jane's mother. "All I can see is his feet."

"Oh," said Jane's father, "how awful!"

"Yes," said Jane's mother. "Good-by."

So then Jane's father went back to his work again. He signed his name some more, and blotted it, and threw lots and lots of papers on the floor. But all the time he was thinking about William and Jane. All afternoon he thought: "How dreadful it is to have William acting the way he is and Jane acting the way she is. I do wish Jane's mother would call me again . . ."

Pretty soon she did.

"Hello," said Jane's father when the telephone rang, "hello, hello."

"Hello," said Jane's mother. Her voice was quite weak.

"What's happening?" asked Jane's father.

"Jane has on her waist," said Jane's mother, "and her panties and one shoe, and now she's putting on her dress."

"Do you think she'll be dressed before it's time for her to go to bed?" asked Jane's father.

"I don't know," said Jane's mother.

"But what shall we do if she isn't dressed by the time it's time for her to get *undressed* again?"

"Oh, I don't know," said Jane's mother. "But won't you please hurry home?"

"What's William doing?" asked Jane's father.

"He's up in a tree," said Jane's mother. "Won't you please hurry home?"

"I'll come right away," said Jane's father. "Good-by."

So he hurried home as fast as he could, and when he got inside the gate he looked up in all the tops of the trees for William.

"William," he called. "William! Come down, William. Nice William. Come down."

But William wasn't in a tree. No, William was leaning against the side of the house with his head hanging over.

"Why, William," said Jane's father, "Jane's mother just telephoned me that you were up in a tree, so I hurried home to get you down again. Why did you climb up a tree, William?"

"Well," said William very slowly, "I wish I never had."

"Are you sorry that you did it, William?" asked Jane's father.

"Yes," said William, "very."

"And you won't climb up trees or roll in hay or hop or skip or jump rope any more the way you did today?"

"No," said William, "never. What I feel like doing," he said, "is standing very still for a long, long time." And he began to do it.

Then Jane's father went to look for Jane. He found her in her mother's room. She was all dressed with her hair ribbon on and both shoes laced. And she was skipping as hard as she could.

"Hello, Father," she said without stopping her skipping.

"Hello, Jane," said her father.

"I'm all dressed now," said Jane, giving her father a kiss without stopping her skipping.

"Isn't it funny? Suddenly she got dressed very quickly," said Jane's mother, "and started this skipping."

"I'm hopping now," said Jane. And she was.

"And pretty soon I'm going to jump," she said. And she did. And then she started climbing up, and crawling under and wriggling over, and squirming through. Just the way she always used to do.

"I'm never going to stand still again," said Jane.

And she never, never did.

LITTLE EDDIE GOES TO TOWN

by Carolyn Haywood

It was half-past three of a Saturday afternoon when Mrs. Wilson remembered that she needed a jar of cold cream. She looked around the house to see if one of the older boys was at home, but she only found little Eddie. Eddie was busy oiling an old typewriter that he had picked up in a junk shop for a dollar. It was his most recent treasure. About half of the keys were gone, and the rest made a noise like a string of freight cars going over a bridge. Eddie thought a little oil would help. He was busy pumping sewing machine oil into every rack in the typewriter when his mother found him.

For a few minutes she stood watching him. He looked very little. She wondered whether to send him for the cold cream. He had never been to the center of the city alone. He would have to change buses, and Mrs. Wilson wondered whether Eddie was big enough to change buses. At last she said, "Eddie, do you think you could go to the city for Mother? I need a jar of cold cream from Potter's Drug Store. Mr. Potter makes his own cold cream, and I like it much better than any other."

Eddie looked up with his eyes sparkling. "Oh, Mamma!" he cried. "Sure, I can go to the city."

"You know, you have to change buses," she said. "You have to change to the H bus."

"Sure! I know," said Eddie, wiping his hands on his trousers.

"Eddie!" cried Mrs. Wilson. "How often do I have to tell you not to wipe your hands on your trousers?"

"I'm sorry," said Eddie. "I forgot."

"Well now, don't forget that you are going to get cold cream.

And remember that you change to the H bus and get off at Twelfth Street."

"I know. I know," said Eddie. "And Potter's Drug Store is right on the corner."

"That's right," said his mother. "I'll write a note for you, and you can give it to Mr. Potter."

"Oh, that's the way babies go to the store," said Eddie. "I'm no baby. I'm not going to hand Mr. Potter a piece of paper. I can remember cold cream."

"Well, run along and get washed, and put on a clean blouse and your other trousers," said his mother.

Eddie went off to wash. In about ten minutes he was ready.

"I'll put you on the bus," said Mrs. Wilson, handing Eddie his bus fare. "And I'll ask the bus driver to put you off to change to the H bus."

"Oh, Mamma," said Eddie, "let me tell him. He'll think I'm a baby if you tell him. When I get in I'll say, 'I want to change to the H bus.' "

"No, Eddie," said his mother, "you must say, 'Will you please tell me where I get off to take the H bus.' Then sit close to the driver."

"Okay," said Eddie.

"And don't lose your yellow transfer that the bus driver will give you. That's your fare on the H bus."

"Okay," said Eddie.

"And ask Mr. Potter to show you where you get the bus to come home. Don't forget you have to change to the E bus to come home."

"I know," said Eddie. "I know."

"And don't forget what it is you are going for," said Mrs. Wilson. "Cold cream."

"I won't forget," said Eddie. "Rudy says if you want to remember something, you think of something that goes with it. You know. If you want to remember eggs, you think of chickens. I'll keep thinking of milk, and then I'll remember cold cream."

"You just keep thinking of cold cream," said his mother. "And tell Mr. Potter to charge it on my bill."

"But I want to do it Rudy's way. I want to think about milk," said Eddie.

"Here comes the bus," said his mother.

The bus swung up to the curb, and before the door opened Eddie said, "You won't tell the bus driver, will you, Mamma? I want to tell him."

The door opened, and Eddie stepped into the bus. He handed his fare to the driver and said, "I'm going to the city for my mother. I have to change to the H bus. I think I know where to get off, but I guess you had better tell me." Then he added, "Please."

"All right," said the driver. "Here's your transfer. Hold on to it. And sit right there."

Eddie sat down in the seat the driver pointed out. Beside Eddie sat a very fat man, so there wasn't much room for Eddie. He wriggled back on the seat, and his legs dangled over the edge.

In the seat behind Eddie sat a woman with a baby on her lap. On the seat beside her lay a large green watermelon.

The bus rolled rapidly along, and Eddie bounced a little on his seat and swayed from side to side. The straw-covered seat was very slippery, and the fat man took up the greater part of the seat.

Suddenly the bus gave a terrible lurch as it swung around the corner. All of the passengers swayed with the bus. The watermelon on the seat behind Eddie rolled off the seat. The lurch of the bus threw it forward, and it landed with a smack in the aisle of the bus. A split second later Eddie shot off his seat and "Kerplunk!" he sat right on the watermelon. The fall to the floor had already cracked the watermelon, so when Eddie sat on it, it smashed into pieces, splashing in all directions.

The bus driver drew up to the curb and stopped. "Anybody hurt?" he called out, as he turned in his seat.

Everyone in the bus was standing up. The fat man was leaning over Eddie. "Are you hurt, son? Are you hurt?" he was saying to

Eddie. Eddie was lying flat on the floor now, surrounded by pieces of watermelon. He didn't look exactly scared, but he looked terribly surprised. The man held out his hands to him and Eddie took hold of them. "There's something the matter with the seat of my trousers," he said.

"Well, stand up," said the bus driver, who had left his wheel. "Let's have a look."

Eddie got up and turned his back on the driver. Then he leaned over. The whole seat of his trousers was wet.

"Does it hurt?" said the bus driver.

"Is it blood?" asked Eddie, hoping that it was.

"No," replied the bus driver. "It's watermelon. I said, does it hurt?"

"No," said Eddie. "Just awful wet."

When the lady with the baby found that Eddie was all right, she began to think about her watermelon. "What about my watermelon?" she said to the bus driver. "I paid a dollar for that watermelon."

"I'm sorry, madam," said the bus driver, "but you had no right to have the watermelon on the seat. We charge for those seats, and you didn't pay any fare for the watermelon."

"Well!" said the lady. "We'll just see about this. I'll take it up with the company."

"Very well, madam," said the driver, as he picked up the pieces of watermelon and put them in a newspaper. When he had gathered it all up, he turned to the lady. "Madam," he said, holding out the bundle, "your watermelon."

"Throw it out," said the lady.

As he opened the door of the bus, Eddie said, "Hey! What are you going to do with it?"

"I'm going to throw it down the sewer," said the bus driver.

"Oh, Mister!" Eddie cried. "Wait a minute! Can I have a piece?"

"Sure!" said the bus driver. "Help yourself!"

Eddie selected one of the larger pieces and settled back in

his seat, while everyone, even the lady with the baby, laughed.

The fat man on the seat beside him bounced up and down when he laughed. "Here," he said, placing his newspaper on Eddie's lap, "have a napkin."

Eddie hadn't half finished his piece of watermelon when the bus driver called out, "Walnut Street. Change to the H bus. This is it, son."

Eddie scrambled off his seat, knocking the newspaper from his lap. The bus stopped, and Eddie stepped out.

"So long!" the bus driver called to him.

"So long!" Eddie called back. Then, as the door was closing, he held up the piece of watermelon and shouted, "Thanks!"

He finished the watermelon while he waited for the H bus. As it came into sight, he threw the watermelon rind down a near-by sewer. He stepped into the bus, and hoped that no one would notice his trousers. They still felt wet, and they were beginning to feel sticky.

"Fares!" said the bus driver. And then Eddie thought of his transfer ticket for the first time. He looked in both of his hands but it wasn't there. He put his hand in his trouser pocket, and pulled out a handful of odds and ends. A bunch of rusty keys, some bottle tops, a few marbles, a couple of large screws, some nuts and bolts, a small flashlight, a piece of white chalk, some broken crayons, a ball of string, and a quarter. But there was no transfer ticket.

"Sit down," said the bus driver. "I can't wait all day."

Eddie sat down and plunged his hand into his other pocket. He pulled out a handful of cornflakes. He had put them there after breakfast to nibble on. Then he had forgotten them. Now in the excitement of looking for the transfer ticket, the cornflakes fell in a shower to the floor.

At the next stop the bus driver looked around. "How are you coming?" he said to Eddie.

"I've got it some place," said Eddie.

"Try the pocket of your blouse," the driver suggested.

Eddie poked his fingers into his blouse pocket. A wide grin spread over his face, and he pulled out the yellow transfer ticket. "I knew I had it," he said, as he handed it to the driver. Then he added, "Oh, I forgot. We didn't go past Twelfth Street, did we?"

"Two more stops," said the driver.

Eddie ate his few remaining cornflakes, and at the second stop he jumped out the moment the doors opened.

He walked into Potter's Drug Store and up to the counter. Mr. Potter came out from behind a glass window through which Eddie could see shelves filled with bottles. Every time he came into Potter's he wished that he could go behind that window and play with all of those bottles.

"Hello!" said Mr. Potter. "You're Mrs. Wilson's little boy, aren't you?"

"Yes, sir," replied Eddie. "I'm Eddie."

"Well, what can I do for you, Eddie?" Mr. Potter asked.

"Mamma sent me for some . . . some . . . some . . ."

"Yes?" said Mr. Potter. "Some what?"

"Uh, some . . ." What was it his mother had sent him for? Eddie couldn't remember.

"Did she write it down for you?" asked Mr. Potter.

"No," said Eddie. "But I remember what it was."

"You do?" said Mr. Potter.

"Yes. It was, ah . . . It was, ah . . . Milk!"

"Milk!" exclaimed Mr. Potter. "Eddie, I don't think your mother sent you here for milk."

"Well, it wasn't just milk, but it was some kind of milk," said Eddie.

"Oh, I know!" said Mr. Potter. "Milk of magnesia." And with this, Mr. Potter placed a package on the counter.

"I don't think it was milk of magnesia," said Eddie.

"Maybe it was shoe milk," said Mr. Potter. "There's a shoe milk to clean white shoes. Do you think it was shoe milk?" Mr. Potter lifted a package off a shelf and placed it beside the milk of magnesia.

"Shoe milk. Shoe milk," repeated Eddie. "It didn't sound like that."

Mr. Potter's face lighted up. "I know," he said, "it was probably malted milk. Was it malted milk, Eddie?"

"Malted milk," said Eddie. "Malted milk. Well, now, maybe it was." Mr. Potter brought out the bottle of malted milk.

"No," said Eddie, wrinkling up his brow. "I don't think it was malted milk."

Mr. Potter placed his palms on the counter and leaned towards Eddie.

"Eddie," he said, "do you think it was buttermilk soap? Try to think hard. Was it buttermilk soap?"

"Buttermilk soap," muttered Eddie. "Buttermilk soap."

Mr. Potter placed a cake of buttermilk soap beside the other packages.

"Maybe it was," said Eddie, "but I'm not quite sure."

"You're sure it wasn't milkweed lotion?" said Mr. Potter.

"What's that for?" Eddie asked.

"It's for your hands. Keeps them soft," replied Mr. Potter.

"Milkweed, milkweed," Eddie mumbled to himself. "Milkweed."

"Well, one of these must be right," said Mr. Potter. "Tell you what we'll do. I'll put all of these things in a bag and you take them home to your mother. She can bring back the ones she doesn't want."

"Okay!" said Eddie, joyfully. "That's a good idea, Mr. Potter."

Mr. Potter placed all of the packages in a large paper bag. "I'll charge this on your mother's bill," he said. "You tell her she can return what she doesn't want."

Eddie took the bag in his arm. Then he said, "My mother said, 'Will you please show me where to get on the bus to go home?' "

"Why, of course," replied Mr. Potter, coming out from behind the counter. "Come along."

Mr. Potter walked outside with Eddie. "You get the H bus right over on that corner. Now wait until the light changes."

Eddie watched the traffic signal. When it turned green, Mr. Potter said, "Now, go ahead. And remember to change to the E bus at Walnut Street."

Eddie ran across the street with his large package. As he reached the pavement he could see the H bus coming. Just as it swung up to the curb, Eddie thought of milk again. Milk. The door opened and he put one foot on the step. Then he jumped back. He looked at the traffic signal. It was green. He dashed across the street and into the drug store. He ran up to the counter and put down his bundle. Then he shouted, "Cold cream! It was cold cream!"

Mr. Potter came out from behind his window. "So! It was cold cream! Are you sure?"

Eddie nodded his head very vigorously. "Yes, Mr. Potter. I know it was cold cream. Do you want to know how I know?"

"Yes," said Mr. Potter. "How do you know it's cold cream?"

" 'Cause I kept remembering milk," said Eddie.

THE GOOD LITTLE BAD LITTLE PIG

by Margaret Wise Brown

Poor little pig. He lived in a muddy pigpen, in an old pigpen of garbage and mud, with four other little pigs and an old mother sow. He was a little white-pink pig, but the mud all over him made him look pink and black and gray-pink.

Then one day a little boy named Peter asked his mother if he could have a pig.

"What!" said Peter's mother. "You want a dirty little bad little pig?"

She was very surprised.

"No," said Peter. "I want a clean little pig. And I don't want a bad little pig. And I don't want a good little pig. I want a good little bad little pig."

"But I never heard of a clean little pig," said Peter's mother. "Still, we can always try to find one."

So they sent the farmer who owned the pig a telegram:

"Farmer, Farmer
I want a pig
Not too little
And not too big
Not too good
And not too bad
The very best pig
That the mother pig had."

The farmer read the telegram, and then he went out to the pigpen and looked at the five little pigs. Three little pigs were fast asleep. "Those," said the farmer, "are good little pigs." And one little pig was jumping all around. "That," said the farmer, "is a bad little pig." And then he heard a little pig squeak, and then he heard a little pig squeal. But when he looked, there was just one little gray-pink pig standing on an old tin pan in the corner of the pen. "That," said the farmer, "is a good little bad little pig." And he reached in and grabbed the little pig by the hind legs and put him in a box and sent him by train to Peter.

When the express man brought the little pig to Peter's front door, his mother said, "What a dirty little pig!" And the pig said, "Squeak squeeeeeeeeeeeee ump ump ump." And Peter said, "Wait till I give this little pig a bath." But when they let the little pig out, he ran all over the room squealing like a fire engine.

"What a bad little pig!" said Peter's father, and he had to catch the little pig by the hind leg to make him hold still while Peter put the red leather dog harness around the little pig's stomach.

"Wait," said Peter, "until the little pig knows us. He is not a bad little pig." And he clipped a red leather leash on the little pig's harness.

The little pig stared at Peter out of his blue squint eyes, and then he shook himself and trotted after Peter on the leash.

"What a good little pig!" said Peter's mother, as she came in the room with a pan of bread and milk for the little pig to eat after his journey.

"Wait," said Peter. "Remember this is a good little bad little pig."

"Galump gump gump gump gump." The little pig was eating. He seemed to be snuffling and sneezing into his food as he ate.

"What a bad little pig!" said the cook, who had come in to see how the little pig was enjoying the bread and milk. "What terrible eating manners he has!"

"But he does enjoy his food," said the little boy.

"Yes," said the cook, "he does enjoy his food." And she beamed with a smile all over, for the cook did dearly love for anyone to enjoy his food. "What a good little pig," she said. "He has eaten up everything in the pan."

"Come on, you good little bad little gray-pink pig," said Peter, "I will give you a bath so you will be a clean little white-pink pig."

So Peter and his mother and his father and the cook all went into the bathroom and put the little pig right into the bathtub and let the warm water run all over him. The little pig squeaked and squealed and wiggled all around. But Peter's mother held his front legs and his father held the little pig's hind legs, so that the little pig couldn't kick himself or the people who were bathing him. The little boy took a big cake of white soap and rubbed it all along the pig's back until he was all covered with pure white soapsuds. Then he took a scrubbing brush, and he scrubbed and he scrubbed right down through the bristles on the little pig's back to the little pig's skin. He scrubbed and he scrubbed until the pure white soapsuds were all black and gray. Then he poured warm water over the pig's back until there was no soap on it. Then he put some more soapsuds all over the little pig's back. And he scrubbed and he scrubbed and he scrubbed and he scrubbed and he scrubbed until the pure white soapsuds were all gray and black again. Then he rinsed off the pig's back with warm water and put more soapsuds on. But this time the soapsuds stayed almost pure white. So he left them on the little pig's back and washed his stomach and his feet until he was all clean

and white and pink from the tip of his tail to the tip of his nose. Then they dried the little pig with a great big bath towel, and Peter took him for a walk in the sunshine.

"Look," said Peter as he showed his little pig to the policeman on the corner. "Did you ever see such a fine little clean little pig?"

"I never did," said the policeman, "see such a good little pig." And he blew his whistle and stopped all the automobiles so that Peter and the little pig could get across the street.

But the little pig did not want to get across, and he pulled back on the red leather leash and refused to budge. Peter pulled and he pulled, but the little pig would not go across the street.

"What a bad little pig!" said the people in the automobiles, and they began to honk their horns. And the little pig began to squeal and squeak. "Squeak squeeeeeeeeee ump ump ump." But the policeman held up his hand and wouldn't let the automobiles go. Then he came over to Peter and his pig.

"You pull him, Peter," he said, "and I'll get behind him and push." So they did. And when they got to the middle of the road, the little pig trotted on after Peter just as nice as you please. "What a good little pig," said the people on the other side of the street.

And so it was that Peter got just what he wanted. A good little bad little pig. Sometimes the little pig was good and sometimes he was bad, but he was the best little pig that a little boy ever had.

HOW THE SINGING WATER
GOT TO THE TUB

by Lucy Sprague Mitchell

Once there was a little singing stream of water. It sang whatever it did. And it did many things from the time it bubbled up in the faraway hills to the time it splashed into the dirty little boy's tub. It began as a little spring of water. Then the water was as cool as cool could be for it came up from the deep cool earth all hidden away from the sun. It came up into a little hollow scooped out of the earth and in the hollow were little pebbles. Right up through the pebbles, bubbling and gurgling it came. And what do you suppose the water did when the little hollow was all full? It did just what water always does, it tried to find a way to run down hill! One side of the little hollow was lower than the others and here the water spilled over and trickled down. And this is the song the water sang then:

"I bubble up so cool
 Into the pebbly pool.

Over the edge I spill
And gallop down the hill!"

So the water became a little stream and began its long journey to the little boy's tub. And always it wanted to run down—always down, and as it ran, it tinkled this song:

"I sing, I run,
In the shade, in the sun,
It's always fun
To sing and run."

Sometimes it pushed under twigs and leaves; sometimes it made a big noise tumbling over the roots of trees; sometimes it flowed all quiet and slow through long grasses in a meadow. Once it came to the edge of a pretty big rock and over it went, splashing and crashing and dashing and making a fine, fine spray.

It sang to the little birds that took their baths in the spray. And the little birds ruffled their feathers to get dry and sang back to the little brook. "Chin-a-ree!" they sang. It sang to the bunny rabbit who got his whiskers all wet when he took a drink. It sang to the mother deer who always came to the same place and licked up some water with her tongue. To all of these and many more little wild wood things the little brook rippled its song:

"I sing, I run,
In the shade, in the sun,
It's always fun
To sing and run."

But to fish in the big dark pool under the rocks it sang so softly, so quietly, that only the fishes heard.

Now all the time that the little brook kept running down hill, it kept getting bigger. For every once in a while it would be joined by another little brook coming from another hillside spring. And, of course, the two of them were twice as large as each had been alone. This kept happening until the stream was a small river—so big and deep that the horses couldn't ford it any more. Then people built bridges over it, and this made the small river feel proud. Little boats sailed on it too—canoes and sail boats and row boats. Sometimes they held a lot of little boys without any clothes on who jumped into the water and splashed and laughed.

At last the river was strong enough to carry great gliding boats, with deep, deep voices. "Toot," said the boats, "tootoot-toooooooooot!"

And now the song of the river was low and slow as it answered the song of the boats:

"I grow and I flow
 As I carry the boats,
 As I carry the boats of men."

After the little river had been running down hill for ever so long, it came to a place where the banks went up very high and steep on each side of it. Here something strange happened. The little river was stopped by an enormous wall. The wall was made of stone and cement and it stretched right across the river from one bank to the other. The little river couldn't get through the wall, so it just filled up behind it. It filled and filled until it found that it had spread out into a real little lake. Only the people who walked around it called it a reservoir!

Now in the wall was just one opening down near the bottom. And what do you suppose that led to? A pipe! But the pipe was so big that an elephant could have walked down it swinging his trunk! Only, of course, there wasn't any elephant there.

Now the little river didn't like to have his race down hill stopped. So he began muttering to himself:

"What shall I do, oh, what shall I do?
 Here's a big dam and I can't get through!
 Behind the dam I fill and fill
 But I want to go running and running down hill!"

If the pipe at the bottom will let me through
I'll run through the pipe! That's what I'll do!"

So he rushed into the pipe as fast as he could for there he found he could run down hill again! He ran and he ran for miles and miles. Above him he knew there were green fields and trees and cows and horses. These were the things he had sung to before he rushed into the pipe. Then after a long time he knew he was under something different. He could feel thousands of feet scurrying this way and that; he could feel thousands of horses pulling carriages and wagons and trucks; he could feel cars, subways, engines—he could feel so many things crossing him that he wondered they didn't all bump each other. Then he knew he was under the Big City. And this is the song he shouted then:

"Way under the street, street, street,
I feel the feet, feet, feet.
I feel their beat, beat, beat,
Above on the street, street, street."

And then again something queer happened. Every once in a while a pipe would go off from the big pipe. Now one of these pipes turned into a certain street and then a still smaller pipe turned off into a certain house and a still smaller pipe went right up between the walls of the house. And in this house there lived the dirty little boy.

The water flowed into the street pipe and then it flowed into the house pipe and then—what do you think?—it went right up that pipe between the walls of the house! For you see even the top of that dirty little boy's house isn't nearly as high as the reservoir on the hill where the water started and the water can run up just as high as it has run down.

In the bathroom was the dirty little boy. His face was dirty, his hands were dirty, his feet were dirty and his knees—oh! his knees were very, very dirty. This very dirty little boy went over to the faucet and slowly turned it. Out came the water splashing, and crashing and dashing.

"My! but I need a bath tonight," said the dirty little boy as he heard the water splashing in the tub. The water was still the singing water that had sung all the way from the faraway hills. It had sung a bubbling song when it gurgled up as a spring; it had sung a tinkling song as it rippled down hill as a brook; it had crooned a flowing song when it bore the talking boats; it had muttered and throbbed and sung to itself as it ran through the big, big pipe. Now as it splashed into the dirty little boy's tub it laughed and sang this last song:

"*I run from the hill—down, down, down,*
  Under the streets of the town, town, town,
  Then in the pipe, up, up, up,
  I tumble right into your tub, tub, tub."

And the dirty little boy laughed and jumped into the Singing Water!

THE RABBIT HUNT

by Muriel Fellows

Sah-mee had never been on a rabbit hunt, but he had heard Father tell about it many times, so he knew just what to do. Father had said that the men and boys would beat the bushes and make a great noise. This would frighten the rabbits and they would try to get away. Then the men and boys would throw their rabbit sticks or shoot their arrows and kill the rabbits.

Sah-mee was excited. His black eyes sparkled. He beat the bushes and shouted. Just then a little animal ran out of the bushes. It was very much frightened. It ran toward Sah-mee instead of running away from him. Sah-mee saw that the little animal was a baby fox. Sah-mee forgot that he wanted to kill a rabbit. He forgot that he wanted to be a great hunter. He thought only of the poor, little, frightened baby fox.

Sah-mee saw that the little thing was too tired and frightened to run away. He took it up in his arms. "Poor little fox," he said gently. He stroked its ears, and the little animal tried to get away. "I will not harm you," he whispered. "I will take you home to Moho and she will keep you for a pet." Sah-mee looked around for Father but could not find him. Father and the others had gone farther away into the desert in search of rabbits. Sah-mee was not frightened. He knew the way home. He could not hunt and take care of the baby fox, too. Besides he was more tired than he had ever been before.

Sah-mee started up the steep trail to the village. He held the baby fox tightly in his arms. When he was about halfway up the trail, Sah-mee remembered that he had left his rabbit stick lying under a sage bush in the desert. "I will go back and get it tomorrow," he thought to himself.

The trail seemed very steep and rough and rocky to Sah-mee. He could feel the heart of the frightened little fox thumping against his own. "We will soon be home," he whispered into the little brown ear.

Sah-mee's little sister, Moho, was waiting for Sah-mee to come home. When she saw him coming, she ran out of the house to meet him. "How many rabbits did you bring home, Sah-mee?" she called.

Then suddenly, she caught sight of the little brown bundle of fur in Sah-mee's arms. Moho was very much excited. "What have you there?" she asked.

"It isn't a rabbit," answered Sah-mee. "It is a little fox. I couldn't kill him, Moho, for he is only a baby. I brought him to you for a pet."

Moho understood. She reached out and took the little animal

in her arms. "I always wished for a little fox for a pet," she said.

By and by Father and the other men and boys came home, bringing many rabbits with them. They had missed Sah-mee and had hoped to find him at home, so they were glad to see him waiting for them.

The Indian women were all ready to make the rabbit stew.

Sah-mee was a little worried. He wondered what Father and the others would say. To go on a rabbit hunt and not bring home one rabbit! To go on a rabbit hunt and bring home a fox! He hoped that the boys would not laugh at him.

"I caught a little fox," said Sah-mee to Father. "I could not kill him because he is just a baby. I brought him to Moho for a pet."

Father smiled. He put his hand on Sah-mee's head. "You are a good boy, Sah-mee," he said. "We killed so many rabbits that there will be food enough for all for many days. I am glad that you remembered that a good Indian never kills a baby animal."

THE LITTLE BOY
WHO WASN'T LOST

by Julilly House Kohler

Once upon a time there was a boy named Peter, who lived on a farm in the country. Not a very big farm, but a pleasant one, with fields and brooks and a river, and woods near enough to have fun in.

One day in the late summer Peter said to his mother, "Mother, this afternoon I want to pick blackberries in Mr. Buck's woods."

"Very well," said his mother. "There's nothing your daddy

loves better than a blackberry pie. Run along, but don't go too far in the woods and come home in time for supper."

So Peter took a berry pail and off he went toward Mr. Buck's woods. First he crossed the road, looking very carefully in both directions to make sure there was no truck or tractor or hay-wagon coming. Next he trudged across Mr. Jensen's big oat field, hot and rough and full of stiff stubble left after the tall oats had been cut. Then he squeezed, very carefully, under the barbed wire fence, and there he was at last, at the edge of Mr. Buck's woods.

Then he saw the blackberries, dark and ripe. "Plup!" went each fat berry as it slipped neatly from its greenish-white stem. "Pling!" went each fat berry as it bounced merrily into the tin berry pail. Sometimes there wasn't any "Pling!" because the berry went into Peter's mouth, instead. The pail grew heavy and the sun was hot. Peter looked around for a place to cool off.

Down at the bottom of the slope the brook twisted and flashed in the sun. Down he raced. Quickly he pulled off his shoes and socks and scrunched his toes in the sandy bottom of the cool water.

Finally he went back to get his berry pail. "I have enough berries for the biggest pie in the world," he thought. Suddenly he heard a rustle behind him. Out of the bushes marched five baby pheasants. They were going for a walk all by themselves. "Look at that!" breathed Peter. "They haven't even grown their tail-feathers." He picked up his berry pail and followed the pheasants into the woods.

But baby pheasants can run fast. In a few minutes Peter was deep in the pine woods, and too tired to take another step. He threw himself down on some soft moss under a big tree and soon he was fast asleep.

When he opened his eyes again it was almost dark. The birds had stopped chirping. The woods were very still. Peter felt around for his berry pail. He took a few steps one way; then he took a few steps another way, but he really did not know which way to go. Down he sat under the big tree again.

"There is no sense in walking in the woods at night," he thought. "I'll just have to wait here for Daddy to come and take me home."

Being a sensible boy he was really not the least bit afraid. He had lost his way, but he himself was not lost. He knew exactly where he was. He was in Mr. Buck's woods—which was at one end of Mr. Jensen's oat field—which was across the highway—which ran along in front of his own farmhouse. That's where he was, all right, and his mother knew it and would tell his daddy, who would soon come and get him if he didn't come home for supper.

Just the same, Peter began to feel hungry. He thought of the blackberry pie his mother was going to make. Then he began to think of all the other beautiful things to eat in the world.

"Maybe, if I say them out loud," he said to himself, "it will make me feel more cheerful." So he took a deep breath and began.

"Hamburgers," he said, "in crunchy buns; orange-pop, like at the circus.

"Spaghetti," he said, "with lots of cheese and tomatoes; and baked potatoes, bursting in the middle." His tummy gave a little groan, and he hurried to cheer it up some more.

"Corn on the cob," he said, in a louder voice, "and lamb chops that you eat with your fingers; and peach ice cream; and oatmeal in the winter time; and devil's food cake; and thick vegetable soup; and carrots, with oodles of butter. . . ."

"Carrots?" said a curious voice not two inches away from Peter's ear. "Did I hear somebody mention carrots?"

"Yes," said Peter in surprise, trying hard to see who was speaking to him, "I mentioned carrots, with lots of butter and salt."

"Waste of time," said the voice, this time close to Peter's other ear, "putting anything on 'em. Eat 'em the way they grow; the more the better. Shall we go and get some now? I was just about to start when I saw you sitting here."

"Who are you?" asked Peter, more surprised than ever. But he need not have asked, for at that very moment the big, round, cherry-colored moon rose full above the edge of the world and Peter could see who it was.

It was a big, gray rabbit.

"Why, you're a rabbit!" said Peter in amazement. But the rabbit did not seem amazed at all.

"Of course, I'm a rabbit," he said rather scornfully, "and you're a boy. Anybody can see that. Now shall we go for those carrots? I can't wait all night."

"Well . . . I'm not sure that I'd better go with you," said Peter slowly. "You see, I'm waiting for somebody to come and find me."

"What do you mean 'find you'? I found you, didn't I? And besides," said the rabbit, "why do you have to be found? You know where you are, don't you?"

"Oh, yes, I know where I am. I'm just not sure where my home is," Peter explained. "You see, I came to the woods to pick blackberries, and——"

"Boys are silly," the rabbit interrupted rather rudely. "If they ate more carrots and less blackberries they could see much better in the dark. And if they weren't so particular they could find any number of good homes right here in these woods. I do. Oh, I have nothing against blackberries. Their bushes and briars make about the best kind of house that a rabbit could ask for; but I'd never waste a minute on the berries themselves. Carrots, now; there's something you can really put your teeth in."

The rabbit looked at Peter, and Peter looked at the rabbit, and for a moment neither one spoke. The moon was climbing steadily up the sky, not quite so close and friendly now, but pinky silver and cool. The woods were lighter, and the lighter they became the bigger the rabbit seemed to become, too. Peter began to feel he would miss the rabbit very much if he went without him. Besides, he rather thought the rabbit really wanted him to come along. So——

"All right," said Peter, and he smiled at the rabbit. "Thank you very much. I will come with you and I do like carrots just as they grow, particularly if they're good ones."

"Good ones? These carrots are the best carrots in the country; and I should know. I've tasted a lot of carrots in my days and nights, and I think I can positively say that, for crispness and sweetness and size and color, the carrots I'll take you to right now would take a prize at Rabbit Hill itself. Come along. Follow me!"

With a jump and a turn and a twist the big, gray rabbit streaked away into the shadows so fast that Peter didn't even see which way he went.

"Wait!" he cried. "Wait for me! I must get my berry pail and I can't go as fast as you."

"Oh, of course," said the rabbit, bouncing back into a patch of moonlight, "I forgot. You're only a boy. I'll try to go more slowly."

"Fence here!" shouted the rabbit over his shoulder a minute later, without slowing up. "Slide under fast." And he was through in a flash.

"Oh, I can't," cried Peter. "Wait! Wait for me! I must push the berry pail through first, and then step down on this bottom wire, and lift up the next one, like this, and squeeze between very slowly—— Oh, dear, I almost caught my shirt on one of these sharp points."

"Boys!" snorted the rabbit. "I suppose I'll never understand them." And off he went through the plowed field that stretched out ahead in the moonlight.

The plowed field was very long, and really, Peter thought, very plowed. He never could seem to find one furrow to walk in, but had to walk crossways over the deep ridges, up and down, stumbling and dropping unexpectedly from a high spot to a low spot. The rabbit, however, scooted like lightning ahead of him, and hardly seemed to touch the ground. Peter hated to ask him to wait or to stop to rest and did his best to keep up, but finally his shoes were so full of dirt and stones and sandy stuff that he felt he simply could not walk any further.

"Wait!" he called to the rabbit. "Oh, please wait just once more. You see, my shoes are full of stones and dirt and I think I'll just have to stop a minute to take them off and dump them out. I'll try not to be very long." And he sat right down and struggled with the knots in his shoelaces and tugged and tugged and finally got his shoes off and poured simply buckets of stuff out of them. The gray rabbit meanwhile sat and looked at him and seemed to grow bigger every minute. But all he said was "Boys!"

After that, it wasn't so bad. They reached the end of the field and walked on solid grass for a while and then, for some reason, they stopped. Only this time, it was the rabbit who stopped.

"Now here," said the rabbit, and his voice, for the first time, sounded rather scared, "this is really the most dangerous place on the whole trip. Right here—on this enormous, hard path— there are monsters roaming."

"Monsters?" said Peter.

"Monsters," repeated the rabbit. "Tremendous monsters with eyes as big as moons that shoot fiery lights as they look for you. Monsters with voices that sometimes roar and sometimes bellow. Look out! Here comes one now."

Peter looked and what he saw made him grin and then giggle and then pretty soon he was shouting with laughter until there were tears in his eyes.

"Silly!" he said, when he could get his breath. "Those aren't monsters. Those are automobiles. Those are not eyes shooting fire; they're headlights to keep the driver from hitting you. They don't roar or bellow. They just sound a horn to tell you to get out of the way." And Peter looked at the rabbit as though he really liked him for the first time and the rabbit looked back the same way.

But all Peter said was "Rabbits!" and he grinned.

When they had crossed the road, with Peter's help, the rabbit said, "Well, we're here at last, and I, for one, think it's about time. Just follow me, now, and don't make a noise, and in a few minutes we'll be in clover. Or rather, carrots. I can smell them already. Isn't it heavenly? Look! There they are just waiting for us. I'll take this row and you can take the next. Well, here goes." And the only thing Peter heard after that was a pawing and a nibbling and a munching, as the hungry gray rabbit settled down to his feast.

But Peter didn't so much as bend down and pull one crisp, sweet carrot. Peter just stood there and looked all around and strained his eyes to see in the pale moonlight.

"Rabbit," he said softly, "Rabbit, are there, by any chance, beans growing in the next row to this?"

"Don't bother with them," said the rabbit, with his mouth full. "They're old and woody and the new ones are just coming along."

"Rabbit," went on Peter, and he began to sound very excited, "Rabbit, are there big Spanish onions in the row next to that? Are there?"

"Onions? Yes, there are," said the rabbit without raising his head, "but who in the world would want onions?"

"I would. Oh, I would!" shouted Peter. "I would want onions and beans and carrots. Because I planted them and this is my very own garden and I am home!"

And he began to run as fast as he could toward the pretty white house gleaming in the moonlight. Just as he reached the front steps, the door swung open wide and there stood his mother and daddy, and his daddy had a big lantern in his hand.

"Mother," said Peter, and the words came so fast he could hardly say them, "I didn't mean to go too far or stay too late, and I brought the blackberries for Daddy's pie, and a rabbit brought me home and is eating carrots this very minute in my garden."

"I know," said his mother softly. "I know. And when he gets through with the carrots in your garden, he's welcome to the carrots in mine."

"I like blackberry pie much better, anyway," said his daddy.

And they all went into Peter's warm, pleasant house and closed the door behind them.

THE TUGBOAT

Picture Scripts

Puff, puff, puff!
The busy little tug, Jo Anna, steams along the river.
Swish! She cuts the water in front of her.
She splashes white spray all around.
Little ripples run along behind.
Out the Jo Anna hurries into the bay.
Her tall captain is up in the pilot house.
He steers the Jo Anna's shining brass wheel.
His eyes are watching, watching every minute.
He looks far out over the water.
He is looking for the bell buoys that tell him where danger is.

He watches all the boats that are coming into the harbor.
He watches the boats that are going out.
Toot! He blows one long whistle to a ferry boat near him.
The whistle says to the ferry boat, "Look out, ferry boat.
   I am going to pass you on the port side."

The ferry whistles back, "Toot! Go ahead!"
On goes the Jo Anna.
She leaves the ferry boat far behind.
The Jo Anna's captain looks out over the harbor.
His eyes keep watching, watching.

Suddenly he says,
　　"Ah, here she comes!
　　Here is the Nancy Brown.
　　Now, Jo Anna, you must get to work.
　　Come along and pull
　　that clumsy old giant
　　into her dock."

Slowly the Jo Anna steams along toward a great big freighter.
The freighter is the Nancy Brown.
She has a cargo of bananas in her hold.
She comes from South America.

The Nancy Brown sees the Jo Anna coming.
She waits.
Her propellers hardly turn.
The little Jo Anna puffs up
　　along the side
　　of the big freighter.

The Jo Anna's captain calls out to the mate high up on the deck of
　　　　the Nancy Brown,
"Stand by, Mr. Mate.
　　Here comes our rope."
Up shoots a rope from the Jo Anna,
　　high up to the bow of the Nancy Brown.
A seaman on the Nancy Brown catches it.
He makes it fast to the freighter.
Chug, chug!
Along comes another tug.
She shoots her rope high up to the freighter.
The seamen on the Nancy Brown fasten it tight.
The tug bumps its nose up against the stern of the freighter.

The tugs have pads of rope on their bows and on their sides.
The rope keeps the big boats from getting scratched.
It protects the tugs too.

The Jo Anna's captain goes aboard the Nancy Brown.
He climbs up a rope ladder to the bridge of the freighter.
He waves his hands at the tugs.
He blows his whistle.

Soon the freighter is on its way to its dock.
The tugs puff hard at their work.
They leave a white froth in the water.
They puff and they push at the big giant.
The Nancy Brown comes close to its dock.

The seamen throw big ropes down from the Nancy Brown to the dock.
The ropes are tied fast to the dock.
The Nancy Brown is safe at home.
Soon she will unload all of her bananas.
But the little tugs have other work to do.
They turn and chug away.

Off puffs the Jo Anna.
Her captain says,
> *"Do you know what you have to do next,*
> *Jo Anna?*
> *You have to help push a big liner*
> *out of her dock.*
> *So chug along now."*

The Jo Anna chugs along up the river.
A big liner is waiting at her dock.
She is ready for her long ocean voyage to Europe.

Six other tugs are there to help, too.
The great liner lets the ropes go which hold her to her dock.

Her engines begin to roar.
The little tugs push their noses up against her.
They puff and they tug and they pull.
The tugs push the liner out into the river.

Then they swing her around toward the bay.
Her propellers kick up a white froth.
Off steams the liner. Too-oo-oot!
The Jo Anna has helped her off on her long voyage.

Ding! Dong! The Jo Anna's cook rings the bell for lunch.
"Good," says the captain.
"Lunch is what this captain needs."
He turns and calls, "Hey there, Mr. Mate!
    It's your turn at the wheel."

The mate comes running up to the pilot house.
The captain turns the wheel over to him.
Then he rushes downstairs to the galley.
Some of the crew are there already.

The captain and the crew sit down at a long table.
The cook brings them meat and potatoes and other good things to eat.
There are eight men in the crew of the Jo Anna—all big and strong.
They work hard all day long
    and they must have plenty of good food.

The Jo Anna works hard all day long too.
She brings in big freighters.
She starts great liners off on long voyages.
She takes ships out of dry dock.

She tows barges up the river.
She starts oil tankers off to South America.

It is late in the day
  when the Jo Anna's work is done.
She goes to her own dock
  and is tied there safely for the night.

Her crew leave the decks scrubbed clean.
They take off their work clothes.
Then they go to their own homes.
Now the Jo Anna may rest
  after her long day's work.

PELLE'S NEW SUIT

by Elsa Beskow

There was once a little Swedish boy whose name was Pelle. Now, Pelle had a lamb which was all his own and which he took care of all himself.

The lamb grew and Pelle grew. And the lamb's wool grew longer and longer, but Pelle's coat only grew shorter!

One day Pelle took a pair of shears and cut off all the lamb's wool. Then he took the wool to his grandmother and said:

"Granny dear, please card this wool for me!"

"That I will, my dear," said his grandmother, "if you will pull the weeds in my carrot patch for me." So Pelle pulled the weeds in Granny's carrot patch and Granny carded Pelle's wool.

Then Pelle went to his other grandmother and said: "Grandmother dear, please spin this wool into yarn for me!"

"That I will gladly do, my dear," said his grandmother, "if while I am spinning it you will tend my cows for me." And so Pelle tended Grandmother's cows and Grandmother spun Pelle's yarn.

Then Pelle went to a neighbor who was a painter and asked him for some paint with which to color his yarn.

"What a silly little boy you are!" laughed the painter. "My paint is not what you want to color your wool. But if you will row over to the store to get a bottle of turpentine for me you may buy yourself some dye out of the change from the shilling." So Pelle rowed over to the store and bought a bottle of turpentine for the painter, and bought himself a large sack of blue dye out of the change from the shilling.

Then he dyed his wool himself until it was all, all blue.

And then Pelle went to his mother and said:

"Mother dear, please weave this yarn into cloth for me."

"That I will gladly do," said his mother, "if you will take care of your little sister for me." So Pelle took good care of his little sister, and his mother wove the wool into cloth.

Then Pelle went to the tailor:

"Dear Mr. Tailor, please make a suit for me out of this cloth."

"Is that what you want, you little rascal?" said the tailor. "Indeed I will, if you will rake my hay and bring in my wood and feed my pigs for me." So Pelle raked the tailor's hay and fed his pigs. And then he carried in all the wood. And the tailor had Pelle's suit ready that very Saturday evening.

And on Sunday morning Pelle put on his new suit and went to his lamb and said:

"Thank you very much for my new suit, little lamb."

"Ba-a-ah," said the little lamb, and it sounded almost as if the lamb were laughing.

THE POPPY SEED CAKES

by Margery Clark

Once upon a time there was a little boy and his name was
Andrewshek. His mother and his father brought him from the
old country when he was a tiny baby.

Andrewshek had an Auntie Katushka and she came from the
old country, too, on Andrewshek's fourth birthday.

Andrewshek's Auntie Katushka came on a large boat. She
brought with her a huge bag filled with presents for Andrewshek
and his father and his mother. In the huge bag were a fine feather
bed and a bright shawl and five pounds of poppy seeds.

The fine feather bed was made from the feathers of her old

green goose at home. It was to keep Andrewshek warm when he took a nap.

The bright shawl was for Andrewshek's Auntie Katushka to wear when she went to market.

The five pounds of poppy seeds were to sprinkle on little cakes which Andrewshek's Auntie Katushka made every Saturday for Andrewshek.

One lovely Saturday morning Andrewshek's Auntie Katushka took some butter and some sugar and some flour and some milk and seven eggs and she rolled out some nice little cakes. Then she sprinkled each cake with some of the poppy seeds which she had brought from the old country.

While the nice little cakes were baking, she spread out the fine feather bed on top of the big bed, for Andrewshek to take his nap. Andrewshek did not like to take a nap.

Andrewshek loved to bounce up and down and up and down on his fine feather bed.

Andrewshek's Auntie Katushka took the nice little cakes out of the oven and put them on the table to cool; then she put on her bright shawl to go to market. "Andrewshek," she said, "please watch these cakes while you rest on your fine feather bed. Be sure that the kitten and the dog do not go near them."

"Yes, indeed! I will watch the nice little cakes," said Andrewshek. "And I will be sure that the kitten and the dog do not touch them." But all Andrewshek really did was to bounce up and down and up and down on the fine feather bed.

"Andrewshek!" said Andrewshek's Auntie Katushka, "how can you watch the poppy seed cakes when all you do is to bounce up and down and up and down on the fine feather bed?" Then Andrewshek's Auntie Katushka, in her bright shawl, hurried off to market.

But Andrewshek kept bouncing up and down and up and down on the fine feather bed and paid no attention to the little cakes sprinkled with poppy seeds.

Just as Andrewshek was bouncing up in the air for the ninth

time, he heard a queer noise that sounded like "Hs-s-s-sss," at the front door of his house.

"Oh, what a queer noise!" cried Andrewshek. He jumped down off the fine feather bed and opened the front door. There stood a great green goose as big as Andrewshek himself. The goose was very cross and was scolding as fast as he could. He was wagging his head and was opening and closing his long red beak.

"What do you want?" said Andrewshek. "What are you scolding about?"

"I want all the goose feathers from your fine feather bed," quacked the big green goose. "They are mine."

"They are not yours," said Andrewshek. "My Auntie Katushka brought them with her from the old country in a huge bag."

"They are mine," quacked the big green goose. He waddled over to the fine feather bed and tugged at it with his long red beak.

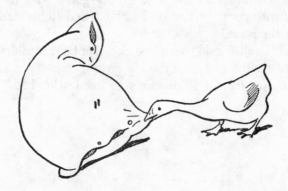

"Stop, Green Goose!" said Andrewshek, "and I will give you one of Auntie Katushka's poppy seed cakes."

"A poppy seed cake!" the green goose quacked in delight. "I love nice little poppy seed cakes! Give me one and you shall have your feather bed."

But one poppy seed cake could not satisfy the greedy green goose.

"Give me another!" Andrewshek gave the green goose another poppy seed cake.

"Give me another!" the big green goose hissed and frightened Andrewshek nearly out of his wits.

Andrewshek gave him another and another and another till all the poppy seed cakes were gone.

Just as the last poppy seed cake disappeared down the long neck of the green goose, Andrewshek's Auntie Katushka appeared at the door, in her bright shawl. "Boo! hoo!" cried Andrewshek. "See! that naughty green goose has eaten all the poppy seed cakes."

"What? All my nice little poppy seed cakes?" cried Andrewshek's Auntie Katushka. "The naughty goose!"

The greedy goose tugged at the fine feather bed again with his long red beak and started to drag it to the door. Andrewshek's Auntie Katushka ran after the green goose and just then there was a dreadful explosion. The greedy goose who had stuffed himself with poppy seed cakes had burst and all his feathers flew all over the room.

"Well! well!" said Andrewshek's Auntie Katushka, as she gathered up the pieces of the big green goose. "We soon shall have two fine feather pillows for your fine feather bed."

BALLET

by Emma L. Brock

A rms one, arms side."

That was Madame Olga Samovar giving directions to her class. Seven little girls stood with their right hands resting on a wooden rail on one side of the room. Mary, Mildred, Judy and Betty-Lou and Joan and Harriet and little fat Elizabeth. Seven little girls wearing leotards that looked like bathing suits, and black ballet slippers.

"*Plié,*" said Madame Samovar. "*Demi-plié;* half-bend."

All the little girls bent themselves part way to the floor and up again.

"Keep your feet in a straight line. No, Joan. One of your feet is turned in. Not both pointed in the same direction. Turn both feet out, way out, in a straight line. That's it.

"Now, *plié,* one, two, three, four. One, two, three, four. Second position. Slide left foot out. Weight on both feet. *Plié.*"

Down and up again bobbed Mildred and Mary and all the others. Fourth position. Fifth position. Down, up, down, up.

"One, two, three, four," counted Madame Samovar. "Now turn, left hand on *barre,* light as a butterfly. One, two, three, four. Head up, don't watch your feet."

Madame was always telling them things that made it harder, Mary thought. Like "stomach in, hips in." How could you do both at the same time? "Don't bend like a kangaroo." And "always turn out your feet." If you turned them out too far, you were sure to tip over. Mary knew. She had done it and finished on all fours.

It was like that all through June, right up to the Fourth of July. Always turn out your feet.

"Are we soon going to be dancing?" Mary asked.

"Before long," Madame Samovar said. "We must get our ankles and legs strong, and our backs and our feet.

"Now *relevé*; up on the balls of your feet, down," she said. "Up, down, up, down. One, two, one, two. Second position. One, two, one, two."

Mary wanted to ask when they would be wearing the fluffy stand-out skirts, but she kept still. These ugly black things, just bathing suits. Ugh! Uglier than bathing suits.

Madame Samovar's dancing costume was better. It was a bathing suit, too, but it had a belt around the waist and long stockings that looked like fish nets. Mary thought she was really beautiful. Her hair was black and tight to her head. Her eyes were huge, and black, too, and they made her face look small and pointed. Mary liked to look at her.

There were more exercises at the *barre*. Mary pushed her damp bangs from her forehead. It was as hot as playing tag.

"One, two, three, four," said the music. "One, two, three,

four." It made you want to dance. Dance, dance, when would they begin to dance?

"Now, out in the center," Madame Samovar said. "Two lines. Mary, Mildred, and Elizabeth in front. Ready, arms in first position, arms out to the side. First position, feet out in a straight line."

Mary leaned forward and waved her arms like pinwheels. Harriet took two little extra steps to keep from falling.

"Fifth position, right foot front. Now, positions of the arms—*port de bras.*"

The music sang out with a slow, swaying tune, like grasses in the wind.

"Ready, one, two, three, four, five, six, seven, eight," counted Madame Samovar. "Front, up, side, down, front, up, side, down. One, two, three, four, five, six, seven, eight."

Harriet's arms wobbled in the wrong direction as they usually did. *Port de bras* was a little like dancing, Mary thought.

"Now this is *glissade*," Madame Samovar said. "It's new, but it is not hard. Do it slowly, first. I will show you."

All their eyes were fastened on the feet of Madame Samovar.

"Fifth position, right foot front, arms side, *demi-plié*, up. Stretch right foot to side, toe pointed—that's *battement tendu* with the right foot. Now transfer weight to right foot. Close left to right to fifth position, in *demi-plié*."

They all practiced it slowly. Again and again.

"Now faster and repeat. Ready, one, two, three. One, two, three. *Plié*, point, close."

Across the floor they bobbed and slid. One, two, three. One, two, three. The music was gay and dancy. *Plié*, *tendu*, close. Harriet was putting in a few extra motions. She always did, no matter how many times Madame showed her the steps.

"Fun?" asked Madame Samovar.

"Oh," gasped Mary, pushing back her hair. "It's dancing! We're dancing! It's just like a ballet, a real ballet!"

That was the way it went, two days a week all through July. Each time more like dancing.

One day it was *arabesques*, standing on one leg with the other extended behind, and one arm extended forward and the other back. Mary kept jumping to keep from falling.

"Just stand still, Mary," Madame said. "Don't try to dance."

"I'm not dancing, but my feet have to try to keep up with my head."

Hop, hop, hop.

"Or I'll fall on my nose!"

Hop, hop, hop!

"Try again," said Madame Samovar. "Don't lean forward so much. There, that's better."

And another day there were turns. *Piqué* turns across the floor.

"That's real dancing," panted Mary.

"Shorter steps, Mary. You're galloping. Now do it with rhythm," Madame said. "One of you start, then another, and another, the way a ballet company does. Each one start when the same place comes in the music. Ready, go. Mary."

Mary danced *piqué* turns across the floor with hands out, stepping right foot front, left foot to ankle, turn on right toe, arms front, head flipping around like a weathercock in a gale to keep eyes front.

"Mildred."

Mildred danced *piqué* turns across the floor with hands out, right foot front, left to ankle, turning with hands front, head snapping around to face the front.

"Elizabeth."

Little fat Elizabeth danced *piqué* turns across the floor with hands out, right foot front, left to ankle, turning with arms front, head flipping around to face the front.

Joan, Judy, Betty-Lou, and Harriet one after another whirled across the floor.

It was just like the *corps de ballet* in a real theater. Mary's grin was so wide that it almost flew off when she whirled her head around to face the front. As they finished, they walked back on the edge of the floor and danced off again. *Piqué* turn, *piqué* turn. The turns were rather wild. The whirling dancers zigzagged across the room, but it was real dancing.

"When do we have our *tutus*, our standy-out skirts? When, Madame, when?" gasped Mary.

Madame Samovar's voice rang out in laughter.

"You are in a hurry. You are in such a hurry, Mary!"

Mary felt a little silly.

"I like them," she said, her face pink. "I want to wear one and see it flapping around me."

"All right. Keep on working hard and some day you will. Some day we'll give a recital," said Madame Samovar.

"A recital?" said Mary. "Oh, goody!"

"We'll dance and people will come to see us and they will clap. Maybe we'll even give a play. Act a play out with dances."

"Oh, when?" cried Mary.

"When?" shouted the others with one voice.

"Let's see," Madame said. "Maybe at Christmas time. We can choose what we want to do and practice and practice. We should know it by that time."

"Oh, Christmas is a long time from now," Mary said. "An awful long time off. Way after school begins."

"Maybe Thanksgiving. Yes, Thanksgiving. There will perhaps be a program at school at Christmas time. So we'll choose Thanksgiving."

"Oh, goody, goody!" and they all began to do *piqués* and *pirouettes*, everything but handsprings, all up and down the room.

"Now Jimmy won't tease me any more," Judy said.

"Tease you? Jimmy?" asked Madame Samovar.

"He's my brother. He laughs at me when I'm practicing. He says, 'One, two, buckle my shoe, three, four, shut the door,' and that silly rhyme. Now I can say: 'I'm practicing for a play, stupid!' He likes plays."

"We'll show him," Mary said.

"And we'll practice every day," said Madame, "no matter how many Jimmys there are."

"Yes, Madame, we will," said Mary and Judy and all the others.

And they all did a révérence to Madame Samovar. Plié with the back leg, pointing the front toe forward, a low bow, arms out at the side.

THE CAP THAT MOTHER MADE

A Swedish Tale

There was once a little boy called Anders. One day Anders' mother gave him a present, a cap that she herself had knit for him. It was a very pretty cap! It was red except for a little part in the middle which was green because there wasn't enough red wool to finish it all. And the tassel was blue.

Anders put the cap on his head and his mother and father told him that he looked very fine in it. Then his brothers and sisters walked around him to see how he looked from the front and the back and from each side. They, too, agreed that Anders looked very fine. So Anders put his hands in his pockets and went out for a walk, for he wanted everyone to see the lovely cap his mother had made him.

The first person he met was a farmer. The farmer was walking beside his cart which was loaded with peat, but when he saw Anders' new cap he stopped walking and made a deep bow. Anders kept right on walking and he held his head very high for he was proud to be wearing his pretty new cap.

The next person he met was Lars, the tanner's boy. Lars was

a big boy, much bigger than Anders. He was so big, in fact, that he wore high boots and carried a jack-knife. But when Lars saw Anders and his splendid new cap, he stood still and looked at it and then went up close to feel it and to play with the blue tassel.

"I'll give you my jackknife if you give me your cap," he said.

Now Anders knew that as soon as one has a jackknife one is almost a man. But he couldn't give up, even for the knife, the cap his mother had made him.

"I'm sorry, Lars," he said. "But I cannot give you my cap."

And off he went down the road. At the crossroads he met a little old lady. She made a deep curtsey to Anders and said, "Little boy, you look so fine, why don't you go to the king's ball?"

"I think I will," Anders replied. "With this cap on my head, I am certainly fit to visit the king."

And off he went to the king's palace. But at the gate of the palace two soldiers stopped him.

"Where are you going, little boy?" one of the soldiers asked.

"I am going to the king's ball," Anders replied.

"You cannot go to the king's ball," said the soldier. "No one can go without a uniform."

"Surely," thought Anders, "my cap is as fine as any uniform!"

But the soldiers didn't think so and Anders felt very sad. Just then the princess came to the gate of the palace. She saw the splendid red cap on Anders' head and said to the soldiers,

"What is wrong? Why won't you let this little boy come to the king's ball?"

"He has no uniform," one of the soldiers told her. "No one can go without a uniform."

"His fine cap will do just as well as a uniform," the princess said. "He shall come to the ball with me."

So the princess took Anders by the hand and together they went through the gate, up the broad marble steps, down the long hall and into the ballroom. In the ballroom ladies and gentlemen wearing fine clothes of silk and satin stood about talking with one another. But when they saw Anders walking beside the princess and saw the red cap on his head, they bowed very low and they probably thought that he was a prince.

At the end of the ballroom was a long table with rows of golden plates on it and rows of golden goblets. On large silver platters there were tarts and cakes and all manner of fine things to eat and in the goblets there was red wine. The princess sat down on a golden chair at the end of the table and Anders sat down on the chair beside her.

"But you cannot eat with your cap on your head," said the princess, and she started to take it off.

"Oh yes! I can eat just as well with it on," Anders said, and he held on to it with both his hands.

"Will you give it to me if I give you a kiss?" the princess asked.

Anders shook his head. The princess was beautiful and he would like to be kissed by her, but he would not give up the cap that Mother made.

But the princess filled his pockets full of cakes and cookies and she put her own golden necklace around his neck and then she bent down and kissed him.

"Now," she said, "will you give me the cap?"

Anders thanked her for the cakes and cookies, the necklace and the kiss, but he wouldn't take his hands from his head.

Just then the king himself entered the ballroom. He was wearing a mantle of blue velvet, bordered with ermine, and on his head was a large gold crown. When he saw Anders sitting in the golden chair, he smiled at him.

"That is a very fine cap you have," he said.

"Yes it is," said Anders. "My mother made it for me, but everyone wants to get it away from me."

"Surely you would like to change caps with me," said the king.

He took off his large golden crown and held it out to him. With his other hand he reached for Anders' little red cap.

Anders didn't answer a word. He jumped out of his chair and dashed across the ballroom and ran down the long hall and skipped down the broad marble steps, and went out of the gate that led to the king's palace. He ran so fast that all the cakes and cookies fell out of his pocket and the golden necklace that the princess had given him fell from his neck.

But he had his cap! He had his cap! He had his cap! He held it tight with both his hands and ran home to his mother's cottage. When he got there he told his mother and his father, his brothers and his sisters all that had happened to him during the day. He told them how everyone admired his lovely red cap, but how everyone tried to get it away from him.

When he came to the part about how the king offered his golden crown for the little cap, Anders' big brother said, "You were very foolish, Anders! Think of all the things you could buy if you were king! High leather boots, a jackknife or a sword, even a cap finer than your own—one that is red all over and has a feather in it."

But Anders grew very angry and his face grew very red. "I was not foolish!" he cried. "Nowhere in the world is there a finer cap than the one my mother made me!"

And then his mother took him on her lap and kissed him.

HOW LITTLE PEAR WANTED
BOTH A TOP AND A TANG-HULUR

by Eleanor Frances Lattimore

For some time after Little Pear's trip to the city he was very good. Perhaps he was sorry to have frightened his family so. Anyway, he was very good, and one day his mother said, "Little Pear, here are some pennies. Run along and buy yourself a pretty toy."

"Thank you!" said Little Pear, reaching out in delight for the pennies. They had holes in the middle and were all strung on a string which was tied so that they could not slip off. Little Pear started forth in great excitement, almost tripping over the high doorstep. As he hurried along the street he counted his pennies—one, two, three, four—four pennies! He couldn't remember ever having been so rich before.

On each side of the street were walls made of sun-baked bricks. Over the top of the walls you could see the roofs of the houses. Some were made of gray tiles, and some were made of straw. In the walls were many gateways, leading into the courtyards of the houses. They had different-colored doors: red doors and black doors and once in a while a green door dotted with gold paint.

"Little Pear! Little Pear!" called a voice suddenly. Little Pear turned around, and there was his friend Big Head, calling to him from his gateway. "Come and see my new top!" he cried. "It is the most beautiful top in the whole world, and the fastest spinner!"

"Ay-ah!" exclaimed Little Pear, and he looked at the top admiringly. It was certainly a beauty—a great pear-shaped silver top, with stripes of scarlet, pink, and green.

Big Head proudly spun it, and it twirled round and round,

while a crowd of children gathered to watch. Little Pear slipped away toward the street where the shops were, thinking, "Perhaps I can find a beautiful top like that! I have four pennies."

Little Pear walked along the street, humming happily, and the very first shop that he came to sold tinware. There were little tin teapots and tin saucepans, and they hung in bunches in front of the open shop and rattled merrily in the breeze. Little Pear stopped and looked at the tinware and thought that he would like a teapot of his own. But then he looked at his four pennies and thought of the top, and so he walked on.

"Hot chestnuts, hot chestnuts!" called a man in a loud singsing voice, standing behind a tray of smoking hot chestnuts, just off the charcoal. Little Pear wrinkled his nose in joy as he sniffed the delicious smell. But he looked at his four pennies and thought of the toy shop at the end of the street, and he walked on.

"Tang-hulurs! Tang-hulurs!" called a man coming toward him, and this time Little Pear stopped short with his mouth wide open.

For the man was simply laden down with the tang-hulurs, which were Little Pear's favorite candy. He looked at the red fruit, eight or ten on a stick, all covered with candied syrup, and he jingled his string of pennies. He thought that he would be perfectly happy if he could have a tang-hulur.

"How much?" he asked the man.

"Two pennies a stick!"

Little Pear untied the string and gave the man two of his precious pennies. Then he started on toward the toy shop, nibbling at his tang-hulur.

The toy shop was very wonderful. There were wooden swords painted in pink and green and gold. There were funny little monkeys made of clay covered over with chicken feathers, and round boxes made of gourds, all delicately carved. The boxes were stained orange or green or brown, and they had crickets inside of them that made a queer little singing noise with their wings. There were cloth tigers, with smiling faces and green glass eyes. And, yes, there were tops! Tops of all colors, striped and plain.

"This one," said Little Pear to the shopman, pointing to one as large and beautiful as Big Head's.

"The tops," said the man, "are four pennies."

"Oh, dear! Oh, dear!" cried Little Pear, " and I bought a tang-hulur with two of my pennies! There are not enough left."

"Come back some day when you have more money," said the shopman; but suddenly Little Pear had a much better idea. He ran down the street until he met the tang-hulur man again.

"Another tang-hulur, please!" he said, and handed the man his last two pennies in exchange for another delicious stick of candy.

Then very happily he trotted along till he came to the home of Big Head. Big Head was sitting on his doorstep alone, holding his top. He looked very much surprised when he saw Little Pear with two tang-hulurs.

One tang-hulur was almost gone, but the other hadn't had a single bite taken out of it. "Oh, Little Pear, how good they must taste!" said Big Head. "I do love tang-hulurs!"

"So do I," replied Little Pear, "but I will trade you my whole tang-hulur that isn't eaten for your top."

But that Big Head would not do. He was a little older and wiser than Little Pear; so he said, "I cannot give you my precious top, but I will share it with you if you will share your tang-hulur with me."

So that is what they did. They took turns eating the tang-hulur until it was gone, and then they took turns spinning the top, and they were perfectly happy.

THE RED GASOLINE PUMP

by Lucy Sprague Mitchell

Once there was a road. It was a long road. It was a well-paved road. It was a road which automobiles like to speed along. Whirr, whirr; honk, honk, honk! All day long, many automobiles went whizzing over the road. Fast, fast, fast!

In the road was a bend. The automobiles slowed up as they came to the bend. Around the curve they went. Slowly, slowly, slowly around the bend.

On the side of the road, right by the bend, stood a gasoline pump. It was a brand new pump. Its paint was bright red. It had a hose, a marker and a grinding handle. Underneath the ground out of sight it had a big tank full of gasoline. The pump was owned by a man who lived in a little house near by. Early one morning he came down to the gasoline pump. He walked up to it and touched it with his finger. No red spot of paint on his finger tip! Good! it was dry.

When would the first automobile come? The owner of the pump looked down the road one way. Far away he could see a little speck. Far away he could hear a faint sound. Bigger and bigger grew the speck. Louder and louder got the sound. Yes, it was a Ford! On it came bouncing and jouncing merrily down the long, well-paved road. The driver slowed up as he came near the bend of the road. For he saw the new red gasoline pump!

He turned the wheel and ran the Ford close to the side of the bright red pipe.

"Want some gasoline?"

"Yes. I need about five gallons. Nice new pump you have."

"You're the first man to use it. The paint's just dry. Let's see if it works all right."

By this time the driver had jumped out and lifted a hinged lid near the engine. That was where the Ford kept its gasoline tank. The owner of the pump put the end of the long hose into a hole in the tank. Then he set the marker at 5. Slowly, slowly he ground the handle. Around and around and around. The little arrow moved down to 5. There it stopped. The owner of the pump lifted up the hose to let all the gasoline run into the tank. Then he took the hose out. The driver put his hand into his pocket, pulled out some money and paid the owner of the pump.

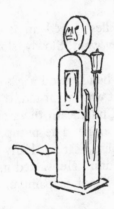

"Your pump is certainly a good one," he said. "Good-by." And off went the Ford around the curve and up the road. The owner of the pump watched it. Smaller and smaller it grew. Fainter and fainter it sounded. At last he couldn't see it or hear it. But he could still smell it.

When would the next automobile come? The owner of the pump looked up the road the other way. Far away he could see a little speck. Far away he could hear a faint sound. Bigger and bigger and still bigger it grew. Louder and louder and still louder it got. This was not a Ford! No, it was a truck! On it came rumbling and grumbling up the long, well-paved road. The driver slowed up as he came near the bend of the road. For he saw the new red gasoline pump!

He turned the wheel and ran the truck close to the side of the bright red pipe.

"Want some gasoline?"

"Yes, I'll take about ten gallons. Nice new pump you have."

"You're the second man to use it. It seems to work all right."

By this time the driver had lifted up the cushioned seat where he had been sitting. That was where the truck kept its gasoline tank. The owner of the pump put the end of the long hose into a hole in the tank. Then he set the marker. Slowly, slowly he ground the handle. Around, and around, and around, and around, and around, and around. The little arrow moved down to 10. There it stopped. The owner of the pump lifted up the hose to let all the gasoline run into the tank. Then he took the hose out. The driver put his hand in his pocket, pulled out some money and paid the owner of the pump.

"Your pump is certainly a good one," he said. "Good-by." And off went the truck around the curve and down the road. The owner of the pump watched it. Smaller and smaller it grew. Fainter and fainter it sounded. At last he couldn't see it or hear it. But he could still smell this one, too!

Before long a third automobile came. That was a taxi. Then a fourth automobile came. That was a bigger car with four children and a driver in it. All day long autos came up the road and autos came down the road. Some went right by though they slowed up going around the curve. Some stopped to get gasoline at the bright red pump. And when their tanks were filled, off they went getting littler and littler, and fainter and fainter, until they disappeared on the long, well-paved road.

The pump worked all day while the owner ground the handle to make the gasoline flow. After a long time it grew dark on the long, well-paved road. The automobiles got fewer and fewer. Whirr, whirr; honk, honk, honk! That was the last one. They had all stopped whirring and honking for that day. The owner had gone to bed. And the bright red pipe, looking all dim and dull, stood alone by the bend in the long, well-paved road.

That was the end of the pump's first day.

A *bright red pipe,*
    A long strong hose,
A marker that shows how the gasoline flows.
    That's a gasoline pump
        As everyone knows,
For the auto that needs gasoline when it goes.

BIG FELLOW'S FIRST JOB

by Dorothy Walter Baruch

Ned went riding along on his bicycle. He whistled joyously as he rode. Today was no ordinary day. Today was a great and thrilling day—a most important day; for today something that meant a great deal to Ned was going to happen.

Ned was happy. Ned's hopes were high. He was on his way to see his best friend.

Now, this best friend of Ned's, you must know, was no ordinary friend, but a certain very special friend. And, if you were to guess from now until your next birthday and longer, you would never be able to guess what his friend's name was, unless, of course, you knew.

You see it wasn't a boy's name, nor a girl's name, nor a dog's name, nor a pony's, because Ned's friend wasn't a boy or a girl or a dog or a pony. No, indeed! His friend was something quite different and much, much bigger. It was a great, enormous machine. It was a noisy, rumbly, giant machine—a huge gasoline shovel. And its name was Big Fellow.

No doubt you know shovels like it. No doubt you've seen them often enough cutting and scooping the ground, digging ditches, or burrowing deep holes, or helping build roads.

But Ned had never seen Big Fellow doing these things. He had never seen the great shovel at work on any job, because, fact was, the shovel had never yet worked on any job. It was too new.

Ned had met Big Fellow in the machine factory where it had been made. He had actually seen parts of it being made out of iron and steel. Since that time Ned had gone to the factory over and over again to visit Big Fellow, and to admire it as it stood in its corner—strong and gleaming and new.

Ned loved the great shovel. He loved to feel the smooth cool iron and steel of it. He was anxious to see it at work and was impatient for it to set out on its first job.

"Just wait till you're sold, Big Fellow," Ned would say, "then you'll be leaving this factory. Then you'll be starting your work."

And Ned would laugh and add: "You'll show them what you can do, won't you, Big Fellow? I'll bet you'll be the best working shovel ever made. You'll do the finest jobs ever done."

And Ned would fondly touch the sharp iron teeth of the shovel's dipper and would declare, "Oh what a day that will be, Big Fellow, when you start to work on your very first job."

For a long time Big Fellow had stayed at the factory. But one day a man called Sandy Stone had come along. He had looked the shovel up and down. He had inspected every one of its working parts, from the teeth of its dipper to the tractor base on which it moved. And Sandy had decided to buy Big Fellow.

Ned was overjoyed when he heard this. He watched the shovel being loaded onto the low, flat trailer which was to move it from the factory to Sandy Stone's place.

Sandy Stone owned many machines beside Big Fellow. He rented his machines to people who were building and who needed the machines to help.

Sandy kept his machines, when they were not at work, in his equipment yard under whitewashed sheds. There were several shovels like Big Fellow, and several concrete-mixers and several dump trucks and several other kinds of machines.

The morning on which Sandy had bought Big Fellow, Ned heard him say:

"Loads of builders want to rent machines for jobs these days. Now *this* shovel—why, I'll be sending it pretty quick to the new aviation field they're starting over at Oak Road."

Ned had almost jumped up and down for joy. Imagine! Just imagine! Big Fellow was to help build the new aviation field. *That* was to be Big Fellow's first job. Ned knew Big Fellow would be happy working at such a grand job.

He had gone over to the shovel and laid his hand on its long steel boom.

"You'll show how you can work, you will, Big Fellow!" Ned had proudly declared.

That had been three days ago. Ned had waited patiently during those three days. He thought constantly of Big Fellow's first job. He was going to be right on hand to see the shovel begin work. Sandy had said he might be.

And now at last the day was here!

Ned was on his way to Big Fellow's first job!

Ned whistled joyously as he rode along on his bicycle. He was going to see Big Fellow work; he was going to see Big Fellow work. The sound of his bicycle's wheels going over the road seemed to whisper: "Sssee Big Fellow work. Sssee Big Fellow work. SSee, SSee, ssssssee Big Fellow work."

Presently, however, Ned's whistle died down. The smile left his face. Suppose something were to go wrong with Big Fellow. Suppose one or another of its parts were to get out of order and not start properly. Such things did happen with machinery. You never could tell.

Sometimes the engines would spit and sputter. Sometimes the shovel dippers would get stuck in the earth. Sometimes the turning parts just wouldn't turn. Sometimes even the strong rope cables would snap. Oh, how Ned hoped that none of these things would happen to his friend, Big Fellow.

By now he had only a little way left to go. There were trees ahead and a curve. He knew that around that curve he would find . . . Big Fellow.

His heart beat faster. His bicycle wheels turned faster. He skimmed past the trees. He swept around the curve. And there, ahead, stood his friend, Big Fellow.

The shovel gleamed in the morning sun! Sharp teeth ready to cut the earth! Strong dipper ready to scoop! Long boom ready to move up and down! While through the door of the square cab Ned could see the driver's seat, and the engine, and the levers!

Workmen were gathered around. A man was climbing up into the cab. That was Blake, the driver.

What were they doing? Yes, Ned knew. They were getting ready to start Big Fellow. It wouldn't be long now! If only, only everything would go all right!! If only Big Fellow wouldn't fail!

Ned could hear two men who stood near him talking.

"Sure's going to be a great job!" said one.

"Best aviation field ever," answered the other.

"It'll have concrete runways for the airplanes to taxi on, and hangars, and a station where you can buy airplane tickets. But that shovel has lots of work to do before the field's finished."

"Yes," nodded the other man, "it has to cut away the humps and bumps so the field'll be level."

Ned's eyes were fastened on Big Fellow. Now Blake was up in the cab, ready to start the machinery. At last Big Fellow's first job was to begin.

Ned waited for the engine to turn on. Would it work properly? Oh, would it?

"Jrr," went the starter.

"Putta-put," went the engine, "Putta-putta-put."

Ned breathed a sigh of relief. Thank goodness, the engine was working all right!

And would the tractor base carry Big Fellow over the ground to where it was to begin digging?

Ned saw Blake pull a lever. Rumpety-clump, rumpety-clump, the shovel crawled across the field.

Thank goodness, its tractor base was working all right!

And now, would the great shovel turn and swing into place in response to the levers Blake pulled?

Blake pulled the levers, Clackety-clack, around went the great shovel body.

Thank goodness, the shovel's turning was all right!

But now came the keenest test of all. Those iron teeth on the shovel's dipper! They had never yet bitten into earth or rock. This was to be their first trial. Would they do it? Oh, would they?

Down toward the ground went the teeth of the shovel. Burra-burrrrr! They were going in . . . going in. Chrrra-chrrrr sang the engine, faster, louder, speeding up to give the dipper more power. Downward went the teeth, biting into the earth, boring in—deeper, deeper. . . .

And then with a mighty heave up came the dipper, up and out of the ground filled to the top with chunks of rich brown earth.

Ned threw back his head. He laughed aloud with joy. His friend, Big Fellow, could work. His friend, Big Fellow, hadn't failed. Good for Big Fellow!

And that was how Big Fellow started on its first job.

THE TWINS AND TABIFFA

by Constance Heward

Tabiffa was a big black cat with a coat like velvet, a beautiful tail, and handsome whiskers. She walked daintily, like a princess.

She belonged partly to Peter, who was seven years old—a thin boy with red hair and freckles.

But mostly to Binkie and Dinkie. They were twins, four years old, with round red faces and black hair which looked in front as if it had been nibbled by a mouse. They were exactly alike, so, to tell one from the other, Binkie's jersey and breeches were always brown and Dinkie's blue.

Now, one day a dreadful thing happened. Tabiffa disappeared, and Binkie and Dinkie cried and cried and cried, till their cheeks got all big and puffy and nearly buried their eyes.

Mother petted them and loved them and said she would go and buy a new cat, but Binkie and Dinkie said they wanted Tabiffa.

Father came in, and told them to stop crying at once.

They stopped then, and Peter took them to search the house for Tabiffa, though he knew she wasn't in it, because he had looked in every room and closet more than once that day.

For a whole week Tabiffa was lost, and Binkie and Dinkie began to look pale and thin with sorrow.

But one night, after the twins had cried themselves to sleep, Peter lay in his bed beside theirs, and racked his brain for a plan to get Tabiffa back.

And while he lay there something came softly in through the half-open door. It was Tabiffa, and in her mouth she carried a small black kitten.

She sprang onto Binkie and Dinkie's bed, scraped a nice little nest at the foot of it in the eiderdown, and put the kitten gently in.

Then she went away looking very large and black and important, while Peter sat up in bed hugging himself with excitement, because he was sure that she had gone to fetch more kittens.

And he was right, for she fetched them, one at a time, in her mouth, till there were four little, soft, black, mewing things in the nest in the eiderdown.

Then Tabiffa curled herself up beside them, purring loudly, and Peter got out of bed and was just going to wake the twins, when Nurse came walking into the room, and when she saw Tabiffa and her kittens on the bed she was so angry that she smacked Peter for being out of bed, and scolded so hard that Binkie and Dinkie woke up. "She's come back!" screamed Binkie.

"Wif some dear likkle babies!" screamed Dinkie, and they knelt at the foot of the bed in their pajams, and kissed Tabiffa and never even heard Nurse's scolding.

But Father and Mother did, and they came up to see whatever could be happening.

Binkie and Dinkie rushed at them and hugged them 'round their knees, and begged and begged that Tabiffa and the kittens might stay, while Peter tried to explain at the top of his voice how Tabiffa had brought them, and Nurse said she never knew such goings-on.

The end of it was that Tabiffa and the kittens were put into an old work-basket, with a piece of blanket in it, on the floor beside the twins' bed, and everybody went to sleep, full of happiness. Except Nurse, and her face under her nightcap was enough to turn the milk sour if there had been any near enough.

Now, in the middle of the night, when the moon was peeping in at the windows, Peter was awakened by something poking and patting his face. He was dreadfully frightened till he heard a loud, pitiful "Miaow! Miaow-ow-ow!" right in his ear, and he knew it was Tabiffa.

And, as he tried to push her away, his eyes smarted and he smelt smoke, and he jumped out of bed and ran to Nurse and shouted in her ear that the house was on fire.

Then he ran to wake Father and Mother, and the children were bundled up in blankets and carried on to the lawn, and Nurse's nightcap had come off and her curling-pins were showing.

And Mrs. Moriarty, the cook, came running out, holding her pet frying-pan under her arm.

And Susan, the housemaid, came out in a raincoat and bare feet, and her best Sunday hat in a green paper bag.

And they all stood and watched the smoke come curling out of the attic windows, and Tabiffa sat in her basket with the kittens in it and watched it, too.

And then the fire-engine dashed wildly up, and the firemen ran up ladders and squirted great streams of water out of their hose-pipes onto the fire, and it did not take very long to put it out.

But the children went to sleep in their blankets on the summerhouse floor, with their feet in the middle like soldiers in a tent.

Tabiffa wears a beautiful red leather collar now with a silver plate on it, and on the plate is written: "I am Tabiffa, who saved the house from burning."

Her four kittens are getting dreadfully big, but they still sleep in the basket by Binkie and Dinkie's bed, though it is a tightish fit; and Tabiffa makes a little nest for herself at the foot of the bed in the eiderdown.

CHARLIE RIDES IN THE ENGINE
OF A REAL TRAIN

by Helen Hill and Violet Maxwell

One day Charlie and his mother and his auntie and Topsy and Bingo and Jane went to stay in the country.

It was a very interesting place where they were going to stay in the country. What do you think? It was the place where Charlie's daddy had lived when he was a little boy!

Yes, that is where they were going, and, as it was Saturday, Charlie's daddy was going with them too. He was not going to live with them in the country, because on weekdays he had to go to the office every day. But he said that he would come down every Saturday and stay in the country till Sunday night.

So they all went to the railway station in a taxicab. Jane traveled in a cat basket and Charlie's auntie carried her. Topsy also traveled in a cat basket and Charlie's mother carried him, but Bingo had to travel in the baggage car and he had a ticket all to himself because he was a dog. Charlie thought that he ought to feel very proud.

When they got to the station they all went straight through the gate to the platform, and there the train was waiting for them. It was a great enormous train with ever so many coaches. First, Charlie and his daddy took Bingo to the baggage car, and the baggage man fastened Bingo's leash to the end of a trunk and promised Charlie to be good to Bingo.

Then they all got into the day car, and the train gave a loud whistle and steamed out of the station. My goodness! How fast it went! Everything just seemed to go flying past.

Soon the conductor came walking down the aisle and he took everybody's ticket. He was a very grand-looking man; he was tall and stout, and he had a beautiful blue uniform on. He soon came to the seat where Charlie and his daddy were sitting, and he took the tickets. Yes, the conductor took all the tickets and he stuck Charlie's daddy's ticket in his hatband, but as his mother and his auntie had no hatbands, he stuck *their* tickets into the top of the seat in front of them. Then he took Charlie's ticket, and he stuck it in Charlie's hatband. Charlie felt very proud, and he would not take his hat off. No, he kept his hat on all the time because he wanted everybody to see that *he* had a ticket in his hatband just like all the other men.

Then Charlie said to his daddy, "Daddy, what exactly makes the train go?"

And his daddy said, "It's the steam that makes the engine work, and it is the engineer and the fireman who look after the steam and the engine."

Then Charlie said, "What I want to know is exactly what the fireman and the engineer do when they are making the engine go."

But what do you think? His daddy did not know exactly what they did—he said that he had never ridden in an engine in his life, so how could he know what they did? And Charlie's mother and his auntie did not know either. That was very surprising.

Well, after they had been on the big train for about a whole hour, they came to a station where there were a lot of tracks. This station was called a junction, because there were so many tracks.

Some of the trains went to the North and some to the South and some to the East and some to the West. The train that Charlie and his daddy and his auntie and his mother were on was going toward the West; but now they wanted to go to the North, so they had to change trains and go on a train that was going toward the North.

The train was already waiting on its own track. It was a very little train, it had only two coaches!

Charlie's mother and his auntie and Jane and Topsy got into the train, and they took Bingo with them, because, as it was such a little unimportant train, the conductor said that Bingo could travel in the day coach instead of being tied in the baggage car, and Bingo was very glad. But Charlie and his daddy waited on the platform till it was time for the train to start, and they looked at all the interesting things about them.

Then a man came up. He wore overalls and a peaked cap. And —you never can guess who it was! It was the fireman who helped work the engine of the train they were going to take. And what do you think? The fireman knew Charlie's daddy! Yes, the fireman came up to them, and said to his daddy, "Hello, Bob!" Bob was his daddy's name that his mother and his auntie always called him! And his daddy said, "Why, hello, Bill," and shook hands.

Charlie was very much surprised that the fireman and his daddy knew each other, but it was not so very surprising after all. The fireman lived in the village where Charlie's daddy had lived when he was a little boy, and where Charlie and his mother and his auntie were going to live for a whole month, and his daddy and the fireman had gone to the same school when they were little boys!

Well, the fireman then looked at Charlie, and he said, "And is this your boy?"

Then Charlie's daddy said, "Yes, this is Charlie, and you are the very man he wants to meet. Charlie wants to know exactly what the fireman and the engineer do to make the train go—and he can't find anybody who knows. So go ahead and tell him all about it."

But the fireman said, "I can do better than that. Suppose you and Charlie take a ride on the engine with me; then he can see everything with his own eyes, and learn all there is to know in case he wants to be a fireman himself."

Yes, the fireman actually said those words! And Charlie's daddy said, "That will be fine. I'll just go and tell Charlie's mother and his auntie what has become of us, so they won't worry."

And he did so. Then the fireman, and Charlie and his daddy all got into the cab, which is back of the engine, where the engineer and the fireman sit.

The engineer was already sitting in his place, which is on the right of the cab. He was very pleased to meet Charlie and his daddy, but he said that after the train had started nobody must speak to him. Yes, nobody must ever speak to the engineer when he is driving the engine, because if anybody spoke to the engineer it might distract his attention and then the train might be wrecked!

All the time that the train is going the engineer has to sit on his seat with his hand on the throttle, which is the thing that makes the train stop in a hurry, and all the time he has to look out of the window to see what the signals say, and to see that there is nothing on the track ahead of him.

If he sees a green signal on the signal post that means that the engine can go straight ahead, but if the signal is red, then it means "Stop"—and the engineer presses on the throttle, and the train stops.

The engineer told all this to Charlie while they were waiting for the train to start. Then the engineer got the signal from the man on the platform; he blew the whistle, and the train started, and he could not say another word.

Well, the fireman's place is on the left side of the cab, and Charlie's daddy sat between him and the window, and Charlie sat on his daddy's knee.

The fireman has to work very hard, but when he is not working he can talk if he wants to. This fireman was very kind and, when he was not working, he explained everything to Charlie and his daddy—but all the time he was explaining he had to keep looking out of the window, too, in case he should see anything that the engineer didn't see. There are a great many windows in the cab of an engine—it has windows all round, because it is so very important that the engineer and the fireman shall see all that there is to see.

Well, I will now tell you what the fireman was doing all the time that Charlie and his daddy were riding in the engine with him.

In front of the fireman was the steam gauge, which is a round thing like a clock, and it has a hand like a clock hand, too, and the steam makes the hand move—so that you can see how much steam is coming out of the boiler. When the steam is getting low the hand drops, and when the hand of the gauge drops to one hundred and fifty the fireman knows it is time to put more coal in the fire box.

Every time that the hand of the gauge dropped to one hundred and fifty the fireman got up and opened the little door in the back of the cab, which opened right into the fire box, so that you could see the fire all red and glowing, and the fireman scooped a great shovel full of coal into it. The fireman told Charlie that it was very important how one shovels coal into the fire box. It has to be shoveled very evenly, so that it is not all black with coal in one place and all red hot with ember in another place. Yes, the fireman told Charlie that it needs a lot of practice before one can shovel the coal just exactly right.

Then the fireman also had to watch the water gauge, which shows how much water there is in the boiler.

When he saw by the water gauge that the water was getting low in the boiler, then the fireman had to turn a valve, which is a sort of handle that starts a pump working, and the pump pumps water into the boiler.

Charlie very much wanted to turn the valve himself, but the fireman said No, that it needed a whole lot of practice before one could pump water into the tank—as it is very important just how much water to pump. If too much cold water is pumped into the boiler it might cool the water already in the boiler so that no more steam would come out—and then the train would stop!

Do you think that the fireman on an engine is a busy man? Indeed he is.

But that is not all that the fireman has to do. Oh, dear, no! The fireman has a lot more work to do.

When the train is coming to a steep place—and there were a lot of steep places on the railroad that Charlie was traveling on —the fireman has to make the fire *red hot,* so that lots and lots of steam can come out of the boiler. He makes the fire get hotter and hotter until the steam gets so strong that the "safety valve" pops off—and this shows the engineer that there is enough steam to push the train up the steep place. Yes, you can see that it would need a lot of extra steam to push a train up a steep, high hill.

The fireman also has to blow a whistle, whenever the train comes to a crossing or to the station. And when they got to the last stop—which was the village where Charlie and his mother and his auntie and Bingo and Topsy and Jane were going to live for a whole month—the fireman let Charlie blow the whistle

himself! Yes, he did, and you should have heard what a loud whistle Charlie blew.

Well, at last they had come to the end of their journey, and Charlie had certainly learned a whole lot about engines. Yes, Charlie had learned a whole lot more than most people know. Of course he told his mother and his auntie about everything, so that they, too, should know all about what the fireman and the engineer do to make the train go.

And Charlie said, "Now, when I get home to the city I will be able to play with my train in just the right way. I will be able to play that I am the fireman and the engineer, and I will know exactly what they do, and I will practice and practice being a fireman so that I can be one when I grow up!"

LISA'S SONG

by Ruth Kennell

When Lisa's mother asked her what she wanted for her birthday, she answered without a moment's hesitation.

"One of Mrs. Puff's canaries, Mamma!" and then she added doubtfully, "If it wouldn't be too expensive. . . ."

The canaries sold for three dollars apiece, sometimes more. Liza knew three dollars would buy a fine laying hen, or two dozen baby chicks.

All the families in this colony of one-acre ranches on the San Francisco Peninsula raised things in order to make a living. Mr. Garten, Lisa's father, raised hens, and marketed the eggs. The people across the road raised rabbits. Mr. Puff raised pigeons, and Mrs. Puff, canaries. Lisa always thought of her as "Mrs. Cream-Puff," for she was short and plump with a soft, pretty face.

Mrs. Garten smiled at her little daughter. "I don't think it would be too expensive, honey. You've been a big help to your papa and me, and you deserve a nice present. Stop in at the Puffs' on your way from school tomorrow and pick one out."

As soon as school was out next day, Lisa ran so fast across the fields to the Puff ranch that when she arrived, she had no breath left to explain her errand. But Mrs. Puff seemed to be expecting her. She had baked her favorite cookies, full of almonds from their own tree, and while Lisa munched a cooky, she led her to the sun-porch where the cages hung.

Lisa tried not to make any noise, for she knew that some of the birds were nesting. The mother birds sat on their nests made in wire strainers, while the fathers from a high perch kept a sharp lookout. In one cage both parents busily hopped about. Lisa could see their young in the nest, stretching their bare necks and opening their beaks for the food which their mother and father had to chew up for them.

"Your Mamma phoned you were coming to pick out a canary for your birthday," said Mrs. Puff, going toward a large cage full of yellow song-birds.

Lisa's eager eyes searched among them. "Where's Heinie?" she inquired anxiously.

"Heinie? Oh, I've put him in a cage by himself in my room."

"I know why!" Lisa giggled in delight. "You guessed that *he* is the one I want, didn't you?"

Mrs. Puff's pink and white face looked troubled. "I declare I didn't, dearie. Most people like this kind the best."

She stepped close to the cage and whistled a few notes. At once, an alert little songster on the swing took up the air and the others followed him, trilling until their tiny throats seemed ready to burst.

"Wouldn't you like one of these, Lisa? You may have Fritzie the leader, if you want."

Lisa was silent. She did not like to seem unappreciative, but it was Heinie, and no other, that she wanted. Birds were like people. Each one was different, and Heinie was so very different. She loved the dark green of his coat, the perky black cap on one side of his head, and his voice, especially. It was not high, as were the voices of the more delicate yellow canaries, but low and sweet like something dreamed.

It seemed that whenever she came to see him and spoke to him in a soft, cooing voice, his bill would open wide and start quivering, and out would come a melody like nothing she had ever heard. It was a song especially for Lisa.

"You're disappointed, I can see that, dearie, and I'm sorry," Mrs. Puff was saying gently. "To tell the truth, you picked my choicest canary. The dark green are favored by fanciers and judges. I expect to get a good price for him at the conservatory in San Francisco. A dark green contralto like Heinie might bring as much as fifty dollars."

Fifty dollars! Lisa turned away disconsolately. "Thank you just the same, but I guess I don't want a canary, Mrs. Puff," she said politely.

Mrs. Puff followed her to the door, trying to think of something to say to comfort her. As she started down the walk beneath the blossoming acacia tree, Mrs. Puff called after her: "Wouldn't you like to go along when we take Heinie up to the conservatory next Saturday?"

Lisa nodded, pressing back her tears.

They started out early Saturday morning. An hour's drive up the Peninsula brought them to the door of a gray frame house with a stucco front. It stood in a long row of identical houses which ran up a steep hill. In the bay window hung a gold-lettered sign: "UPHAUS CONSERVATORY. VOICE TRAINING SCHOOL FOR CANARIES." When they had parked the car, Mrs. Puff carried the large cage covered with thin muslin. Lisa followed with Heinie's small covered cage.

While they waited to see the director, Mrs. Puff showed Lisa about. In a large room, one glass wall of which looked out on the Golden Gate and the gleaming new bridge, hung many large cages, a dozen yellow canaries in each. These were the ordinary singers, Mrs. Puff explained. Cards on each cage gave their grading as to tone and range of notes.

"Will Henie be put here?" Lisa inquired timidly.

"Oh, no. In that room with the glass door are the gifted birds. Each is kept in a sound-proof cage."

Lisa stood on tiptoe and peered through the glass at the rows of closed, silent cages.

"On each cage is a card giving the bird's pedigree," continued Mrs. Puff. "They're all descended from dark green canaries imported from Germany many years ago."

"But why are these canaries kept in sound-proof cages?" faltered Lisa.

"Because canaries have such sharp ears, they imitate the sounds they hear when very young, before their own natural song comes to them. They begin their training when only a month old. For three months they're kept in these cages where they don't hear a sound except when the doors are opened for them to listen to a phonograph record of the artificial song they're to learn. This lot are being taught to whistle 'Yankee Doodle.' At the end of three months those that have mastered the human song are graduated from the conservatory. Graduates sell for as much as a hundred to five hundred dollars apiece!"

Lisa's spirits sank even lower. She understood now that Heinie had a brilliant career ahead of him, but it seemed to her a dreary life for a little bird. She had planned to hang Heinie's cage among the plants in the sun-room overlooking her mother's garden, and perhaps later on to get a quiet mate for him so that his happiness would be complete.

The director called to them and they returned to the office. Mrs. Puff took the covering off the large cage and the yellow warblers performed for Mrs. Uphaus, who made notes on a card.

"They'll do," she decided crisply. "We're paying three dollars for natural singers now. There's always quite a demand for them."

"I have one bird I'd like you to test as a possible pupil in your special training course," Mrs. Puff said to the director a little breathlessly.

She removed the muslin cover from the small cage, over which Lisa hovered like an anxious mother hen. Inside sat Heinie looking so dejected that Lisa bent over him and spoke in tender, cooing tones. The green canary lifted his head and, with wide-open bill quivering, uttered a few low notes of liquid sweetness. Then in one prolonged breath he rolled inside his pulsing throat the melody that Lisa had believed was a special greeting to her.

"How very original!" exclaimed the director, coming quickly to the cage. "A contralto of unusual quality. How old is he?"

"Six months," admitted Mrs. Puff reluctantly.

Mrs. Uphaus expressed doubt that such a mature bird could be trained to sing an artificial song.

"Suppose you leave the bird here for a week on trial, Mrs.

Puff," she said. "When you come next Saturday, I'll be prepared to make you an offer. In any case, we'll buy him. That's definite."

Lisa was silent on the ride home. She thought of Heinie, imprisoned in a dark, soundless cell, and forced to learn a human song.

"Just think, dearie," Mrs. Puff was chattering cheerfully, in an effort to break her silence, "movie stars and other famous people are customers for Mrs. Uphaus's rollers. Wouldn't it be wonderful if Heinie should go to the White House?"

But even the idea that Heinie might sing "Yankee Doodle" for the President failed to comfort Lisa.

Her birthday was the following Saturday, but when you are ten you already have responsibilities. She worked in the garden most of the lovely, spring day, for it was her special task to keep the weeds pulled in her mother's luxuriant bed of bulbs and fuchsias. Overhead, the birds flew to and from their nests in the Italian cypress trees. Lisa loved them all, but with an impersonal affection quite different from the feeling she had for Heinie. The silly doggerel

"Heinie, oh, Heinie,
 I love but you . . ."

ran through her head like a lament.

The sparrows and linnets chirped and trilled in hushed tones as their day's work drew to a close. Soon it was time for Lisa to gather the eggs. It was no small task, going in and out of pens among a thousand hens. Still it was a pleasant one, groping to feel the smooth, warm eggs in the nests, and counting them one by one as she put them in the bucket.

She heard a car in the driveway.

"Lisa!" called her mother from the house. She came slowly, not feeling in the mood for visitors.

Mrs. Puff sat in the living room with a cage on her knees wrapped in light muslin. Papa Garten was there in his overalls; Mamma Garten in her kitchen apron.

"I've brought your birthday present, dearie!" Mrs. Puff beamed at her.

Lisa turned her face away. Why did they insist upon giving her another canary when they knew it was only Heinie she wanted? Mrs. Puff was talking in pleased tones as she removed the cover.

"All week in the conservatory he refused to sing a note. So today the director told me they couldn't pay more than five dollars for him. A temperamental singer is too much of a risk, she said. Of course, I refused. I couldn't disappoint Lisa for a difference of two dollars!"

Lisa turned quickly and dropped to the floor beside the uncovered cage.

"Heinie, oh, Heinie—it's you . . ." she sang joyously.

Heinie smoothed his ruffled feathers, opened wide his quivering bill, and trilled his lovely melody.

"There it is!" Mrs. Puff whispered to Lisa's parents in something like awe. "He sings it only for her. It's Lisa's song!"

P-PENNY AND HIS
LITTLE RED CART

by Amy Wentworth Stone

Have you ever heard of a Peleg?

Does it sound like a big bird with long legs?

Well, it wasn't. It was just a little boy, whose whole name was Peleg Penniman.

He did not like his name at all, so almost everybody called him P-Penny instead, except his granddaddy, who called him P-leggins.

"Mummy, why did they name me Peleg?" he asked his mother one day.

"Because that was Daddy's name," said his mother.

"But why did they name Daddy that?" asked P-Penny again.

"Because that is Granddaddy's name," replied his mother.

"And why was Granddaddy named that?" went on P-Penny.

"Because Great-Granddaddy was," said his mother.

"Oh dear!" sighed P-Penny, "what a lot of poor little Pelegs."

But P-Penny did not let his funny name make him unhappy. He was a very cheerful little boy, who smiled at everybody, and so everybody liked him. Whenever he went down street with his little red cart, as he did nearly every day, there were always friends at their windows to wave to him, and when they met him they said:

"Well, P-Penny, how is business today?"

For P-Penny did a good deal of business with his little red cart. He carried groceries up the street, and packages to the post office, and sometimes he even dragged heavy books home from the Library for people. It was a very fine little cart, with rubber tires on the wheels, and strong straight sides, on which were painted these words:

P. PENNIMAN

—BUNDLES CALLED FOR AND DELIVERED

2 CENTS A MILE—5 CENTS FOR TWO MILES

P-Penny and his little red cart had already earned two dollars and thirty-five cents. He was saving all this money in a little iron bank for something especial, which was a secret. It was a funny little bank, shaped like an owl, with a slit under its beak where you could put in your nickels and your dimes. When you put them in, it snapped its bill, just like a real owl. Granddaddy, who had given it to P-Penny, called it "Penny-Wise." P-Penny put all his nickels and dimes into Penny-Wise when Mummy was not looking, for the secret was that P-Penny was going to buy a ring for Mummy for her birthday. Mummy had a plain gold ring already, but other mothers sometimes wore rings with pretty, bright stones in them, and he wanted his to have one, too. He had seen a row of them in the watchmaker's window, and the watchmaker had told him that he could have his choice for five dollars.

One sunny afternoon in the fall, when the fruit was ripe on the trees, P-Penny put on his red sweater and his round red cap and went out under the pear tree that grew in front of the little white house where he lived, to find a nice pear to eat. The ground under the tree was covered with goldy-brown pears, and up in the tree there were ever so many more—more, thought P-Penny, than he and Mummy and Granddaddy could possibly eat up, if they ate and ate and ate all the time until Christmas.

"Oh," said P-Penny suddenly to himself, as he took his first juicy bite. He had a fine idea! He would sell pears. He would be a fruit man, like the one who came to the back door every morning, with lots of dimes and nickels jingling in his pocket. He would earn a lot more nickels and dimes to jingle inside Penny-Wise.

So he set to work, and very soon he had picked up enough pears to cover the bottom of the little red cart. He was careful not to take any that had been bruised by falling off the tree, and he rubbed every one on his sweater to make it clean and shiny. As soon as he had a good load, he walked off down the street, dragging the little red cart behind him.

As he went along, he looked into all the gardens, to see if there were any houses that did not have fruit trees of their own, but nearly all of them did, for the street where P-Penny lived had once been a big orchard, and through the gates and hedges he could see pears and apples piled here and there on the grass.

After a while he met Mr. Rafferty, the postman. P-Penny and Mr. Rafferty were great friends.

"How's the fruit business?" said Mr. Rafferty, looking at the little red cart.

"Pretty good," replied P-Penny. "Would you like a pear? They're a cent apiece."

"Whew!" said Mr. Rafferty, "that's too much for me. I'm poor. But you can put one in my Uncle Sam's bag. He's rich and he likes pears. He'll pay it for me." And he put his hand in his pocket, and took out one cent and gave it to P-Penny.

P-Penny chose a pear out of the little red cart, and dropped it into the big leather bag which hung from Mr. Rafferty's shoulder. Then he picked up another and dropped that in, too.

"That's for your Uncle Sam," he said.

Mr. Rafferty laughed. "Thanks," he said. "When I get another cent from Uncle Sam I'll bring it to you."

Then P-Penny walked on, getting farther and farther away all the time from the little white house where he lived.

After a while he came to a street where there were very big houses indeed. They had fine trees around them, but P-Penny could not see any pears. The people must be very rich, thought P-Penny, to live in such grand houses—rich enough to be able to buy a great deal of fruit. At the very end of the street was the finest house of all. It was built of brick, with two big stone lions on each side of the high gate, and a curving driveway instead of a front walk. P-Penny dragged the little red cart in between the lions, and up the driveway to the great white door. He had to stand on tiptoe to reach the high brass knocker, and when he knocked, it made such a loud noise that he almost wished he had not come at all. After a few moments the door was opened, just a little way, by a large woman, with a white apron and a sour face.

"Do you want to buy some pears?" asked P-Penny, in a very small voice.

"No," said the woman, "we never buy anything at the door," and she closed it a little.

"Oh," said P-Penny, "but wouldn't you like a pear to eat? They're very nice. I'll give you one."

"No," said the woman again, with a faint, sour smile, "we don't eat pears here," and she closed the door entirely.

P-Penny picked up the handle of the little red cart, and walked soberly down the driveway. He thought it was very queer not to like pears, and he wondered if all the people in the other big houses didn't like them. Just as he reached the stone lions he heard a shrill voice behind him, from one of the upper windows.

"Hi, scalawag!" it called. "Come back."

P-Penny looked up at the windows. There was nobody to be seen, but, feeling a little scared, he turned and walked back with the little red cart. Just as he reached the great white door again, it was suddenly opened, and a very tall man stood in the doorway.

"Why, hello, P-Penny," said the man, looking down in surprise. "What are you doing here?"

P-Penny was surprised, too, for he saw that the man was Mr. Norman Ames, who came sometimes in the evening to see Mummy and Granddaddy. P-Penny did not like Mr. Norman Ames at all, because when he came to call Mummy never had time to play dominoes. P-Penny had hoped that he should never see Mr. Norman Ames again, and here he was!

"I'm selling pears," said P-Penny.

"Well, that's great," said Mr. Norman Ames. "I am out of pears, and Pauline likes them."

"I—I don't think she does," said P-Penny.

"Oh, yes, she does, she's crazy about them," said Mr. Norman Ames.

"Is Pauline the fat lady?" asked P-Penny, looking behind Mr. Norman Ames into the dark hall, where he thought that he saw a white apron.

"Who?" said Mr. Norman Ames. Then he laughed—such a jolly laugh. "Oh, no, that's Mrs. Pickens. Pauline is upstairs. How much are the pears?"

"One cent each," said P-Penny.

"Have you a hundred of them? Pauline wants a hundred," said Mr. Norman Ames.

"I—I don't think so," said P-Penny, bending over the little red cart, "but I'll count them."

"No, don't stop to do that," said Mr. Norman Ames. "We'll let Mrs. Pickens count them. While she's doing it, let's take one upstairs and see how much Pauline likes it."

So P-Penny took a pear from the little red cart, and followed Mr. Norman Ames into the big hall and up the broad velvet-covered stairs. At the top they went into a big, cheerful room, filled with sunshine and books. P-Penny could not see anyone in it, but as soon as he went through the door a voice said:

"Poor Pauline, oh, poor Pauline. Have you got it? Have you got it?"

"Yes, Pauline, we've got it," said Mr. Norman Ames.

Then across the room, on a table by the open window, P-Penny saw a large wire bird-cage, with an enormous white parrot in it. As they came up to the cage, the parrot edged along on its perch and bent its head, putting its beak through the wires.

"Scratch Pauline," she said.

Mr. Norman Ames scratched the back of her head gently with his finger, while P-Penny looked on, breathless.

"Now, Pauline, talk to P-Penny while I fix your pear," said Mr. Norman Ames, as he took his knife out of his pocket.

"Won't!" said Pauline. And she wouldn't. She just watched

with beady eyes, while Mr. Norman Ames cut up the pear with his pocketknife.

When it was ready, P-Penny held up a piece to the wire, and Pauline took it in her beak. Then, standing on one leg, and holding the pear in the other claw, she ate it quickly and daintily.

"What do you say to P-Penny, Pauline?" said Mr. Norman Ames. "I'm ashamed of your manners."

"Tanks," said Pauline. "Pitty good. More."

So P-Penny kept on handing in bits of pear, and Pauline kept on eating, and saying, "Pitty good. More," until every bit of it was gone.

"Shall I get another one?" asked P-Penny.

"No," said Mr. Norman Ames, "but you see she does want a cartload."

"Poor Pauline. More! More! More!" cried Pauline, looking right at P-Penny with her beady eye.

"She likes me, doesn't she?" said P-Penny, delighted.

"She's a wise old bird," said Mr. Norman Ames, as he went out of the room to answer the telephone.

"Poor, poor Pauline. Scratch Pauline," she coaxed, putting her head down very low.

P-Penny stuck one finger carefully through the wires, and scratched the soft white feathers ever so gently.

Suddenly Pauline lifted her head and nipped P-Penny's finger with her great sharp bill.

"Ouch!" said P-Penny.

"Got it! Got!" shrieked Pauline. "More. More!"

P-Penny ran out of the room as fast as he could, and downstairs with his nipped finger in his mouth. He did not stop until he reached the front door. Mr. Norman Ames was still talking at the telephone at the back of the house, but the little red cart had been emptied of pears, and in it instead, weighted down with a little stone so that the wind should not blow it away, was a fresh, crisp dollar bill.

P-Penny's eyes shone, and he forgot all about the nipped finger.

Never in his life had he earned so much money at one time, and he felt like a very big businessman indeed. He was not sure just how many nickels and dimes there were in that dollar bill, but he knew that there were a lot. He folded it up and put it in his pocket. Then he picked up the handle of the little red cart and started for home.

"Hi, scalawag. Come back!" cried a shrill voice again from the window upstairs.

"Oh," laughed P-Penny to himself, "it was Pauline!"

But this time he did not go back.

THE TRADING POST

by Ann Nolan Clark

Doli peeped shyly from the deep folds of her mother's wide skirts. Her black eyes shone.

Here was no home hogan, no rounded mud-plastered walls, no friendly center fire on which the supper mutton stew slowly bubbled and steamed. This place was the Trading Post, a great room of boarded walls with corners. The walls were lined with ladderlike shelves filled with hard things and soft things. At one end were Navajo blankets of many numbers, folded and stacked in piles of colors. On the side in back of the counter were cans on cans of foods. Some of the cans were covered with papers the colors of sunset and others were beautiful with pictures of green growing things.

Doli's mouth watered for the good food the cans held, she could almost taste their goodness.

Father was looking at the glass case full of silver rings and bracelets, coral and shell necklaces, and strings of turquoise. Father stood there, not talking, not moving, just looking at those things within the case.

Mother had come to the Post to sell a blanket of her weaving and to buy cans of tomatoes and peaches, sacks of wheat flour and cane sugar, bags of salt and coffee. If the day was a lucky one and Mother received many of the round, silver money pieces for her blanket, she would buy more things, perhaps candy, lard, baking powder.

Doli could not remember that she had been to this Trading Post before, although her mother said she had. Hobah, the elder sister, had told her of it many times as they sat together in the shade of the twisted juniper and lazily watched Sun-Carrier going on his day-long journey through the blue above them.

Doli was afraid, but very curious. Soon she ventured out from the shelter of her mother's many skirts and found a better place between the knees of her tall father where he stood looking at the turquoise and silver.

She leaned far out from the gateway of his knees, her stiffly gathered yellow-brown calico skirts petaled flower-like above her bare brown feet. Turquoise earbobs swung gently against her thin brown cheeks. Her velvet blouse was the color of a bluebird's wing, for she was a Bluebird child of the yellow sand country. Her thick black hair was smoothed back in a fat queue and tied with strings of white yarn, for she was a woman child and must look and act like Mother and like Elder Sister, Hobah.

Doli thought to herself, "This is a great place, this Trading Post." Her heart sang, "Beautiful. Beautiful. Things here are beautiful."

Flies buzzed in and out the doorway. Mother looked at many things and marked in her mind those it was good that she should buy. Doli watched her mother as she bought, one by one, the things she needed.

Through the open door she could see Navajo men squatting in the sand. Slowly, slowly, step by step, Doli went over to see what they were doing. They were playing a game. They drew a circle in the sand and placed small stones around its line. Two sticks made a little door in the circle of stones. Doli peeked around the side of the Trading Post door. There was Uncle! He was playing with the other men. He had three chips which were painted black on one side. Uncle tossed the chips and they came down with the unpainted side showing. That gave him one mark for each chip so he could place his little stick three stones from the door of the circle. The men spoke little. Their game was silent and swift. Doli liked watching them, but she was afraid to stay long for fear she might miss something else exciting.

She went around the wall, back to where her mother was buying things from the Trader's shelves and bins. Doli stood on tiptoe with her big eyes just above the counter. Mother's shopping was a game, too. Mother put a bag of cornmeal to one side and gave the Trader some silver pieces from the small pile which he had given her for the blanket. Mother waited a long time, looking and thinking. Then she put a box of matches beside the cornmeal and paid the Trader some more round money, this time a little piece.

Mother pulled her blanket closer about her. She went outside to the wagon to get another blanket in which to carry the things she bought. Doli went with her. They did not hurry. Going to the Trading Post was not an everyday happening. It was a day that had been looked forward to and planned for and it must be enjoyed slowly. Doli and her mother did not intend to treat it lightly or hurriedly. Buying things was fun enough and important enough to take a long time to finish.

They did not seem to be looking, but they saw the men who were still playing their game. Uncle was tossing the chips again. This time all the black sides came up. Each black chip gave three marks, so Uncle moved his little stick nine stones around the circle. Uncle was good at tossing chips. His little stick was way ahead. He was winning.

Mother went into the store to unfold her blanket on the

counter and put into it her bundles and bags. This done, she bought a bag of coffee and looked longingly at some bright velvet.

Doli watched her father. He was not talking to the Trader. He was not looking at the Trader, but the Trader was looking at him. The Trader was looking at the new bracelet Father was wearing. Father had just finished it this morning before they had started for the Post. He had made it to sell, but now he acted as if he had forgotten that he had it. Doli looked up at him. His eyes were still. Suddenly she knew something. Father was playing a game, too. He was playing that he did not want to sell his bracelet.

The Trader was very busy. When he was not taking round silver money from Mother's pile for the things she bought, he was trying to make Father want to sell his bracelet. Doli ducked her head. She had to put her hand over her mouth to hide a smile. At last Father said, Yes, he would sell the bracelet and the Trader gave him four round silver money pieces for it. Father took also, for good measure, some little brown papers and a bag of tobacco for the cigarettes which he liked to smoke.

The Trader gave Father a square of paper with black marks on it. He said it was a letter from Big Brother in the far-distant School land where he had gone so long ago. The Trader made the paper talk for Father, saying words of greeting from Big Brother to his home people.

Doli suddenly had a great longing for the home hogan and for tall, laughing Big Brother, who used to bring her gifts of bluebird feathers and colored stones. But that was long ago before he had gone to the School. Only once since then had he returned to visit them.

Doli took the candy which the Trader gave her, but the wonders of the Trading Post were gone. She no longer saw the cans of food, the blankets, the silver-trimmed saddles, the beautiful blue kettles and pans. She wanted to go home to her sheepskin bed by the friendly center fire. She was tired. She was hungry, so hungry that she could almost smell the hot, woolly smell of the supper mutton stew. She remembered the first supper with Big Brother the time he had come back to visit. There was mutton stew that night, but he had not eaten. He had sat in the shadows of the darkening hogan, not laughing, but quiet with a kind of anger that was frightening. When he spoke at all it was of a table and dishes and chairs and beds. Doli had not understood. What were these things of which he talked, she wondered. Why did he want them for this home place which always had felt so right?

Big Brother's second going had been in the season of the corn-growing-large. Corn-growing-large time had come again, but Big Brother had not returned.

Doli looked up. She had forgotten that she was here at the Trading Post. The Trader was looking down at her. He had given her candy. Father spoke to her in Navajo. He said in his low kind voice, "This White Man likes children, I think."

Little Bluebird pushed against her father's knees. In English she said to the Trader, "Big Brother." It was all the English she knew. Big Brother, himself, had taught her Navajo tongue to say it. "Big Brother," she repeated softly, shyly, but with great courage to show him that she was pleased with his gift of candy.

Tall Father moved toward the door. Doli went with him. He lifted her into the wagon and untied his horses from the bar. By and by Mother finished shopping and came out with her blanket bundle. She, too, climbed into the wagon. She pulled her blanket high up around her head and from within its shelter she looked out at the wagons and horses and people around the Trading Post. Doli pulled up her blanket but she, too, saw the happenings around her.

Navajos sitting in the door shade looked up from their game and nodded. Navajos standing by the watering trough looked back and nodded. Father said to them, "The People speak as they pass. My way lies in this direction."

It was sun-hot time of day. Far away a whirlwind danced across the sand. Doli held the bag of candy tightly in her thin brown hand. Father called to the horses a high-pitched, long-drawn "A-ya-an-na."

They started toward home. The horses moved slowly along the sandy ruts. Yucca bloomed by the side of the road. A road runner ran a race with the wagon. A prairie dog sat by his front door and watched their passing. A jackrabbit loped across the road.

Father sang as he drove along. Doli was sleepy. Her head nodded to her father's singing and to the lurchings of the wagon.

It had been a long day. It had been a good day, but now the journey to the Trading Post was over.

THE MIDDLE BEAR

by Eleanor Estes

When a play was given at the town hall, Sylvie was usually the only one of the four Moffats who was in it. However, once in a while the others were in a play. For instance, Rufus had been the smallest of the seven dwarfs. And once Janey had been a butterfly. She had not been an altogether successful butterfly, though, for she had tripped on the sole of her stocking, turning a somersault all across the stage. And whereas Joey was rarely in a play, he was often in charge of switching the lights on and off.

Jane liked the plays at the Town Hall. In fact she liked them better than the moving pictures. In the moving pictures Jane always found it difficult to tell the good man from the bad man. Especially if they both wore black mustaches. Of course the pianist usually played ominous music just before the bad man came on the scene, and that helped. Even so, Jane preferred the plays at the Town Hall. There she had no trouble at all telling the good from the bad.

Now there was to be a play at the Town Hall, "The Three

Bears," and all four of the Moffats were going to be in it. Miss Chichester, the dancing-school teacher, was putting it on. But the money for the tickets was not going into her pocket or into the Moffats' pocket, even though they were all in the play. The money was to help pay for the new parish house. The old one had burned down last May and now a new one was being built. "The Three Bears" was to help raise the money to finish it. A benefit performance, it was called.

In this benefit performance, Sylvie was to play the part of Goldilocks. Joey was to be the big bear, Rufus the little bear, and Janey the middle bear. Jane had not asked to be the middle bear. It just naturally came out that way. The middle Moffat was going to be the middle bear.

As a rule Joey did not enjoy the idea of acting in a play any more than he liked going to dancing school. However, he felt this play would be different. He felt it would be like having a disguise on, to be inside of a bear costume. And Jane felt the same way. She thought the people in the audience would not recognize her as the butterfly who turned a somersault across the stage, because she would be comfortably hidden inside her brown bear costume. As for Rufus, he hoped that Sylvie, the Goldilocks of this game, would not sit down too hard on that nice little chair of his and really break it to bits. It was such a good chair, and he wished he had it at home.

Mama was making all the costumes, even the bear heads. A big one for Joey, a little one for Rufus, and a middle-sized one for Jane. Of course she wasn't making them out of bear fur; she was using brown outing flannel.

Now Jane was trying on her middle bear costume. She stepped into the body of the costume and then Mama put the head on her.

"Make the holes for the eyes big enough," Jane begged. "So I'll see where I'm going and won't turn somersaults."

"Well," said Mama, "if I cut the eyes any larger you will look like a deep sea diver instead of a bear."

"Oh, well . . ." said Jane hastily. "A bear's got to look like a bear. Never mind making them any bigger, then."

Besides being in the play, each of the Moffats also had ten tickets to sell. And since Rufus really was too little to go from house to house and street to street selling tickets, the other three Moffats had even more to dispose of. Forty tickets!

At first Jane wondered if a girl should sell tickets to a play she was going to be in. Was that being conceited? Well, since the money was for the new parish house and not for the Moffats, she finally decided it was all right to sell the tickets. Besides, she thought, who would recognize her as the girl who sold tickets once she was inside her bear costume?

Sylvie sold most of her tickets like lightning to the ladies in the choir. But Joey's and Janey's tickets became grimier and grimier, they had such trouble disposing of them. Nancy Stokes said she would help even though she went to a different parish house. She and Joey and Jane went quietly and politely up on people's verandas and rang the bell.

"Buy a ticket for the benefit of the new parish house?" was all they meant to say. But very often no one at all answered the bell.

"They can't all be away," said Nancy. "Do you think they hide behind the curtains when they see us coming?"

"Oh, no," said Jane. "You see it'd be different if the money was for us. But it isn't. It's a benefit. Why should they hide?"

One lady said she was very sorry but she was making mincemeat. "See?" she said, holding up her hands. They were all covered with mincemeat. So she could not buy a ticket. Not possibly, and she closed the door in their faces.

"She could wash her hands," said Nancy angrily. The children called this lady "mincemeat," ever after. Of course she never knew it.

Yes, the tickets were very hard to sell. But little by little the pile did dwindle. If only everybody were like Mrs. Stokes, they would go very fast. She bought four tickets! Jane was embarrassed.

"Tell your mother she doesn't have to buy all those tickets just 'cause all of us are in the play," she instructed Nancy.

But all the Stokes insisted they really wanted to go. And even if none of the Moffats were in it, they would still want to go, for the play would help to build a new parish house. What nice people! thought Jane. Here they were, a family who went to the white church, buying tickets to help build a parish house for Janey's church. She hoped she would be a good middle bear, so they would be proud they knew her.

At last it was the night of the play. The four Moffats knew their lines perfectly. This was not surprising, considering they all lived in the same house and could practice their lines any time they wanted to. And, besides this, they had had two rehearsals, one in regular clothes and one in their bear costumes.

When Jane reached the Town Hall, she was surprised to find there were many features on the program besides "The Three Bears." The Gillespie twins were going to give a piano duet. "By the Brook," it was called. A boy was going to play the violin. Someone else was going to toe dance. And Miss Beale was going to sing a song. A big program. And the Moffats, all of them except Mama, were going to watch this whole performance from behind the scenes. They could not sit in the audience with the regular people with their bear costumes on, for that would give the whole show away.

Jane fastened her eye to a hole in the curtain. Mama had not yet come. Of course Mama would have to sit out front there with the regular people, even though she had made the costumes. The only people who had arrived so far were Clara Pringle and Brud. They were sitting in the front row and Jane wondered how they had gotten in because the front door that all the regular people were supposed to use wasn't even open yet.

When Jane wasn't peering through a hole in the curtain, Joey or Rufus was. Each one hoped he would be the first to see Mama when she came in. Or now and then they tried to squeeze through the opening at the side of the asbestos curtain. But the gnarled little janitor shook his head at them. So they stayed inside.

Sylvie was busy putting make-up on herself and on the dancers' faces. Jane watched them enviously. The only trouble with wearing a bear costume, she thought, was that she couldn't have her face painted. Well, she quickly consoled herself, she certainly would not have stage fright inside her bear head. Whereas she might if there were just paint on her face. "Somebody has been sitting in my chair," she rehearsed her lines. She stepped into her bear costume. But before putting on her head, she helped Rufus into his bear uniform. He didn't call it a costume. A uniform. A bear uniform. Jane set his head on his shoulders, found his two eyes for him so he could see out, and the little bear was ready.

Joey had no difficulty stepping into his costume and even in finding his own two eyes. Now the big bear and the little bear were ready. Jane looked around for her head, to put it on. Where was it?

"Where's my head?" she asked. "My bear head."

Nobody paid any attention to her. Miss Chichester was running back and forth and all around, giving an order here and an order there. Once as she rushed by, causing a great breeze, Jane yelled to make herself heard, "How can we act 'The Three Bears' unless I find my middle bear head?"

"Not just now. I'm too busy," was all Miss Chichester said.

Everybody was too busy to help Jane find her head. Sylvie was helping the toe dancer dress. Joey was busy running around doing this and doing that for Miss Chichester. And the little old janitor was busy tightening ropes and making sure the lights were working. Rufus could not be torn from a hole in the curtain. He was looking for Mama.

Jane sighed. Everybody's busy, she thought. She rummaged around in a big box of costumes. Maybe her bear head had been stuck in it. She found a dragon head and tried it on. How would that be? She looked in the mirror. The effect was interesting. But, no, she could not wear this, for a bear cannot be a dragon.

Goodness, thought Jane. The curtain will go up, and the middle bear won't be a whole bear. This was worse than tripping over her stocking the time she was a butterfly. Maybe Joey and Rufus somehow or another had two heads on. They didn't, though, just their own. Phew, it was warm inside these bear costumes. Jane stood beside Rufus and looked through another small hole in the curtain. Oh! The big door was open! People were beginning to arrive. And what kind of a bear would she be without a head? Maybe she wouldn't be allowed to be a bear at all. But there certainly could not be three bears without a middle one.

"Don't worry," said Rufus, not moving an inch from his spot. "Lend you mine for half the play. . . ."

"Thanks," said Jane. "But we all have to have our heads on all through the whole thing."

The Stokes were coming in! Jane felt worried. The only person who might be able to fix a new bear head for her in a hurry was Mama. Oh, if she had only made a couple of spare heads. But Mama wasn't coming yet. Jane resolved to go and meet her. She put on her tam and her chinchilla coat over her bear costume. Then she ran down the three narrow steps into the Hall. She crouched low in her coat in order not to give away the fact that she was clad in a bear costume. Nobody on this side of the curtain was supposed to know what people on her side of the curtain had on until the curtain rolled up. Surprise. That's what was important in a play.

Mr. Buckle was coming in now, walking towards the front row. Jane stooped low, with her knees bent beneath her. In front her coat nearly reached the ground. From the way she looked from the front, few would guess that she was the middle bear. Of course her feet showed. They were encased in the brown costume. But she might be a brownie or even a squirrel.

"Hello, Mr. Buckle," said Jane. "I'm in a hurry. . . ."

"Where are you going, middle Moffat?" he asked. "Aren't you the prima donna?"

"No. Just the middle bear."

"Well, that's fine. The middle Moffat is the middle bear."

"Yes. Or I was until I lost my head."

"Oh, my," said Mr. Buckle. "This then is not your head?" he asked, pointing to her tam.

"Yes, but not my bear head. I don't mean bare head. Bear head! B-e-a-r. That kind of head."

"Mystifying. Very mystifying," said Mr. Buckle, settling himself slowly in a seat in the front row.

"You'll see later," said Jane, running down the aisle.

She ran all the way home. But the house was dark. Mama had already left. And she must have gone around the other way or Jane would have passed her. Jane raced back to the Town Hall. There! Now! The lights were dim. The entertainment had begun. Jane tried to open the side door. Chief Mulligan was guarding this entrance. He did not want to let her in at first. He thought she was just a person. But when she showed him her costume, he opened the door just wide enough for her. The bear costume was as good as a password.

The toe dancer was doing the split. Jane tiptoed up the three steps and went backstage, wondering what would happen now. The show always goes on. There was some comfort in that thought. Somehow, someone would fix her head. Or possibly while she was gone her middle bear head had been found. She hoped she would not have to act with her head bare.

Miss Chichester snatched her.

"Oh, there you are, Jane! Hop into your costume, dear."

"I'm in it," said Jane. "But I can't find my middle bear head."

"Heavens!" said Miss Chichester, grasping her own head. "What else will go wrong?"

Jane looked at her in surprise. What else *had* gone wrong? Had others lost worse than their heads?

"Where's the janitor?" Miss Chichester asked. "Maybe he let his grandchildren borrow it."

Jane knew he hadn't, but she couldn't tell Miss Chichester for she had already flown off. And then Janey had an idea.

"I know what," she said to Joey. "Pin me together." And she pulled the neck part of her costume up over her head. Joey pinned it with two safety pins, and he cut two holes for her eyes. This costume was not comfortable now. Pulling it up and pinning it this way lifted Jane's arms so she had trouble making them hang down the way she thought a bear's should. However, at any rate, she now had a bear head of sorts.

"Do I look like a bear?" she asked Rufus.

"You look like a brown ghost," Rufus replied.

"Don't you worry," said Sylvie, coming up. "You look like a very nice little animal."

INDIANS IN THE HOUSE

by Laura Ingalls Wilder

Early one morning Pa took his gun and went hunting.

He had meant to make the bedstead that day. He had brought in the slabs, when Ma said she had no meat for dinner. So he stood the slabs against the wall and took down his gun.

Jack wanted to go hunting, too. His eyes begged Pa to take him, and whines came up from his chest and quivered in his throat till Laura almost cried with him. But Pa chained him to the stable.

"No, Jack," Pa said. "You must stay here and guard the place." Then he said to Mary and Laura, "Don't let him loose, girls."

Poor Jack lay down. It was a disgrace to be chained, and he felt it deeply. He turned his head from Pa and would not watch him going away with the gun on his shoulder. Pa went farther and farther away, till the prairies swallowed him and he was gone.

Laura tried to comfort Jack, but he would not be comforted. The more he thought about the chain, the worse he felt. Laura tried to cheer him up to frisk and play, but he only grew more sullen.

Both Mary and Laura felt that they could not leave Jack while he was so unhappy. So all that morning they stayed by the stable. They stroked Jack's smooth, brindled head and scratched around his ears, and told him how sorry they were that he must be chained. He lapped their hands a little bit, but he was very sad and angry.

His head was on Laura's knee and she was talking to him, when suddenly he stood up and growled a fierce, deep growl. The hair on his neck stood straight up and his eyes glared red.

Laura was frightened. Jack had never growled at her before. Then she looked over her shoulder, where Jack was looking, and she saw two naked, wild men coming, one behind the other, on the Indian trail.

"Mary! Look!" she cried. Mary looked and saw them, too.

They were tall, thin, fierce-looking men. Their skin was brown-ish-red. Their heads seemed to go up to a peak, and the peak was a tuft of hair that stood straight up and ended in feathers. Their eyes were black and still and glittering, like snake's eyes.

They came closer and closer. Then they went out of sight, on the other side of the house.

Laura's head turned and so did Mary's, and they looked at the place where those terrible men would appear when they came past the house.

"Indians!" Mary whispered. Laura was shivery; there was a queer feeling in her middle and the bones in her legs felt weak. She wanted to sit down. But she stood and looked and waited for those Indians to come out from beyond the house. The Indians did not do that.

All this time Jack had been growling. Now he stopped growling and was lunging against the chain. His eyes were red and his lips curled back and all the hair on his back was bristling. He bounded and bounded, clear off the ground, trying to get loose from the chain. Laura was glad that the chain kept him right there with her.

"Jack's here," she whispered to Mary. "Jack won't let them hurt us. We'll be safe if we stay close to Jack."

"They are in the house," Mary whispered. "They are in the house with Ma and Carrie."

Then Laura began to shake all over. She knew she must do something. She did not know what those Indians were doing to Ma and Baby Carrie. There was no sound at all from the house.

"Oh, what are they doing to Ma!" she screamed, in a whisper.

"Oh, I don't know!" Mary whispered.

"I'm going to let Jack loose," Laura whispered, hoarsely. "Jack will kill them."

"Pa said not to," Mary answered. They were too scared to speak out loud. They put their heads together and watched the house and whispered.

"He didn't know Indians would come," Laura said.

"He said not to let Jack loose." Mary was almost crying.

Laura thought of little Baby Carrie and Ma, shut in the house with those Indians. She said, "I'm going in to help Ma!"

She ran two steps, and walked a step, then she turned and flew back to Jack. She clutched him wildly and hung on to his strong, panting neck. Jack wouldn't let anything hurt her.

"We mustn't leave Ma in there alone," Mary whispered. She stood still and trembled. Mary never could move when she was frightened.

Laura hid her face against Jack and held on to him tightly.

Then she made her arms let go. Her hands balled into fists and her eyes shut tight and she ran toward the house as fast as she could run.

She stumbled and fell down and her eyes popped open. She was up again and running before she could think. Mary was close behind her. They came to the door. It was open, and they slipped into the house without a sound.

The naked wild men stood by the fireplace. Ma was bending over the fire, cooking something. Carrie clung to Ma's skirts with both hands and her head was hidden in the folds.

Laura ran toward Ma, but just as she reached the hearth she

smelled a horribly bad smell and she looked up at the Indians. Quick as a flash, she ducked behind the long, narrow slab that leaned against the wall.

The slab was just wide enough to cover both her eyes. If she held her head perfectly still and pressed her nose against the slab, she couldn't see the Indians. And she felt safer. But she couldn't help moving her head just a little, so that one eye peeped out and she could see the wild men.

First she saw their leather moccasins. Then their stringy, bare, red-brown legs, all the way up. Around their waists each of the Indians wore a leather thong, and the furry skin of a small animal hung down in front. The fur was striped black and white, and now Laura knew what made that smell. The skins were fresh skunk skins.

A knife like Pa's hunting-knife, and a hatchet like Pa's hatchet, were stuck into each skunk skin.

The Indians' ribs made little ridges up their bare sides. Their arms were folded on their chests. At last Laura looked again at their faces, and she dodged quickly behind the slab.

Their faces were bold and fierce and terrible. Their black eyes glittered. High on their foreheads and above their ears where hair grows, these wild men had no hair. But on top of their heads a tuft of hair stood straight up. It was wound around with string, and feathers were stuck in it.

When Laura peeked out from behind the slab again, both Indians were looking straight at her. Her heart jumped into her throat and choked her with its pounding. Two black eyes glittered down into her eyes. The Indian did not move, not one muscle of his face moved. Only his eyes shone and sparkled at her. Laura didn't move, either. She didn't even breathe.

The Indian made two short, harsh sounds in his throat. The other Indian made one sound, like "Hah!" Laura hid her eyes behind the slab again.

She heard Ma take the cover off the bake-oven. She heard the Indians squat down on the hearth. After a while she heard them eating.

Laura peeked, and hid, and peeked again, while the Indians ate the cornbread that Ma had baked. They ate every morsel of it, and even picked up the crumbs from the hearth. Ma stood and watched them and stroked Baby Carrie's head. Mary stood close behind Ma and held onto her sleeve.

Faintly Laura heard Jack's chain rattling. Jack was still trying to get loose.

When every crumb of the cornbread was gone, the Indians rose up. The skunk smell was stronger when they moved. One of them made harsh sounds in his throat again. Ma looked at him with big eyes; she did not say anything. The Indian turned around, the other Indian turned, too, and they walked across the floor and out through the door. Their feet made no sound at all.

Ma sighed a long, long sigh. She hugged Laura tight in one arm and Mary tight in the other arm, and through the window they watched those Indians going away, one behind the other, on the dim trail toward the west. Then Ma sat down on the bed and hugged Laura and Mary tighter, and trembled. She looked sick.

"Do you feel sick, Ma?" Mary asked her.

"No," said Ma. "I'm just thankful they're gone."

Laura wrinkled her nose and said, "They smell awful."

"That was the skunk skins they wore," Ma said.

Then they told her how they had left Jack and had come into the house because they were afraid the Indians would hurt her and Baby Carrie. Ma said they were her brave little girls.

"Now we must get dinner," she said. "Pa will be here soon and we must have dinner ready for him. Mary, bring me some wood. Laura, you may set the table."

Ma rolled up her sleeves and washed her hands and mixed cornbread, while Mary brought the wood and Laura set the table. She set a tin plate and knife and fork and cup for Pa, and the same for Ma, with Carrie's little tin cup beside Ma's. And she set tin plates and knives and forks for her and Mary, but only their one cup between the plates.

Ma made the cornmeal and water into two thin loaves, each shaped in a half circle. She laid the loaves with their straight sides together in the bake-oven, and she pressed her hand flat on top of each loaf. Pa always said he did not ask any other sweetening, when Ma put the prints of her hands on the loaves.

Laura had hardly set the table when Pa was there. He left a big rabbit and two prairie hens outside the door, and stepped in and laid his gun on its pegs. Laura and Mary ran and clutched him, both talking at once.

"What's all this? What's all this?" he said, rumpling their hair. "Indians? So you've seen Indians at last, have you, Laura? I noticed they have a camp in a little valley west of here. Did Indians come to the house, Caroline?"

"Yes, Charles, two of them," Ma said. "I'm sorry, but they took all your tobacco, and they ate a lot of cornbread. They pointed to the cornmeal and made signs for me to cook some. I was afraid not to. Oh Charles! I was afraid!"

"You did the right thing," Pa told her. "We don't want to make enemies of any Indians." Then he said, "Whew! what a smell."

"They wore fresh skunk skins," said Ma. "And that was all they wore."

"Must have been thick while they were here," Pa said.

"It was, Charles. We were short of cornmeal, too."

"Oh well. We have enough to hold out awhile yet. And our meat is running all over the country. Don't worry, Caroline."

"But they took all your tobacco."

"Never mind," Pa said. "I'll get along without tobacco till I can make that trip to Independence. The main thing is to be on good terms with the Indians. We don't want to wake up some night with a band of the screeching dev——"

He stopped. Laura dreadfully wanted to know what he had been going to say. But Ma's lips were pressed together and she shook a little shake of her head at Pa.

"Come on, Mary and Laura!" Pa said. "We'll skin that rabbit and dress the prairie hens while that cornbread bakes. Hurry! I'm hungry as a wolf!"

They sat on the woodpile in the wind and sunshine and

watched Pa work with his hunting knife. The big rabbit was shot through the eye, and the prairie hens' heads were shot clean away. They never knew what hit them, Pa said.

Laura held the edge of the rabbit skin while Pa's keen knife ripped it off the rabbit meat. "I'll salt this skin and peg it out on the house wall to dry," he said. "It will make a warm fur cap for some little girl to wear next winter."

But Laura could not forget the Indians. She said to Pa that if they had turned Jack loose, he would have eaten those Indians right up.

Pa laid down the knife. "Did you girls even think of turning Jack loose?" he asked, in a dreadful voice.

Laura's head bowed down and she whispered, "Yes, Pa."

"After I told you not to?" Pa said, in a more dreadful voice.

Laura couldn't speak, but Mary choked, "Yes, Pa."

For a moment Pa was silent. He sighed a long sigh like Ma's sigh after the Indians went away.

"After this," he said, in a terrible voice, "you girls remember always to do as you're told. Don't you even think of disobeying me. Do you hear?"

"Yes, Pa," Laura and Mary whispered.

"Do you know what would have happened if you had turned Jack loose?" Pa asked.

"No, Pa," they whispered.

"He would have bitten those Indians," said Pa. "Then there would have been trouble. Bad trouble. Do you understand?"

"Yes, Pa," they said. But they did not understand.

"Would they have killed Jack?" Laura asked.

"Yes. And that's not all. You girls remember this: you do as you're told, no matter what happens."

"Yes, Pa," Laura said, and Mary said, "Yes, Pa." They were glad they had not turned Jack loose.

"Do as you're told," said Pa, "and no harm will come to you."

AIRPLANE ANDY

by Sanford Tousey

Andy and his father drove to LaGuardia Field and Captain Armstrong parked his car in the space reserved for those who work for the air lines. Andy was excited as he followed his father through the waiting room where passengers and their forty pounds of luggage were being weighed.

"Uncle Sam's Civil Aeronautics Board is very particular to see that passenger planes are not overloaded, Andy," said his father. "Then they have a better chance for a safe landing in an emergency." He led Andy out onto the flying field where several big planes were parked. Others were floating down from the sky and landing on the runways ready to land the passengers. Some of them had slept all night on the planes that flew from coast to coast.

"That plane is exactly like the model I made last winter!" Andy told his father. He was happy to recognize the original and to realize how closely his model resembled the real thing.

"Why is that big orange and blue truck rushing up to the plane?" asked Andy.

"Watch them get that long hose out," advised his father, "and you'll see them fuel the plane. Just as the gas-station man does to our car, only this gas pump is movable. See the hose being run up to the tank in the wing? And there comes the U. S. Mail truck."

Andy watched the mail truck drive up to the nose of the ship where attendants threw the sacks in through the open door of the mail compartment in front of the pilot's cabin. Then the passengers' baggage arrived on a small truck called a "donkey" and was placed in a baggage compartment behind the passengers' cabin. Air express packages went with it.

Andy heard a loudspeaker shouting, "Flight Number 25 now loading. Passengers for Washington and points South go aboard."

"That is my regular flight, Andy," said his father. "Come aboard and I'll show you where I sit when I'm not having my days off."

Before they could walk up the loading steps which had been wheeled to the open door of the plane, a uniformed attendant ran up to Captain Armstrong.

"They want to see you in the office, sir," he said. "There's heavy traffic today and they're putting on an extra plane. Too bad, on one of your days off."

"Come along, Andy," said his father. "We'll go to the office and see what's doing."

Captain Armstrong found that, in order to help out in the emergency, he must take out another plane within a half-hour.

"You'll have to go along with me, Andy," he said. "We'll telephone your mother not to expect us home for dinner. Then we'll telegraph your grandfather Armstrong in Washington. He can meet the plane at the airport and you can stay with him till I return."

When the plane was all ready they walked up the steps. A flight-stewardess in uniform was inside showing passengers to their seats.

"Come forward to the pilot's compartment, Andy," said his father.

The co-pilot was not yet aboard so Andy sat in his seat for a few minutes. What a thrill that was! He put his hands on the wheel, which looked like an automobile's steering wheel with part of the rim cut off. This controlled the upward or downward movements of the plane in flight. The instrument panel was filled with dozens of dials.

"I must make a little panel like that for my new model and paint the instruments on it!" thought Andy. He studied the panel as his father watched him.

"What are all these instruments?" asked Andy.

"That's a compass, and just below is the artificial horizon to show whether you are flying on an even keel. This is an air-speed indicator. Next to it is the bank-and-turn indicator and the rate-of-climb indicator. That's the altimeter to show our flying height. These others are gasoline gauges, oil-temperature gauges, ammeters, pressure gauges, a tachometer to show how fast the motor is turning over, switches, throttles, and the radio. I haven't time to explain all of them now, but someday you'll know them all and what they're for. Big planes on some lines have an automatic pilot that is called Iron Mike."

"That's a funny name for an instrument!" said Andy.

"Yes, and it's almost human," replied his father. "It's a mechanical pilot that works the controls of the plane and flies it automatically."

The co-pilot came in, so the flight-stewardess led Andy to a seat in the passenger cabin and strapped the seat belt. These belts were always used by the passengers at the time of taking off or landing, just in case the plane bumped.

Then Andy heard his father speed up, first one motor, then the other, to be certain they had been properly warmed. Mechanics had already made sure that the engines were working properly.

"Eastern Flight 25 to Tower! Ready for taxi." Captain Armstrong called the radio tower on his radio.

From the radio tower came back: "Tower to Flight 25. Clear to taxi to Runway 7." It was time for the plane to move.

When the motors were slowed down to normal Captain Armstrong heard in his earphones:

"O.K., Flight 25. You may proceed when ready. You're clear from here to Newark. Proceed east to one thousand feet and then make your turn."

"All right," replied Captain Armstrong, and they were off.

Very soon they were high above the city and Andy looked down with amazement at the patterns made by the parks and their small lakes. The tall skyscrapers stuck up like irregular fingers.

The stewardess, who had been passing chewing gum, matches, and magazines to the passengers, now came over to Andy.

"Your father just told me to have you look below, out of your window. We are passing your home."

Andy was all excited! Would he know their house? Would his mother be looking for them? Yes! there was a little figure stepping off the front porch. The landing lights were flashed twice by Pilot Armstrong and at once the little figure waved a white towel, so Andy knew that his mother had seen the flashes.

"It's Mother!" he shouted to the stewardess.

"We're getting away up in the blue now," thought Andy. "I've never sent one of my models up *this* high!"

After a while, the stewardess looked at her watch.

"How would you like something to eat?" she asked smiling.

This sounded good to Andy, and he settled back in his chair to be served sandwiches and warm bouillon by the stewardess.

Captain Armstrong took the plane in "on the beam" and Andy found his grandfather awaiting him at the airport all ready to show him the sights of Washington. It was all exciting, but Grandpa could scarcely drag Andy away from the interesting exhibit of planes, old and new, at the Smithsonian Institution.

These old planes of an earlier flying period fascinated Andy, including the Spirit of St. Louis, the first plane to fly non-stop from New York to Paris.

Captain Armstrong was flying on to Richmond to complete the morning's flight. The next day he returned to Washington on another plane and picked up Andy.

When they reached home Andy filled his mother's ears with the account of his adventures. And when he had finished telling her he dashed downstairs to the workbench to finish another part of his model plane.

One evening Andy's father came home with a broad smile on his face.

"Look at this letter," he said to Mrs. Armstrong. "The company has made me Flight Superintendent of this division. When the transport planes are crowded I'll have a smaller Stinson plane for my own use. Maybe I'll take you along someday, Andy. How would you like that?"

"When?" shouted Andy. "I can hardly wait!"

One morning his father took him to the airport where a sturdy little cabin monoplane had been taxied out of the big hangar. It was all warmed up and ready to go. They got in, took off, and headed southward. In New Jersey his father circled twice around their home while his mother waved to them. In less than two hours they had crossed New Jersey and were flying over Delaware Bay, nearly out of sight of land. Andy saw water to his left, land to his right.

They were flying near the Atlantic coast now and Andy could see two thin strips of sand extending southward. When they reached the spot where one of these two strips ended Andy's father said, "From here, Andy, you can see two very historic spots. That monument below us is at Kitty Hawk, North Carolina. It was erected in honor of the Wright brothers' first flight in a powered airplane in 1903. I doubt if either of the Wrights guessed the changes that would be made in planes during the lifetime of one of them. They did not vision companies of soldiers jumping out of transport planes and parachuting to earth, nor a man bailing out at 31,400 feet and dropping 29,300 feet before opening a parachute; planes that could fly four hundred miles per hour would cause no astonishment. Their own little flying box kite had to be handled very carefully to keep it in the air at all."

"Even the designs for my model planes change so fast I can hardly keep up with them!" replied Andy.

After a while his father said, "Now we'll stop at Wilmington, North Carolina, and pick up gas."

They landed at Bluethenthal Field where a gray-haired man prepared to fill their tank.

"You look like an old-timer," said Captain Armstrong. "We

just passed over Kitty Hawk. I wanted my son Andy here to see the country's tribute to a pair of real flyers."

"Yes, they were smart boys, the Wright brothers," said the attendant. "I knew them. They had everything—patience, persistence, courage, and resourcefulness. When they needed a lighter gasoline engine than could be bought they weren't stumped—they made it themselves! They studied the early efforts of Canute and Lilienthal at gliding and learned what not to do.

"I was down there on the Kitty Hawk sands that cold December seventeenth in 1903 when they got their kite into the air and made the first airplane flight. It was a big day for the world—bigger than any of us realized, even the Wrights. For they had done a lot of gliding before ever they flew and they knew what it was to be in the air."

Andy was thrilled to listen to a man who had seen the first powered flight.

Andy's father paid for the gasoline and they took off to westward. When they reached the route of the Eastern Air Lines Captain Armstrong made his inspection.

Andy thought the day had passed all too fast as they headed for home.

"Looks stormy ahead, Dad," he remarked.

"Yes," replied his father. "But we'll fly around it. Have to do it to get my report in tonight."

The air got bumpier and bumpier as they attempted to skirt the storm area. The little plane rose and fell, rose and fell, until Andy's stomach began to feel funny. He didn't feel like taking the controls now, even if his father had let him. And Captain Armstrong was too busy at that moment, controlling the ship, to think of anything else.

Andy could see the sharp streaks of lightning over to the right as the plane bucked the rising gale. Andy's father had once told him that early flyers like Farman sent up toy balloons at the airfield. If the wind blew them away at fifteen or twenty miles per hour the aviator refused to fly. Yet here they were, bucking a fifty-mile gale. As gusts hit the plane it seemed to shiver and shake.

The vibration made Andy uneasy, and then he saw the serious look on his father's face.

"Can we make it, Dad?" he asked.

"Don't worry, Andy," came the answer. "I've been through worse than this, and in an open cockpit, too."

Andy's worry was relieved. He watched his father handle the controls with all the skill acquired in his years of flying. But his imagination pictured what would happen to one of his model planes aloft in such a gale. In all probability he would never see it again.

Watching the storm kept Andy on the edge of his seat. At last they were leaving the storm area now and Captain Armstrong said, "A few more minutes and we'll be in sight of the airport."

"Oh, boy!" called Andy shortly afterward, "there it is."

Captain Armstrong made a perfect three-point landing and shut off his motor.

Mrs. Armstrong had watched the storm and she was happy to see them safe when they drove into the yard later on.

"I'm so glad you're home," she exclaimed as she gave each one a hearty hug.

Andy had enjoyed his trip immensely but he could hardly wait for morning to come so could get to work on his model plane. He felt like a real pilot now and even his models seemed more real after his voyage in the air. Andy's little planes had won many contests held by the local model airplane club, and his parents were proud of his good record and planes.

His mother came downstairs to see how he was getting along. When she saw his neat work on the Flying Wing she said, "Well, Andy, you're certainly outdoing yourself!"

"This time I want my model to be good enough to be sent to the national contest at Chicago," Andy said eagerly. "This Flying Wing ought to do it. It's the best model I've made. Dad bought me this pair of motors that are whizzes, and I'm trying to scheme some way so that the ship won't fly out of sight and be lost."

Andy was busy the next day trying to work out this problem when his father arrived home with a box under his arm.

"What do you think I have here, Andy?" he asked. "It's a radio control for your model plane!"

He unwrapped the package, and there before Andy was the solution of his big problem.

"Oh, boy, Dad!" Andy cried. "I didn't know there was such a thing. Maybe it will help my Flying Wing get a chance at the national model contest. Wouldn't that be great?"

"You've worked hard for it, Andy, and with all your experiments with other models you ought to have a good chance. Your mother and I wish you luck. We hope you win the trophy."

"Me, too!" said Andy as he began studying the printed plan for installing the radio control.

ANIMAL CRACKERS

by Christopher Morley

Animal crackers, and cocoa to drink
That is the finest of suppers, I think;
When I'm grown up and can have what I please
I think I shall always insist upon these.

What do you choose when you're offered a treat?
When Mother says, "What would you like best to eat?"
Is it waffles and syrup, or cinnamon toast?
It's cocoa and animals that I love the most!

The kitchen's the coziest place that I know:
The kettle is singing, the stove is aglow,
And there in the twilight, how jolly to see
The cocoa and animals waiting for me.

Daddy and Mother dine later in state,
With Mary to cook for them, Susan to wait;
But they don't have nearly as much fun as I
Who eat in the kitchen with Nurse standing by;
And Daddy once said he would like to be me
Having cocoa and animals once more for tea!

THE CUPBOARD

by Walter de la Mare

I know a little cupboard,
  With a teeny, tiny key,
And there's a jar of Lollypops
  For me, me, me.

It has a little shelf, my dear,
  As dark as dark can be,
And there's a dish of Banbury Cakes
  For me, me, me.

I have a small fat grandmamma,
  With a very slippery knee,
And she's the Keeper of the Cupboard,
  With the key, key, key.

And when I'm very good, my dear,
  As good as good can be,
There's Banbury Cakes, and Lollypops
  For me, me, me.

GENERAL STORE

by Rachel Field

Some day I'm going to have a store
With a tinkly bell hung over the door,
With real glass cases and counters wide
And drawers all spilly with things inside.
There'll be a little of everything:
Bolts of calico; balls of string;
Jars of peppermint; tins of tea;
Pots and kettles and crockery;
Seeds in packets; scissors bright;
Kegs of sugar, brown and white;
Sarsaparilla for picnic lunches,
Bananas and rubber boots in bunches.
I'll fix the window and dust each shelf,
And take the money in all myself.
It will be my store and I will say:
"What can I do for you today?"

Stories about Animals

Everybody is interested in animals, even those who have no pets of their own. We like to know what animals do, and what other boys and girls do with animals.

Some of these stories are about real happenings to real animals, but even the made-up stories are about what real animals could do and about things that really happen in their lives.

I have picked out a few animal stories and, if you like any of these, you will be able to find many more of the same kind.

THE HORSE WHO HAD
HIS PICTURE IN THE PAPER

by Phyllis McGinley

There is a city called New York, so crowded with tall buildings that you must tilt back your head and look straight up to see the sky.

So of course there isn't room for green fields or fat red barns. Nearly everybody lives upstairs—even the horses.

In one of the buildings lived a horse named Joey.

Joey was a contented horse. He liked his upstairs stable and he liked his stall, which was sunny, with a window to look out of.

He liked working for Mr. Polaski who sold fruit and vegetables to city people.

He liked the folks he met as he pulled his cart about the city streets.

And he was fond of his friend, the Percheron, who lived in the left-hand stall.

In fact, he was as contented as a horse can be, until the day that Brownie moved into the right-hand stall next door to his.

Brownie was a Police Horse, and he never let anyone forget it. He was shining brown all over except for his mane and his tail, which were black. And he was very proud. He was proud of his mane and proud of his tail and proud of being on the Force. And he was very, very proud because he had had his picture in the paper.

He treated the other horses coolly because they were ordinary fellows who pulled carts like Joey or hauled great drays like the Percheron. He himself carried a Police Sergeant on his back and was much admired by all the passersby.

Sometimes he led parades up Fifth Avenue and sometimes he

kept the crowds in order when something exciting was going on. And he had been to school to learn how to jump over bars and how not to be afraid of loud noises, and how to act like a policeman.

"It isn't just any horse who gets on the Force," he told Joey haughtily. "We're picked for our brains, you know. Besides, I'm a hero. That's why I had my picture in the paper."

"Is that good?" asked Joey, who had lived a sheltered life.

"Of course it's good," said Brownie. "It got my Sergeant a promotion. So now he has more money in the bank and I have more apples with my lunch."

Joey didn't care about the apples. Mr. Polaski gave him all the apples he wanted, anyhow. But he knew that Mr. Polaski had six children at home who were always needing new shoes, and that sometimes he was worried about money. "A vegetable cart is no gold-mine," Joey often heard him say.

Now Joey wished he could have *his* picture in the paper. Maybe then Mr. Polaski would get a promotion, too.

He thought and he thought, but he couldn't decide how to go about it.

"How do you get to be a hero?" he said timidly to Brownie.

"Save a man's life, like me," answered Brownie.

"Did you rescue him from a burning building?" asked Joey, who had a romantic mind.

"Not at all," Brownie snorted. "I saved his life by not stepping on him. When a crowd pushed him, he fell under my feet. And I stood still as a statue. It's the way they taught me in school."

He looked so pleased with himself that Joey decided just standing still must be quite difficult for a Police Horse.

But the Percheron nearly strangled on his oats.

"Think of the lives *I've* saved," he whispered to Joey. "Thousands and thousands! Why the city is *filled* with people I haven't stepped on."

But Joey didn't laugh. He just went on wondering how he could be a hero and get his picture in the paper.

Whenever he saw a crowd he trotted toward it, hoping some-body would fall under his feet. But Mr. Polaski always pulled him back to the curb again. And although he stood as quietly as a statue while Mr. Polaski sold his vegetables, *that* didn't make him a hero. It just brought him pats on the nose and an extra carrot or two.

Once a lady with a camera took his picture as he was nibbling a lump of sugar from the hand of a friendly little girl. Unluckily, a fly was buzzing around him and he had to swish his tail and wrinkle his nose just as the lady snapped the shutter. So prob-ably it wasn't a good likeness. At any rate, he didn't hear of the picture's appearing in any paper.

Then one day he thought his chance had come.

Mr. Polaski was selling a cauliflower to a woman in front of an apartment house and Joey was saying hello to a pigeon.

Suddenly a little boy, just learning to walk, came down the apartment house steps ahead of his nurse, and wobbled into the street. It was a busy street, with cars whizzing by and trucks rushing to reach the corner before the light turned red.

The nurse called to the little boy but he didn't stop. The lady was too busy pinching the cauliflower to notice him. And Mr. Polaski was too busy with the lady.

But Joey saw. And quick as a flash, he reached out and caught the little boy by the seat of his bright blue sun-suit.

"Now I'm a hero!" he thought to himself. "And my picture will surely be in the paper."

But the little boy began to cry and the nurse came running after him, shrieking, "Help." The lady dropped the cauliflower and said, "I do believe your horse bit that child!"

And since Mr. Polaski hadn't been watching, he couldn't ex-plain that Joey was only rescuing the little boy from the cars and the trucks.

Mr. Polaski had to apologize to the nurse, and on the way down the street he scolded Joey as if he had done something wrong.

"A vegetable cart isn't a gold-mine," he said crossly. "And now you have lost me a customer." And he didn't even give Joey an apple with his lunch.

Joey knew Mr. Polaski didn't understand, and forgave him. But it made him quite downhearted.

"How am I to get my picture in the paper?" he asked the Percheron that night.

"Join a circus!" snapped the Percheron, throwing a bit of hay crossly onto the floor. He was fond of Joey but he believed that Brownie was putting foolish ideas into his head.

"Join a circus," Joey said to himself, thoughtfully. "Why yes, circus horses *do* get their pictures in the paper. I could learn to walk on my hind legs and do tricks."

But when he practiced walking on his hind legs in the stall, he frightened the man who was bringing him his oats.

And after he had tried to bow and kneel on one leg as he had heard that circus horses do, he ached so badly all over that he limped as he pulled the cart.

So he had to give up the idea of becoming a circus performer. But his hope of helping Mr. Polaski led him into trouble one June morning.

It was a very pleasant morning. Joey was jogging along, enjoying the sunshine, while Mr. Polaski from the front seat of the cart sang out, "Strawberries! Strawberries! Nice fresh Strawberries!"

A lady called to them from the upstairs window of a house and Mr. Polaski, stopping the cart, climbed the steps to sell her two boxes of berries. He left Joey standing still as a statue.

But just as Mr. Polaski was counting his change in the hall, Joey heard a sound that made his ears stand straight up on his head. It was the exciting sound of trumpets and drums and marching feet.

"A parade," thought Joey. He knew about parades. Brownie had often told him that the horse who led one was bound to have his picture taken. It was like a law.

"Boom!" went the drums. "Tarara, tum-tum, tara!" tootled the horns and the bugles. It was too much for Joey.

Lifting his feet smartly and trailing his reins to one side, off he trotted in the direction of the music. He reached the corner just as the marchers reached it, too. The crowds watching the parade were too surprised to stop him. Even the policemen noticed him too late. Before they knew it, Joey was there at the head of the line, ready to lead the paraders up the avenue.

The only trouble was that he had taken a left turn while the parade was trying to turn to the right. There he was in the way of everybody!

The fife-players stopped so suddenly that the buglers stepped on their heels. The drummers stepped on the heels of the buglers. And the men who were only marching, stepped on the heels of the drummers. The whole parade came to a standstill.

When Mr. Polaski ran panting up to the corner, the policeman was holding Joey by the bridle, the crowd was laughing, and the paraders were very angry. It was a dreadful moment.

Mr. Polaski explained that Joey meant no harm. So the policeman let them go with a warning and the parade started up again. But Mr. Polaski seemed so frightened and upset that Joey realized he had made a terrible mistake.

"Whatever has got into you, Joey?" asked Mr. Polaski, sorrowfully. "A vegetable-cart is no gold mine. But you'll make me poorer than I am, if you don't behave yourself. Then what will happen to my six children?"

Poor Joey! He felt very sad; especially since Brownie's Sergeant had received another promotion and Brownie was prouder than ever. He swished his black tail and tossed his black mane and boasted about how well he had pushed back the crowds one day when the President of the United States drove by.

He even had his picture again—in the *Daily News*. He was leading a parade.

"I'll never be a hero and I'll never amount to anything," Joey confided to the Percheron. "I'm just an ordinary city horse with no talent. It's too bad for Mr. Polaski."

"You're a good fellow, Joey," said the Percheron. "Just cheer up and get that nonsense out of your head about newspaper pictures. Do your duty and everything will be all right."

So Joey made an effort to be cheerful and obedient, and Mr. Polaski didn't have to scold him again.

But things weren't going too well with the vegetable-cart. It was now the middle of the summer and very hot in the city. It was so hot that many of Mr. Polaski's best customers moved right out into the country to be comfortable. The vegetables and the fruit wilted in the heat, and new customers would not buy them. But Mr. Polaski's six children ate just as much as ever and needed as many pairs of shoes.

So, Mr. Polaski's face grew longer and longer.

One morning, earlier than usual, Mr. Polaski came into the stable and took Joey out to the cart.

"We're going to New Jersey, Joey," he said as he fastened the harness and put a hat over Joey's ears to keep off the sun. "I've heard of a place where I can get fresh vegetables cheaper than here. We'll drive over and look at them."

Joey was pleased to be having an adventure. In spite of the heat, he trotted along briskly in the direction that Mr. Polaski told him was New Jersey.

He trotted for blocks and blocks, weaving his way through the throngs of cars and trucks and busses. The streets were new and exciting to him and he liked it when they came to one which ran as far as he could see, beside a river.

Finally he trotted up a sort of hill and all of a sudden found himself on a great bridge flung across the water. It might have frightened another horse but Joey wasn't frightened at all. He only slowed to a walk, the better to enjoy the sight of the river and the boats skimming busily along below him.

Mr. Polaski enjoyed it too, and they were both sorry to see the tollhouse at the end of the bridge coming into sight. There seemed to be a crowd gathered there; and the cars, too, were moving slowly. Joey hurried a little so he could see what was going on. In fact, he edged right in front of a truck which was shifting gears, and the driver shouted at him. But Joey didn't mind, he was so interested.

The cart stopped at the tollhouse, which was decorated with flags. And then, just as Mr. Polaski started to take out his purse to pay the toll, a man with a red carnation in his buttonhole stepped up to them.

He wore a silk hat and carried a bouquet of flowers. Behind him came several other men, some with cameras and some with pencils and pads of paper in their hands.

"Congratulations!" said the man with the silk hat. "These flowers are for you. You have also won the fifty-dollar prize. What is your name, sir?"

"Polaski," said Mr. Polaski, much surprised. "Please—I don't understand."

"We are from the Department of Bridges," the man said, "and this prize is being given to the millionth vehicle to pass the toll-house.

"Your cart was the millionth."

"And we're reporters," said one of the men who carried pencils and paper. "We'd like your address, too. There's quite a story for our papers in this. You see we had expected a car or a truck or a bus to get the award. We didn't count on a horse and cart."

"What's your horse's name?" another reporter asked. When Mr. Polaski told him, he wrote down "Joey" on the pad of paper. Then he shook Mr. Polaski's hand and several people cheered.

It was almost as good as leading a parade. The first man put the flowers in front of the cart and handed Mr. Polaski five ten-dollar bills. Then the men with cameras crowded around and cars halted to watch and people shouted cheerful remarks.

"Smile, now," said a cameraman. "And hold on to your horse. We especially want a good shot of him."

"That's quite a bonnet he's wearing," said another. "But he

needs just one more touch. He's the hero of the day, you know."

He whispered something to the man in the silk hat. Then that gentleman took the red carnation out of his buttonhole and tucked it behind Joey's ear.

"Don't let him move," said the cameraman. But Joey wouldn't have moved for anything, not even for a hundred flies. He stood still as a statue and looked straight into the cameras, while the bulbs flashed like fireworks. He wasn't going to take a chance on spoiling *this* picture.

Afterwards the reporters patted his neck and complimented Mr. Polaski on driving such a well-behaved horse.

"We're holding up traffic, I'm afraid," said the silk-hatted man. "You'll have to move on. But look in the papers tomorrow —you'll be sure to see yourselves."

And with everybody gaily waving and the cars tooting their horns good-naturedly, Mr. Polaski and Joey moved on.

When they got back to the stable that night, Joey didn't say a word to the other horses about his adventure. Something might go wrong—perhaps the papers wouldn't use the picture after all. Besides, he was afraid his hat wasn't really becoming.

But the next morning Mr. Polaski burst in, waving half a dozen newspapers.

"Look, Joey!" he cried. "Here we are! We're famous!" He opened one of the papers and there, almost on the front page was a picture of Joey, handsome as a circus horse, with his hat becomingly tilted, and the red carnation behind his ear.

Underneath the picture it said:

NEW YORK ONLY ONE-HORSE TOWN AFTER ALL—
CART-HORSE JOEY WINS FIFTY DOLLAR PRIZE

All the horses craned their necks over their stalls to see. Even Brownie was impressed. He murmured, "Excellent likeness." And the Percheron said dryly, "Well, you made it."

"But that's not all, Joey," Mr. Polaski said. "Maybe a vegetable-cart *is* a gold mine after all. A friend of mine—he knew me in the old country—saw that picture first thing this morning and he telephoned me right away. He's got a farm on Long Island and he needs somebody to help him in the city. He says I'll be his partner. Every day he'll bring me his fresh vegetables and you and I will sell them. Now I won't mind if my six children grow so fast out of their shoes."

My, but Joey was happy! He said later to the Percheron, "Of course it would have been nice to have been a real hero. But I expect this is nearly as good."

"There are all sorts of ways of being a hero," the Percheron told him kindly. "You did your duty every day and didn't complain and that's as good a way as I know of. And," he added with a side glance at Brownie, still tossing his black mane in the right-hand stall, "it's certainly just as good as saving a man's life by standing still."

"Anyhow," said Joey contentedly, "I got Mr. Polaski his promotion."

THE SILVER FLOWER

by Rhea Wells

Peppi wanted a friend. Everyone in the world needs a friend, why shouldn't a little duck want one too? He counted over all the fowls and animals in the courtyard, and then he thought of the people whom he saw every day. After a long time, he decided to make friends with a boy named Franz. Franz was the gardener's son. Each morning he came into the courtyard and got his tools before he went to help his father work in the garden. Every noon he came and washed his hands and face in the fountain which always ran in the court. At evening he came again and filled a big pot with water which he took to the garden to give the plants a drink before they went to sleep.

After supper, Franz came into the court and sat down on the curb by the fountain. He had a piece of bread and butter which he was eating. As he ate, the bread crumbs fell on the ground. Peppi came and watched Franz eat his bread. Peppi came up very close because he wanted to make friends with Franz. After a while Franz gave Peppi a piece of the bread and butter. It was only a little piece, but Peppi was so pleased he almost choked. Every evening after that Franz came and gave Peppi some of his bread.

Peppi was sure Franz was the nicest boy in the world. Franz wore woolen stockings, short leather trousers, a white shirt, and a green hat with feathers and three silver flowers on it. Peppi would look at the silver flowers and wonder if the flowers in the garden where Franz worked could ever be as beautiful.

One thing worried Peppi. He thought it very generous of Franz always to give him some of the bread and butter which Franz had for his supper. "But," thought Peppi, "it is not nice of me always to take the bread and give nothing in return. One must do something for a friend."

One morning Franz came running across the court. He had got up late and was in a great hurry to go to work. In his haste, his hat fell off, and when he picked it up he did not notice that one of the silver flowers had dropped off.

Later in the day, Peppi found the silver flower. "Now," thought Peppi, "I can do something for Franz. In the evening, when he sits by the fountain, I will give him the flower and he will be pleased."

That evening, when Franz sat by the fountain, he did not eat his bread. He sat and looked over the treetops at the great mountains behind the castle and wondered where he had lost the silver flower. His mother had given it to him on his last birthday. Peppi came up to Franz with the silver flower in his bill. After a long time, Franz looked down and saw him.

"What shall I do?" said Franz. "I have lost the beautiful flower which Mother gave me for my hat."

Then Peppi came quite near, and Franz saw the silver flower in his bill. "Oh, Peppi, you found my flower," cried Franz. He put out his hand, and Peppi let the flower drop into it. Peppi stood there and let Franz stroke his fuzzy head and back. He was so happy he felt warm and cuddly all over.

"You can have all my bread," said Franz, putting the bread on the ground. "Tomorrow I will bring you some worms from the garden." But at that moment Peppi was not thinking about worms.

PUDDLE

The Real Story of a Baby Hippo

by Ruth Ann Waring and Helen Wells

A new baby at the zoo! Everyone was excited, for it was a baby hippo, the first one ever born at the Chicago Zoological Park.

All the boys and girls went out to see him, and they laughed and laughed as they watched the fat little hippo playing in the water with his great big mama.

The baby hippo's mother's name is Bebe. The father's name is Toto. Both of them are American born, so the baby hippo is an all-American hippo.

Toto was only four years old, and Bebe five and a half, when the little hippo was born. Mama Bebe weighed four thousand pounds, and her baby weighed forty pounds. People said they looked just like a Zeppelin and a tiny blimp.

At first the baby hippo was not safe in the deep pool. So the zoo keepers let out some of the water. The baby could wade in the shallow places, or swim where it was a little deeper. And he could lift his head out of the water to take a breath of air very often. The baby hippo would splash and splash until he was tired. Then he would rest with his chin on Mama Bebe's back.

Every day crowds of people visited the zoo and stayed for hours watching the big and little hippos.

The new baby could swim and dive as soon as he was born. Mama Hippo always kept the baby close by her side.

Everyone was asked to help name the baby hippo. Some wanted to call him Bubbles, or Chunky, or Blimpo, or Tobe, or Pompey, or Dodo, or Poochie. But finally they named him PUDDLE.

There probably isn't another hippopotamus in the world called

Puddle. And it is just the right name because a baby hippo likes nothing better than a very large puddle or pool to play in.

When Puddle was eight days old, his mother led him out of the water for the first time. Then everyone could see what wrinkly, loose pinkish-gray skin he had, and what rolls of fat.

"Look, look!" everyone said, as the baby hippo wobbled on his short legs along the sandy path, slowly following Mama Bebe. While they were on land, Bebe and Puddle took a walk and enjoyed a little sun bath.

Mama Bebe and Puddle went back into the pool. There were little splashes and then big splashes as first Puddle and then Bebe plunged into the cool water.

Puddle wiggled his pink little ears to shake off the water.

After the first trip on land Puddle and Bebe came out of the water every once in a while. Before long Bebe had shown Puddle every corner of their big yard with its trees and bushes and grass and rocky caves. But they still spent most of the time in the pool. Puddle always loved to go back there to play in the water.

On warm summer days Bebe would lie dozing in the shallow water near the edge of the pool with her huge body half out of water. She was like a big island for little Puddle to swim and play around.

Puddle would duck and scoot along under the water, then bob up and nip Bebe's ear.

When Puddle was eight months old he weighed about one hundred and fifty pounds. He now looked much bigger and less wrinkly. His skin had grown thicker and darker on top but was still very pink underneath and around his ears and chin.

When Puddle was nearly a year old he had teeth that he could eat with. His first teeth were too far back to be easily seen even when he opened his mouth to yawn or squeal.

On each side, near the front of his mouth, you could see the places where his big tusks were going to grow out.

Some day Puddle will have fierce-looking tusks.

When a big hippo opens his huge pink mouth it looks as though he could swallow you in one small gulp.

After he was ten months old Puddle was fed only once a day, like a big hippo, instead of taking a drink of his mother's milk whenever he was hungry. For this one meal, at five o'clock in the afternoon, the keeper would give him three gallons of milk made into porridge with cornmeal and oatmeal, and a big pail of fresh-cut grass with bananas and apples, or sometimes spinach and carrots. Puddle gets as far in as he can go when he drinks his porridge.

A hippo keeps growing until he is about fifteen years old.

At one year Puddle weighed two hundred and fifty pounds. The husky young hippo was given a birthday cake of grass and hay, with one big candle.

Soon after his first birthday Puddle had another surprise. He was invited to take a long journey to the San Diego zoo to live, and to make friends with the children there.

THE COMING OF MAX

by Mabelle Halleck St. Clair

The house stood on a hill. It was broad and low, with eaves that hung over like bushy eyebrows. In it lived Billy and Jane, their father and mother, the white dog, and the little black bear. The bear had a room of his own, which was underneath the sunny back porch where they all played.

Behind the house was a forest of tall pine trees with the ground covered with soft pine needles. The hill in front was covered with poplar trees, green in the summer and pure gold in the fall. The house was proud of this dark cloak of pine with its trimming of green and gold. Its own color was green too. It had so many casement windows that when the snow fell and covered everything outside with many feet of soft white, it seemed to Billy and Jane that they were out in the snowstorm and yet snug and dry by the great roaring fire.

The little white dog was Sunny Jim. Jim was to be his grown-up name, and Sunny his baby name. Billy thought of the name when he was eating his morning cereal. There was a picture called Sunny Jim on the box. And the name did fit, for if ever there was a dog like a streak of sunshine, it was this little collie puppy. He had a tail that he carried proudly like a flag, and his soft long hair was all white except for two golden tan spots, one over one eye, and one on his back.

Sunny was six months old when the little bear came. He had stopped being nothing but a ball of fluff who rolled and tumbled in the snow and begged to be carried when the snowballs got between his toes. He was quite a wise puppy now, who knew his way around and felt that the house and everyone in it were his particular property.

Then came the wonderful day in May when Father came to Jane's bedroom one morning and dropped into it a little black dot, no bigger than the smallest kitten you ever saw. Most of it was head and ears, with a tiny round body and an inadequate tail; so it looked rather like an animated comma. That was Max, and Jane loved him at once, though she rolled out of bed in terror when she heard he was a bear. For she had read about bears in her animal book. But Father told her that this bear was a lonely little orphan whose mother and father had been shot.

"Let us give him to Sunny," said he. "Sunny will show him how to be a little puppy bear."

Billy and Jane were charmed with the idea, and soon a procession came out on the sunny lawn. First came Father, carrying baby bear, then Mother with a saucer of warm milk, then Billy and Jane, and Sunny jumping excitedly around. They all sat in a circle with Sunny close to Father and the bear between them.

"Now, Sunny," said Billy, "this is your own baby bear. You must take care of him and play with him and teach him everything."

Sunny wagged his tail in excited agreement and touched the little black head with his nose.

"He is saying yes," cried Jane. "I am sure he is."

"What shall we name the little bear?" asked Billy, wriggling with excitement.

"How would you like to call him Max after Uncle Max? I am sure Uncle Max would like that, and it would be a good name to grow up to."

The children were delighted, and Max he was.

Meanwhile little Max wept on, such lonely moanings and whimperings.

"He wants his mother," said Jane.

"He is afraid," said Billy, trying to stroke him gently, but there wasn't much to stroke; so Billy had to rub his ears.

"He is certainly hungry," said Mother. "We must try to get him to lap some of this warm milk."

But Max didn't know how to lap. No matter how much they pushed his nose into the warm milk, he couldn't swallow any.

"If he only had a bottle with a rubber end, like Aunt Ruth's baby," cried Jane. But the house on the hill was a long way from town, and Mother said they must find some way to feed Max right away or he might die.

"Jane, run into the house, and get some brown sugar and a nice little piece of clean white cloth," said Mother.

When Jane came running back, Mother tied a little lump of brown sugar in the cloth, wet it in the milk and put it in Max's mouth. At once he began to suck on it.

Then Mother poured the rest of the sugar into the basin of milk, stirred it well, and took the little bag away. She pushed Max's nose into the sweetened milk. Out came his red tongue this time and he began to lap the milk, awkwardly at first, but soon with a businesslike regularity. Sunny wagged his tail excitedly, and Billy and Jane rolled over on their backs in the grass with shrieks of joy.

After Max had finished the milk, he looked about, ran to a tree, lay down and was asleep in an instant.

"Why did he run to the tree, Mother?" asked Billy.

"Do you think it was because his mother and father and grandmother and grandfather always lived in the woods and found the foot of a tree the safest place to sleep? If they hear any animal coming to harm them, they could run up to the top of the tree and be safe."

"Can bears climb trees?" asked Billy. "Can our Max climb these big tall pines?"

"We shall see. And now while he is asleep we must find a little house for him to live in."

But Jane wasn't satisfied. "How would Max know about climbing the trees? He is such a baby. Did his mother tell him?"

"It must be just born in him," answered Mother. "When you were old enough you were able to walk without anyone teaching you. How would you like to use Sunny's little old kennel for Max?"

So Billy, Jane, and Sunny ran off to get the kennel, while Max slept under his tree.

THE BLUE-EYED PUSSY

by Egon Mathiesen

Translated by Karen Rye

Once upon a time a little cat with blue eyes and a cheerful disposition went out into the world to find the Land of Many Mice.

Puss set out on the journey with a high heart because he knew that whoever found that land would never go hungry.

First he came to a lake. A fish stuck his head up out of the water. "Do you know where I can find the Land of Many Mice?" Puss asked.

But the fish laughed aloud when he saw the blue eyes, and flipped his tail so that Puss got all wet.

"Never mind," said Puss, and went on his way. "A fish cannot know everything."

On the way he caught a fly, and after all a fly is better than nothing.

A little later Puss came to an enormous cave. "Perhaps," he thought, "this is the entrance to the Land of Many Mice."

And he went straight into the darkness. The only light came from his own two blue eyes.

But suddenly he saw two eyes that were much bigger than his own.

And he sprang out of the cave and never learned what kind of beast lived in it.

"Never mind," said Puss, and went on his way. "I will meet someone else whom I can ask."

This time the only thing he caught was a little mosquito. But that, too, is better than nothing.

As he went on his way he heard a rustling in a wheatfield. "Perhaps it is a mouse," thought Puss.

No, it was a little porcupine. "But a porcupine likes mice, too," Puss thought. "Here I can surely learn where the Land of Many Mice lies."

But as soon as the porcupine saw Puss's blue eyes he rolled himself up into a ball. Puss would never get a word out of him. That was plain enough. So he went on his way.

This time the only thing he caught was a little plant louse. It was so sticky that he could not get it off his paw. That was almost worse than nothing.

It began to grow dark, and Puss went on his way, dreaming delightful dreams of the Land of Many Mice. Suddenly he heard the miaowing of many cats.

"Here is the land," he said. "Where there are so many cats there must be many mice." And he sprang into the darkness where the sounds came from.

In the black night he saw ten yellow eyes shining. Joyfully he miaowed: "Is this the Land of Many Mice?" But the cats with yellow eyes answered only: "Mia-a-a-ow, he has blue eyes."

There was not another sound that night. And all the cats closed their eyes.

But when daylight came, there sat five cats with yellow eyes, peering at Puss, who had asked about the Land of Many Mice.

"We, too, have searched for the Land of Many Mice," they sneered. "And you think that you can find it—you with your blue eyes."

"It may be that they are right," Puss thought, rubbing himself behind the ear. "Perhaps it cannot be found at all." And so he stayed among the cats with yellow eyes.

"I think I will have a little fun," Puss decided one day. "Even if one has nothing else, one can still have a cheerful disposition."

He put a pair of sunglasses on his nose, and he curled his tail. But the others did not think that that was funny. "You have blue eyes," they said. "We can see that plainly. And proper cats have yellow eyes."

So little Puss went to a pool and looked at his reflection. It did not seem to him that blue eyes were ugly, or that he was not a proper cat.

That made him so happy he ran home to tell the others that they had made a great mistake.

But when he came home they were all sitting in a tall tree, shaking with fear. A monstrous dog was after them, and they called down to Puss with the blue eyes: "Drive that dog away!"

What should Puss do? How can a little cat drive away a big dog? Puss lay down to think it over.

But—W-R-R-OOF! It came with the sound of thunder, and Puss flew up in the air with fright.

W-R-R-OOF!

When he came down again he landed on the dog's back, and dug in his claws so that he would not fall off.

The dog streaked away, uphill
and downhill
and uphill
and downhill
and uphill
and downhill

And then the dog could go no farther. Puss jumped down, and what did he see?

A field full of holes, and out of the holes were peeping little mice. Puss had come to the Land of Many Mice.

And Puss went hunting till he grew round and fat.

And then he returned to the cats with yellow eyes, who had so long sat shaking in the tree that they had grown thin and gaunt. "Where is the dog?" they miaowed.

"Gone," said Puss. "Oh, you and your blue eyes," they said.

"I have blue eyes," said Puss. "That is true. But blue eyes can also see, and I have seen the Land of Many Mice."

"Let us go with you then and see," said the cats. "But if what you tell us is not true we will scratch out your blue eyes."

And so they followed Puss, up and down all the hills.

How they leaped and jumped when they came to the field full of mouseholes! Here was the land they, too, had been seeking.

And when they had run hither and thither for many days and nights, and had at last grown fat again, they laid down beside Puss and purred: "Thank you for the mice, good Puss. We have found out that you are a cat just like ourselves.

"You can be hungry and playful and thin and fat. You can find fields full of mice and you can see just as we do, even if your eyes are blue."

HIS FIRST BRONC

by Will James

Billy was a born cowboy; the only kind that ever makes the real cowboy. One day Lem told him he could have a certain black horse if he could break him. It was a little black horse, pretty as a picture. Billy went wild at the sight of him, and ran into the corral to get as close a view of the horse as he could.

"By golly!" he said. "I've always wanted to break in a horse. That'll be lots of fun."

The next morning Lem found Billy in the corral with the new horse.

"Well, I see you're busy right early, Billy."

"You bet you," he said. "He's some horse, ain't he?"

"He sure is," agreed Lem. "And your first bronc, too."

An hour or so later Billy had his saddle on the black horse, and cinched to stay. By this time quite a crowd had gathered around. The foreman, the cowboys, all the ranch hands were watching. All was set but taking the hobbles off the horse's front feet and climbing on. Some of the men offered to do that for Billy but that young cowboy refused. He wanted to do it all himself; it was his bronc.

Billy gathered his hackamore rope and a hunk of mane to go with it, grabbed the saddle horn with his right hand and, sticking his foot in the stirrup, eased himself into the saddle. He squirmed around until he was well set, like an old bronc fighter saw that the length of reins between his hands and the pony's head was just right, then he reached over and pulled off the blindfold.

Billy's lips were closed tight; he was ready for whatever happened. The pony blinked at seeing daylight again, looked back at the boy sitting on him, snorted, and trotted off.

A laugh went up from all around. Billy turned a blank face toward his father and hollered.

"Hey, Dad, he won't buck!"

Another laugh was heard and when it quieted down Lem spoke up.

"Never mind, son," he said trying to keep a straight face, "he might buck yet."

The words were no more than out of his mouth, when the little black lit into bucking. Billy was loosened the first jump for he'd been paying more attention to what his dad was saying than to what he was sitting on. The little pony crowhopped around the corral and bucked just enough to keep the kid from getting back in the saddle. Billy was hanging on to all he could find, but pretty soon the little old pony happened to make the right kind of a jump for the kid and he straightened up again.

Billy rode pretty fair the next few jumps and managed to keep his seat pretty well under him, but he wasn't satisfied with just sitting there; he grabbed his hat and began fanning. All went fine for a few more jumps and then trouble broke loose. Billy dropped his hat and made a wild grab for the saddle horn.

But the hold on the saddle horn didn't help him any; he kept going, up and up he went, a little higher every jump, and pretty soon he started coming down. When he did that he was by his lonesome. The horse had gone in another direction.

"Where is he?" said Billy, trying to get some of the earth out of his eyes.

"Right here, Son," said his father, who'd caught the horse and brought him up.

He handed the kid the hackamore reins and touched him on the hand.

"And listen here, young feller, if I catch you grabbing the horn with that paw of yours again, I'll tie it and the other right back where you can't use 'em."

Those few words hit the kid pretty hard. There was a frown on his face and his lips were quivering at the same time. He was both ashamed and peeved.

His father held the horse while Billy climbed on again.

"Are you ready, cowboy?" Lem looked up at his son and smiled. After some efforts the kid smiled back and answered.

"Yes, Dad, let him go."

The pony lit into bucking the minute he was loose this time and seemed to mean business from the start. Time and again Billy's hand reached down as if to grab the saddle horn, but he kept away from it.

The little horse was bucking pretty good, and for a kid Billy was doing mighty fine, but the horse still proved too much for him. Billy kept getting further and further away from the saddle till finally he slid along the pony's shoulder and to the ground once again.

The kid was up before his dad could get to him and began looking for his horse right away.

"I don't think you'd better ride him any more today, Sonny," Lem said as he brushed some of the dust off the kid's clothes. "Maybe tomorrow you can ride him easy."

But Billy turned and saw the horse challenging him, it seemed, and he crossed the corral, caught the black, blindfolded him and climbed on again.

Then Lem walked up to Billy and said so nobody else could hear,

"You go after him this time, Billy, and just make this pony think you're the wolf of the world. Paw him the same as you did that last calf you rode."

"Y-e-e-ep!" Billy hollered as he jerked the blind off the pony's eyes. "I'm a wolf!"

Billy was a wolf; he'd turned challenger and was pawing the black from ears to rump. Daylight showed plenty between him and the saddle but somehow he managed to stick on and stay right side up. The horse, surprised at the change of events, finally let up on his bucking, he was getting scared and had found a sudden hankering to start running.

After that it was easy for Billy; he rode him around the corral a couple of times and then, all smiles and proud as a peacock, he climbed off.

Billy had ridden his first bronc.

CASEY JOINS THE CIRCUS

by Dorothea F. Dobias

Casey was a little black and white dog who had no home.

One day the circus came to town and there was a big parade with brass bands playing, beautiful white horses prancing, clowns running up and down, and all sorts of wild animals in cages. There were elephants in a long line holding on to each other's tails. At the very end, holding on to its mother's tail, was a little baby elephant.

It was a beautiful sight and made Casey so happy he barked for joy.

He liked the band, he liked the horses, he liked the elephants holding on to each other's tails, but best of all he liked Peter, the baby elephant, at the very end. So Casey followed the parade all the way back to the big white tents, for he had decided that he would join the circus.

Casey wanted most of all to stay with the elephants, but he did not dare, as they already had a big dog named Leo guarding them. Although elephants are so big and strong, most small animals frighten them. They are particularly afraid of a mouse or a barking dog.

Because of this the circus men give the elephants a dog of their own, who lives with them always; he guards them when they walk through town, and sleeps in the straw with them on the train.

When the elephants become used to their own dog, other dogs do not frighten them so much.

So when Casey crept into the elephants' tent, Leo saw him and barked, "Go away! You are not allowed in here!"

"But I would like to stay here and join the circus," said Casey.

"Go away," growled Leo again. "In the circus everyone has work to do, and I'm too busy to be bothered with you."

Then Casey walked all around the big tents and thought he still wanted to join the circus more than anything in the world, so he began to look for work then and there.

First he went to see the black and white ponies.

"Have you anything for me to do?" asked Casey. "For I would like to join the circus."

"Come with us, if you can dance on your hind legs," neighed the ponies.

Of course Casey could not dance on his hind legs, so he went on to see the lions.

But the lions just yawned and shook their heads.

Next came the tigers' cage. The tigers walked up and down—up and down.

"We could find something to do with you, if you would just step inside our cage," growled the tigers.

But Casey did not care to step inside the cage, so he went to the seals.

They said if he could juggle a ball on his nose, as they did, he could stay and help them perform.

Casey could not juggle a ball on his nose, so there was nothing for him to do there.

Then Casey saw the tall giraffe, and waited until he bent down to drink.

"Have you any work for me?" he barked.

The giraffe did not answer him. Although they are the tallest animals and have the longest necks they cannot make a sound. He just rolled his big eyes and shook his head sadly, so Casey went away.

He went to the monkey cage.

"Have you anything for me to do?" asked Casey.

They all chattered at once.

"Can you swing by your tail?" screamed the little spider monkey.

"Can you eat with a knife and fork?" asked the long-armed orangutan.

"Can you count up to five?" inquired the educated chimpanzee.

But Casey could not swing by his tail, could not eat with a knife and fork, and could not count at all.

He looked up at the acrobats in their spangled tights. He watched them swinging on the high trapeze and flying through the air. It was wonderful to see, but Casey knew it was nothing a dog could do.

As he watched, the trained pig came by.

"Perhaps you know of something I could do?" he said to the pig.

"Have you a clown to ride on your back?"

"I have no clown," answered Casey.

"Then," said the pig, "there's nothing for you to do in the circus, but you might go and see the performing bear."

"Now let me see," said the bear, scratching his nose. "Can you ride a bicycle?"

Casey could not ride a bicycle, so he went to the hippopotamus.

"Do you think you could eat a bale of hay?" asked the hippopotamus. "That's what draws the crowds."

"Why, I think you have the hardest work in the circus!" exclaimed Casey. "I sleep on hay, but I could never eat it."

The camels were standing nearby, chewing their cuds.

"Perhaps you know of something I could do," Casey said to them.

"You have no humps on your back," they sneered, spitting disgust, "so of what use would you be around here?"

The camels were so disagreeable, Casey ran away without answering them.

He heard the trained dogs barking, and when he found them, he was very happy. "Because," thought he, "now I will surely find something I can do."

But these sleek dogs with their red harnesses, white frills and polished toenails were the worst of all. They could not bear the sight of the little tramp dog, although most of them had once been like him, and had joined the circus the same way. They snapped and snarled and chased Casey away before he had time to ask them anything.

Now Casey was very much discouraged, as there did not seem to be a place for him in the whole circus.

"At least," he thought, "I will go back and look at the long line of elephants once more before I leave. I particularly want to see the baby elephant at the very end."

It was dark when Casey got back to the elephants, and there was Leo running around in circles barking.

"What is the matter?" said Casey.

"There is a storm coming up," howled Leo. "The elephants are afraid of storms when they are inside, and I am trying to keep them quiet!"

Suddenly the lightning flashed, the thunder growled, and the wind swept through the tents.

The elephants swayed back and forth at their stakes. They rolled their eyes in fright and flapped their big ears.

Casey looked around for Leo, but he was nowhere in sight. Leo was more afraid of the storm than the elephants. At the very first crash of thunder he crawled far under the straw, and there were the frightened elephants, with no dog to guard them.

The wind blew still harder, the sides of the tent slapped and billowed, and suddenly blew straight in at the elephants. They squealed in terror, reared on their hind legs, dragging their stakes out of the ground, and off they went in a wild stampede.

Casey ran around them, barking and jumping to head them back. Men came running with elephant hooks and soon they had the frightened animals quieted, with their stakes hammered into the ground once more.

But Peter, the baby elephant, was gone.

The men took lanterns out into the dark hills to look for him. They searched all night but they could not find Peter.

Of course, no one missed Casey, although he was gone, too.

In the morning, when the men came back without Peter, everyone was very, very sad. It did not seem the same with Peter, the baby elephant, gone.

But everything has to go on as usual in a circus, no matter what happens. So when it came time for the big parade, the elephants all formed in line, holding on to each other's tails—all but Peter, the baby elephant, whose place was at the very end.

Suddenly the dogs barked, the elephants trumpeted, and the circus men shouted for joy! Coming over the fields was Peter, a very tired and dirty baby elephant, and at his side was Casey, guiding him back.

Right up to his place at the end of the line, Casey took Peter. Then he sat down to rest, for he was very tired, too.

The whole circus was glad. Everyone hugged and petted Peter. For a treat they fed him carrots and bananas, as well as quite a lot of hay.

But they did not forget Casey. They remembered how he had helped when the elephants broke loose, and that he was not afraid of the thunder and lightning, as Leo was, and that he had worked all night to find Peter and bring him back.

So they decided to give Casey charge of the elephants instead of Leo, as he took much better care of them, particularly the baby elephant at the very end.

And that was how Casey joined the circus.

THE SANDY MOUND
BY THE THICKET

by Alice Gall and Fleming Crew

Close to the edge of a thicket, where the sun shone down through scrubby trees and bushes, stood a low mound of sand. It was one of the hills of the black ant people and inside it Little Black Ant was making her toilet one morning.

Like all the ant people, this little black ant thought that nothing was more important than keeping perfectly clean. So now she washed herself with her tongue and brushed herself with the hairy bristles on her front legs, until her glossy coat shone and glistened.

Though the day had already come, the little ant was in darkness, for no ray of light ever found its way down the long winding corridors that led from the outside world. But she did not mind the darkness; she was used to it. She did not need to see in order to find her way about the hill, for she knew just where all its snug little rooms were. And she knew every twist and turn of its crooked hallways.

Hundreds of worker ants were astir this morning. They ran up and down the corridors and darted busily in and out of the dark little rooms, doing the things that must be done each day in an anthill. Little Black Ant heard them and hurried on with her toilet—she, too, had work to do and she must be about it.

Each day she had her own particular task to perform; sometimes it was one thing, sometimes another. This morning she was going into the outside world to forage for food. She would walk through the tall grass that grew like a green forest all around the hill. She would hurry through dark caves hidden among tangled roots. And she would not stop until she had found the food she wanted.

When her toilet was finished she went swiftly along one of the narrow corridors until she came to a small gallery that opened into one of the royal chambers. Here she paused, as though trying to decide whether or not she should enter.

These royal chambers were places of the greatest mystery to the little ant. They were the rooms in which the queens lived—the queens who meant so much to the hill and its people—and she could never pass one of them without stopping.

Was there a queen in there now? she wondered. Should she go in and see?

No, she decided, she must not take time for that this morning; she was going to gather honey from the great white blossoms that grew on a thorny bush she knew, and she must be on her way.

Hurrying up the corridor, she went out through one of the gateways of the hill, stopping only long enough to greet the sentinel ant who stood guard there. Other workers were now swarming out through the gates, but Little Black Ant did not wait to see which paths they took. Her own path led to the thorny bush, so she hurried off through the tall grass.

It was not an easy journey. The way was rough and in many places her path was blocked by stones or by thick stalks of weeds, so that she had to make her way around them. Sometimes there were fallen trees to be climbed over, sometimes there were gullies to be crossed; but she kept patiently on.

When at last she reached the thorny bush, she found other insects already busy gathering honey. The bumblebees, the butterflies and the wasps; all were there.

"Go away, Ant," a bumblebee called out to her. "Go away and find another place. There is no room for you here."

But Little Black Ant paid no attention to the bumblebee. She had come a long way to find these blossoms and, now that she was here, she meant to stay. There was room enough for all of them, she knew, and there was honey enough for all of them, too.

She had climbed almost to the top of the bush where the blossoms were finest, when there came such a whirring of wings and such a rush of air that she was nearly blown to the ground.

"Hummingbird!" exclaimed a wasp crossly. "I wish those creatures would stay away from here. They frighten me with their whirring wings, and I don't like their long bills, either; they look dangerous."

But the hummingbird darted away as suddenly as it had come, and the wasps, and the bumblebees and the butterflies went on with their feasting, not noticing that Little Black Ant had squeezed herself in among them and was sipping the sweet honey water as fast as she could.

When the honey water was gone, she visited another blossom, and then another. And when, at last, she climbed down to the ground again, she was so full of honey that she could not have held another drop.

"I should hate to be as greedy as she is," said a butterfly, as the little ant went hurrying away. "Of all creatures in the insect world the ants are the greediest."

"That is where you are wrong," spoke up a beetle. "I am well acquainted with the ways of ants for I once dug my way into one of their hills and spent a winter there, and I know they are not in the least greedy."

"But didn't you just see that little black ant sipping the honey from these blossoms?" asked the butterfly. "She didn't stop for a moment, but sipped and sipped and sipped and kept on sipping until I wonder she managed to find room for it all. She must have a great appetite."

"Wrong again!" declared the beetle. "Why, that little black ant scarcely tasted a drop of the honey that she swallowed."

"Then why did she swallow so much of it?" demanded the butterfly.

"That is hard to understand," answered the beetle. "Now when I swallow food, it is because I am hungry. Down it goes and that is the end of it! But with the ants it is different. That little black ant has a way of storing up, inside her body, the honey that she gathers. And the strange part of it is, she does not gather it for herself at all."

"I never heard such nonsense!" exclaimed the butterfly. "Why does she gather it if it isn't for herself?"

"You will be surprised when I tell you," answered the beetle. "She takes this honey home to her hill and shares it with the other ants who live there. To each ant who asks her for food, she gives a little of the store of honey she has put away."

"That doesn't seem fair," the butterfly said. "Why don't the other ants go out and find their own food?"

"I don't know," admitted the beetle, "unless it is because they are so busy working inside their hill all day long that they haven't time to go out and look for food and must have it brought to them. I don't understand it very well myself; I only know that it is the way of ants."

"Well, it sounds foolish to me," said the butterfly. With a flutter of her yellow wings, she floated away in the sunshine, feeling sorry for the little ant who must go creeping around over the ground, carrying food for someone else to eat.

But the little ant did not mind working. She was glad to come into the outside world and gather food, and she was glad to carry it back to the hungry workers who were waiting for her inside the hill. So now she hurried on toward the sandy mound at the edge of the thicket.

But she had not gone far when suddenly she stopped and, raising herself as high as she could on her six small legs, she stood for a moment waving her silken feelers in every direction.

A strange power lay in those tiny feelers that reached out, one on each side of her head, like delicate little arms. All ants have them, but no ant quite understands the secret of their magic. They are more than eyes, they are more than ears, and there is little the ant people need to know that these magic feelers cannot tell them.

They were telling Little Black Ant something now; something that terrified her. These silken feelers were telling her that an enemy was near, and that she must get away quickly if she wished to live.

But could she get away? For an instant she stood there remembering the dreadful things that happened every day out here in this forest of tall grass. It was a dangerous place for little ants, and she knew that many of the workers who had left the hill that morning would never return to it. Would she be one of these? Would the sentinel at the gate wait for her in vain?

"I must get back to the hill," she said. "I must get back to the hungry workers who are waiting for the honey I have found for them."

Climbing quickly up a blade of grass, she looked around anxiously. Just in front of her a leaf of dockweed stirred a little and she caught a glimpse of a dark shapeless creature, so terrible that for a moment she could do nothing but stare at it. It was half hidden by the weeds and she could not see it plainly enough to make out what it was, but she could see its great round eyes and the crease of its enormous mouth.

From a near-by blade of grass a small green insect rose into the air. "Toad! Toad!" it cried as it flew away.

"Toad!" Little Black Ant shivered with fear at that name. For the toad is a creature that can dart its long tongue far out of its mouth and seize small insects and eat them!

She must not wait an instant, she knew, if she wanted to save herself and, without another glance at the creature in the weeds, she turned and went swiftly down the blade of grass.

Quick as a flash the toad shot out its tongue, but it was just a moment too late. In that moment Little Black Ant had been near to death, but the toad had not been quite quick enough to catch her and, for this time at least, she was quite safe.

It was not her first narrow escape and it would not be her last, but she did not stop to think of this now. Today her life had been spared; today she would carry to the hungry workers in her hill the honey she had gathered for them. Little Black Ant was very thankful as she hurried away through the grass.

BLACK FACE

by Thelma Harrington Bell

Once upon a time there was a field with a wooden fence all around it.

Beside the field ran a railroad track.

Across one corner of the field was a ditch filled with blackberry brambles, and birds, and birds' nests, and field mice, and little green snakes, and blue beetles, so that it was all very gay with squeaks and twitterings and bright colors.

Every morning a prim little shepherdess with a yellow crook led her sheep through a gate into the field. After she had closed the gate she neatly dusted a brown log and sitting down took out her bag of knitting.

Every day while the shepherdess knitted the little lambs frisked and kicked up their heels and played.

Every day the older lambs tried jumping across the ditch and sometimes fell in. The mother birds and the baby birds in their nests did not like this at all. But the little shepherdess put her crook around the lamb that had fallen into the ditch and hooked him out. Then she straightened the birds' nests, and sprinkled crumbs for the field mice, and went back to her knitting.

And every day just as the little shepherdess had put down her knitting and was opening her lunch basket packed with bread, and butter, and yellow cheese, and milk, the noonday train passed on the railroad track beside the field.

Later, when the sun began to sink low in the sky, the shepherdess walked to the gate and called her sheep. All the sheep passed through the gate into the sleeping shed for the night, all the sheep but one. This one had black hoofs and a black face and he always wanted to stay and play in the field a little longer than the others.

When he reached the gate he stopped, and flicking his tail asked, "Why?"

But the little shepherdess primly waiting did not say a word, and so he went through the gate.

This was not the only time that the black-faced lamb asked, "Why?" Often when he watched the noonday train chugging into sight he asked himself many "whys."

It was a shiny clean little train. Its engine was always fresh and green, with rods and knobs of brightly polished brass. All the carriages where the people sat were painted glossy black. Sometimes hands waved at the windows and the shepherdess waved her crook in return.

Black Face was the only lamb that paid any attention to the train. He liked the chugging engine. He asked himself why it came and where it was going and why it was so soon out of sight. He wondered if it ever stopped and what could make it stop.

He always ran to the fence, and standing on his hind legs, put his forefeet on the rail, and watched until the last car with its bright green flags was whisked out of sight around a hill.

Every day he found more questions to ask himself, even such questions as, "Why can't I chug on around the hill with the shiny green engine?"

Late one morning he walked all around the field close beside the fence, just to see if there were any holes under the fence big enough for a black-faced lamb to squeeze through. But there weren't any. Then he thought of the ditch. Out of the corner of his eye he saw the little shepherdess watching him from under the brim of her big straw hat, so he stopped to nibble some grass.

As soon as the shepherdess took up her knitting again, Black Face slipped quietly down into the ditch. The brambles caught in his fluffy wool and held on so tightly that he left quite a few of his curls on the bushes behind him.

When he reached the spot where the ditch went under the fence, sure enough, there was room for him to squeeze through, and squeeze through he did as fast as he could, and scrambled up the bank on the other side.

When the noonday train chugged into sight, there was Black Face in the middle of the track waiting for it.

Now Black Face found out what could stop a train, for the train was stopping. In fact, it stopped quite still just before it reached him, and he and the little engine stood looking at each other, face to face.

The engineer leaned out of his window and shoo-ed at Black Face. Black Face leaped lightly upon the cowcatcher where he could not be seen. The engineer thought that the lamb had scrambled down the bank, and so he rang his bell, put on steam, and started up again, chug-chug-chug, chug-chug-chug, chug-chug-chug, chug-chug-chug, faster and faster, while Black Face stood on the cowcatcher with the wind whistling through his wool.

The shepherdess dropped her lunch basket and ran up to the fence waving her crook, but no one saw her except the people in the train and they waved back.

Soon Black Face was whizzing past smooth meadows, and the

next minute looking dizzily down into deep valleys, or fast-flowing rivers. He stood very still with his four feet planted firmly, and would not move even when the wind stood his ears on end.

Here and there he could see the roof of a cottage among the trees, or perhaps a pleasant farmhouse by a roadside. But after a half hour he saw many houses clustered together. There were big chimneys, and little chimneys, and buildings with hundreds of windows. The train was coming to a town.

"Chug-chug-chug, chug-chug-chug, chug-chug-chug, chug-chug-chug," said the engine, and slowly stopped at a station beside a long platform.

Everyone got off the train so Black Face jumped off, too.

He did not know where to go, but close beside him was a little girl carrying a small hat box and a basket in one hand, while she held her mother's hand tightly with the other.

Black Face walked quietly by her side. Once she felt the touch of his moist nose on her hand and looked around. She smiled at him. When they reached the street, there was a carriage waiting for the little girl and her mother.

"Come, Patricia," said the mother. "Jump in and we shall soon be home."

But Patricia, still holding her mother's hand, pointed to the lamb. Black Face stood very close to her, and tried to look as if he belonged to her. He heard Patricia's mother laugh.

"Where did that black-faced lamb come from?" she exclaimed.

She asked the station master, and the passengers who had alighted from the little train. No one knew anything about Black Face. Even the engineer did not know that Black Face was the very same lamb that had stopped his train beside the green field.

"Since he belongs to no one, you may keep him," said the mother.

Black Face was lifted into the carriage and lay quietly at Patricia's feet. Away they drove through the bustling town, out into the country until they came to a red-roofed cottage.

All around the cottage was a wide lawn where kittens and puppies were playing together. The puppies barked at Black Face. The kittens pranced sideways with their tails sticking up straight and bristling. One of them even jumped upon the lamb's back and tried to scratch him through his thick wool, but Black Face leaped about so quickly that the kitten was glad to jump safely to earth again.

After a supper of fresh grass and a romp with Patricia, Black Face lay down alone in the barn to sleep. Patricia said good night to him and closed the barn door.

The next morning when she came to take him out for breakfast, he was already standing close to the barn door waiting for her. They scampered out together on the lawn to play. But soon it was time for Patricia to go shopping with her mother and Black Face was left alone.

He began to think about the little green engine. It would chug past the green field and he would not be there to see it. He would like to see the little engine again, now that he knew it so well, now that he had met it face to face.

He trotted to the gate, and looked down the road to where a cloud of dust moved in the bright sunlight.

What could it be?

Why, a flock of sheep. And they were going toward the town!

They would see the little green engine! Why couldn't he go, too?

He watched the flock as it went by. His little black hoofs pranced in the grass, and his long ears wriggled as he saw the last tails bob-bobbing toward town.

With a snort and flick of his woolly tab of a tail, Black Face went romping after the flock. No one noticed him, not even the shepherd who was driving the sheep to town. He was busily filling his long pipe.

"Where are you going? Why are you all walking down the road stirring up so much dust?" Black Face asked the sheep next to him.

The sheep looked at him in surprise.

"I don't know," he replied. "Early this morning, just after the sun rose, when the grass was still very wet with dew, the shepherd brought us from our farm out on to the road. We have been walking ever since, past houses, water-falls, and mills, and over bridges, but I do not know where we are going."

"I can tell you where you are headed for," said Black Face. "See those tall chimneys ahead of us? That is a large town, with busy people, big shop windows, and a train, a shiny, friendly train with a little green engine. I have seen it."

Soon they reached the beginning of town: houses, large buildings filled with the whir and clank of machinery, mamas, daddies, baby carriages, and children. Black Face found that he had missed many interesting things the day before, when he had ridden through town high up in the carriage. Walking slowly down along the street was quite different. In fact, he began to feel very well acquainted with all the new sights and sounds.

Of course, the sheep did not go through the center of town, not down the main street. Indeed, no, there were too many wagons and carriages rushing about. Where would there be room for a whole flock of slowly moving sheep in the middle of a busy street? They were driven by the shepherd down quiet side streets where round-eyed children watched them curiously.

Suddenly, as they were passing a shop window, Black Face saw something large and white and woolly.

A lamb! In a shop window! What was he doing there? What would it be like to live in a glass house? He would find out.

He lagged behind the other sheep and scampered over to the window. It was a pretty window filled with brightly colored toys. Black Face pranced around to attract the snowy-white lamb's attention, but the lamb was staring straight ahead of him at a red-and-yellow rocking horse. He did not turn his head, not even when Black Face stood on his hind legs and tapped the window with his forefeet.

"I wouldn't live in a shop window," thought Black Face, "if it made me as stupid as that," and he trotted on down the street.

But the flock of sheep had turned down another street and were nowhere to be seen.

He went this way and that, and here and there, looking for them, but they were nowhere to be found.

At last he came out into the middle of a wide street and saw horses and wagons coming toward him in all directions.

Even when the people shouted at him he did not move. A burly driver from a farm truck jumped down and picked him up.

"I know where this lamb belongs," he said, "with that flock of sheep that went down toward the station. I'll take him there."

He whipped up his horse and away they drove.

When they reached the station the flock was just going through the gate. A train was waiting. Not the train that Black Face knew, full of people. This train had cars of all kinds. There were cars for carrying fruit, and coal, and animals, and machinery.

Suddenly the shepherd called out sharply from behind the flock, and the sheep all ran crowding together up a slanting wooden walk into a cattle car, Black Face with them. The door of the car was closed fast, and after a few minutes there was a creaking and rattling, and the car began to move.

Here was Black Face back again on a train with the engine puffing and chugging.

Although he was jammed tightly among the other sheep, Black Face managed to stick his nose through the side bars of the car and look out. Houses, rivers, valleys, and meadows rushed past for the longest kind of a time. Then a green field with a fence around it came into sight. There were sheep in it—and yes, a prim little shepherdess with a yellow crook. Could it be?

Now the train was slowing down because the prim shepherdess was standing beside the track waving her crook.

"Where is my lamb?" she asked the engineer. "The lamb that jumped upon the cowcatcher of the noonday train yesterday."

The engineer did not know. He had not heard of such a lamb.

Black Face was prancing up and down with excitement, but no one noticed him, crowded as he was behind the bars of the cattle car. Would the little shepherdess never look his way? No, she was turning sadly away. With all his bobbing of ears and pressing his nose through the bars, the shepherdess had not seen him. With a last frantic effort Black Face opened his mouth and a high piping bleat came forth:

"Baa-aa-aa-aa-aa!"

Round whirled the shepherdess.

"There he is," she cried. "That is the one. Did you have a black-faced lamb in your flock?" she asked the shepherd who had come to see what was the matter.

"No, only white sheep," said the shepherd. "This lamb with the black face does not belong to me."

And so Black Face was taken out of the car and given to the little shepherdess. Down they went to the green field, side by side.

How nice it was to be back in the green field with the other lambs. And when noon came, how nice it was to be watching again for the little green engine.

As for the little green engine, it nearly turned around on its track, so surprised was it to see Black Face back again in the field with his forefeet on the fence rail.

THE SHIRE COLT

by Zhenya Gay and Jan Gay

Penny Farm is in the Cotswold Hills in England. There is a big stone house, and a little stone church, and three stone barns. There are acres and acres of green fields that roll over the hills and down into the valleys. There are orchards and meadows, berry brambles, a lily pond, a brook.

No one knew Penny Farm better than Djuna, the big Shire mare. All through the year she worked for Farmer Penny. In the spring she plowed the fields. In the summer she carted the hay. In the autumn she brought in the fruit from the orchards. In the winter she drew the wagon of heavy cordwood down from the hills. Djuna had a long flowing mane, a long tail, and clusters of curls around her feet. She was strong and beautiful as she went down the road with her mane flying in the breeze, and her great hooves pounding clip-clop, clip-clop.

Last spring another horse plowed the fields of Penny Farm. Djuna was busy with something else. She had a new foal. He was a weak little fellow so she had to take a great deal of care of him. This colt had a brown coat and brown eyes, a curly brown mane, and a curly brown tail. When Farmer Penny saw the colt he said, "There's nothing else to do but to call this colt Brownie."

Brownie had little pointed ears, and a soft inquisitive nose. At first he wasn't strong. When he tried to stand up, his legs wobbled. When he tried to walk, he fell down. For quite a long time he lived in the stable, in a box stall with a bed of yellow straw. When he was tired he lay down in the straw. Djuna lay beside him to keep him warm.

One day in April when the sun shone brightly, Farmer Penny led Brownie and Djuna out of the stable into the farmyard. Brownie was frightened, and stayed close to his mother. He saw a great many things that were new to him. He saw the outside of the stone stable where he lived. He saw tall stacks of cordwood. He saw a big pig and her little pigs. He saw a rooster and hens and little chickens. He saw ducks that waddled when they walked.

After Brownie had spent several days in the farmyard, he knew the chickens and ducks and pigs. He knew another horse and a cow. He was afraid of the cow's horns. He knew which door of the stable led to his stall. Then he discovered the gate. Beyond the gate there was a great green world stretching as far as he could see. There were hills and valleys with hedgerows between the fields. He didn't know what all these were, but he was eager to find out.

Now Brownie was strong enough to go and live in the fields. Farmer Penny put a halter on Djuna and led her out of the farmyard. Brownie followed at her side. He could walk now without falling down. He could even run a little way if he didn't try to go too fast. They went past the pond where the ducks were swimming, past the orchard where the apple trees were in bloom. They went through a gate, across a field, through another gate. Then Farmer Penny left them.

The summer was so fine that they stayed out of doors all day and all night. They made their home under a special chestnut tree. Farmer Penny put a water trough there, so Djuna and Brownie could have a drink when they wanted one. During these first days in the field, everything that Brownie saw surprised him. He would prick up his ears and kick up his heels to see what would happen next.

When it grew dark, Brownie wondered why they didn't return to the stable. That was what he had done when he stayed in the farmyard. Now that they had moved to the field, he found that they were going to sleep under the chestnut tree. Djuna lay down on the ground. Brownie lay beside her. He saw the stars twinkling far away in the sky. He saw his mother warm and comforting beside him. Then he went to sleep.

The next morning, and all of the first days in the field, he kept close beside Djuna. She was happy to be in the meadow, and wandered from place to place, munching the tender grass. When Brownie saw her eating grass, he thought it must be good, so he tried to nibble it, too. But his teeth weren't big enough yet, and he had to wait until he was a little older to find out how good grass tasted.

Brownie was growing stronger every day. After a run in the field he would come back and lie down under the tree. One day he discovered the flowers growing in the grass. "This is a wonderful world," he said to himself, "the grass is soft, the flowers smell sweet, and all I have to do this summer is lie here and kick my heels."

Now Brownie grew bolder. He didn't stay beside Djuna all the time, but went off by himself through the field to see what he could find. One day he discovered that other animals lived in his field. The first one he found was a queer spotted fellow that sat on the grass and looked at him with big bulging eyes. As usual when Brownie was surprised he pricked up his ears and was ready to run to his mother when the frog hopped away through the grass.

Just then Djuna came up to him, and Brownie peeped fearfully around her to see whether the frog had come back. Djuna said to him, "You mustn't be afraid of the other animals. They won't hurt you. Make friends of them and play with them. One day soon I expect you will meet a rabbit. There are many rabbits in this field."

A few days later Brownie was taking a nap in the sun. A noise wakened him and he turned to see what it was. There beside him was the strangest animal he had ever seen. It had two long flopping ears bigger than his own. For a few minutes they stared at each other. Then Brownie went back to sleep. He soon wakened again. This time he saw half a dozen rabbits. The first one had called in all his brothers and sisters to see this strange long-legged colt sleeping in the grass.

Then Brownie remembered that his mother had told him to make friends with the other animals and play with them. He stood up, and was just going to invite them to play when all the rabbits hopped quickly away. Brownie was so much bigger than they were that the rabbits thought he might step on them. The colt was disappointed. He tried to find the rabbits, but they had all disappeared into their burrows.

Brownie decided that if no one would play with him, he would play by himself. There was a new game he had invented several days ago, the game of Rolling on Your Back. He lay down in the grass and pawed the air with his four feet. M-m-m, how good that felt, he thought, as he rolled over and over on the grassy knoll.

One day as he walked along behind his mother, Brownie sniffed at the hedgerow. He had admired the May blossoms and the glossy holly leaves for a long time. Djuna was busy eating grass, walking along with her head close to the ground. Brownie stuck his nose into the thorn tree. With a whinny of pain he ran to his mother. He had a thorn in his nose. Oh-oh, how it hurt! Finally the thorn fell out. Djuna took him to the water trough to cool his poor nose in the water. "You must be careful," she said, "about poking your nose into unknown places."

Farmer Penny took Djuna and Brownie to a new field. A lovely field. A brook ran along one side of it. Brownie went for a walk through the long grass that grew beside the brook. All at once he saw something very strange at his feet. It looked like a little umbrella. Not one umbrella but dozens. All this corner of the field was sprinkled with mushrooms.

Brownie found the mushrooms most exciting. He put his hoof on one, and it disappeared. He wanted to eat one. Quickly he snapped it off with his lips. He was afraid to eat it in front of the others, for fear they would chase him. He galloped off to another corner of the field with the mushroom in his mouth. When he got there he had lost it, but he had great fun taking it, just the same.

Another day when he was out exploring, he went back to the brook. He slid down the steep bank. To his surprise, he found water in the brook. He slipped and got quite wet. He switched his tail and shook his head to get the water out of his ears. While he was there he took a long drink. Then he climbed up the bank and scampered off to tell his mother his latest discovery—that the brook was full of water like the trough.

While he was running away from the brook, he heard something buzzing, and felt a bumping on his back. He tried to shake it off, but it wouldn't go. He ran and jumped, and tried to switch his tail, but his tail wouldn't reach the fly. The only thing to do was to go to Djuna who had such a splendid long tail that with just one flick she got rid of the fly for him.

One day Brownie found himself quite alone in a far corner of the field. The wind blew and ruffled up his ears. Little drops hit him, pat pat, drop drop, on his head and his back and in his face. The rain came on harder. He was frightened and hugged up close against a tree trunk. The wind howled. The rain came down in sheets. He was very frightened.

Finally he heard Djuna neighing. She came galloping across the field to him. She stood beside him, and nuzzled him, and told him everything was all right. How warm she was! How big and strong! He never felt afraid when she was beside him. She stayed with him until the storm was over. Then she went on eating grass.

After the rain everything smelled so good. He stood on a little knoll and sniffed the rain-washed air. Then he went on a journey of exploration. The gate to the next meadow had been left open. He crossed a bridge over the brook. He had never walked on anything but grass before. His hooves made a hollow sound on the planks of the bridge.

Brownie had been curious about some little white specks that moved about in this field. Now that he was close to them, he saw that they had four legs. They ran and jumped. He ran after these lambs, to play with them. But like the rabbits, the lambs ran away from him. They didn't disappear in the holes in the ground, they just played by themselves. Brownie was sorry they wouldn't play with him, they looked so white and fluffy.

In another corner of the field he saw some of those strange beasts that he just barely remembered seeing in the farmyard a long time ago. The big ones wore long horns and were not nearly as nice as his mother. The little ones were about his own size, but they couldn't run as fast. He chased them, and they ran bawling away to their mothers.

Brownie walked over toward the next field. Beyond the fence he saw what he had been wanting for a long time, a playfellow who looked like himself. Another colt stood in the next meadow. The trouble was that the gate wasn't open, so the two little colts stood on either side of it, whinnying to each other and wishing that they could play together.

Farmer Penny was crossing the fields, going home to his tea. He opened the gate and let the colts into the same field. They started to play together. They gamboled and raced, kicking their heels high into the air. Brownie said to the other colt, "I don't care if the rabbits and the lambs and the calves won't play with me. You are the best playmate of all."

Then Farmer Penny took Brownie back to his own field by the brook. Djuna was waiting there for him. Brownie told her all his adventures. "You are growing up," she said to him. "It is a good thing, too, because soon I am going to leave you in the daytime and go back and work in the fields. This is the haying season. I am going to draw the cart to carry the hay to the barns so we will have something to eat next winter."

Brownie was really very sorry to see his mother go away, although he now had the other colt to play with. But when he saw her pulling the cart, he was proud of her because she was so beautiful and strong. He ran back to the field to play with the other colt.

Next year, perhaps, when Brownie grows big and strong like Djuna, he too can help with the haying.

KAROO, THE KANGAROO

by Kurt Wiese

Karoo, the kangaroo, was born in a land where it rains but once a year. The sands there are so thirsty that they drink up all the water, and there are few rivers that run between green banks down to the sea. Australia is a pleasant place, in spite of that, for the sun is warm. When little Karoo was born, there was no fur at all on his smooth little body, no bigger than a squirrel's, and he was glad about the warm sun, and glad there was no rain, as he curled on the ground waiting for his mother. Presently she came jumping through the tall grass. She picked him up tenderly with her strong soft lips. Then she dropped him in a pocket inside herself. That is what mother kangaroos are famous for!

Inside his mother, in her warm, dark, deep, soft pocket, Karoo went sound asleep as children do in bed. It was very cozy. And after a while, velvety brown fur began to grow on his bare little body. And his hind legs grew longer and longer. But his front legs stayed short. And his tail grew even faster than his hind legs, and it grew strong enough to use as a brace. He could sit upon his tail almost as if it were a stool, when his mother was standing still. When she hopped about, that was different. But when she was listening, or sunning herself, or quietly eating, Karoo practiced mightily with his short front legs, and his long hind legs, and his fine strong tail.

By and by he could sit up, and he thought "Maybe I can hop." So he pulled himself up by his front paws, and poked his head out of his mother's pocket to have a look at the world. What he saw was one of the great rolling grassy plains of Central Australia. Hundreds of beautiful kangaroos were nibbling the tender green grass. It was a most exciting luncheon. Not far away, well balanced on his stout and useful tail sat an old, old kangaroo, Captain Kango Kangaroo. Suddenly Captain Kango wiggled his ears and waggled them and whistled through his nose. And when he whistled, all the hundreds of kangaroos went plop and hop, hoppity hop. They went in a herd. They went in a rush. Hop, hop. Ploppity hop. Karoo's mother pushed him inside her, plop, fast quick into her pocket, and hop, hop, off she went as fast as the rest. She didn't want to be left behind. Hop, hop! Little

Karoo wondered what it was all about. But nobody stopped to tell him what the hurry was for.

By and by there came a day when Karoo's mother let him out of her pocket and began to teach him the ways of a proper kangaroo. He learned to jump. Just at first he often tumbled and landed on his velvet nose. Then he learned to leap and land in elegant curves like Captain Kango's. He nibbled at the sweet green grass, that grew higher than his head, and he watched all the others out of the corner of his eye. "I am growing up," he said to himself, "and I am a part of this great big wonderful herd." It was very fine to be a kangaroo in the spring of the year on the wide plains of Australia.

Karoo's mother gave him rules to keep him safe. "Karoo, my little kangaroo," she said, admiring his bonny little velvet coat, "eat plenty of fine, green, tender grass, but never, never wander out of your mother's sight. Between nibbles look and see just where I am, and at any strange sight, or any strange sound, steer with your tail, and jump for my pocket.

"And most particularly, ever and always, beware the barking dingo. The dingoes are wild dogs. They are fierce and always hungry, and they eat kangaroos. Never waste a second when you hear a dingo bark. Fly for my pocket. And all your life, when you hear the bark of a dingo, make haste. The dingoes run so fast themselves that kangaroos must always hurry out of their sight. Dingoes are dreadful. Every proper kangaroo knows that!"

Little Karoo was much impressed. And every day he watched his mother out of the corner of his eye. But one day, when the sun was very bright, and the wind played tunes among the grasses, he forgot. He was practicing with his stout tail, and jumping more and more like Captain Kango, when he heard a warning whistle, and far across the plain the terrifying bark and yelp of the dingoes. He looked for his mother. She was nowhere to be seen. "Mother! Mother!" cried Karoo, but there was no answer, and the whole herd came through the grasses with a sound like thunder and the big flying feet of Captain Kango, leaping, leaping, knocked poor little Karoo into the sand under the grass. The bristling, barking, snarling dingoes in a great pack came bounding after. The noise was terrible. The dust was, too. By and by, Karoo stopped trembling and sat up. Far away in the distance all the kangaroos and all the dingoes were vanishing. Little Karoo was alone.

Karoo was sad. He did not wish to be all alone in the world. So he decided to follow the footprints of the dingoes and the kangaroos. As he hopped along over the plain, the grasses seemed to grow taller and taller. "I think this must be the forest," he said, when he came to a big eucalyptus tree. He was very tired so he sat down under the tree and went to sleep. When he woke up it was dark. The white trunks of the gum trees frightened him. The loose bark on the trees scratched in the wind and made flapping sounds. All sorts of noises that he did not know the why of, worried him. All night he shivered, and his little heart ached whenever he thought of how kind his mother was and how warm and soft her body used to be when he slept in her pocket.

Long before the sun was golden, when the day was still gray, Karoo made up his mind to go back to the grassy plain. The forest was too strange and different. Out on the plain, even being lonely was not so bad. The sun was warm. The dew dried. He was nibbling at his breakfast in a most contented way, when he heard a sly slither in the grass. It was a snake! A coiled black snake with wicked eyes and darting tongue. With all the strength of his whole young life in his sturdy little tail, Karoo pushed off and leaped into the air. Over the snake and away like hopping lightning, little Karoo made for the forest.

When he reached the shady woods his heart began to beat more slowly. He caught his breath and hopped to a clearing in the forest. Karoo looked around, and lo, climbing a young gum tree was his mother's friend, Koala, the chunky Australian bear, with a baby bear on her back. "Koala, Good One," shouted Karoo. "Help me. I lost my mother when the dingoes came barking upon us. Where has the herd gone?" "That I cannot say," said Koala, kindly, "but Anteater will know. Look for him in his cave beyond the three eucalyptus trees. He comes out in the open to feed. I stay hidden in the leaves, and see no one pass. But Anteater knows everything that goes on in the grass and on the plain." So Karoo hopped off toward the three trees.

Sure enough, there was a cave door in the sunny patch beyond the three trees. "Anteater, Good One," shouted Karoo, "come out and help me. Show me the way to the herd. I lost my mother when the dingoes came barking upon us." Then Karoo became very frightened for the anteater seemed to him more ugly than any other creature, with his back like a stubby bobbed porcupine, skin as thick and tough as shoe soles, and a nose that was as long as a policeman's club. "That I cannot say," said the anteater kindly, "but Duck's Bill will know. She spends her days swimming up and down the little river which is the only one for hundreds of miles around. All the animals come to the river; she can hear under water and she will tell you where the kangaroos spoke of going. Go West until you come to the river, Karoo, and then shout."

So Karoo hopped West. By and by, he smelled water. A few more jumps and he came to a flowing river with gum trees green along the bank. "Duck's Bill, Good One," he shouted. Bubbles came up from the water. Karoo's mother had told him many things about Duck's Bill—how she laid eggs like a bird, and had a mouth like a beak. Yet she was an animal and fed her babies with her own milk. Duck's Bill rose from the water and looked out of small cross eyes at Karoo. "Duck's Bill," said Karoo politely, "where has the herd gone? I lost my mother yesterday when the dingoes came barking upon us." But Duck's Bill said, "Only the dingoes have drunk of the river since yesterday. When they come all creatures stay away." And she started to slip under the water again. But Karoo looked so tired that she added, "Go deep into the jungle and call the kiwi—an old wise bird who knows all things without seeing or hearing any of them."

So Karoo hopped straight into the forest, and the trees grew thicker and thicker and the path very dark. "Kiwi," he shouted. "Kiwi," and by and by, suddenly right in front of him was Kiwi— a portly fellow with a very long beak, with a thin mustache all around it. His legs were strong and his feet were like a giant's rake and very good for scratching. "Kiwi, Good One, you who know all things, which is the way to the herd? Yesterday I lost my mother when the dingoes came barking." "The herd is very far away," said Kiwi slowly. "You must go and ask the birds who live in the tops of the trees. The Kookaburra will know for he lives on the edge of the forest and he has very big eyes." Then Karoo began to cry. "That is where the snake lives. I cannot go there to ask." "Don't be silly," said the kiwi. "Don't you know that Kookaburra is the great Snakekiller? Clever snakes never come near the nest of the kookaburra."

So Karoo turned around and hopped back through the forest toward the grassy plain. He was growing tired, and feeling very blue when he came to the red gum tree. He sat down sadly and waited for the sun to set. Soon the light faded and the kookaburra and his wife arrived. When kookaburra saw the little kangaroo, he began to laugh. "HaHaaHaHaa! Haw Haw Hoo Hoo Hoo!" It was the most terrible and cruel noise Karoo had ever heard. Karoo stopped trembling long enough to shout, "Kookaburra, Good One, where has the herd gone? Yesterday I lost my mother." "Haw Haw Hoo Hoo Ha Ha!" crowed

Kookaburra. "The dingoes almost got your mother, but she is where the herd is now. Due East across the desert." Karoo pushed hard on his strong tail and started off Due East.

He had not leaped very far when he saw that it was night so he hopped straight back to the red gum tree, where he could see the kookaburra up in the tree. Safe from the snakes, he slept all night, and early in the morning when the stars were still in the sky he started off again, after a mouthful of delicious grass, Due East across the desert. He hopped all morning, and he did not stop at noon. There was not a single leaf to munch nor any blade of grass. All around him was the desert. So he hopped Due East all night long, and in the morning licked a little dew from the rock for his breakfast and hopped Due East, as if he were running away from the little black shadow that was the only company he had. When the sun was red in the sky and just going down, he caught sight of something green and knew that the rim of the desert was just ahead. Karoo was too tired to jump any further, so he lay down in the cold sand and did not open his eyes until daybreak.

Karoo woke with a start and there all around him was the herd. Karoo leaped high in the air. He was surprised himself that he could jump so high. Old Captain Kango caught sight of him and made a most familiar toot. Karoo heard a sound like rushing and thunder. The herd jumped toward him, and there was his mother, looking lovelier and kinder than all the rest. She snatched him up and dropped him in her soft warm pocket. It was almost too small for him. He knew then that he was almost grown up. But it was very nice to be there, cozy and safe, with their two hearts throbbing like two parts of the same tune. He could hear her voice saying, "I think it will never happen again!" "Absolutely," said Karoo to himself as he snuggled down to rest from his trip across the desert.

ALMOST AN AMBUSH

by Le Grand Henderson

Tom Perkins and his army were holding a council of war in a thick grove of the young pines that covered Eagle Hill. Pinned to each shoulder of Tom's shirt, four silver-paper stars gleamed in the sunlight, indicating that he was a full general.

One of the other two boys also wore silver stars on his shoulders. That was Herb Wilks who had the three stars of a lieutenant general, and so was next in rank to Tom.

Only Peewee Davis had no stars at all. Peewee had no marks of rank of any kind. As the youngest and smallest boy in Tom's army, he was naturally a private. Peewee didn't mind, because he was more than just one private. He was all the privates.

There was one other member of the army who, like Peewee, had no marks of rank. This was Tom's small, bright-eyed, black-and-white dog, Floppy.

Tom thought Floppy was stationed a little way off as a sentinel, to bark a warning if Stubby Johnson's enemy army appeared while the council of war was in session. Floppy thought he was out there to look for a rabbit.

"Now, look," Tom said to the council. "Stubby's army is over there on the other side of the hill." He pointed out a position on a smudged, roughly penciled map.

The others nodded in agreement, and Tom went on, "Now what I say is, we have to surprise 'em."

Peewee said, "Yep," and crawled around on his hands and knees to show how he thought it should be done.

Tom scowled and shook his head warningly. "The idea is, we have to be quiet about it. Anybody that makes a noise is just the same as a traitor."

Unfortunately, at that moment, Floppy found the rabbit he had been looking for and started out after it, barking shrilly.

Herb snorted at Tom and said, "What did I tell you? Didn't I say we shouldn't bring him? How we going to surprise any one with him yapping like that?"

Tom didn't answer. He set out after his dog and soon came back with Floppy under his arm. The little dog's eyes sparkled from behind the shaggy hair that nearly hid them. He wriggled and pushed against Tom with all four feet as he tried to get back to the fine new game of chasing a rabbit and being chased by Tom at the same time.

Herb looked at Floppy sourly.

Tom said, "Just you wait. Floppy'll be a big help yet. Just wait, you'll see."

Noticing that Herb's expression didn't change, Tom went on, "Listen. All armies have dogs, don't they? Didn't the gov'ment say that our army needs lots of dogs to train for sentries an' for— well, for sentries an' for uh—well—things?"

Herb couldn't deny that, but he could and did say, "Yeh, but not little noisy dogs like that."

Floppy suddenly raised his ears and looked as if he understood what Herb had said and his feelings were hurt. When Floppy raised his long ears, the ends drooped over and hung nearly to his eyes. That gave him a sad expression. He let his tongue hang out of the side of his mouth and that made him look so mournful that Herb shuffled his feet and looked away. Although Herb liked big dogs best, he and Floppy were old friends and his objections to the little dog now were purely for military reasons.

Tom decided it was a good time to change the subject.

"Look," he said, "we don't have time to stand here and talk. The enemy's coming up over the hill. They'll be here in a little while. Now here's my plan. We'll retreat down this path, toward the old quarry . . ."

Herb broke in, "The old quarry? Huh, that's just where they'll expect us to go."

Tom grinned. "Yeh—only we'll fool them. We'll stop before we get to the quarry and dig in beside the path. Then, when they come running after us, they'll run right into an ambush."

To make sure the enemy would follow, Tom dropped his hat beside the path and, a little farther, Herb dropped his handkerchief.

At a place where the path curved in a bend, Tom said, "This is a good spot for our ambush. Now the best way is to dig foxholes. They'll never see us if we do that."

Without any tools but bare hands and one dull knife, the foxholes were hard to dig. Tom, Herb, and Peewee studied their bruised hands when the shallow holes were done.

Tom licked a brier scratch. "Well, that was a tough job, but it'll be worth it when the enemy comes along. Boy, they'll never know what hit them." He reached in to a bag at his side and drew out a pine cone. "Better get your ammunition ready."

Herb and Peewee opened their bags of pine-cone ammunition.

Herb looked hopeful. "Uh-huh," he said. "They'll be along any time now. We'd better get in those good ol' foxholes right away——" He stopped suddenly and looked around as a curious expression crossed his face. "Say, where's that noisy little dog of yours?"

Tom looked around quickly. Floppy was not in sight.

"Aw, *now* what's he up to?" Herb asked bitterly.

They didn't have to wait long for the answer to that question. Back up the path Floppy's shrill, eager bark broke out and was followed immediately by the voice of Stubby Johnson. "Hey, here's Tom's dog. The enemy's right around here somewhere. Make a big circle and we'll surround 'em."

There was no chance for an ambush now. A retreat was the only way to avoid being surrounded.

Herb looked bitterly at his foxhole. "All that work for nothing," he grunted. "And it's all that dog's fault."

That was not a good time for Floppy to come back but he did, bouncing merrily up to Tom, his eyes shining and his tail paddling the air happily. The look Tom gave him stopped him in his tracks. His tail stopped waving. It drooped, and so did his ears. His expression said, "I don't know what I did wrong, but I'm sorry. Please stop looking at me like that."

Herb and Peewee had already started down the path. Tom started after them and Floppy brought up the rear, jogging along in a slow and subdued manner. There was no bounce in his gait. Sometimes he looked up at Tom with a puzzled, sorrowful expression. Clearly, he knew he was in disgrace, but if he was not a good soldier, Floppy was no deserter. Soberly, but steadily, he followed, keeping just behind Tom's heels.

Tom's spirits were as low and troubled as Floppy's. He knew that the only way he could redeem himself was to think up some brilliant plan that would turn defeat into a spectacular victory. The trouble was that he couldn't think of any plan at all. The only thing that seemed possible was to continue down the path which led to the abandoned quarry. In the quarry there would be good hiding places behind the scattered blocks of stone and maybe a plan would come.

The path slanted downward and grew rocky. The quarry was just ahead, at the bottom of the slope.

Scattered over the quarry floor were the big blocks of rocks that had been blasted away from the cliffs. Tom sprinted ahead of Herb and Peewee and peered behind one of the rocks. Right there would be a good place to make a defensive stand. The trouble was that Tom didn't want to make a defensive stand. He wanted some bold surprise move that would win the battle brilliantly, and would leave no doubt as to who deserved the credit for winning it!

His glance went past the big rock to the hillside beyond it. He started to run on, stopped and came back, his eyes squinting with the beginning of an idea.

He stopped Herb and Peewee. "Look," he said. "The tunnel's dry."

They all stared at the hole that led into the hillside. Always before, the five-foot opening had been half full of water brought from a stream on the other side of the hill. They knew that, when the quarry was worked, the tunnel had been dug especially to bring that water here to wash the crushed rock.

"Hey," Tom said. "With no water in the tunnel, we could go through it and come out back of the hill."

Herb saw what he had in mind. "Yeh, then we could get back to the path and we'd be back of Stubby's army."

"That's it." Tom's face glowed with the joy of a great idea. "We'd be back of them and they wouldn't know it 'till we attacked them. Boy, that'd be the end of this battle."

He pushed Peewee toward the tunnel saying, "Get in there quick. Say, this is the best war-plan anybody ever had, I bet!"

Herb was following Peewee into the tunnel when a sudden thought struck him and he looked around warily.

"Where's that Floppy?" he asked. "We don't want him hanging around here showing them where we went and spoiling *this* plan."

"Here he is." Tom lifted Floppy and carried him into the tunnel behind Herb. "Now," he said. "This time nothing can go wrong with our plan."

It was black dark in the tunnel. Tom looked back toward the entrance and noticed something.

"Look," he said. "See that big rock? It's just balanced there, and I bet we could push it down so's it would nearly cover the entrance."

"Yeh," Herb agreed. "And then nobody would ever think we came in here. That would fool 'em all right."

Tom was right. The big rock was delicately balanced, and after the second push it began to roll. The tunnel sloped down toward the entrance and, after the rock began to move, it rolled faster than Tom had expected. It lurched sideways and hit the wall, knocking loose another rock. A clod of earth fell into the place where the other rock had been. A small stone fell from the top of the tunnel, and several lumps of earth followed it. A rumbling, grinding sound echoed through the tunnel. Stones and clods of earth were falling like a dark snowstorm. Near the entrance, the whole top of the tunnel shifted, swayed, and collapsed with a thump like a heavy explosion.

The noise died away. It was very quiet in the tunnel. Floppy whined a little. The air was thick with dust and Tom sneezed. Suddenly Peewee sniffled.

"How we going to get out of here?" he wailed.

Tom's attempt to laugh sounded queer. "Huh," he said uneasily. "We'll go on out the other end the way we planned."

"Yeh," Herb said. "C-come on, let's go. It—it might get late, or something."

Tom found himself in the lead. As he couldn't see, he had to feel his way along. Sometimes he bumped into the sides and had to grope around until he could find his direction again.

He had done this several times when Herb heard him mutter excitedly, "Blame ol' tunnel must bend here. I can't find it— keep bumping into the side."

Herb came up to him and they both groped along the wall. They could feel the bend in the wall, but when they followed it they came back to where they had started from. They knew that, because finally they bumped into Peewee who was standing still and so must be where they had left him.

Even Peewee knew what had happened. The tunnel was blocked ahead of them just as it was blocked behind.

No one said anything until Peewee wailed, "I want to go home."

Tom had a terrible feeling that he might say something like that himself. To avoid that he tried to find something else to say, anything at all that would sound steady and unafraid.

His voice didn't quiver very much. "I guess that's why the tunnel is dry. That cave-in is damming up the water so it can't come through."

Peewee's sniffles grew louder. "What we going to do?"

Neither Herb nor Tom answered that question. They were

both afraid they knew what they were going to do. It looked as if they were going to stay there, buried alive in the tunnel.

"Come on," Tom blurted out desperately. "Let's go back to the other end. Maybe there's some way out there. We didn't stop to look."

Tom found himself thinking about the bright, sunny world above; how the birds were singing up there in the warm sweet air, so different from the damp, moldy underground smell.

It seemed miles back to the other end of the tunnel, but when he reached the blocked entrance Tom could see the wall of earth and stones ahead.

He could see again, very dimly, but well enough to make out the caved-in mass ahead. That meant there was light here and light could only come from a hole that led to the outside world.

Now he saw it. A little patch of sky shone gloriously blue at the far end of a slanting crack in the roof. The crack was about ten feet long and it was narrow.

He scrambled up the sloping wall of caved-in dirt and tried to force himself into the opening. His shoulders stuck and no matter how hard he pushed he could not wedge himself up any farther.

He dropped back and watched Herb and then Peewee try to wriggle into the hole. Even Peewee was too big to make it.

They shouted and their voices boomed back at them and died away in rustling echoes along the length of the dark tunnel.

"Prob'ly no one could hear us no matter how loud we holler," Herb said despairingly. He scrambled toward the opening again and tripped over something soft, something that yelped. The sound startled all of them. They had forgotten Floppy.

"Blame ol' dog," Herb said bitterly. "It's all his fault we're in here. I told you all along not to bring him today."

Tom hardly heard him. "Floppy!" he said to himself. "That's it—Floppy—he's small enough." He turned to Herb. "So Floppy's no good, huh?" he asked. "Well, let me tell you something. Floppy's going to get us out of this."

Herb snorted scornfully. "That dog! How's he going to do anything? He's too small to——" Herb stopped suddenly, then went on, "Yeh, Floppy can get out maybe, but that won't help us."

Tom fished in his pockets and located a stub of a pencil and his map. He turned the map over and wrote on the blank side of the paper. "We are stuck in the tunnel at the old quarry, the one the water comes through. Come to the quarry end of the tunnel and holler. There is a small hole and we can hear you, I guess. We will holler back. Faithfully yours, Tom Perkins, Herb Jenkins, and Peewee Davis. P. S. Holler good and loud."

Tom thought for a minute and then took off his shirt. It was a bright blue shirt. He tied one sleeve to Floppy's collar and knotted the other sleeve around the note.

"There," he said. "I guess someone will wonder what a dog is doing with a shirt, and then they'll see the note."

He picked the little dog up and pushed him into the narrow opening, spanked him once and shouted. "Go home. You hear me, Floppy? You go home."

Floppy wriggled and his paws made a scraping, clawing sound. Loose bits of dirt showered down behind him. For a while the light in the opening was blotted out, and then the little patch of blue sky appeared again. A high, thin bark sounded faintly in the tunnel.

Floppy was gone. Would he come back? And more important, would he bring someone back with him?

The minutes dragged by and grew into what seemed like years.

Tom was conscious that he was very thirsty. He wondered if it would rain before it was too late and if enough rain water would trickle down through the hole to do any good. He looked up to see if he could tell by the way the hole sloped. And there at the other end of the opening was Floppy's shaggy face staring down at him.

"He's come back alone," was Tom's first thought. "Maybe he's just been standing around up there all the time."

Then Floppy's face disappeared and a man's voice shouted down the hole. It was Tom's father's voice. A shovel thudded into the ground, and the boys took a deep breath.

After that Tom didn't remember anything that happened until he dragged himself up the enlarged hole and stood sighing and blinking at a little dog that seemed more beautiful than any dog possibly could be.

Floppy, however, was not through redeeming himself. When Tom had finished explaining to his father how they had been trapped in the tunnel, he noticed that Floppy had pricked up his ears and was staring excitedly down into the quarry. Tom looked where the little dog's nose was pointing.

Stubby Johnson and his army were marching by at the base of the hill.

Tom motioned to Herb and Peewee. They all drew pine-cone ammunition out of the bags they had forgotten about until that minute.

"Fire," Tom yelled, and for a little while the air was thick with whizzing cones that thudded into the surprised enemy.

Mr. Perkins blinked in amazement as the three boys, apparently forgetting what they had been through, whooped and jeered at Stubby Johnson and his defeated army.

"You're dead, you're dead, you're dead," they yelled. "We win the battle."

Tom picked up Floppy. "Boy, oh boy, what a dog!"

Herb and Peewee very respectfully shook Floppy's paw and repeated, "Boy, what a dog!"

PONY PENNING DAY

by Marguerite Henry

Pony Penning Day always comes on the last Thursday in July. For weeks before, every member of the Volunteer Fire Department is busy getting the grounds in readiness, and the boys are allowed to help.

"I'll do your chores at home, Paul," offered Maureen, "so's you can see that the pony pens are good and stout."

Paul spent long days at the pony penning grounds. The pens for the wild ponies must be made safe. Once the Phantom was captured, she must not escape. Nothing else mattered.

Paul and Maureen Beebe lived on their grandfather's pony ranch on the island of Chincoteague, just off the Virginia shore. Across a narrow channel lay another island, Assateague, which was the home of the wild herds. They were said to be the descendants of a bunch of Spanish horses off a Spanish galleon which had been shipwrecked there several hundred years ago. Once every July the men of Chincoteague crossed the channel to Assateague and rounded up the wild ponies. They swam them across the channel to Chincoteague to be sold on Pony Penning Day.

Paul and Maureen had gentled many a wild colt. But just as the colt was learning that they were his friends, Grandpa Beebe would sell it and the children would never see him again. They had earned a hundred dollars to buy a horse of their own—and the horse they wanted was the Phantom. This was the mysterious wild mare about whom so many stories were told. None of the roundup men had ever been able to capture her. But this year Paul was old enough to go with the men and he was determined to get her.

"When I do," he said, "I'll tie a rope around her neck to show she's already sold. To us."

The night before the roundup, he and Maureen made last-minute plans in Phantom's stall. "First thing in the morning," Paul told Maureen, "you lay a clean bed of dried sea grass. Then fill the manger with plenty of marsh grass to make Phantom feel at home."

"Oh, I will, Paul. And I've got some ear corn and some 'lasses to coax her appetite, and Grandma gave me a bunch of tiny new carrots and some rutabagas, and I've been saving up sugar until I have a little sackful."

It was dark and still when Paul awoke the next morning. He lay quiet a moment, trying to gather his wits. Suddenly he shot out of bed.

Today was Pony Penning Day! He dressed quickly and thudded barefoot down to the kitchen where Grandma stood over the stove, frying ham and making coffee for him as if he were man-grown! After a hurried breakfast, he ran out the door. He mounted Watch Eyes, a dependable pony that Grandpa had never been able to sell because of his white eyes. Locking his bare feet around the pony's sides, he jogged out of the yard.

Maureen came running to see him off.

"Whatever happens," Paul called back over his shoulder, "you be at Old Dominion Point at ten o'clock on a fresh pony."

"I'll be there, Paul!"

"And you, Paul!" yelled Grandpa. "Obey yer leader. No matter what!"

Day was breaking. A light golden mist came up out of the sea. It touched the prim white houses and the white picket fences with an unearthly light. Paul loped along slowly to save his mount's strength. All along the road, men were turning out of their gates.

"Where do you reckon you'll do most good, Bub?" taunted a lean sapling of a man. He guffawed loudly, then winked at the rest of the group.

Paul's hand tightened on the reins. "Reckon I'll do most good where the leader tells me to go," he said, blushing hotly.

The day promised to be sultry. The marsh grass that usually billowed and waved stood motionless. The water of Assateague Channel glared like quicksilver.

Now the cavalcade was thundering over a small bridge that linked Chincoteague Island to little Piney Island. At the far end of the bridge a scow with a rail fence around it stood at anchor.

In spite of light talk, the faces of the men were drawn tight with excitement as they led their mounts onto the scow. The horses felt the excitement, too. Their nostrils quivered, and their ears swiveled this way and that, listening to the throb of the motor. Now the scow began to nose its way across the narrow channel. Paul watched the White Hills of Assateague loom near. He watched the old lighthouse grow sharp and sharper against the sky. In a few minutes the ride was over. The gangway was being lowered. The horses were clattering down, each man taking his own.

All eyes were on Wyle Maddox, the leader.

"Split in three bunches," Wyle clipped out the directions loud and sharp. "North, south, and east. Me and Kim and the Beebe boy will head east, Wimbrow and Quillen goes north, and Harvey and Rodgers south. We'll all meet at Tom's Point."

Paul touched his bare heels into Watch Eyes' side. *They were off!* The boy's eyes were fastened on Wyle Maddox. He and Kim Horsepepper were following their leader like the wake of a ship.

As they rode on, Paul could feel the soft sand give way to hard meadowland, then to pine-laden trails. There were no paths to follow, only openings to skin through—openings that led to water holes or to grazing grounds. The three horses thrashed through underbrush, jumped fallen trees, waded brackish pools and narrow, winding streams.

Suddenly Paul saw Wyle Maddox's horse rear into the air. He heard him neigh loudly as a band of wild ponies darted into an open grazing stretch some twenty yards ahead, then vanished among the black tree trunks.

The woods came alive with thundering hoofs and frantic horse calls. Through bush and brier and bog and hard marshland the wild ponies flew. Behind them galloped the three riders, whooping at the top of their lungs. For whole seconds at a time the wild band would be swallowed up by the forest gloom. Then it would reappear far ahead—nothing but a flash of flying tails and manes.

Suddenly Wyle Maddox was waving Paul to ride close. "A straggler!" he shouted, pointing off to the left. "He went that-away! Git him!" And with a burst of speed Wyle Maddox and Kim Horsepepper were after the band.

Paul was alone. His face reddened with anger. They wanted to be rid of him. That's what they wanted. Sent after a straggler! He was not interested in rounding up a straggler that couldn't even keep up with the herd! He wanted the Phantom. Then Grandpa's words flashed across his mind, "You, Paul, obey yer leader. No matter what!"

He wheeled his pony and headed blindly in the direction Wyle had indicated. He rode deeper into the pine thicket, trying to avoid snapping twigs, yet watching ahead for the slightest motion of leaf or bush. He'd show the men, if it took him all day. His thin shirt clung to him damply and his body was wet with sweat. A cobweb veiled itself across his face. With one hand he tried to wipe it off, but suddenly he was almost unseated. Watch Eyes was dancing on his hind legs, his nose high in the air. Paul stared into the sun-dappled forest until his eyes burned in his head. At last, far away and deep in the shadow of the pines, he saw a blur of motion. With the distance that lay between them, it might have been anything. A deer. Or even a squirrel. Whatever it was, he was after it!

Watch Eyes plunged on. There was a kind of glory in pursuit that made Paul and the horse one. They were trailing nothing but swaying bushes. They were giving chase to a mirage. Always it moved on and on, showing itself only in quivering leaves or moving shadows.

What was that? In the clump of myrtle bushes just ahead? Paul reined in. He could scarcely breathe for the wild beating of his heart. There it was again! A silver flash. It looked like mist with the sun on it. And just beyond the mist, he caught sight of a long tail of copper and silver.

He gazed awestruck. "It could be the Phantom's tail," he breathed. "It is! It is! It is! And the silver flash—it's not mist at all, but a brand-new colt!"

The blood pounded in his ears. No wonder the Phantom was a straggler! No wonder she let herself be caught. "She's got a baby colt!" he murmured.

He glanced about him helplessly. If he could only think! How could he drive the Phantom and her colt to Tom's Point?

Warily he approached the myrtle thicket. Just then the colt let out a high, frightened whinny. In that little second Paul knew that he wanted more than anything in the world to keep the mother and the colt together. Shivers of joy raced up and down his spine. His breath came faster. He made a firm resolution. "I'll buy you both!" he promised.

But how far had he come? Was it ten miles to Tom's Point or two? Would it be best to drive them down the beach? Or through the woods? As if in answer a loud bugle rang through the woods. It was the Pied Piper, the pinto stallion in command of the herd. And unmistakably his voice came from the direction of Tom's Point.

The Phantom pricked her ears. She wheeled around and almost collided with Watch Eyes in her haste to find the band. She wanted the Pied Piper for protection. Behind her trotted the foal, all shining and clean with its newness.

Paul laughed weakly. *He* was not driving the Phantom after all! She and her colt were leading him. They were leading him to Tom's Point!

Tom's Point was a protected piece of land where the marsh was hard and the grass especially sweet. About seventy wild ponies, exhausted by their morning's run, stood browsing quietly, as if they were in a corral. Only occasionally they looked up at their captors. The good meadow and their own weariness kept them peaceful prisoners.

At a watchful distance the roundup men rested their mounts and relaxed. It was like the lull in the midst of a storm. All was quiet on the surface. Yet there was an undercurrent of tension. You could tell it in the narrowed eyes of the men, their subdued voices and their too easy laughter.

Suddenly the laughter stilled. Mouths gaped in disbelief. Eyes rounded. For a few seconds no one spoke at all. Then a shout that was half wonder and half admiration went up from the men. Paul Beebe was bringing in *the Phantom and a colt!*

The roundup men were swarming around Paul, buzzing with questions. "Beats all!" he heard someone say. "For two years we been trying to round up the Phantom and along comes a spindling youngster to show us up."

" 'Twas the little colt that hindered her."

" 'Course it was."

"It's the newest colt in the bunch; may not stand the swim."

"If we lose only one colt, it'll still be a good day's work."

The man accepted Paul as one of them now—a real roundup man. They were clapping him on the shoulder and trying to get him to talk. "Ain't they a shaggy-lookin' bunch?" Kim Horsepepper asked.

"Except for Misty," Paul said, pointing toward the Phantom's colt. "Her coat is silky." The mere thought of touching it sent shivers through him. "Misty," he thought to himself wonderingly. "Why, I've named her!"

He looked out across the water. Two lines of boats were forming a pony-way across the channel. He saw the cluster of people and the mounts waiting on the shores of Chincoteague and he knew that somewhere among them was Maureen. It was like a relay race. Soon she would carry on.

"Could I swim my mount across the channel alongside the Phantom?" Paul asked Wyle Maddox anxiously.

Wyle shook his head. "Watch Eyes is all tuckered out," he said. "Besides, there's a kind of tradition in the way things is handled on Pony Penning Day. There's mounted men for the roundup and there's boatmen to herd 'em across the channel," he explained.

"Tide's out!" he called in clipped tones. "Current is slack. Time for the ponies to be swimmed across. Let's go!"

Suddenly the beach was wild with commotion. From three sides the roundup men came rushing at the ponies, their hoarse cries whipping the animals into action. They plunged into the water, the stallions leading, the mares following, neighing encouragement to their colts.

"They're off!" shouted Wyle Maddox, and everyone felt the relief and triumph in his words.

On the shores of Chincoteague the people pressed forward, their faces strained to stiffness, as they watched Assateague Beach.

"Here they come!" The cry broke out from every throat.

Maureen, wedged in between Grandpa Beebe on one side and a volunteer fireman on the other, stood on her mount's back. Her arms paddled the air as if she were swimming and struggling with the wild ponies.

Suddenly a fisherman, looking through binoculars, began shouting in a hoarse voice, "A new-borned colt is afeared to swim. Wait! A wild pony is breaking out from the mob! Swimming around the mob! Escaping!"

An awed murmur stirred the crowds. Maureen dug her toes in her mount's back. She strained her eyes to see the fugitive, but all she could make out was a milling mass of dark blobs on the water.

The fisherman leaned far out over the water. "It's the Phantom!" he screamed.

The people took up the cry, echoing it over and over. "It's the Phantom! She's escaped again!"

Maureen felt tears on her cheek, and impatiently brushed them away.

The fisherman was waving for quiet. "It's the *Phantom's* colt that won't swim!" he called out in a voice so hoarse it cracked. "The Phantom got separated from a bran'-fire new colt. She's gone back to get it!"

The people whooped and hollered at the news. "The Phantom's got a colt," they sang out. "The Phantom's got a new colt!"

Again the fisherman was waving for silence.

"She's reached her colt!" he crowed. "But the roundup men are closing in on her! They're making her shove the colt in the water. Look at her! She's makin' it swim!"

Grandpa Beebe cupped his hands around his mouth. "Can the little feller make it?" he boomed.

The crowd stilled, waiting for the hoarse voice. For long seconds no answer came. The fisherman remained as fixed as the piling he stood on. Wave after wave of fear swept over Maureen. She felt as if she were drowning. And just when she could stand the silence no longer, the fisherman began reporting in short, nervous sentences.

"They're half-ways across. Jumpin' Jupiter! The colt! It's bein' sucked down in a whirlpool. I can't see it now. My soul and body! A boy's jumped off the scow. He's swimming out to help the colt."

The onlookers did not need the fisherman with the binoculars any more. They could see for themselves. A boy swimming against the current. A boy holding a colt's head above the swirling water.

Maureen gulped great lungfuls of air. "It's Paul!" she screamed. "It's Paul!"

On all sides the shouts went up. "Why, it's Paul!"

Grandpa leaped up on his mount's back as nimbly as a boy. He stood with his arms upraised, his fists clenched.

"God help ye, Paul!" his words carried out over the water. "Yer almost home!"

Grandpa's voice was as strong as a tow rope. Paul was swimming steadily toward it, holding the small silver face of the colt above the water. He was almost there. He *was* there!

Maureen slid down from her mount, clutching a handful of mane. "You made it, Paul! You made it!" she cried.

The air was wild with whinnies and snorts as the ponies touched the hard sand, then scrambled up the shore, their wet bodies gleaming in the sun. Paul half-carried the little colt up the steep bank; then suddenly it found its own legs. Shouts between triumph and relief escaped every throat as the little filly tottered up the bank.

For a brief second Paul's and Maureen's eyes met above the crowds. It was as if they and the mare and her foal were the only creatures on the island. They were unaware of the great jostling and fighting as the stallions sorted out their own mares and colts. They were unaware of everything but a sharp ecstasy. Soon the Phantom and her colt would belong to them. Never to be sold.

Dodging horses and people, Grandpa Beebe made his way over to Paul.

"Paul, boy," he said, his voice unsteady, "I swimmed the hull way with you. Yer the most wonderful and the craziest young'un in the world. Now git home right smart quick," he added, trying to sound very stern. "Yer about done up, and Grandma's expectin' ye. Maureen and I'll see to it that the Phantom and her colt reach the pony pens."

NEW FOLKS COMING

by Robert Lawson

All the Hill was boiling with excitement. On every side there rose a continual chattering and squealing, whispering and whistling, as the animals discussed the great news. Through it all could be heard again and again the words, "New Folks coming."

Little Georgie came tumbling down the Rabbit burrow, panting out the tidings. "New Folks coming," he shouted. "New Folks coming, Mother—Father, new Folks coming into the Big House!"

Mother looked up from the very thin soup that she was stirring. "Well, it's high time there were new Folks in the Big House, *high* time, and I do hope they're planting Folks, not shiftless like the last ones. Three years now since there's been a good garden on this place. Never enough to put anything up for the winters and last winter the worst in years. I don't know how we ever got through it and I don't know how we'll ever make out if they're not planting Folks, I just don't know, with food getting scarcer all the time and no place to get a vegetable except the Fat-Man's-at-the-Crossroad, and him with his dogs and all, and crossing the Black Road twice a day to get there. I just don't know, I just don't know——" Mother was quite a worrier.

"Now, my dear," said Father, "do try to adopt a more optimistic attitude. This news of Georgie's may promise the approach of a more felicitous and bountiful era. Perhaps it would be well if I were to indulge in a short stroll about the neighborhood and seek confirmation of this most auspicious rumor." Father was a Southern Gentleman and always talked like that.

As he picked his way through the long neglected garden the big brick house loomed up dark and lonely in the twilight. It looked very gloomy, no lights in the windows, no Folks about. The roof shingles were curled and rotting, blinds hung crookedly. In the walks and driveway tall, dried weeds rattled and scraped whenever a breeze stirred. Now that all the earth was stirring with spring it seemed even more depressing.

There had been a time, he remembered it wistfully, when things had been quite different here on the Hill. The lawns then had been thick carpets of delicious grass, the fields heavy with clover. Garden vegetables had been plentiful; he and Mother and all their numerous offspring had lived well, all the Little Animals had lived well.

There had been good Folks there in those days, children too, who had played tag with them evenings, who had squealed with delight when mother skunks, their little ones strung out behind in solemn Indian file, had paraded across the lawn. There had been a Dog, a lady Spaniel, old and fat, who carried on endless noisy arguments with the woodchucks, but had never been known to harm anyone. In fact she had once found a lost fox cub and nursed it and raised it with her own puppies. Let's see, that cub would be Foxy's uncle, or was it his father? He couldn't remember, it seemed so long ago.

Then evil days had fallen upon the Hill. The good Folks had moved away and their successors had been mean, shiftless, inconsiderate. Sumac, bayberry and poison ivy had taken over the fields, the lawns had gone to crab grass and weeds, and there was no garden. Last autumn even they had gone, leaving the empty house with its desolate black windows and its shutters flapping through the winter storms.

He passed the tool-house where in the old days bags of seed and chicken feed had always rewarded the hungry field mice. It had been empty for years, every grain of food had been searched out during the cold, hard winters. None of the animals ever went there anymore.

Porkey the Woodchuck was on the side lawn, hungrily snatching at the straggly patches of grass. His fur looked moth-eaten and he was quite thin—a very different animal from the fat, waddling Porkey who last fall had squeezed himself down his burrow to sleep away the winter. Now he was trying to make up for lost time. After each mouthful he would raise his head, look all around and grumble, then snatch another mouthful. It made his grumbling come in short bursts. "Look at this lawn," he growled, "just *look* at it—gulp-gulp—not a leaf of clover in it, nothing but crab grass and chickweed—gulp-gulp—*time* new Folks was coming—gulp-gulp—*high* time." He paused and sat up as Father courteously greeted him.

"Good evening, Porkey, *good* evening. It is indeed a pleasure to see you about again. I trust you passed a comfortable winter and that this pleasant spring evening finds you in the best of health."

"Dunno," grumbled Porkey. "Health's all right, I guess, but I'm thin as all get out and how in tarnation's a fellow going to put any fat on his ribs with this stuff?" He waved disgustedly at the weed-choked fields, the patchy lawn. "Them last Folks were slops, that's what they were, slops. Never done nothing, never planted nothing, never took care of nothing, let everything run down. Time they were gone, good riddance *I* say, time there was new Folks coming, *high* time."

"That is precisely the subject on which I wished to consult you," said Father. "I have heard certain talk concerning the possibility of new arrivals and wondered if you had any definite knowledge of the facts of the case. Is there any clear proof of this most desirable addition to our neighborhood, or is it mere hearsay?"

"Hearsay, hearsay?" said Porkey a little doubtfully. He scratched his ear and spat thoughtfully. "Well now, I'll tell you. I hear say as how that real-estate fellow was up to the house two-three days ago with a couple of people, going all around inside and outside. I hear say as Bill Hickey, the carpenter fellow, was up here yesterday a-poking at the roof and at the tool-house and the chicken house and figgerin' figgers on a bit of paper. I hear say as Louie Kernstawk, the mason, was up here today kicking and poking around them old stone walls and them tumbledown steps and figgerin' figgers too. And I hear say this, and this is important." He hitched himself closer and banged the ground with his paw. "This is *real* important. I hear say as Tim McGrath —you know, the fellow in the cottage down to the fork, does plowing and planting and such—I hear say as he was up here this afternoon looking over the old garden and the lawn and the North field here, and he was figgerin' figgers too. Now what do you think of that?"

"I think," said Father, "that it all sounds extremely auspicious. There seems no doubt that new Folks are coming and all signs seem to indicate that they are planting Folk. We could well do with some good planting Folk hereabout. A nice field of bluegrass now——" Father had come from Kentucky many years ago and his talk of the bluegrass had become just a trifle tiresome.

" 'Twon't grow good here," Porkey interrupted, " 'twon't grow good here in Connecticut at all. Myself I could do with a good field of clover and timothy, though, I could do fine. Timothy and clover and maybe some decent lawn grass—and a garden." His eyes grew watery at the thought. "Some beet tops now, and maybe some green peas and a mouthful of verbena to top off with." He suddenly went back to his frantic tearing at the sparse grass patches.

Father continued his stroll in a happier frame of mind. After all, times *had* been pretty hard these last few years. Many of their friends had deserted the Hill, all their married children had sought other homes, Mother really was looking peaked and seemed to worry more and more. New Folks in the House might bring back the good old days——

"Good evening, sir, and good luck to you," said the Gray Fox, politely. "New Folks coming, I understand."

"A pleasant good-evening to you, sir," answered Father. "All indications seem to point to that happy event."

"I must thank you," the Fox went on, "for taking those dogs off my trail yesterday morning. I wasn't in very good condition to deal with them. You see, I had been away up Weston way to bring home a hen—pickings are pretty scarce hereabouts these days. Eight miles it is, there and back, and she was a tough old girl. She was sitting pretty heavy and I was tuckered out when those dogs jumped me. You handled them very skillful, very, and I am obliged to you."

"Not at all, my boy, not at all. Pray don't mention it," said Father. "I always enjoy a run to hounds. Brought up on it, you know. Why down in the Bluegrass Country——"

"Yes, I know," said the Fox hastily. "What did you do with them?"

"Oh, just took them on a little romp down the Valley, through a few brier patches, ended them up on that electric fence of Jim Coley's. Stupid brutes, though. Hardly could call it sport, very low class. Now down in the Bluegrass Country the hounds were real thoroughbreds. Why, I can remember——"

"Yes, I know," said the Fox, melting into the bushes. "Thanks just the same though—"

The Gray Squirrel was digging around rather hopelessly. He never could quite remember where he'd buried his nuts, and there had been very few to bury last autumn anyway.

"Good evening, sir, and good luck to you," said Father. "The good luck, however, seems to be what you most require." He smiled as he eyed the futile diggings. "Your memory, old fellow, if you'll forgive my saying so, is not what it used to be."

"It never was," sighed the Squirrel. "Never *could* recollect where I put things." He paused to rest and looked out over the valley. "I can recollect other things, though, real clear. Do you remember the old days when things were good here on the Hill, when there was good Folks here? Mind the tree the young ones always used to fix for us, come Christmas? That spruce over there it was, only smaller then. Little lights onto it, carrots and cabbage leaves and celery for your folks, seed and suet for the birds (used to dip into them a bit myself), nuts, all kinds of nuts for us—and all hung pretty-like on the branches?"

"Indeed I do," said Father. "The memory of those times is deeply cherished by all of us, I am sure. Let us hope that the anticipated arrival of new Folks may, in some degree, bring about a renaissance of the old and pleasanter days."

"New Folks coming?" inquired the Squirrel quickly.

"It is so rumored, and recent developments seem to indicate such a possibility."

"Good," said the Squirrel, resuming his explorations with more energy. "Hadn't heard of it—been too busy scrabbling around. I've got the *most* forgetful memory——"

Willie Fieldmouse galloped along to the end of the Mole ridge and whistled shrilly. "Mole," he shouted, "Mole, come up. News, Mole, news!"

Mole heaved head and shoulders up out of the earth and turned his blind face toward Willie, pointed snout quivering. "Well, Willie, well," he said, "what's all the excitement? What news is news?"

"News enough," Willie cried breathlessly. "Oh, Mole, what news! Everybody's talking about it. New Folks coming, Mole, NEW FOLKS COMING! In the Big House, new Folks. . . . Everybody says they're planting Folks, Mole, and maybe there'll be seeds again in the tool-house, seeds and chicken feed. And it'll fall through the cracks and we'll have all we can eat all winter, just like in summer. And there'll be heat in the cellar and we can build burrows right against the walls and be warm and snug again. And maybe they'll plant tulips, Mole, and scillas and chionodoxas. Oh, what wouldn't I give for a nice crisp tulip bulb right now!"

"Oh, that old bulb game," chuckled the Mole. "I know. I do all the digging and you follow up the burrow and eat the bulbs. That's fine for you, but what do I get out of it? Nothing but the blame, that's all I get."

"Why, Mole," said Willie, very hurt. "Why, Mole, that's unfair of you, it really is. You know what pals we've always been, always share and share alike. Why, Mole, I'm surprised——" He was snuffling slightly.

The Mole laughed and clapped Willie on the back with his broad, leathery paw. "Come, come," he laughed, "don't be so everlastingly sensitive. I was only joking. Why, how could I get along without you, how could I know what was going on? How could I see things? What do I say when I want to see anything?"

Willie wiped away his snuffles. "You say, *Willie, be eyes for me.*"

"Of course I do," said the Mole heartily. "I say, *Willie, be eyes for me,* and you are eyes for me. You tell me just how things look and the size of 'em and the colors of 'em. You tell it real good too. Nobody could tell it better."

Willie had lost his hurt now. "And I *do* tell you when mole traps have been set, don't I, or poison put out, and when they're going to roll the lawn, though nobody's rolled *this* lawn in a long time?"

"Of course you do," laughed the Mole, "of course you do. Now blow your nose and run along. I've got my dinner to get and grubs are scarce around here nowadays." He ducked back into his run and Willie watched the ridge lengthen slowly down the lawn, the end of it heaving and quivering with the Mole's digging. He scampered down and rapped on the ground. "Mole," he cried, "I'll be eyes for you when *they* come. I'll tell you real good."

"Of course you will," Mole's voice was muffled by the earth, "of course you will—and I wouldn't be surprised if there was tulips."

Phewie the Skunk stood up by the edge of the pine wood looking down at the Big House. There was a slight rustle and the Red Buck appeared beside him. "Good evening, sir, and good luck to you," said Phewie. "New Folks coming."

"So I understand," said the Deer. "So I understand, and high time too, not that it matters to me especially. I roam a lot, but things have been poorly here on the Hill for some of the little fellows, very poorly."

"Yes, you roam," Phewie answered, "but you're not above a mess of garden sass now and then, are you?"

"Well, no, not if it's right to hand," the Buck admitted. He sniffed slightly. "I say, Phewie, you wouldn't mind moving over a bit, would you, a little to the leeward? There, that's fine. Thanks lots. As I was saying, I'm fairly fond of a mess of greens now and then, a row of lettuce, say, or some young cabbage, very young— the old ones give me indigestion—but of course what I really crave is tomatoes—are tomatoes. You take a nice young ripe tomato now——"

"You take it," interrupted Phewie. "Personally myself I don't care whether they're planting Folks or not, except for the rest of you, of course. Gardens are nothing in my life. What *I'm* looking forward to is their garbidge."

"You do have such low tastes, Phewie," said the Buck. "Er—by the way, the breeze seems to have shifted—would you mind? —there, that's fine, thanks. As I was saying——"

"Low taste nothing," answered Phewie indignantly. "You just don't understand garbidge. Now there's garbidge *and* garbidge, just like there's Folks and Folks. Some Folks' garbidge just ain't fit for—well, it ain't even fitten for garbidge. But there's other garbidge now, you couldn't ask for anything nicer."

"*I* could," said the Deer firmly, "much nicer. By the way, just to change the subject, Foxy's rather counting on there being chickens, perhaps ducks, even. That ought to interest you."

"Chickens is all right—young ones," admitted Phewie, "and ducks is all right. But to get back to garbidge——"

"Oh dear," the Buck groaned, "the wind's changed *again*," and backed into the woods.

Deep down in the cold ground where some frost still lingered, the old Grandfather of all the cutworms uncoiled his dirty gray length and stretched his stiff joints. His voice was a hissing whisper, but it served to waken from their winter sleep all the thousands of his offspring.

"New Folks coming," he hissed. "New Folks coming." Through all the sluggish mass the sound spread. Slowly a quiver ran through their ugly forms, slowly they uncoiled and began the long climb up through the clammy earth to be ready at the surface when the tender new plants should appear.

So it went on all over the Hill. Through the bushes and the tall, unkempt grass there was a continual stirring and rustling as the Little Animals rushed about, gossiping and speculating on the great event. The squirrels and chipmunks skittered along the stone walls, barking out the news. In the dark pinewood the owl, the crow and the blue jays argued over it loudly. Down in the burrows there was a ceaseless coming and going of visitors and above it all the ever recurring phrase, NEW FOLKS COMING.

Stories of Make-Believe

Everybody likes to pretend. When we are children we like to pretend we are grown up. When we are grown up we sometimes like to pretend that we are children again. But, however young we are or however old, we like to think: "Wouldn't it be fun if horses could talk!" or, "Just suppose a house could fly!"

All these stories were written by people who were "just supposing." And when you read them you have to pretend and suppose too. That is why they are called stories of make-believe.

AND TO THINK THAT I SAW IT ON MULBERRY STREET

by Dr. Seuss

When I leave home to walk to school,
Dad always says to me,
"Marco, keep your eyelids up
And see what you can see."

But when I tell him where I've been
And what I think I've seen,
He looks at me and sternly says,
"Your eyesight's much too keen.

"Stop telling such outlandish tales.
Stop turning minnows into whales."

Now, what can I say
When I get home today?

All the long way to school
And all the way back,
I've looked and I've looked
And I've kept careful track,
But all that I've noticed,
Except my own feet,
Was a horse and a wagon
On Mulberry Street.

That's nothing to tell of,
That won't do, of course . . .

Just a broken-down wagon
That's drawn by a horse.

That can't be my story. That's only a start.
I'll say that a ZEBRA was pulling that cart!
And that is a story that no one can beat,
When I say that I saw it on Mulberry Street.

Yes, the zebra is fine,
But I think it's a shame,
Such a marvelous beast
With a cart that's so tame.
The story would really be better to hear
If the driver I saw were a charioteer.
A gold and blue chariot's something to meet,
Rumbling like thunder down Mulberry Street!

No, it won't do at all . . .
A zebra's too small.

A reindeer is better;
He's fast and he's fleet,
And he'd look mighty smart
On old Mulberry Street.

Hold on a minute!
There's something wrong!

A reindeer hates the way it feels
To pull a thing that runs on wheels.

He'd be much happier, instead,
If he could pull a fancy sled.

Hmmmm . . . A reindeer and sleigh . . .

Say—anyone could think of that,
Jack or Fred or Joe or Nat—
Say, even Jane could think of that.

But it isn't too late to make one little change.
A sleigh and an ELEPHANT! There's something strange!

I'll pick one with plenty of power and size,
A blue one with plenty of fun in his eyes.
And then, just to give him a little more tone,
Have a Rajah, with rubies, perched high on a throne.

Say! That makes a story that no one can beat,
When I say that I saw it on Mulberry Street.

But now I don't know . . .
It still doesn't seem right.

An elephant pulling a thing that's so light
Would whip it around in the air like a kite.

But he'd look simply grand
With a great big brass band!

A band that's so good should have someone to hear it,
But it's going so fast that it's hard to keep near it.
I'll put on a trailer! I know they won't mind
If a man sits and listens while hitched on behind.

But now is it fair? Is it fair what I've done?
I'll bet those wagons weigh more than a ton.
That's really too heavy a load for one beast;
I'll give him some helpers. He needs two, at least.

But now what worries me is this . . .
Mulberry Street runs into Bliss.

Unless there's something I can fix up,
There'll be an awful traffic mix-up!

It takes Police to do the trick,
To guide them through where traffic's thick—
It takes Police to do the trick.

They'll never crash now. They'll race at top speed
With Sergeant Mulvaney, himself, in the lead.

The Mayor is there
And he thinks it is grand,
And he raises his hat
As they dash by the stand.

The Mayor is there
And the Aldermen too,
All waving big banners
Of red, white and blue.

And that is a story that NO ONE can beat
When I say that I saw it on Mulberry Street!

With a roar of its motor an airplane appears
And dumps out confetti while everyone cheers.

And that makes a story that's really not bad!
But it still could be better. Suppose that I add . . . .

. . . A Chinaman
Who eats with sticks . . .
A big Magician

Doing tricks . . .
A ten-foot beard
That needs a comb . . .
No time for more,
I'm almost home.

I swung 'round the corner
And dashed through the gate,
I ran up the steps
And I felt simply GREAT!

FOR I HAD A STORY THAT NO ONE COULD BEAT!
AND TO THINK THAT I SAW IT ON MULBERRY STREET!

But Dad said quite calmly,
"Just draw up your stool
And tell me the sights
On the way home from school."

There was so much to tell, I JUST COULDN'T BEGIN!
Dad looked at me sharply and pulled at his chin.
He frowned at me sternly from there in his seat,
"Was there nothing to look at . . . no people to greet?
Did nothing excite you or make your heart beat?"

"Nothing," I said, growing red as a beet,
"But a plain horse and wagon on Mulberry Street."

THE TURTLE WHO COULDN'T
STOP TALKING

by Ellen C. Babbitt

A Turtle lived in a pond at the foot of a hill. Two young wild Geese, looking for food, saw the Turtle, and talked with him. The next day the Geese came again to visit the Turtle and they became very well acquainted. Soon they were great friends.

"Friend Turtle," the Geese said one day, "we have a beautiful home far away. We are going to fly back to it tomorrow. It will be a long but pleasant journey. Will you go with us?"

"How could I? I have no wings," said the Turtle.

"Oh, we will take you, if only you can keep your mouth shut, and say not a word to anybody," they said.

"I can do that," said the Turtle. "Do take me with you. I will do exactly as you wish."

So the next day the Geese brought a stick and they held the ends of it. "Now take the middle of this stick in your mouth, and don't say a word until we reach home," they said.

The Geese then sprang into the air, with the Turtle between them, holding fast to the stick.

The village children saw the two Geese flying along with the Turtle and cried out: "Oh, see the Turtle up in the air! Look at the Geese carrying a Turtle by a stick! Did you ever see anything more ridiculous in your life!"

The Turtle looked down and began to say, "Well, and if my friends carry me, what business is that of yours?" when he let go, and fell dead at the feet of the children.

As the two Geese flew on, they heard the people say, when they came to see the poor Turtle, "That fellow could not keep his mouth shut. He had to talk, and so lost his life."

HOW ICE CREAM CAME

by Carolyn Sherwin Bailey

Once upon a time, in the Land-Of-Never-Was-But-Might-Have-Been, the fashion of having birthday parties for the children began, but there was no ice cream.

The children had birthday presents and birthday cakes and birthday games and birthday books, but at the beautiful time during a party, when all children sit quietly and wait with shining eyes for the chocolate, or the vanilla, or the peach, or the strawberry ice cream to be served in large saucers, it was not served. And that was a pity, for, as every little boy and girl knows, ice cream *is* the party.

There was a Brindled Cow in the Land-Of-Never-Was-But-Might-Have-Been who loved the children of that Land. The Brindled Cow loved the children because they never threw sod at her or chased her, but always pulled tufts of green grass for her to eat, and led her home safely to her barn at night. And when the Brindled Cow heard that the children were going to have birthday parties, she moo-ed:

"How I would like to do something to make such a party happier! I wonder if I could give some extra cream every day that would be useful for the children's birthdays."

The Brindled Cow moo-ed her plan so loudly that the Grocer, driving past her barn in his little green delivery cart, heard her, and she gave him an idea. The Grocer loved the children of that Land, for the little boys were quite willing to help him by carrying baskets full of groceries when there were too many to fill his delivery cart; and the little girls never, never touched his raisins or citron or peppermint drops when they came to his grocery shop. So the Grocer, when he heard the plan of the Brindled Cow, whistled softly to himself.

"The Brindled Cow is going to give some extra cream every day for the children's birthday parties," said the Grocer to himself. "I have a barrel of white sugar in my shop. I wonder if I could be of use at a birthday party by giving the children some sugar to sweeten the cream from the Brindled Cow."

The Grocer was so pleased with his plan, that he told it over and over to himself as he made his rounds, and even talked about it when he took his way through the countryside. And after he had passed, there was such a rustling and whispering in the orchards and along the roads as you never heard! The Peach Tree and the Cherry Tree and the Sugar Maple Tree and the Strawberry Vine and the Raspberry Bush all whispered secrets to one another.

The Fruits and Berries loved the children of that Land, because they tended the trees and the vines and the bushes, never tearing off their buds or picking their fruits until the peaches and the strawberries and the rest were ripe. So these tree and vine friends of the children laid a plan.

"The Brindled Cow is going to give some extra cream every day, and the Grocer is going to give some sugar from his barrel to sweeten the cream for the children's birthday parties," rustled and whispered the trees and the vines. "Shall we not give of our flavors as well?"

This happened one summer and harvest time in the Land-Of-Never-Was-But-Might-Have-Been. Presently it was the winter time, but a birthday party was to be held just the same. The children arrived. There were birthday presents and a birthday cake and birthday games, and then, when the party was almost over, a tiny, tiny rapping at the door of the house was heard. The child who was having the birthday party peeped out of his window and then he came back to the warm fireplace and told the others what he had seen.

"There is a frosty, chilly, white-as-snow boy outside," said the birthday child. "His hair is made of icicles and his cloak of snow crystals. He is carrying a frozen bucket on his arm and knocking at our door as if he wanted to come in."

Some children at a birthday party might not have opened their door to let in so frosty a little boy as this. Some children would not have opened the door to one who had not been asked to the party. But these were the good-natured children of the Land-Of-Never-Was-But-Might-Have-Been.

"Open the door and let the frosty child come in beside our fire!" they shouted, crowding to see which could be the first to greet the stranger who was so cold. So in came the little frozen boy with his frozen bucket, but he was laughing as merrily as possible and he set the bucket down on a table and skipped out again. He was little Jack Frost, and he had brought the first ice cream to a birthday party!

Yes, Jack Frost had frozen the ice cream made of the Brindled Cow's cream, and the Grocer's sugar, and some Fruits who had preserved themselves for this particular party. The children got out saucers and spoons. They had two saucerfuls each, and that was the beginning of ice cream, which has been going on making birthday parties ever since!

PUDDLEBY

by Hugh Lofting

Once upon a time, many years ago—when our grandfathers were little children—there was a doctor; and his name was Dolittle—John Dolittle, M.D. "M.D." means that he was a proper doctor and knew a whole lot.

He lived in a little town called Puddleby-on-the-Marsh. All the folks, young and old, knew him well by sight. And whenever he walked down the street in his high hat everyone would say, "There goes the Doctor!—He's a clever man." And the dogs and the children would all run up and follow behind him; and even the crows that lived in the church-tower would caw and nod their heads.

The house he lived in, on the edge of the town, was quite small; but his garden was very large and had a wide lawn and stone seats and weeping-willows hanging over. His sister, Sarah Dolittle, was housekeeper for him; but the Doctor looked after the garden himself.

He was very fond of animals and kept many kinds of pets. Besides the goldfish in the pond at the bottom of his garden, he had rabbits in the pantry, white mice in his piano, a squirrel in the linen closet and a hedgehog in the cellar. He had a cow with a calf too, and an old lame horse—twenty-five years of age— and chickens, and pigeons and two lambs, and many other animals. But his favorite pets were Dab-Dab the duck, Jip the dog, Gub-Gub the baby pig, Polynesia the parrot, and the owl Too-Too.

His sister used to grumble about all these animals and said they made the house untidy. And one day when an old lady with rheumatism came to see the Doctor, she sat on the hedgehog who was sleeping on the sofa and never came to see him any more, but drove every Saturday all the way to Oxenthorpe, another town ten miles off, to see a different doctor.

Then his sister, Sarah Dolittle, came to him and said,

"John, how can you expect sick people to come and see you when you keep all these animals in the house? It's a fine doctor would have his parlor full of hedgehogs and mice! That's the fourth personage these animals have driven away. Squire Jenkins and the Parson say they wouldn't come near your house again— no matter how sick they are. We are getting poorer every day. If you go on like this, none of the best people will have you for a doctor."

"But I like the animals better than the 'best people,'" said the Doctor.

"You are ridiculous," said his sister, and walked out of the room.

So, as time went on, the Doctor got more and more animals; and the people who came to see him got less and less. Till at last he had no one left—except the Cat's-meat-Man, who didn't mind any kind of animals. But the Cat's-meat-Man wasn't very rich and he only got sick once a year—at Christmas time, when he used to give the Doctor a sixpence for a bottle of medicine.

Sixpence a year wasn't enough to live on—even in those days, long ago; and if the Doctor hadn't had some money saved up in his moneybox, no one knows what would have happened.

And he kept on getting still more pets; and of course it cost a lot to feed them. And the money he had saved up grew littler and littler.

Then he sold his piano, and let the mice live in a bureau-drawer. But the money he got for that too began to go, so he sold the brown suit he wore on Sundays and went on becoming poorer and poorer.

And now, when he walked down the street in his high hat, people would say to one another, "There goes John Dolittle, M.D.! There was a time when he was the best-known doctor in the West Country—— Look at him now—— He hasn't any money and his stockings are full of holes!"

But the dogs and the cats and the children still ran up and followed him through the town—the same as they had done when he was rich.

THE LION-HEARTED KITTEN

by Peggy Bacon

Once there was a striped kitten with yellow eyes and a black nose. He was only a very little kitten but he had the heart of a lion. He was as brave as he could be, and one day he started out to conquer the world. The path he took led through a big black wood, and down this path the kitten stalked very proudly, with his head held high as possible.

Pretty soon, along came a big gray wolf.

"Grumble tumble in the jungle, I'm hungry!" growled the wolf, for this is what the wolves say when they are going to eat you up.

Now it is all very well to be brave in a crisis, but it is even better to be clever too. This the kitten knew, so without showing any fear he said boldly:

"O Mr. Wolf, I was just looking for you. My great-aunt the tigress told me to ask you the way to roast lamb. She says you know so much more about such things than she."

The wolf was impressed and a little flattered. But he was also a bit suspicious of this small kitten, and so he said:

"Tell your great-aunt the tigress that I roast lamb the same way that I roast kitten."

This really frightened the kitten, but he pretended great unconcern and retorted:

"Of course, Mr. Wolf, if you really wish me to tell her that, I will do so; but my great-aunt the tigress is rather short of temper and she might take offense at what you say; she has some kittens of her own and a great many little nieces and nephews."

"Hmmm," murmured the wolf gazing thoughtfully at the kitten who had begun to wash its face, "you may tell her that roast lamb tastes nice with sage and onions." He turned and ran into the wood.

The kitten trotted on along the path and suddenly around a corner he came face to face with a great big enormous snake who was hanging from the branch of a tree just over the path.

"Hiss swich, wish a dish for dinner!" hissed the snake, for that is what the snakes say when they are going to eat you up.

"O Miss Boa Constrictor," cried the kitten (for that was the snake's name), "I have been looking for you everywhere. My great-aunt the tigress wishes to know what is the best way to catch birds. She says that you are so clever at it, and she would be much obliged for some advice on the subject."

Now snakes catch little creatures by staring in their eyes till they are so frightened they dare not move; the boa constrictor said:

"Watch me and I'll show you," for she thought the little kitten looked quite fat and delicious.

But the kitten was far too wise for that, so he simply looked hard beyond the snake and called out:

"Well, I do declare, if that isn't my great-aunt the tigress herself coming this way now!"

The snake whipped round quickly for fear the tigress was creeping up behind her, and while she looked back, the kitten escaped into the wood.

The brave little kitten ran on and on till by and by very suddenly round a big tree he came face to face with the tigress herself.

This time the kitten for all his courage was much alarmed. His breath came fast and his heart beat rapidly, but his wits did not forsake him.

"O Aunty Tigress," he gasped, "I have been hunting and hunting for you till I am all out of breath. My mother, the golden tigress of the next forest but one, wishes to know what it is your kittens eat which make them so big and fat. She is worried about me because I am so very small."—After this speech the kitten held his breath, waiting for the tigress to reply.

For a long time the tigress looked at the kitten and sniffed at the kitten and put her head on one side and considered the kitten. And after a while she came to the conclusion that this kitten certainly did look quite like her kittens save for size; and since her own children had grown up and left her she decided it would be nice to adopt another; so giving the kitten a motherly lick of a large kind she said:

"You certainly are much too small, and if you will come home with me I will feed you up and fatten you up and see what I can do."

Away they walked together, the kitten not without misgivings, going through the big black wood till they came to the tigress' cave. There the tigress gave the kitten all kinds of meat and bones; and sure enough the kitten began to grow, and he grew and grew and grew until he got to be about as big as a cat. The tigress was then well satisfied, for she said: "You are now exactly the size of my own kittens; this diet has agreed with you."

And so the kitten continued to live happily in the cave cared for and protected by the tigress, but he never grew to be any bigger than a cat.

THE FIERCE YELLOW PUMPKIN

by Margaret Wise Brown

There was once a small pumpkin in a great big field, a very small pumpkin the size of an apple, just a little green pumpkin. But the sun burned down on the big field, warm on the little pumpkin, and the little pumpkin grew and he grew and he grew under the fierce burning sun. And pretty soon there was a fat little, round little, yellow little pumpkin in a great big field.

Now this fat little, round little, yellow little pumpkin grew so fat and full of himself that he began to think he was a very fierce vegetable, as fierce as the sun that warmed his fat round sides. "Ho! Ho! Ho!" he would say. "When I grow up and go out into the world Ho! Ho! Ho! I will frighten all the mice and all the vegetables that grow. I'll even frighten the old scarecrow."

For the little pumpkin would dearly have loved to make a fierce ferocious gobble-gobble face like the scarecrow at the far end of the field; but try as he would, his own pumpkin face stayed smooth and yellow and shining.

Then one day the sun did not shine as hot as fire. And black birds, skies full of black birds, began flying over the big field. There was a burning smell of leaves in the air and a crisp tingle that tickled the fat little pumpkin's sides. There were so many birds in the sky that the scarecrow was busy from before daylight until after daylight when it got dark, chasing the birds out of his field. His gobble-gobble face became droopy and dreadful. The wind blew whoo through his hair. He lost one scarecrow eye. For the old scarecrow knew that if there is anything that a black crow is scared of it is a one-eyed scarecrow. How the little pumpkin wished he were a one-eyed pumpkin! He would scare all the field mice out of the field if he were a one-eyed pumpkin! And then that night and the night after, something began to happen. The first cold frosts came in the night. And the fat little, round little, yellow little pumpkin woke up one of those mornings and discovered that he was a fiery orange yellow pumpkin. The color of the sun. A fierce burning orange.

Then the children came galloping through the big field and the old one-eyed scarecrow couldn't even make them jump, because they didn't even look at him. They ran right up to the fat little, round little, orange little pumpkin, and one little girl called out, "Here he is, here is our terrible pumpkin!"

So they cut the pumpkin's heavy stem with a little saw knife; and each taking turns, they carried the pumpkin home, across the field to their house. The little pumpkin liked that. And then with the little saw knife they hollowed him out all empty inside, clean as a whistle, and as sweet smelling as the inside of a pumpkin. They hollowed him all out. Then they cut one big round eye in the side of his face. A big round hole. And the little pumpkin liked that.

"Ho! Ho!" laughed the pumpkin
The fierce yellow pumpkin
"I'm a one-eyed pumpkin
For sure."

Then they cut another big round hole in the other side of his face.

"Ho! Ho!" laughed the pumpkin
The fierce yellow pumpkin

"I'm a fierce yellow pumpkin
For sure."

But that wasn't all. The children cut a sharp shape in the pumpkin for a nose, the shape of a witch's hat. And that wasn't all, either. They took the little saw knife and they sawed zigzag up and zigzag down until the pumpkin had a whole mouthful of sharp zigzag teeth.

Then with a loud Ho! Ho! the little pumpkin laughed a dreadful zigzag laugh across his zigzag teeth.

"Ho Ho Ho
He He He
Mice will run
When they see me."

He was certainly a fierce and ferocious pumpkin with a terrific terrible face.

After a while it was night. There was black darkness all around, inky black darkness.

The children came in with a lighted candle and stuck it inside the pumpkin so that the light shined out his big round eyes and his triangle nose. And the light shined over his zigzag teeth. He was a horrible sight to see. Brrrrr in the dark. He grinned a zigzag grin there in the corner of the room. Grrrr. And the children danced about him singing a song to the terrific terrible pumpkin with the zigzag zigzag grin.

And the little pumpkin was fierce and happy, and he sang:

"Ho Ho Ho
He He He
Mice will run
When they see me!"

And they did.

BLUE SILVER

by Carl Sandburg

Long ago when the years were dark and the black rains used to come with strong winds and blow the front porches off houses, and pick chimneys off houses, and blow them onto other houses, long ago when people had understanding about rain and wind, there was a rich man with a daughter he loved better than anything else in the world.

And one night when the black rain came with a strong wind blowing off front porches and picking off chimneys, the daughter of the rich man fell asleep into a deep sleep.

In the morning they couldn't wake her. The black rain with the strong wind kept up all that day while she kept on sleeping in a deep sleep.

Men and women with music and flowers came in, boys and girls, her playmates, came in—singing songs and calling her name. And she went on sleeping.

All the time her arms were crossed on her breast, the left arm crossing the right arm like a letter X.

Two days more, five days, six, seven days went by—and all the time the black rain with a strong wind blowing—and the daughter of the rich man never woke up to listen to the music nor to smell the flowers nor to hear her playmates singing songs and calling her name.

She stayed sleeping in a deep sleep—with her arms crossed on her breast—the left arm crossing the right arm like a letter X.

So they made a long silver box, just long enough to reach from her head to her feet.

And they put on her a blue silver dress and a blue silver band around her forehead and blue silver shoes on her feet.

There were soft blue silk and silver sleeves to cover her left arm and her right arm—the two arms crossed on her breast like the letter X.

They took the silver box and carried it to a corner of the garden where she used to go to look at blue lilacs and climbing blue morning glories in patches of silver lights.

Among the old leaves of blue lilacs and morning glories they dug a place for the silver box to be laid in.

And men and women with music and flowers stood by the silver box, and her old playmates, singing songs she used to sing —and calling her name.

When it was all over and they all went away they remembered one thing most of all.

And that was her arms in the soft silk and blue silver sleeves, the left arm crossing over the right arm like the letter X.

Somebody went to the king of the country and told him how it all happened, how the black rains with a strong wind came, the deep sleep, the singing playmates, the silver box—and the soft silk and blue silver sleeves on the left arm crossing the right arm like the letter X.

Before that there never was a letter X in the alphabet. It was then the king said, "We shall put the crossed arms in the alphabet; we shall have a new letter called X, so everybody will understand a funeral is beautiful if there are young singing playmates."

JOHNNY PING WING

by Ethel Calvert Phillips

Johnny Ping Wing hung in the window of the Daffodil Shop and smiled and twirled and whirled.

Johnny Ping Wing was a little Chinaman made of peanuts. He had been placed in the window by Miss Martha Pretty, who kept the Daffodil Shop, and who now stood watching Johnny as he spun merrily round and round on the end of a string.

"There!" said Miss Martha, smiling as Johnny waved his arms and let his feet kick gracefully into the air. "You will sell quickly, I haven't a doubt. I used to love peanut Chinamen when I was a little girl!"

Then Miss Martha, who herself looked like a daffodil with her bright golden hair and her gay green smock, fell to dusting the pretty vases and candlesticks and cups that filled the window of her yellow and green shop with its bunch of daffodils painted on the door. And Johnny Ping Wing, left to himself, opened his twinkling black eyes to their widest and looked about him to see what he might see.

He was a gay little figure swinging there on the string that was fastened to the tip of his pointed yellow silk hat. His wide silken trousers were golden yellow too. His coat was a lovely blue trimmed with the smallest brass buttons ever seen. His narrow almond eyes were black and bright and full of fun. His nose was a droll little dot, nothing more, and his tiny mouth wore a curious smile, while from under his bright silk hat there hung a long black pigtail, made of shoe thread and braided as nicely as you please. Johnny was proud of his pigtail. He thought it very beautiful and ornamental, as indeed it was. Not many people nowadays can boast such a fine pigtail as did Johnny Ping Wing.

There were many things, both inside the Shop and out, for Johnny Ping Wing to see as he swung smiling there.

Within the Shop were all sorts of colored bowls and pitchers and plates ranged neatly on counters and shelves. There were lamps of many shapes and colors, both large and small. There were work-baskets and scrap-baskets, colored and sweet grass and plain. There were book-ends and door-stops, paper-weights and ink-wells, pepper-pots and salt-cellars, too. There were story-books and picture-books, and even a few toys. Indeed, there were so many pretty objects in the Daffodil Shop that Johnny Ping Wing thought it would take him a week to see them all.

Outside the Shop there was something passing almost every

moment. Automobiles rolled up and down the street. Ladies walked to and fro. Little boys and girls ran gaily by. Often the people stopped and looked into the window of the Daffodil Shop. The little boys and girls flattened their noses against the glass and breathed heavily as they gazed, and when they spied Johnny Ping Wing, they cried "Ah!" and looked wistful, as if they wanted him very much for their own.

As the morning wore on, people began coming into the Shop to buy. Every time the door opened, Johnny Ping Wing gave a fidgety jerk that set him twirling, for every time he thought to himself, "Perhaps that person is coming in to buy *me!*"

But nobody bought Johnny Ping Wing.

"I will take that yellow pitcher, Miss Pretty," said one. "It is just the size to hold our cream for tea."

"How much is that large bowl, Miss Pretty?" asked another. "I would like it for a present for my sister, I think."

"Have you amber glasses for lemonade, Miss Pretty?"

"I want a box of writing paper and a bottle of ink, please."

"Do you keep birthday cards?"

"Mother says please send her a five-cent pencil with a rubber on the end."

So many different people, so many different needs!

"What fun to keep a shop!" thought Johnny Ping Wing to himself. He liked to watch Miss Martha as she stepped about the shop. He liked the way she wrapped and tied her parcels, cutting off the string with a sharp snap of her shears. He liked to see her count out the change, never once dropping a penny on the floor.

Johnny's bright black eyes saw all that was going on. As for the different noises in the street, Johnny soon learned to know what they meant.

With his eyes shut he could tell by the footsteps who was passing by. He knew the tip-tap, tip-tap of the ladies from the trippety, trippety of the children and the occasional thump-bump, thump-bump of the men. Not many men passed the Shop, for most of them went into the City in the morning on the train.

The hoot or wail of the automobiles did not frighten Johnny

once he had learned what to expect from the big shining cars or neat wagons that passed in procession up and down the street.

He was glad to see that dogs were left outside the Shop when their mistresses came within.

"You may bark all you please," said Johnny to the dogs (but not so loud that anyone could hear), "but you can't reach me."

And he even went so far as to wrinkle up his nose at a white curly dog who yelped and snapped and jumped at the window in the hope of catching Johnny in his teeth and having a good play with him.

But presently a strange noise came up the street, a noise that Johnny didn't know at all. It was a loud and piercing and angry noise, and before long the person who was making it came in sight.

It was a little boy who was being jerked along the street by his mother's hand. The little boy's face was red, tears were rolling down his cheeks, his mouth was wide open, and he screamed without stopping. Under his arm he carried a large yellow duck, a duck that would float on the water and not sink.

Just in front of the Shop window, the little boy stood still. His mother tried to pull him along, but he braced his feet on the sidewalk and would not stir. Johnny's eyes popped in his head. He didn't know little boys ever behaved that way.

Then suddenly Johnny gave a startled twitch on his string. For the little boy had thrown his yellow duck on the pavement and was jumping up and down on it with all his might and main.

Crash! Split! Smash!

The duck lay flat on the sidewalk crushed and broken, never to float again.

The little boy still danced on the sidewalk, but his cries were growing fainter, and soon he let his mother draw him aside to the Shop window and wipe the tears from off his face.

As he stood there, he spied Johnny Ping Wing.

"I want him!" he cried, pointing up at Johnny. "I want him, I want him, I want him, I do!"

His face puckered and he opened his mouth to scream again. He scarcely listened as his mother hastily said, "Don't cry! Don't cry! We will go inside and I will buy it for you."

In spite of this it seemed for a moment as if the little boy meant to have another tantrum then and there.

But he let his mother pull him into the Shop with not a look behind at the poor broken duck, who lay on the pavement deserted and forlorn.

Now you may imagine just how frightened was Johnny Ping Wing. If that little boy bought him, he knew what would happen without a doubt.

"He will squeeze me and crush me and tear me to bits," thought Johnny, trembling upon his string.

His arms and legs grew quite stiff with horror. His pigtail stuck out straight behind.

"I'll run away," thought Johnny Ping Wing.

But how could he run when he was fastened tight to his string?

"I'll hide," thought Johnny, looking wildly round.

But one glance showed him that he had no chance to hide at all.

So Johnny hung there on his string, his face screwed into a little knot, as miserable as he could be, and waited to see what was going to happen to him. Already he could feel the clutch of the little boy's hands, pulling and tearing him to bits.

But Johnny had no cause for worry. Miss Martha Pretty had seen the tantrum from the window, though she was far away at the back of the Shop when the little boy and his mother entered the door.

"No, the little Chinaman is not for sale at present," said Miss Martha Pretty in answer to the question the little boy's mother asked. "He is the only sample I have. But perhaps your little boy might like one of these new picture-books, indestructible ones."

"He is upset this morning," murmured the little boy's mother, "because he has a cold, and I couldn't let him go down to the brook with his duck. But I think he will like a picture-book, this one, about fire engines and automobiles."

Yes, the little boy did like the picture-book and went peacefully off with the book tucked under his arm.

Johnny Ping Wing felt more peaceful, too. His face unscrewed, his arms and legs hung limp, his pigtail lay down flat as a pigtail should.

"Miss Martha will look out for me," thought he, giving her a grateful look. "I shan't worry any more."

So he hung and swung and enjoyed the sights, and thought in his heart how kind Miss Martha was to him.

Almost everyone, going in or out, looked up at Johnny Ping Wing in the window smiling and swinging on his string. But when twelve o'clock came, he was still hanging there.

As the whistles blew and the Town clock chimed noon, Miss Pretty slipped on her hat and coat, placed a sign in the window that read "Closed from 12 to 1," and, stepping out, locked the door behind her and walked off up the street.

CARRIE-BARRY-ANNIE

by Rose Fyleman

There was once a little girl called Margery who lived in a house in the country. She had one brother and one sister, but they were a good deal older than she was and were both away at school, so that she was a rather lonely little girl. Her mother and father worked together in London and went off by train every day after breakfast.

Margery had a nurse who took her every morning to a little day school in the small country town a mile away from where they lived. But she was a rather shy little girl and did not make friends very easily. She liked playing by herself.

I said she was lonely; but that isn't quite right.

She wasn't really lonely, because she had an invisible playmate whom she called Carrie-Barry-Annie.

Nobody had ever seen Carrie-Barry-Annie (that was what I meant when I called her invisible), and I don't know where Margery got her queer name from.

I have an idea she may once have lived in Fairyland and got turned out for some kind of disobedience, and was sent into the everyday world to be a companion to little lonely girls until it was thought fit for her to return.

I can't be at all sure about that. It's just an idea I have, as I said.

Anyway, Margery was very fond of her indeed and spent many happy hours with her.

She used to play with her in the garden, and when she went out for walks with nurse Carrie-Barry-Annie came too. They even ran races together.

Carrie-Barry-Annie had her own little bit of garden and her own lilac bush at the end of the croquet lawn, near the tool shed. She had her own chair in the nursery, too, and on wet days or after tea in the winter, when it was too cold to go out, she and Margery used to have long conversations about all the wonderful adventures they had had together.

"Do you remember, Carrie-Barry-Annie," Margery would say, "the time we were shipwrecked on the desert island when we found the perfectly *enormous* treasure cave?" Or, "Do you remember the darling little mermaid we had such a lovely time with on the shores of the Land of Pearl?"

Margery was never quite sure whether she and Carrie-Barry-Annie really had had those adventures or whether they just imagined them. But it was lovely talking about them.

Carrie-Barry-Annie slept in Margery's room. She had her own bed in the corner. You couldn't see it, of course, but there it was.

Margery always turned the bedclothes back when she turned back her own.

Carrie-Barry-Annie was rather careless about things like that, so that Margery had to look after her a bit.

"Have you your raincoat?" she used to say when they were starting off for a walk. And when they were on the desert island she had always to be reminding her to be on the lookout for snakes and lions.

Carrie-Barry-Annie was nearly eaten up by a lion once because she would go out without her bow and arrows. Margery came running after her and shot the lion just as it was going to spring on her. But it was a narrow escape.

Carrie-Barry-Annie was very, very grateful. She gave Margery a beautiful and precious stone in remembrance of her brave deed. Margery kept it in the little wooden inlaid box which her Granny brought her from Tunbridge Wells.

Nobody knew it was a precious stone. Nurse thought it was just a common pebble and actually wanted Margery to throw it away!

When Margery was nine years old her parents moved to a new house, nearer to London.

Of course, Carrie-Barry-Annie moved too, but, somehow or other, she never seemed quite as much at home there as in the old house. Everything was just a little different. For one thing, a family of children lived in the house next door, and Margery got to know them very well, and soon it was arranged that she was to have lessons with them instead of going to school.

She made another friend, too—the Doctor who came to see her when she got German measles and had to stay in bed for a week.

He was a very kind person, and when Margery was better he used sometimes to take her with him when he went out in his car in the afternoon, visiting patients.

Carrie-Barry-Annie didn't care much for motoring, but she went once or twice.

"I hope you didn't feel very lonely," the Doctor said to Margery one of these times, when he happened to stay at one house a rather long time.

"Oh, no," said Margery. "You see, Carrie-Barry-Annie came with me today."

"And who, pray, is Carrie-Barry-Annie?" said the Doctor, much interested.

So Margery told him all about her. He was the kind of person to whom one *could* tell things like that.

Margery never told the children next door about her friend. As a matter of fact, Carrie-Barry-Annie asked her not to. They weren't really quite her sort, though they were very nice and jolly and very kind to Margery.

Carrie-Barry-Annie still slept in Margery's room, and she sometimes sat in her own special chair in the nursery, though not so often.

Margery was rather worried about her. She felt she was not quite kind to her friend, and yet it seemed impossible for things to be just as they had been before.

And then, at the end of the first year in the new house, it was decided that Margery was to be sent away to school.

She knew at once that Carrie-Barry-Annie would have to be left behind, and she was more worried than ever.

At last she decided to ask her friend the Doctor about it. She felt sure that if anyone could help her, he could. He was so very clever and kind and understanding.

And—do you know?—he really did help.

He took Margery to see a little girl patient of his who had to lie in bed all day because she had something the matter with her back.

And he suggested that Carrie-Barry-Annie should go too and be introduced to the little girl and have her for a friend.

And—wasn't it a fortunate thing?—it was the greatest success imaginable.

They liked one another very much indeed, and Carrie-Barry-Annie thanked Margery ever so much for introducing her to

Gennifer, which was the little girl's name.

Oddly enough, when she went to stay with Gennifer she lived in a little china house on the mantelpiece and was quite, quite small. Gennifer said she had wings, too, and used often to fly away at night and not come back till the morning.

Which rather looks—doesn't it?—as if my idea about her being a fairy was right.

I don't know what became of her in the end.

Margery is grown up now, and Gennifer got quite well and is growing up too. I never heard how long Carrie-Barry-Annie stayed with her.

Perhaps she went to live with another little girl later on.

Perhaps she went back to Fairyland.

I do wonder. . . .

LITTLE BOY PIE

by Eleanor Farjeon

Everybody liked Jim, but it was the children who loved him best. For the exciting thing about him was that, long before they were born, he had been a sailor.

He knew all the places on earth, and all the weather in the sky. He could tell you a day ahead what the weather would be like. And he had a wonderful way of telling it to you something like this:

"There's a storm blowing up! Ah, that 'minds me of the big storm off Cape Horn, when I was Mate of the good ship *Rockinghorse!*"

Or: "There's a frost coming at last. You'll be able to skate tomorrow, the ponds will be covered with ice. Never shall I forget the time the *Rockinghorse* struck an iceberg off Newfoundland."

Or: "Wind's on the way. Get home quick afore it comes, Derry, and if it ketches you, just you hold on to your feet!"

"Why, Jim?" asked Derry.

"Why? You don't want to get blown off 'em, to the top of that plane-tree there, do you? It's happened to me afore now."

"What! a big man like you, Jim?"

"Ah, but then I was a little boy like you. And 'twasn't a plane-tree that time, but an elm-tree full of black rooks' nests, and the rooks all trying to caw the life out of me!"

"Tell me about it, Jim!"

Jim moved a few inches on his box, and Derry clambered on the free corner and dangled his legs, while Jim told him about it.

One summer, when I was a small boy, I had to keep the birds out of the peas. The peas were wanted as food for the cattle, and if the birds had their way the cattle would go short in winter. From break of day till dusk I sat in the field, and when the birds came near me to steal the peas I shook my rattle at them and sang:

"Fly, rascals, fly,
 Or I'll make you into pie!"

Maybe they knew what the words meant, and maybe they did not; but whether they did or not, they flew away at once. Then I felt like a hero who had won a battle. The rooks and the starlings were the foe I had put to flight.

But as often as they flew away, back they came again. It seemed as though they would not learn their lesson. I could not think why they kept coming back. It must be for some very strong reason indeed, a reason more strong than their fear of me.

It made me angry to see them defy me, and again I shook my

rattle at them, and sang my song. So all that summer, the birds and I did not love each other.

There was one rook, a bold black chap, the biggest of the lot, who did not mind my rattle or my song. He stayed among the peas eating his fill, till I came so near that I could all but touch him. If ever I did catch him, I said to myself, I would surely take him home to my mother to be made into a pie. Rook Pie would be a tasty dish, no mistake!

I crept like a mouse up to the big black bird, and put out my hand to grab his tail. And at once, as though he could hear my very shadow moving, off he flew with a loud "caw-caw!" for all the world as though he had the laugh of me. But, "You wait, old chap!" I called after him. "I'll have you yet!" And I shook my rattle again, and sang:

"Fly, rascal, fly,
  Or I'll make you into pie!"

One hot day, in the noon, when the sun stood at the top of the sky, I took my dinner out of a bag I had with me, and began to eat. It was the sort of food I liked, two big bits of bread, with a slice of cold bacon inside them. I had to open my mouth wide to bite right through them, and the taste of bacon in the middle of the bite seemed to me as nice as any food could be.

Each bite filled my mouth quite full, and I had to chew and chew before I was ready for the next one. This was hard work on a hot day, and maybe that was why in the middle of a bite my jaws fell idle, my head began to nod, and my eyes to close. Before I had half done my bread-and-bacon, I was fast asleep.

When I woke up, I was not in the same place at all. I was lying at the edge of a field, that was full of as queer a crop as I ever hope to see. It wasn't beans, and it wasn't peas, and it wasn't grass, or corn, or roots of any sort. No, what grew in that field, if you'll take my word for it, was slices of bread and bacon all blowing in the wind.

Dear me, how good they did smell to a hungry boy like me!

As quick as quick, I ran into the field and took a bite out of a slice as it grew. But I had hardly begun to chew it up before I heard a loud flutter of wings, and a harsh voice sang:

"Fly, rascal, fly,
Or I'll make you into pie!"

There, in the middle of the field, was a great black rook, as big as a giant, it seemed to me, and I was but a little tot who did not stand as high as his tail. The rook was rattling his wings, and singing my own song at me; and when I saw how big he was, I took to my heels and ran for dear life.

"I'll never go near *that* place again!" said I to myself.

But in a little while I began to feel my hunger anew, and in spite of the rook I just had to creep back, to try to steal another slice. This time I managed to snatch two bites before he came at me with his wings and his song, and I only got away just in time.

You might think that cured me for good and all from trying to go into the bread-and-bacon field; but when a boy wants his dinner as badly as I did, he forgets to be afraid; and so, for a third time, I stole round the field, slipped in at a new place, and began to eat.

This time I got three bites down, and just as I was feeling that all was going well, down came the rook on me, quicker than rain in April, and before I could run he had the tail of my little coat in his beak.

Up he flew, up, up, up, till I thought he was going to bump into the sun; but no, he only flew as high as the top of an elm-tree, where his nest was swaying in the wind.

Such a great nest it was, as round and as black as a pot. Inside sat his big black wife and his little black family, and when they saw what he'd got in his beak, they all began to caw so loud that I could not hear myself think.

"Why, Daddy," said the Mammy Rook, "you never mean to say you've caught the fat little rogue who is always coming after the bread-and-bacon?"

"That I have!" said Daddy Rook, "and if you want to please us all, you'll make him into pie."

"Little Boy Pie is a tasty dish, and no mistake!" said Mammy Rook; and all the baby rooks cawed with joy.

"Little Boy Pie! Little Boy Pie! Give me a slice of Little Boy Pie!"

"Hand him over, Daddy," said Mammy Rook, "and I'll turn him into pie in a jiffy."

"Catch him, then!" said Daddy Rook, and tossed me across the nest from his strong beak. But he tossed just a little too strong; instead of falling into the nest, I landed on the other edge of it, and before Mammy Rook could seize me in her claws, I jumped!

Yes, I jumped from the very top of that tall elm, and fell down, down, down between the leaves and branches, until at last I came to the ground with a bump.

When I opened my eyes, I was sitting in my own field, with my own bread-and-bacon in my hand, and the rooks all busy at it among the peas.

I jumped up and swung my rattle, and sang my song at the top of my voice:

"Fly, rascals, fly,
  Or I'll make you into pie!"

Off they flew as quick as comets, and when they had gone I ate up my bread-and-bacon.

But now I knew why the birds came back again and again, in spite of me and my rattle. They came back because birds, like boys, are hungry. I must not let them eat the peas, for then the cattle would go short, but when I got home that day I went into my own bit of garden and made a place for the birds to come and eat.

I got my mother to give me a bit of bread to crumble there every day, and I begged my father to bring me a coconut to hang up for the tits. I even saved bits of the bacon-fat out of my sandwich, and threaded them on strings, and hung the strings of fat between two twigs.

So, if I had to keep the birds off with one hand, I fed them with the other; if I frightened them out of the field, I invited them into the garden. After that it seemed to me that the birds and I were not quite such enemies as we had been. Even though the rooks and starlings scolded me, the robins and the tits became my friends.

HE IS OUR GUEST,
LET'S NOT SEE HIS MISTAKES

by Angelo Patri

Hi, yi, i, Camilla. Look what I found."

The shrill voice of an excited little boy made Pinocchio jump inside his faded skin.

"Look. This piece will just fill the bag," and before Pinocchio could wink twice he felt himself seized and thrust head foremost into a bag of driftwood.

"What now?" he groaned. "I did but now call on Christopher Columbus to aid me, and here I am upside down in a bag of kindling. I am faint with hunger and cold as a frog. I hope all this leads to something to eat. My faint stomach bids me hope."

Camilla and Tony trotted along gaily, bumping the bag of wood along the stones as they carried it between them. Bumpity, bump, bump, bump——

"I'm glad we got that big piece, aren't you?" said Tony. "It just filled the bag. It will make a blaze to last all evening."

"Some good saint surely sent it our way," said Camilla, giving a skip and a hop that made Pinocchio close his eyes and groan.

"Let's run. I'm starving, aren't you?" said Tony.

"Starving. I hope there is a big platter of spaghetti."

"M-m-m. And lots of cheese."

"M-m-m, and meat left over from the sauce."

At the thought of the fine dinner waiting for them the two children set off at such a canter that poor Pinocchio gave himself up for dead.

"When things are at their worst, it is always well to hope for the best," said he, trying to hold on to his whirling head with his flapping hands. "All is well that ends well. Let us hope this ends quickly—and well."

At that moment the children let go of the bag and down it went on the kitchen floor with such a thump that Pinocchio hit his nose with his right toe and skinned an ear with his left foot. Then out he tumbled among the sticks on the kitchen floor.

"See this good piece," said Tony, holding up his prize.

"Let me look at that," said his mother, reaching for Pinocchio. "Ah, I thought so. It looked familiar. Children, this is a marionette. Wonderful. See, he is trying to speak. Poor little thing. He is nearly choked with dirt and dust. You must have given him a rough ride," and she held him under the faucet and scrubbed him well.

"There. See? He was once a gay marionette."

"Yes, my friends," said Pinocchio, recovering his breath and with it his speech, "it is I, Pinocchio. I swam the ocean to be with you. I came to your land seeking fame and fortune and freedom.

"To be sure, my dress is not so bright as when I left home, and I have lost my hat and my sword. But what of it? Without them I am still Pinocchio, the greatest marionette in the world. The bravest swimmer, the noblest hero among them all stands before you. I salute you," and placing his hand upon his heart he made such a sweeping bow that the end of his nose scraped the floor and he said, "Ouch!"

"Oh, isn't he lovely? We can keep him, can't we, Mother?"

"We'll see. We'll see. How did you leave your friends, Pinocchio? Your good father, Geppetto, is he well? Did he send any message to us in America?"

Pinocchio hung his head in shame. How was he to tell this good mother that he had run off without a thought of those he left behind? Could he tell the truth and say that Geppetto was at that very moment searching the house for him, behind the door, under the bed, in the wood box, everywhere, calling, calling, calling?

No. He was not brave enough. He lifted his head with what boldness he could gather and said, "He is well and sends you his compliments and begs you to take care of his darling Pinocchio, the pride of his old age who stands starving before you."

"Good, good. We will do our best. Come, come, children. Our guest is tired and hungry. We will serve him a good dinner and then put him to bed. In the morning we shall see what we shall see."

The children ran to set the table and the mother turned again to her cooking.

"Ah!" breathed Pinocchio, happily, "I smell spaghetti boiling. There is also a hint of garlic, and cheese. How my stomach warms at a hint of garlic. My mouth favors a bit of cheese. Who does not love a good piece of cheese? Thank you, my star. Thank you, most gracious Columbus. It was kind of you to lead me here."

Without waiting for an invitation the hungry marionette fell upon his dinner. I am sorry to have to tell you that he was not a pretty sight as he sat at the table gobbling spaghetti, the long ends of it flapping about his face and spattering him with tomato sauce from his eyes to his chin.

"He has not very good manners," whispered Camilla. "See how he glares at the cheese with his mouth full bursting. I think he is greedy and stupid."

"That may be the way of marionettes. You know they have wooden heads. He is our guest. Let us not notice his mistakes," whispered the good mother.

Pinocchio ate all that was set before him, and then, as usual, fell fast asleep.

"Poor little thing. He is tired out. Fix a basket in the corner behind the stove, children. We'll lay him on this soft pillow and let him rest."

So ended Pinocchio's first day in the land he had come so far to see.

THE MAGIC GLASS

by Richard Hughes

There is a little boy I know who always looks very carefully in waste-paper baskets, "because," he says, "you never know what valuable things you may find, that some silly grownup has thrown away."

One day he found what looked like the glass off the end of an electric torch. "That will make a most useful magnifying glass," he said, and put it in his pocket.

That night he woke up; and not being able to get to sleep again he thought he would look at a few things through his glass. The first thing he looked at was a wooden rabbit lying on the end of his bed; but the strange thing was, that, when he looked through the glass, instead of the toy what he saw was a real live rabbit, sitting up on its hind legs and wobbling its nose at him! Then he took the glass from his eye: and lo and behold, it was only a wooden one again.

"This *is* a funny glass," thought the little boy.

Then he looked through it at a china duck there was on the mantelpiece: and, sure enough, there was a real duck, which would have jumped down on to the floor if he hadn't taken the glass from his eye and turned it back into china again.

By this time the little boy was so excited with his glass that he got out of bed and crept down to the room where his father and mother were lying asleep. "For," he thought, "if it turns toys into real, I wonder if it turns real people into toys?" And he put it to his eye and looked at his father and mother. And so it was: they were immediately wooden Mr. and Mrs. Noah out of the Ark. To make sure, he took a pin, and keeping the glass firmly over his eye he tried to stick his mother. But it wouldn't go in, for she was now quite hard: it only scratched a little paint off. Then he took the glass away, and they were his mother and father again. But just to make sure he stuck the pin in again. This time it went right in, and his mother sat up with the most awful yell.

"You naughty boy!" she said. "What are you doing out of bed? And what did you stick a pin into me for?"

"I'm awfully sorry, Mother," he said, "but I thought you were Mrs. Noah! You were, a minute ago, you know!"

"Mrs. Noah?" said his mother. "Stuff and nonsense! You must have been dreaming! Go back to bed at once."

So he went back to bed, and soon was asleep. In the morning, when he went to school, he put the glass in his pocket.

Now, on the way to school there was a dog which the little boy simply hated. Every day when it saw him coming it used to poke its nose through the gate and growl and bark, and he never knew when it might jump out and bite him. So when he got near, and the dog began to bark, he looked at it through his glass, and all at once it turned into one of those funny china dogs you see sometimes on the mantelpiece in cottages. So the little boy picked it up, and threw it on the ground, and smashed it to bits. He wondered very much what would happen, now that it was smashed, when he took the glass away from his eye. What did happen was that it turned into a nice fur rug. So he hid it behind the fence. "Good!" he thought; "I'll pick it up on my way home and give it to Mother, to make up for jabbing her with that pin."

When he got to school he forgot about the glass till halfway through the lessons, when he took it out of his pocket and looked at the mistress through it. Immediately she turned into a golli-wog.

The little boy was not very surprised, but you may imagine all the other children were! They made such a noise in their astonishment that the head mistress came into the room, and hearing her coming he slipped the glass back into his pocket.

"Now then, children!" she said, "what's all this noise?" (It wasn't a very nice school.)

"The mistress has just turned into a golliwog!" shouted the children.

"Nonsense!" said the head mistress, who was a very cross old woman; but just then the little boy looked at the mistress again, and turned her again into a golliwog.

"Good gracious me! What's this?" said the head mistress, and went up to take hold of the golliwog: but when she got close, of course, the little boy could see her through the glass too, and immediately she turned into a Dismal Desmond.

At that, of course, the children were awfully pleased, and wanted to have them to play with: but the little boy said no, they mustn't go near or they'd all be turned into dolls, and all the other children said how clever the little boy was to have done it. So he kept on looking at them until lesson-time was over; and then he went home, not forgetting to pick up the fur rug to give to his mother.

That night, when he was in bed, his mother remembered his trousers wanted a button sewing on, so she came upstairs and fetched them, and then she found the glass in his pocket, and took it downstairs with her.

"What a funny glass," she said, and put it to her eye, and looked at herself in the looking glass.

That was a most awful thing to happen: for not only did she turn into wooden Mrs. Noah immediately, but the glass simply became a painted glass in Mrs. Noah's eye. And so she would have to stay, because the wooden Mrs. Noah, of course, couldn't move, and as long as she didn't move she was staring at herself in the looking glass, and, as long as she stared at herself, Mrs. Noah she would stay.

As a matter of fact she was Mrs. Noah all night, and still Mrs. Noah when the maids came down in the morning to sweep the room.

"There's that naughty boy left one of his toys in the drawing-room," they said, and went to move it: but as soon, of course, as they moved it away from the looking glass it turned back into a person.

"Good gracious!" they said. "It's the Mistress!"

And she rubbed her eyes, and said she felt very sleepy because she had sat up all night. Meanwhile the glass rolled away into a corner, and happened to stop just in the mouth of a mousehole, and no one thought of it any more.

That afternoon the little boy's mother had a whole lot of people coming to tea. They were very stiff and grand people, that the little boy didn't like at all; but all the same he thought he would creep downstairs and have a look at them. So he did, and watched them from where he couldn't be seen. But the little boy wasn't the only inquisitive one. Just at the same moment the little mouse came up his hole, and thought he would have a look at them too: and across the hole was the magic glass, so he looked through that.

Immediately all the people turned into the funniest lot of dolls you have ever seen: Dutch dolls and wax dolls and rag dolls, and even china ornaments. And that wasn't all. There were some pictures on the wall which the mouse could see, too: and while the real people turned into toys, the people in the pictures all stepped down into the room, in their funny old-fashioned dresses, and started to enjoy the tea. At that the little boy was so pleased that he laughed and clapped his hands, and the noise frightened the mouse, who ran away into the back of his hole, and so all was as before.

But presently the mouse came back and thought he would have another look. Just then the little boy's father came in from the office, and was standing in the drawing-room door when all the people turned into toys again, and the pictures started once more coming out of their frames. Meanwhile, the mouse was so excited he kept turning around to tell the other mice what he was seeing, and then looking back, and then turning around again, so that the boy's father was nearly astonished out of his wits, seeing them turn from people into toys and toys into people again as fast as the wink of an eye. But at last the mouse went away: and then they all stayed people, and when the tea-party was over went home as if nothing had happened.

But the little boy's father was really rather frightened. "There's something magic about this house," he said to himself; and as soon as he could he found another house, and they all went to live in that and left the old one empty.

But no one noticed the magic glass sticking in the mouth of the mouse-hole: and if someone else comes and lives in that house, and the mouse comes up his hole to have a look at them, I suppose the same thing would happen to them!

HENRY AND HIS DOG HENRY

by Walter R. Brooks

There was a boy named Henry Tanner, and his uncle sent him a cocker spaniel. He had a hard time thinking up a name for the dog. His mother said, "Well, you can name him anything you want to. What name do you like best?"

"I like my own name best," said Henry.

"But you can't call him 'Henry'," said his mother.

Henry thought a minute and then he said, "Well, I don't know why not. I think it would be fun if we both had the same name." So he called his dog Henry.

It worked at first, because when Henry (the boy) called, "Henry!" Henry (the dog) came. And when Mrs. Tanner called "Henry!" they both came.

But there began to be mix-ups. Sometimes when Mrs. Tanner said, "Henry, do this," or "Henry, do that," the wrong one did it. Like the time Mrs. Tanner was going out for the evening, and as she left the house she called out, "Henry, you go straight to bed at nine o'clock."

So Henry (the dog) went and curled up on his piece of carpet back of the stove at nine, but Henry (the boy) was still up when his mother got home, and he said, "Why, Mother, I thought you meant Henry. You *said* 'Henry'."

Mrs. Tanner was a fair-minded woman, and she said, "Well, I guess I ought to have said *which* Henry. But you go straight to bed now."

The trouble was that Mrs. Tanner was sort of absent-minded, and couldn't seem to remember to say which Henry she meant. And Henry (the dog) was a well-trained dog and always minded and did what he was told. So pretty soon all the minding in the house was done by Henry (the dog).

"Henry," Mrs. Tanner would say, "go get me my sewing basket from upstairs." And Henry (the dog) would go get it, while Henry (the boy) would pretend that he hadn't heard anything.

Now Henry (the dog) didn't mind doing all these things, but he realized that Henry (the boy) was getting pretty lazy.

"Pretty soon," he thought, "that boy won't do anything for himself. He'll be just a shiftless no-account, who'll expect everybody else to do his work for him, and nobody will like him and he won't have any friends. And I don't want to belong to a boy that nobody likes." So he began to think what he could do to help Henry.

Of course, Mrs. Tanner didn't like the way things were going either, and when Henry (the dog) did something that she had asked Henry (the boy) to do, she scolded him. And he would put his tail between his legs and crouch down, apologizing in dog language. But he went right on minding just the same, because he knew if he didn't Henry would be mad at him.

His chance came that night after supper when Mrs. Tanner called, "Henry, there's fifty cents on my dresser if you want to go to the movies."

Henry (the boy) didn't hear her, and Henry (the dog) dashed upstairs and took the fifty-cent piece in his mouth and ran down to the movie.

Well, Miss Schmitt, who was cashier at the movie theater, was pretty surprised when a dog stood up on his hind legs and dropped fifty cents on the little shelf. She jumped and her eyes popped. She knew that her job was to sell all the tickets she could so she grabbed the fifty cents. Then she hesitated and said, "Well, I guess you're under fifteen, aren't you?" And she shoved back a quarter and gave him a ticket.

So Henry went in and gave up the ticket and bought a bag of popcorn. The ticket taker and the popcorn man were so surprised that I guess they didn't realize that Henry was a dog until he had gone in and taken a seat.

The show had started so it was dark and nobody noticed much when the dog sat down. He just sat there and watched the show, and one or two people said, "For Pete's sake, look at that dog!" But that was all. And when the show was over he trotted back home.

But Henry was mad at him. He never licked the dog, but he threatened him, and he said, "You've done me out of a good show. You took that money even though you knew it was meant for me. Now you leave things like that alone, do you understand?"

"Well, I can't do that again," Henry (the dog) said to himself.

"I thought if I did something like that he'd be afraid to have me answer, and when Mrs. Tanner called, 'Henry!' he'd run to answer himself."

One day Henry's uncle came to visit, and, of course, he wanted to see the dog he'd given him.

"What did you name him?" he asked, and Henry said, "Henry."

Well, the uncle thought that was pretty funny and he said, "Good grief, why didn't you give him a regular dog's name? Like—lemme see—well, say 'Rover'?"

"Golly, I wish he had!" Henry (the dog) thought, and he was so pleased at the idea that he wagged his tail hard and went over and licked the uncle's hand.

"There—see?" said the uncle. "He likes a regular dog name. Hey, Rover?"

Henry (the dog) didn't like "Rover," he thought it was terrible. But he thought, "Boy, this is my chance!" and when the uncle said "Rover" the second time he jumped up and down and barked his pleased bark.

"See?" said the uncle. "He likes it."

"Well, I don't," said Henry (the boy). "Here, Henry. Come here, pup."

But the dog paid no attention.

"Henry!" said the boy. "Come here!"

But the dog didn't even look around.

"You haven't trained him very well," said the uncle. "Doesn't even know his own name."

"He does too!" said Henry, and he kept on trying, and even slapped the dog, which was something he had never done before. But Henry (the dog) just lay down and went to sleep. But when the uncle said something about Rover, he jumped up and went to him and put his head on his knee.

By and by the uncle went back to Buffalo, where he lived. Then Henry's (the boy's) troubles began. Henry (the dog) wouldn't do anything that Henry (the boy) told him to. He acted as if he'd never heard the name Henry before. And when Henry (the boy) yelled at him, he just looked bewildered.

Of course this meant that when Mrs. Tanner said, "Henry, do this," or "Henry, do that," Henry (the boy) waited a minute. Then when Henry (the dog) just sat there and didn't even twitch a whisker, Henry (the boy) got up and did what his mother asked him to.

Pretty soon Henry (the boy) was doing quite a lot of minding—even some that belonged to Henry (the dog). Mrs. Tanner would say, "Henry, take that bone outdoors," and when the dog didn't do anything about it, the boy would pick it up and carry it out. He even began doing things before he was told to.

Well, Henry (the dog) was pretty pleased. He had a friend, Jock, a Scotty with whom he often went rabbit hunting. There weren't any rabbits around that neighborhood, but they had fun hunting them just the same. He said to Jock, "That Henry, he's going to turn out all right. He's the kind of boy now that a dog could be proud to belong to."

"Yeah?" said Jock. "The way I heard it yesterday, he says you don't mind any more and he's going to give you away."

"I know," said Henry sadly. "But what can I do? If I start answering to the name of Henry again, we'll be right back where we were."

"If he wasn't so dumb," Jock said, "he'd try calling you other names."

"I know," Henry said again. "But we can't expect a boy to be as smart as we are. Boys just aren't very bright. They talk a lot, but they don't think much. They aren't like dogs."

I guess things might have ended pretty badly for Henry (the dog) if he had been right about boys. But Henry (the boy) really had been thinking. He was pretty fond of his dog, and it made him unhappy that they couldn't seem to get along. And one afternoon he was sitting on the back steps. Henry (the dog) was lying in the grass.

The boy looked at the dog and thought, "I wish I knew why he acts so funny and won't mind any more. We used to have a lot of fun. My goodness, he hasn't wagged his tail since Uncle George was here. That was when Uncle George called him Rover. Rover!" the boy said disgustedly.

He was so disgusted that he said it out loud. To his amazement, the dog jumped up and began to bark and wag his tail.

Henry stared at him and said, "Well, hey! What goes on here?" Then he frowned thoughtfully and picked up a stick and threw it. "Go get it, Henry!" he said. And the dog lay down and pretended to go to sleep.

"Go get it, Rover!" said Henry. And the dog ran and got the stick, and then he pranced around and barked shrill little excited barks until Henry said, "All right, all right. Don't have hysterics. It's a silly name, if you ask me, but you're the one who has to answer to it. Come on, Rover. Let's take a walk."

So that was the end of the trouble, and Henry and Rover had good times together again. Of course, being so absent-minded, Mrs. Tanner couldn't remember half the time that Henry (the dog) was now Rover, and she was a little surprised sometimes to see her son doing something that she thought she had told the dog to do.

Once, when a Mrs. Haskell came in to call, and Henry and Rover were sitting on the davenport, she said, "Henry, get right down off those cushions," and the boy got down on the floor, but the dog stayed where he was.

Mrs. Haskell said, "Gracious! Gracious!" But Mrs. Tanner just said, "Oh dear, I don't know how it is I always get those two mixed up." Mrs. Haskell gave her a funny look, and didn't stay very long, and she never came back again. But Mrs. Tanner didn't care, for she wasn't too absent-minded to realize that Henry was minding a lot better than he used to.

Rover (formerly Henry) was happy, too. Even when Jock, and other dogs of his acquaintance, laughed at his new name and jeered at him on the street, and said, "Oh, see Rover! Oh, see the pretty doggie-woggie!" Even then he didn't care. He didn't even bother to bark at them. And as it isn't fun to tease anybody who doesn't notice it, pretty soon they stopped.

SPACE SHIP TO THE MOON

by E. C. Reichert

Who would like to go to the moon on a space ship?" asked Miss Rose, the teacher, as her class turned a corner in the museum hall. Twenty eager hands waved in the air in answer.

"Well, that is just what we are going to do, or *nearly* going to do," continued Miss Rose. "In the next room we are to see a motion picture that will show us how space ships operate, and the guide will tell us all about a trip to the moon."

Sally and Billy could hardly wait to see the picture. Sally nudged Billy and whispered, "I wonder if it will be like the ones we have seen at home on television?"

"I don't know but I'll bet it will be fun," answered Billy.

Excitedly, the class walked into the large theater with comfortable seats and white screen at the front. The guide went forward and said, "We are going to turn off the lights, and you will see a movie showing how a space ship leaves the earth and goes to the moon and back."

The room was darkened, and the children sat forward on their seats with their eyes fixed on the screen. The guide began, "In this first scene you can see our space ship. You will notice that it does not have wings like an airplane. Can anyone tell me why?"

One of the boys shouted, "Because it is a rocket. It doesn't need wings. It's steered by a gyroscope."

"Right!" said the guide. "That boy knows about space ships. Now, then, notice the holes in the tail. What are they for?"

"They're for the jet blasts to shoot out," said Billy. "The ship gets its power from an atomic engine. I read about it."

"Fine!" said the guide, and he continued, "This diagram shows the ship has a double hull, much like a thermos bottle. That shields the inside from hot and very cold temperatures it must go through. Now we shall see the space ship take off and *if you will use your imagination, I think you can all go along.*"

Sally and Billy saw the ship on the launching platform. Suddenly they heard a loud WHOOSH! Straight out into space the ship sailed, leaving trails of smoke.

Sally and Billy could all but feel the motion of the ship. They heard a man say, "You may unfasten your safety belts. From now on you won't feel any more jars or bolts. We'll ride as easily as a boat does on a calm sea." They unfastened their belts and sat back to enjoy the smooth ride.

"I don't think I know your name," Sally said. "Are you the pilot?"

The man smiled and answered, "I'm one of the pilots, as you call them, but we call ourselves 'astronauts.' I'm Dan."

Billy said, "We're happy to know you, Dan."

"I hope you don't mind questions," Sally continued. "I have about a million to ask you."

"I'll be glad to answer questions," replied Dan, "but right now I think you should look out of the window. You can see the earth dropping away from us, and in just a minute something very exciting will happen."

Sally and Billy looked through the heavy plate-glass window and saw the earth dropping away so quickly that they no longer could see the space port from which they had started. Only lakes and mountains stood out on the rounded surface of the earth.

"What is the very exciting thing, Dan?" asked Sally.

"Well," said Dan, "this is a stage-rocket ship. That means that we are riding in the nose of the ship in one rocket, and there is a bigger and separate rocket for a tail. After five minutes of flight we release the big rocket at our tail, and it parachutes back to earth. Walk up to the front of the ship and you can watch my partner, Bob, release it."

Sally and Billy ran to the front of the ship. Bob, the other astronaut, looked up and said, "Hi, there! Want to see our skyfish lose its tail?"

He pulled back on a big lever at his feet. "Look out the window," he said. Sally and Billy saw the big tail rocket fall away from the ship and a huge parachute billow out behind it.

Bob leaned back and said, "We had to go 25,000 miles per hour for the first five minutes of our flight but now we can coast along. It will take five days to get to the moon. The first part of our trip is very fast, but from now on everything is easy."

Sally and Billy walked back to Dan, who showed them their bunks.

"When you aren't eating or sleeping," Dan said, "you might want to learn more about the moon and the stars. These books above your bunk will tell you a lot of interesting things about them."

The second day passed like the first.

On the third day, after lunch, Dan announced that there was a new adventure ahead. "In just one hour we will arrive at the orbital space station."

"Oh, I've read about that!" said Billy. "It's just like a little moon circling the earth."

"Yes," agreed Dan, "but with one big difference—men made the space station only a few years ago. It was built soon after the first successful space ship flights. It is a very useful place. We can refuel there and talk to the men who send weather reports back home."

Through the window the children watched a shiny object ahead grow larger. As they neared the space station, it looked just like a giant steel umbrella hanging in space.

"Why doesn't it fall back to earth?" asked Sally.

"It isn't that heavy," Dan answered, "and we are already a long way out in space. You know the earth holds everything in its orbit. That's why this is called an orbital station. It will always stay the same distance from the earth and will circle the earth just like a moon."

The ship slowly circled and edged up to the space station. When it was firmly anchored, Bob said, "We will need to wear space suits here. I'll get yours." He went to a closet and took out two suits that looked as if they were made of armor except that they had flexible joints at the elbows and knees and headpieces of plate glass.

"Do we have to wear these all the time we are here?" asked Sally.

"No," replied Bob. "Only when we are not in our ship or under the dome of the space station."

"The air here is too thin to breathe," explained Dan, "and your suits have oxygen tanks attached."

"How can we talk?" asked Billy.

"There's a microphone in the headpiece, and that little rod on top is an aerial," replied Dan.

"What if we fall off the space station?" stammered Sally.

"We won't," Dan hastened to say. "And if we did, we can go

in any direction by using the reaction pistols on the sides of the suits. If you pull the trigger on the pistol to your right, you will turn to the left; the other pistol will send you in the opposite direction."

Sally and Billy put on their suits and helped each other tighten the heavy headpieces. The hatch of the space ship was opened, and they climbed out. While the ship was being refueled, they walked toward the dome in the middle of the station. It was enclosed by glass and topped by high radio and radar towers.

Once inside they removed their headpieces and were introduced to the men who manned the station. One was the radio operator, and he asked the children if they had any message they wished to send home. "Send our mother a message and tell her we are having a heavenly time!" they said.

"O.K.," said the radio operator.

"Now, back to the ship," Dan ordered. "It's time we took off again for the moon."

Back in the ship Sally and Billy got out of their space suits and watched the ship drift away from the space station. They saw the earth getting smaller and smaller, far behind the station, and the moon getting larger and nearer.

On the fourth day Dan said, "Tomorrow is the big day—the day we land on the moon."

The next morning the space ship, instead of going forward and landing like an airplane, backed into the moon with its rocket power as brakes. Soon it was on the ground.

"Here we are!" Dan called. "All out for the moon—but first climb into your space suits."

As soon as they were out of their ship, the walkie-talkie aerials on their suits were sparking questions back and forth.

"What big mountains there are up here!" said Billy.

"Isn't it funny there isn't anything growing?" asked Sally. "Just rock dust as far as you can see."

"There's more than rocks to see," answered Dan. "Look this way and you will see the Lunar Space Station." Sure enough, under a huge glass dome that seemed to stretch for blocks, they saw men moving about. The radio and radar towers loomed high above. In the distance they could see men working in glass-enclosed trucks.

"Now walk slowly and follow me," said Dan. And then came the biggest surprise of all. As Billy stepped forward, to his amazement he jumped nearly ten feet up in the air.

"What happened?" he gasped.

Both Dan and Bob laughed. "You haven't grown any new leg muscles," said Bob. "Everyone can jump high here. The pull of gravity is so much less than on earth. Be careful, though, until you get used to it, or you will fall."

Inside the Lunar Space Station Dan told them to take off their space suits. Sally and Billy met the men who worked in the space port and asked them questions. Then they saw a tremendous rocket ship backing under the glass dome by using its small rockets under the nose of the ship.

"What's that?" asked Billy.

"That is one of the bigger ships that goes on to other planets," Bob explained. "The moon is used mostly as a stopping-off place for flights into farther space. Mining is also an important industry here. Strange and valuable minerals are being discovered all the time. Some are sent back to earth because they are a cheap source of atomic fuel for rocket ships."

"Why is everything under glass or underground here?" asked Billy.

"Because the temperature on the moon varies from much colder at night than it ever gets at the North Pole, to much hotter in the daytime than it gets on the hottest part of the earth," Dan answered.

Sally and Billy stayed two days on the moon and explored every place they could. One day they went into a uranium mine. Too soon the time came for their return trip to the earth. Once again the space ship flew through the sky toward the orbital station, and on the fifth day they arrived at the space port on earth.

Suddenly there was a flash of light, and Sally and Billy jumped.

"We are back on earth," they heard a voice say. They rubbed their eyes and blinked. It was the museum guide talking, and the theater lights had been turned on. Sally gasped, and Billy said, "Whew! That was an exciting trip."

That night, as Sally was getting ready for bed, she looked out of the window and said to Billy, "Look at the beautiful moon! Just think what fun we had at the museum today up there looking down at the earth."

"Yes," Billy answered. "But I'm glad we live where there are trees and grass even if we can't jump as high as we could on the moon."

"Me too!" agreed Sally.

THINKING, THINKING, THINKING
by Moreten Abbott

Six Is Such a Nice Number

I
have six books
and every one
is nice.

I have six
nice aunts
and four
nice uncles.

I wish I had two more uncles.
Then
I'd have six
of everything.

Hottest Day of the Summer So Far

"It's so hot," Mr. Mott said,
"you could fry an egg
on the sidewalk."

"It's so hot, my!" Mrs. Bly said,
"you could fry
an egg
on the sidewalk."

"It's so hot, whew!" Mr. Hugh said,
"you
could fry an egg
on the sidewalk."

But
I
know
that's
just
TALK.

It didn't cook at all.

Things That Turn Round

Some things turn round and make
a noise—
a top, egg-beater, fan.

Other things turn round
and make
no noise.
The world is one.
I
am another.

I can turn round
either way—

    with a noise—
    "Bang! Bang! Bang! Bang! Boom!"
    or without—
    "Sh-h! Sh-h! Sh-h! Sh-h! Shoom!"

Fairy Tales

As long as there have been people there have been wishes. For people are always wishing things were different. They wish the sun were shining when the rain is pouring down, or they wish it were summer in the wintertime. Sometimes they wish for a fine doll or a little pet dog—and these wishes often come true.

Sometimes they wish that they themselves were different. A timid boy or girl wishes to be brave, or a weak one wishes he were great and powerful. Sometimes people even wish trouble for those they do not like. Sometimes people wish for impossible things—like a pumpkin that can turn into a coach, or a mirror that can talk, or a lamp that can provide all sorts of food and drink.

Because people could not make their wishes come true, they made up strange magical folk who could make things happen as they like. They made believe that there were dwarfs and gnomes and fairies who could make anything become something else and who could make any wish come true.

The stories about such magical beings are called fairy stories and, even though they are not really true, I think you will agree that they are fun to hear or to read.

THE THREE BEARS

Once upon a time there were three bears—a great big bear, a middle-sized bear, and a little tiny bear. They all lived together in a house of their own right in the middle of a wood.

One day the three bears sat down to breakfast, but their porridge was so very hot that they couldn't eat it. So they decided to go out for a walk and leave the porridge on the kitchen table to cool off.

While they were away a little girl called Goldilocks came to the house in the wood. She had been picking flowers since early in the morning and was very, very tired. When she saw the little house she said to herself, "Surely the people who live here will let me rest for a while."

So she knocked on the door. But nobody came, for the bears were out walking in the wood. She knocked again, and still nobody came, so Goldilocks opened the door and walked right in.

The first things she saw were three bowls of porridge on the kitchen table. Goldilocks was very hungry, so she started to eat the great big bowl of porridge.

"This is too hot!" she said to herself, and she quickly put down the spoon.

Then she took a taste from the middle-sized bowl.

"This is too cold!" she said to herself, and she quickly put down the spoon.

Then she took a taste from the little tiny bowl.

"This is just right!" she said to herself, and she ate it all up.

Then Goldilocks went into the living room to rest for a while, and there she saw three chairs standing near the fireplace.

First she sat down in the great big chair.

"This is too high!" she said to herself, and she quickly got up again.

Then she sat down on the middle-sized chair.

"This is too wide!" she said to herself, and she quickly got up again.

Then she sat down in the little tiny chair.

"This is just right!" she said to herself, and she sat down so hard that the little tiny chair broke into a hundred pieces.

Then Goldilocks went upstairs and there she saw three beds standing in a row. First she lay down on the great big bed.

"This is too hard!" she said to herself, and she quickly got up again.

Then she lay down on the middle-sized bed.

"This is too soft!" she said to herself, and she quickly got up again.

Then she lay down on the little tiny bed.

"This is just right!" she said to herself, and she fell fast asleep.

After a while the three bears came home from their walk in the wood. They were very hungry now and started to eat their porridge right away. The great big bear took one taste from his bowl and growled, "SOMEONE HAS BEEN EATING MY PORRIDGE!"

The middle-sized bear took one taste from her bowl and said, "SOMEONE HAS BEEN EATING my PORRIDGE!"

The little tiny bear squeaked, "Someone *has been eating* my porridge *and has eaten it all up!*"

Then the three bears went into the living room.

"SOMEONE HAS BEEN SITTING IN MY CHAIR!" growled the great big bear.

"SOMEONE HAS BEEN SITTING IN my CHAIR!" said the middle-sized bear.

"Someone *has been sitting in my chair,*" squeaked the little tiny bear, "*and has broken it all to pieces!*"

Then the three bears went upstairs.

"SOMEONE HAS BEEN SLEEPING IN MY BED!" growled the great big bear.

"SOMEONE HAS BEEN SLEEPING IN MY BED!" said the middle-sized bear.

"Someone *has* been *sleeping* in my *bed*," squeaked the little tiny bear, "*and here she is!*"

His voice woke Goldilocks up and, when she saw the three bears, she was so frightened that she jumped out of bed and bounded down the stairs and ran home to her mother as fast as her legs would carry her. And she never went to the house of the three bears again.

THE UGLY DUCKLING

After Hans Christian Andersen

Once on a lovely spring day, in a farmyard in a beautiful countryside, a Mother Duck sat on her eggs waiting for her ducklings to hatch.

The Mother Duck was getting somewhat tired, because sitting is such a dull business.

But at last the eggshells began to crack, one after the other. "Peep, peep!" cried the new ducklings as they poked out their heads.

"Quack, quack!" said the mother, and quick as quick can be they scurried out looking all around them under the green leaves.

"How big the world is!" said the young ones. They certainly had a great deal more room now than when they were in their shells.

"You think this is the whole world?" their mother asked. "Why, the world goes on and on, far across the other side of the garden, all the way to the pastor's field, farther than I've ever been."

She counted the ducklings and looked in the nest and noticed that one of the eggs, a very large one, hadn't hatched yet. Just then an old Duck, a friend of the Mother Duck, came along and said, "Don't bother with that. It's just an old turkey egg. I was cheated that way once. Baby turkeys are very ugly and they don't know how to swim."

But the Mother Duck wasn't sure that it *was* a turkey's egg. It *might* be one of her own. "I think I'll sit on it a little longer," she said. "I've been at it so long, a few more days won't matter."

At last the big egg broke. "Peep, peep!" said the youngster

scrambling out. The Mother Duck looked at him in astonishment. He was so big and ugly!

"What a large duckling that one is!" she said. "None of the others looks like that! Can he really be a turkey chick? I'll take them to the water and we'll soon find out."

But when she took all the ducklings down to the water, the large, ugly-looking one could swim better than any of the others.

"It must be mine, after all," she thought. "It's really quite pretty if you look at it the right way. See how well he uses his legs and how straight he holds himself. He must be my very own child." And so she took her brood to the farmyard, to show them to the ducks and the other animals living there. But the other ducks just looked at them and said unkind things about the new-

comers. They noticed especially the ugly duckling. "See what a dreadful-looking creature that ugly duckling is! We won't stand for him!" And one duck flew up and bit the poor duckling on the neck.

"Let him alone," said the mother. "He's not harming anyone."

"I know," said the spiteful duck who had bitten him, "but he is so big and so ugly that he should be bitten."

"He isn't so handsome, but he's as good as can be," said the Mother Duck. "And he swims as well as, if not better than, the others. Besides he'll look handsomer when he grows up. He won't seem so big and awkward then. He was in the egg too long, and that's why his figure isn't all it should be."

The Mother Duck tried to make her family feel at home. But the poor duckling who had come out of his shell last and looked so ugly, was bitten and pushed and made fun of, both by the ducks and the chickens. Even his own brothers and sisters made fun of him.

"You are too big!" they said. "And your neck is funny!"

"You are not even a nice color the way we are," they told him. "You are dark and gray while we are bright and yellow."

The poor duckling thought that they would become accustomed to his looks. But they never did. He hoped that some would say, "My, what a lovely disposition you have!" Or, "My, how well you swim!" But they never did.

All they ever said when the poor duckling passed by was, "What an ugly creature! Where do you suppose he came from?"

Each day he grew more unhappy. Soon he stopped trying to show his lovely disposition. And he stopped trying to swim well. All he wanted now was to get away from the farmyard. He wanted to go where there were no animals at all and where no one could call him ugly.

One day he decided to run away. So, half running and half flying, he got over the fence. The little birds in the bushes flew up, frightened. "That's because I'm so ugly," thought the duckling sadly and closed his eyes. But he kept on running till he reached the great marsh where the wild ducks lived. There he lay the whole night long, tired and sorrowful.

In the morning the wild ducks flew up to have a look at their new companion. "What sort of fellow are you?" they asked, as they gathered around him. The duckling turned in all directions, bowing to everybody as nicely as he could.

"You are remarkably ugly!" said the wild ducks, "but you can stay around if you don't come too close."

Poor duckling! He wanted only to be allowed to lie among the reeds and drink a little water from the marsh.

One day along came two wild geese. They were very rude to

him. One of them said, "You're so ugly that I rather like you."
But suddenly two shots rang out—bang! bang! The two ganders
fell dead in the marsh. The water was reddened with their blood.
Bang! bang! sounded again, and a whole flock of wild geese rose
into the air. A great hunt was going on. The poor duckling was
frightened and tried to hide under some bushes. He heard the
dogs coming and tried to hide his head under his wing, when
suddenly a fearfully big dog came up to him. His tongue was
hanging far out of his mouth, and his eyes glared wildly. He
opened his jaws wide, flashed his sharp teeth, and then—splash!
off he went without touching the duckling.

"Thank heaven!" he sighed. "I'm so ugly that even the dog
won't bother to bite me."

So he lay perfectly still, while the shots rattled through the
marsh as gun after gun went off. Late in the day it grew quiet
again.

Late that night he came to a miserable little hut. The door had
come off one of its hinges and hung so crooked that the duckling
could slip into the room through the crack.

In this hut lived an old woman with her cat and her hen. They
were so cruel and harsh to him that he soon left them and ran
off to a pond. He swam in the water and dived into it, but he was
still slighted by the other creatures because he was so ugly.

Autumn came on. The leaves in the forest turned yellow and
brown. The air seemed very cold. The clouds hung low, heavy
with hail and snow. The poor duckling was indeed having a bad
time of it!

One evening, when the sun was setting in all its splendor, a
great flock of handsome birds appeared out of the rushes. The
duckling had never seen anything quite so beautiful as these
birds. They were dazzlingly white, with long graceful necks. They
were swans. They uttered a peculiar cry as they spread their great
wings to fly away, away from this cold land to warmer countries
and to open waters. They went up so high, so very high, that a
strange feeling came over the ugly duckling as he watched them.
He turned around and around in the water like a wheel, craning

his neck to follow their flight, and he made such a strange shrill cry that he frightened even himself.

When he could no longer see them, he dived down to the bottom of the lake and then he came up again; he was beside himself with excitement. He did not know what the birds were called nor where they were flying. Yet he loved them more than he had ever loved anything. He did not envy them in the least. He never thought of wanting to be as beautiful as they. He would have been thankful if only the ducks had put up with him—the poor ugly creature!

And the winter grew cold, and colder. The duckling had to swim around and around in the water to keep it from freezing altogether. But every night the spot where he swam grew smaller and smaller. At last, too tired to move, he sat still and was soon caught fast in the ice.

Early next morning a farmer came by, and seeing what had happened, he broke the ice with his wooden shoe and carried the duckling home with him. There the duckling revived.

The farmer's children wanted to play with him; but the duckling feared they meant to hurt him. In his fright he fluttered into the milk-pail, splashing milk all over the room. The farmer's wife and the children shrieked and clapped their hands. The frightened bird flew into the tub of butter, and then in and out of the flour-barrel. What a sight he was! The children laughed and shouted and tumbled over each other trying to catch him. Luckily, the door was open, and the duckling escaped through it into the bushes. There he lay down in the newly fallen snow, exhausted.

But it would be too sad to tell of all the trouble and sorrow the poor duckling had to suffer during that cruel winter. When the sun began to shine warmly again, the duckling was still alive in the marsh among the weeds. The larks were singing and it was spring, beautiful spring.

Then, one morning as the duckling was flapping his wings, he suddenly found himself up in the air—flying!! Before he quite knew what was happening, he was in a great garden where apple trees were in bloom. Oh, he was happy to be here! He knew now that the Mother Duck was right, that it was a very big world and very beautiful.

Then, from a nearby thicket came three glorious white swans. They ruffled their feathers and swam lightly over the water. The duckling recognized the splendid birds, and a strange feeling of sadness came over him. Although he was very much afraid, he flew out into the water and swam toward the beautiful swans. He tried to hide his head under his wings, but as he bent down, what was this he saw mirrored in the clear water? He saw his own image, but it was not the image of a clumsy, dirty gray bird, ugly and repulsive to look at—he himself was a swan!

So you see, being born in a duck's nest does not matter, as long as you are hatched from a swan's egg!

He rustled his wings and lifted his graceful neck, and from the depths of his joyful heart cried, "I never dreamt there could be such happiness when I was the ugly duckling."

CINDERELLA

There was once a man who married for his second wife a woman who was both vain and selfish. This woman had two daughters who were as vain and selfish as she was. The man had a daughter of his own, however, who was sweet and kind and not vain at all.

Now the stepmother and the two stepsisters could not bear the goodness of this daughter, for it made their own ill-temper seem even more ugly. So they dressed the poor girl in rags and made her work hard from morning till night.

They made her get up early in the morning to start a fire on the hearth. They made her fetch water and wood. And then she had to cook and scour and clean the house. At night, when she was tired and wanted to go to sleep in her own little bed, the wicked stepsisters made her lie in the ashes on the hearth. And so she was called Cinderella, for she was always covered with cinders and ashes.

It is no wonder she was always full of cinders and it is no wonder she was very, very unhappy. Every day when the stepsisters got up they would put on pretty dresses and dainty shoes, but Cinderella had nothing but an old gray dress and heavy wooden shoes.

One day the heralds announced that the King would give a ball in honor of his son, the Prince. All the beautiful maidens in the country were invited.

The two stepsisters were greatly excited when they heard this news. They spent hours walking in the garden or sitting by the fire, talking of the ball and of the beautiful gowns they would wear. The stepmother was very much excited, too, and she ordered a dressmaker to come and make the finest of gowns for her two beautiful daughters.

On the night of the ball the two sisters were even more cross and disagreeable than usual.

"Hurry, Cinderella," said one. "Buckle my shoe."

"Come here," said the other. "Brush my hair."

"Fasten my dress!" ordered the first one.

"Why are you such a slowpoke?" complained the second.

Presently Cinderella started to cry, for she wanted to go to the ball, too.

"May I please be allowed to go?" she asked her stepmother.

"You, Cinderella?" the stepmother replied. "You have only that ugly old dress to wear and those heavy shoes."

"Who would dance with you?" the sisters laughed. "You are all dirty and covered with cinders."

So everyone went to the ball except Cinderella, who was left all alone. She sat by the fire with her face buried in her hands and she cried as if her heart would break.

Suddenly she heard a soft voice near by. It said, "What is the matter, Cinderella?"

The girl looked up and saw a lovely fairy standing before her. There was a star on her forehead and a magic wand in her hand.

"I wish—I wish——" Cinderella sobbed, but she was crying so hard she couldn't finish her wish.

"You wish that you could go to the ball," the fairy said. "Is that right?"

"Oh yes, I do!" Cinderella sighed. "But how did you know and who are you?"

"I am your fairy godmother," was the reply. "Ask me anything you want and your wish shall be granted."

Without waiting a moment Cinderella replied, "Then that is my wish. I want more than anything else to go to the ball!"

"You shall have your wish," said the fairy godmother. "You may go."

"But look at me!" Cinderella cried, almost in tears. "How can I go like this? People will laugh at me and no one will dance with me!"

"Be patient," the fairy godmother told her, "and I will help you. The first thing you must do is to find me a pumpkin."

Without asking any more questions, Cinderella went out into the garden and brought her fairy godmother the largest pumpkin she could find.

"Now find me six white mice."

Cinderella ran down into the cellar and caught six white mice, which she brought up to her fairy godmother.

"Now find me a large gray rat."

Cinderella ran up to the attic and there, in the rattrap, she found a large gray rat which she brought down to her fairy godmother.

"Now bring me the two lizards you will find behind the watering pot."

Cinderella went into the garden and presently came back with a lizard in each hand.

"Now take off your dress and your shoes and leave them with me while you go and wash."

Cinderella did as she was told, and when she came back, with her face all washed and shining and her hair carefully brushed, the fairy godmother said: "You look beautiful already, Cinderella, but just wait until you have your gown on!"

Then she touched the dress and the shoes with the tip of her wand and at once they were transformed. The old gray dress became a beautiful gown made of gold-colored cloth and studded with lovely jewels. The heavy wooden shoes became dainty crystal slippers. Cinderella could hardly wait to put on these beautiful clothes, and when she had done so even the fairy godmother had to exclaim at her loveliness.

"Now come with me," her godmother said, and they went outdoors together.

The fairy godmother put the pumpkin, the six white mice, the rat, and the two lizards on the ground. Then she touched each of them with her wand. The pumpkin at once became a golden coach, the six white mice became beautiful milk-white horses, the rat became a coachman, and the lizards were transformed into handsome footmen.

"Get into the coach, Cinderella," her fairy godmother said, "and go to the ball. Laugh and dance and have a lovely time. But remember this—you must be home at twelve o'clock. For on the stroke of midnight the coach will turn into a pumpkin, the horses will become mice again, your coachman a rat, and your footmen lizards. And you, Cinderella, will be dressed in rags as before."

"Very well, my dear fairy godmother," Cinderella replied. "I shall be back long before midnight. And oh, thank you so much for all you have done for me!"

When Cinderella arrived at the ball everybody noticed her because she was so beautiful in her golden dress. But no one, not even her stepmother and stepsisters, knew she was Cinderella.

They thought she was a foreign princess and were charmed by her loveliness, and all you could hear was "Oh!" and "Ah!"

As soon as the Prince saw Cinderella, he came up to her and, taking her by the hand, led her to the dance. He would not dance with anyone else and he would not let go of Cinderella's hand. When anyone else asked her to dance, he said: "She is my partner."

Cinderella was very happy. She had never been more happy in her life. It was so lovely to be at that wonderful ball and to dance with the charming Prince that she did not notice how late it was getting. As the Prince was speaking to her, the clock suddenly started to strike.

Cinderella looked up and saw that it was midnight. Without even saying good night to the Prince, she dashed out of the ballroom, anxious to be out of sight before the clock would finish striking twelve and before her beautiful gown would turn into rags again.

Cinderella got home safely, but in her hurry she lost one of her glass slippers on the stairway leaving the ballroom. The Prince picked it up and noticed that it was very small and graceful. Only one girl can have a foot as small as this, he thought. So he went to his father, the King, and said: "My bride shall be no other than she whose foot this slipper fits."

A proclamation was issued throughout the land that the Prince was coming to find the beautiful maiden whom he loved so dearly. Every girl in the kingdom would try on the shoe and the one whom it fitted would become his bride.

At last the Prince came to the house of Cinderella's father. The two stepsisters were waiting to try on the glass slipper. They were very excited and very proud for both of them had small feet. But neither of them could get the slipper on, for it was smaller still.

"Have you no other daughter?" the Prince asked their mother.

"Only a little stepdaughter," the mother replied. "But she cannot be your bride."

"Oh no!" the sisters laughed. "She is much too dirty."

But the Prince insisted that every girl in the country must try on the slipper, so Cinderella was called. First she washed her face and hands and then she curtsied to the Prince. Then she sat down on a stool, took off her heavy wooden shoe, and put on the little glass slipper. It fitted her perfectly! Then, for the first time, the Prince looked in her face.

"This is the beautiful maiden with whom I danced!" he exclaimed. "This is my rightful bride!"

The Prince took Cinderella upon his horse and rode away with her to make her his bride and the Queen of the country.

SNOW WHITE

Once upon a time a Queen sat by the window of her castle, sewing. As she looked out at the falling snow she suddenly pricked her finger, and three drops of blood fell on the snow that was on the window sill. The window frame was black, the snow was pure white, and the drops of blood were bright red.

The three colors looked so pretty together that the Queen said to herself, "I wish I had a little daughter as white as this snow, as red as this blood, and as black as this ebony window frame."

Soon afterward a little girl was born to her. And she had skin as white as snow, cheeks as red as blood, and hair as black as ebony. The Queen, remembering her wish, called the baby "Snow White."

When Snow White was still a very little girl her mother died, and a few years later her father, the King, married again.

This second Queen was very beautiful. But she was so vain that she could not bear anyone to be more lovely than she was. Every morning she looked into her magic mirror and said:

"Mirror, mirror on the wall,
  Who is the fairest one of all?"

The mirror always replied:

"Thou art fairest, lady Queen,
  None more lovely can be seen."

Then the Queen was happy, for she knew the magic mirror always spoke the truth.

As little Snow White grew up, however, she grew prettier and prettier, and by the time she was seven years old she was more beautiful than the Queen herself. One day when the Queen looked into her mirror and asked:

"Mirror, mirror on the wall,
  Who is the fairest one of all?"

the mirror replied:

"Thou wert loveliest once, I vow,
  But Snow White's growing fairer now."

The Queen became so angry that she turned green with jealousy. She was so jealous of Snow White that she told a huntsman to take the little girl into the forest and leave her where the wild beasts would destroy her. The huntsman did as the Queen bid him, but he was very very sad, for he hated to be so cruel.

Snow White, alone in the forest, was frightened by all the big trees. She thought that the wild animals would try to devour her, so she started to run. But instead the animals were very friendly. They came from behind the trees to watch the little girl as she ran past.

At last she was so tired that she stopped running and decided to curl up under the nearest tree and go to sleep. Just then she saw a tiny little house right in the middle of the wood.

She went inside and called "Hello!" but nobody was at home. Everything in the cottage was very, very tiny.

In the middle stood a tiny table with seven little chairs around it. On the table were seven little plates, each plate having a knife, a fork, a spoon, and a tiny little mug. Against the wall were seven little beds in a row.

Snow White was both hungry and thirsty, so she went to the table, where she ate a mouthful of porridge and a bite of bread from each plate and took a sip of milk from every cup.

Then, because she was so tired, she decided to lie down and rest. She lay down on the first bed, but it was too short. The second was too long. The third was too hard. The fourth was too soft. The fifth was too narrow. The sixth was too wide. But the seventh bed was just right, and so Snow White tucked herself in and fell fast asleep.

In the evening the owners of the little cottage came home. They were seven little dwarfs who dug for gold all day in the near-by mountains. As soon as they came in, carrying their seven little lamps, they noticed that someone had been there.

"Someone has been sitting in my chair," said the first.

"Someone has been using my spoon," said the second.

"Someone has been tasting my porridge," said the third.

"Someone has been biting my bread," said the fourth.

"Someone has been meddling with my fork," said the fifth.

"Someone has been drinking from my cup," said the sixth.

"Someone has been using my napkin," said the seventh.

Then the first little dwarf started to complain once more. "Someone has been sleeping in my bed," said he.

The others ran to their little beds against the wall and saw that all the sheets had been tumbled. But the seventh dwarf found that Snow White was still sleeping soundly in his bed.

They held their lamps above her so that the light fell on her face and all of them at once cried out, "Oh my, oh my, how pretty she is!"

Snow White was so tired that she kept right on sleeping and didn't wake up until morning. She was frightened at first when she saw the strange little men. But they were so friendly and kind that she smiled and soon felt friendly, too.

"What is your name?" they asked.

"My name is Snow White," was her reply.

"How did you come to our cottage?" they asked and Snow White told them all about the wicked Queen.

When she finished her story they said, "Will you stay and live with us? Will you cook our supper and make our beds? And wash and sew and knit for us? And keep everything neat? If so, we will keep you here and you shall want for nothing."

"Yes, I will," Snow White replied. "And I thank you with all my heart."

So she remained with the seven little dwarfs. Every morning they went to the near-by mountains to dig for gold. Every evening they came back and found their beds made, their supper cooked, and the little cottage as neat as a pin. All of them were very happy together.

But the good dwarfs worried about the wicked Queen. "She will soon know of your being here," they told Snow White. "She will be very angry and will try to hurt you. Therefore, let no one in while we are away."

The dwarfs were right. One day the Queen spoke to her mirror and said:

"Mirror, mirror on the wall,
 Who is the fairest one of all?"

And the mirror replied:

"Thou wert loveliest once, I vow,
 But Snow White is the fairest now.
 She lives in a cottage in the wood
 With the seven dwarfs so kind and good."

The Queen was furious when she heard these words. She determined to kill Snow White, for she wanted to be the most beautiful lady in the world. She dressed herself like an old pedlar woman, put a basket of trinkets over her arm, and went to the little house where Snow White lived.

"Fine things for sale!" the wicked Queen called out. "Lovely things for sale! Laces of all colors, gay as the rainbow, to lace up your bodice." And she held up a loop of gaily colored ribbons.

Snow White peeped out of the window and saw the old pedlar woman. Her face was dyed and she wore a wig, so poor Snow White didn't guess that it was really the wicked Queen.

"This seems to be a nice old woman. Surely I needn't be afraid of letting her in." So she opened the door and bought a pretty new lace to string into her bodice.

"Child," said the old woman, "come and let me lace it properly for you."

Snow White, suspecting nothing, stood up before her and let the pedlar woman lace her with the gay new lace. But the old woman laced so quickly and tightly that in a moment Snow White had lost her breath. She sank to the floor as if dead.

"Now," said the Queen, "I am the fairest one of all!" and she hurried away.

By good luck it was nearly sunset time and the seven little dwarfs soon came home from their work. They were frightened when they saw Snow White lying on the floor as though she were dead. They lifted her up, and when they saw how tightly the lace was pulled, they cut it. Soon she could breathe again.

Snow White told the dwarfs what had happened. "Snow White," they said, "that old pedlar woman was no one but the wicked Queen. You must be careful when we're not here. Do not let anyone into the house, and do not accept any presents."

By this time the Queen had reached home and now she went to her mirror and asked:

"Mirror, mirror on the wall,
Who is the fairest one of all?"

And the mirror replied:

"Thou wert loveliest once, I vow,
But Snow White is the fairest now.
She lives in a cottage in the wood
With the seven little dwarfs so kind and good."

When she heard that, the Queen was furious, for she knew then that Snow White was still alive.

"Now," she said, "I will plan something that will really be the end of her."

By means of witchcraft, at which the wicked Queen was skillful, she fashioned a beautiful comb set with jewels—but the comb was poisonous. Then she dressed herself up to look like another and different sort of pedlar woman, and went to the cottage of the seven dwarfs.

She knocked on the door and called, "Fine things for sale! Lovely things for sale!"

Snow White peeped out the window, but this time she said, "Go on your way, good woman. I must not let you in."

"At least you aren't forbidden to look," answered the old woman. "See this beautiful comb. How nice it would look on you!"

And she held out the gleaming, poisonous comb. Snow White was so delighted with it that she forgot all about the dwarfs' warning and opened the door. The old woman stepped quickly inside, and in a pretended sweet voice said, "Let me show you how to wear it in your lovely hair."

As soon as the Queen put it in Snow White's hair, the little girl fell down on the floor.

"Now she is dead!" said the Queen. "Now I am the fairest one of all!" And she hurried away.

When the dwarfs came home that evening, they found Snow White lying on the floor as though she were dead. They suspected the old Queen had come to harm Snow White and soon found the poisoned comb in her hair. As soon as they pulled it out, she woke up and recovered from the poisoning.

"You must be very careful," the dwarfs told her. "The Queen will try to kill you. Do not let anyone into the house and do not accept any presents."

The very next morning the Queen spoke to her mirror and asked:

"*Mirror, mirror on the wall,*
Who is the fairest one of all?"

And the mirror replied:

"Thou wert loveliest once, I vow,
But Snow White is the fairest now.
She lives in a cottage in the wood
With the seven little dwarfs so kind and good."

This made the Queen so furious that she went to the tower where she kept her poisons. She picked out a beautiful apple which was green on one side and red on the other, and carefully poisoned only the red side. Then she painted her face like that of an old peasant woman, tied a kerchief round her head, and went to the cottage where Snow White lived.

She knocked at the door, but Snow White called through the keyhole, "I dare not let anyone in."

"Look out of the window then," said the wicked Queen. "See my beautiful apples? Here, let me give you one."

Snow White looked out of the window, but she replied, "No, no, no! I dare not take it!"

"What are you afraid of? Poison?" laughed the wicked Queen. "There, I will break it in half and give you the rosy half, eating the green half myself."

The rosy half of the apple looked so nice and juicy that Snow White wanted to eat it. When she saw the old woman eating the green half, she was sure it would be safe. So she reached out her hand for the poisoned half of the apple. As soon as she took one bite she fell down dead.

The Queen was overjoyed, for now Snow White was really dead, and now her mirror on the wall told her what she wanted to hear:

"Thou art fairest, lady Queen
None more lovely can be seen."

When the dwarfs came home that night they wept and wept because their dear Snow White was really dead. She was so beautiful, however, with her skin as white as snow, her cheeks as red as blood, and her hair as black as ebony, that they put her in a glass case for all the world to see.

The animals of the forest and the birds of the heavens came to look at Snow White and to weep because she was dead.

For a long long time she lay there looking as if she were only asleep. Then one day a charming young Prince traveling through the forest happened to see her in her glass case. Snow White looked so beautiful and sweet that he loved her right away.

"Let me have this case," he said to the dwarfs. "I will pay you what you like for it."

"We would not sell it for all the gold in the world," the dwarfs replied.

"Give it to me then," the Prince begged. "I cannot live without Snow White. I will love her and protect her as long as I live."

The dwarfs, who had very kind hearts, took pity on the Prince and gave her to him. He ordered the case carried away on the shoulders of his attendants to his castle over the hill. On the way one of the attendants stumbled over a stone and, with the shock, the piece of poisoned apple fell out of Snow White's mouth.

She woke up, raised the lid of the glass case, and said, "Where am I?"

Full of joy, the Prince told her all that had befallen. He told her also that he loved her and wished her to become his wife.

Joyfully Snow White consented.

And at their wedding, in the castle over the hill, the animals of the forest, the birds of the heavens, and the seven little dwarfs danced and sang to celebrate the happy occasion. The wicked Queen came to the wedding to see the beautiful Princess and, when she saw that it was Snow White, she became so angry that she fell down dead.

THE FROG PRINCE

Adapted from Wilhelm and Jakob Grimm

Long, long ago there lived a King who had three beautiful daughters. But the youngest daughter was the most beautiful of all.

Near the castle of this King was a lovely garden, and in the middle of it was a deep pool. On every hot day the King's youngest daughter played near the pool, throwing her golden ball up in the air and catching it again. This was her favorite game.

Now one day it happened that the little Princess threw her ball up in the air but did not catch it. The golden ball fell on the grass and then rolled right past her into the pool. She ran after the ball and looked into the water, but the pool was so deep that she could not see the bottom.

The poor little Princess knelt beside the pool and started to cry. She cried and cried, her cries becoming louder and louder. Presently a voice called out, "Why dost thou weep, O King's daughter? Thy tears would melt a heart of stone!"

She looked around to see who had spoken, but no one was there. All she saw was a Frog stretching his thick, ugly head out of the water. She started to cry again, and again the voice said, "Why dost thou weep, O King's daughter?" This time it really seemed as if the voice came from the ugly Frog.

"Thou old water-paddler!" said the Princess. "Was it thou that spoke?"

"Yes," the Frog replied. "Thy tears make me very sad. Let me help thee."

"Thou canst not help me, thou stupid Frog," said the Princess. "I am weeping for my golden ball which fell to the bottom of the pool."

"I will fetch it for thee," answered the Frog. "But what wilt thou give me in return?"

"What wouldst thou have, dear Frog?" the Princess asked. "My dresses, my pearls and jewels, or the golden crown I wear?"

The Frog replied: "Dresses and jewels and golden crowns are not for me. But if thou wilt love me, be my friend and play with me, if thou wilt let me sit at thy table, eat from thy golden plate,

and sleep in thy little bed, then I will fetch thy ball for thee. Wilt thou promise me all these things?"

"Oh yes! I promise!" said the Princess.

Instantly the Frog dived to the bottom of the pool and swam up with the golden ball in his mouth. The King's daughter was so happy to see her plaything again that she snatched it from his mouth and ran off with it.

"Stop! Stop!" cried the Frog. "Take me with thee! Don't forget thy promise!"

But his croaking was useless. It was loud enough, but the little

Princess did not listen to him and ran home to the castle. The Frog couldn't run so fast, so he jumped back into the pool.

The next day, when the King and his three daughters and all the courtiers were at dinner, they heard something coming up the marble stairs—splish-splash, splish-splash. When the sound got to the top of the stairs, there was a knock on the door. Then a voice called out, "Open the door, youngest daughter of the King!"

She got up and went to the door, and there stood the Frog before her. She became very angry and slammed the door with a loud bang. When the Princess returned to the table, the King saw that her heart was beating very fast and that she seemed to be afraid. "What is the matter, my daughter?" he asked. "Has a giant come to fetch you away?"

"Oh no," the daughter answered. "It is no giant, but an ugly Frog."

"What does the Frog want?" asked the King.

And so the little Princess told him how she lost her golden ball in the pool, and how the Frog got it for her because she promised he could be her companion. "I never thought he could get out of the water," she said. "But he must have jumped out, and now he wants to come in here and eat off my little golden plate."

At that moment there was another knock on the door and a voice called out:

"King's daughter, youngest,
Open the door.
Hast thou forgot thy promise to me,
After I fetched up thy ball for thee?
King's daughter, youngest,
Open the door."

Then the King said, "What thou hast promised, thou must do. Go and let him in."

The Princess did as her father bid. She opened the door and the Frog hopped into the room. She went back to her chair and the Frog hopped after her.

"Take me up on thy chair," the Frog said. The Princess did not want to, but her father reminded her that she must keep her promise. She took the Frog up on her chair and then he instantly hopped onto the table. "Now push thy plate nearer so we may eat together," the Frog said. And the Princess had to obey.

They ate together off the golden plate, but the King's daughter did not enjoy her dinner. When they had finished the Frog said, "I thank thee, Princess. That was a very good dinner. Now I am sleepy and would like to go to bed. Please take me to thy room."

Then the King's daughter began to cry. She was afraid of the Frog. He was cold and ugly and she didn't want him to sleep in her nice clean little bed. But her tears made her father very angry. "He who helped thee in the time of thy trouble, him must thou help now!" said the King.

So the little Princess picked up the Frog and carried him to her room. She threw him onto her bed and cried, "Now wilt thou be quiet, thou horrid Frog?"

But as he fell, he was changed into a handsome Prince. The Princess was so surprised that she couldn't say a word, but the Prince told her how he happened to be a Frog. "A wicked fairy bewitched me," he said. "She condemned me to live as a Frog in the bottom of the pool until a King's daughter broke the spell."

"Now wilt thou be a handsome Prince forever and ever?" the King's daughter asked. "Or must thou go back to the pool?"

"I shall be a Prince forever," he told her. "Thou hast saved me, beautiful Princess. Wilt thou marry me?"

The King gave his consent, and the following day the Prince and Princess were married. Then they went off in a fine white coach drawn by eight milk-white horses. They went to the Prince's own kingdom where they lived happily ever after.

THE MAGIC FISH-BONE

by Charles Dickens

There was once a king, and he had a queen; and he was the manliest of his sex, and she was the loveliest of hers. The king was, in his private profession, under government. The queen's father had been a medical man out of town.

They had nineteen children, and were always having more. Seventeen of these children took care of the baby; and Alicia, the eldest, took care of them all. Their ages varied from seven years to seven months.

Let us now resume our story.

One day the king was going to the office, when he stopped at the fishmonger's to buy a pound and a half of salmon not too near the tail, which the queen (who was a careful housekeeper) had requested him to send home. Mr. Pickles, the fishmonger, said, "Certainly, sir; is there any other article? Good morning."

The king went on towards the office in a melancholy mood; for quarter-day was such a long way off, and several of the dear children were growing out of their clothes. He had not proceeded far, when Mr. Pickles's errand-boy came running after him, and said, "Sir, you didn't notice the old lady in our shop."

"What old lady?" inquired the king. "I saw none."

Now the king had not seen any old lady, because this old lady had been invisible to him, though visible to Mr. Pickles's boy. Probably because he messed and splashed the water about to that degree, and flopped the pairs of soles down in that violent manner, that, if she had not been visible to him, he would have spoilt her clothes.

Just then the old lady came trotting up. She was dressed in shot-silk of the richest quality, smelling of dried lavender.

"King Watkins the First, I believe?" said the old lady.

"Watkins," replied the king, "is my name."

"Papa, if I am not mistaken, of the beautiful Princess Alicia?" said the old lady.

"And of eighteen other darlings," replied the king.

"Listen. You are going to the office," said the old lady.

It instantly flashed upon the king that she must be a fairy, or how could she know that?

"You are right," said the old lady, answering his thoughts. "I am the good Fairy Grandmarina. Attend! When you return home to dinner, politely invite the Princess Alicia to have some of the salmon you bought just now."

"It may disagree with her," said the king.

The old lady became so very angry at this absurd idea, that the king was quite alarmed, and humbly begged her pardon.

"We hear a great deal too much about this thing disagreeing, and that thing disagreeing," said the old lady, with the greatest contempt it was possible to express. "Don't be greedy. I think you want it all yourself."

The king hung his head under this reproof, and said he wouldn't talk about things disagreeing any more.

"Be good, then," said the Fairy Grandmarina, "and don't! When the beautiful Princess Alicia consents to partake of the salmon—as I think she will—you will find she will leave a fish-bone on her plate. Tell her to dry it, and to rub it, and to polish it, till it shines like mother-of-pearl, and to take care of it as a present from me."

"Is that all?" asked the king.

"Don't be impatient, sir," returned the Fairy Grandmarina, scolding him severely. "Don't catch people short, before they have done speaking. Just the way with you grown-up persons. You are always doing it."

The king again hung his head, and said he wouldn't do so any more.

"Be good, then," said the Fairy Grandmarina, "and don't! Tell the Princess Alicia, with my love, that the fish-bone is a magic present which can only be used once; but that it will bring her, that once, whatever she wishes for, *provided she wishes for it at the right time*. That is the message. Take care of it." The king was beginning, "Might I ask the reason?" when the fairy became absolutely furious.

"*Will* you be good, sir?" she exclaimed, stamping her foot on the ground. "The reason for this, and the reason for that, indeed! You are always wanting the reason. No reason. There! Hoity toity me! I am sick of your grown-up reasons."

The king was extremely frightened by the old lady's flying into such a passion, and said he was very sorry to have offended her, and he wouldn't ask for reasons any more.

"Be good, then," said the old lady, "and don't!"

With those words, Grandmarina vanished, and the king went on and on and on, till he came to the office. There he wrote and wrote and wrote, till it was time to go home again. Then he politely invited the Princess Alicia, as the fairy had directed him, to partake of the salmon. And when she had enjoyed it very much, he saw the fish-bone on her plate, as the fairy had told him he would, and he delivered the Fairy's message, and the Princess Alicia took care to DRY the bone, and to RUB it and to POLISH it, till it shone like mother-of-pearl.

And so, when the queen was going to get up in the morning, she said, "Oh, dear me, dear me; my head, my head!" and then she fainted away.

The Princess Alicia, who happened to be looking in at the chamber door, asking about breakfast, was very much alarmed when she saw her royal mamma in this state, and she rang the bell for Peggy, which was the name of the lord chamberlain. But remembering where the smelling-bottle was, she climbed on a chair and got it; and after that she climbed on another chair by the bedside, and held the smelling-bottle to the queen's nose; and after that she jumped down and got some water; and after that she jumped up again and wetted the queen's forehead; and, in short, when the lord chamberlain came in, that dear old woman said to the little princess, "What a trot you are! I couldn't have done it better myself!"

But that was not the worst of the good queen's illness. Oh, no! She was very ill indeed, for a long time. The Princess Alicia kept the seventeen young princes and princesses quiet, and dressed and undressed and danced the baby, and made the kettle boil, and heated the soup, and swept the hearth, and poured out the medicine, and nursed the queen, and did all that ever she could, and was as busy, busy, busy as busy could be; for there were not many servants at that palace for three reasons: because the king was short of money, because a rise in his office never seemed to come, and because quarter-day was so far off that it looked almost as far off and as little as one of the stars.

But on the morning when the queen fainted away, where was the magic fish-bone? Why, there is was in the Princess Alicia's pocket! She had almost taken it out to bring the queen to life again, when she put it back, and looked for the smelling-bottle.

After the queen had come out of her swoon that morning, and was dozing, the Princess Alicia hurried upstairs to tell a most particular secret to a most particularly confidential friend of hers, who was a duchess. People did suppose her to be a doll; but she was really a duchess, though nobody knew it except the princess.

This most particular secret was the secret about the magic fish-bone, the history of which was well-known to the duchess, because the princess told her everything. The princess kneeled down by the bed on which the duchess was lying, full-dressed and wide-awake, and whispered the secret to her. The duchess smiled and nodded. People might have supposed that she never smiled and nodded; but she often did, though nobody knew it except the princess.

Then the Princess Alicia hurried downstairs again to keep watch in the queen's room. She often kept watch by herself in the queen's room; but every evening, while the illness lasted, she sat there watching with the king. And every evening the king sat looking at her with a cross look, wondering why she never brought out the magic fish-bone. As often as she noticed this, she ran upstairs, whispered the secret to the duchess over again, and said to the duchess besides, "They think we children never have a reason or a meaning!" And the duchess, though the most fashionable duchess that ever was heard of, winked her eye.

"Alicia," said the king, one evening, when she wished him good-night.

"Yes, papa."

"What is become of the magic fish-bone?"

"In my pocket, papa."

"I thought you had lost it?"

"Oh, no, papa!"

"Or forgotten it?"

"No, indeed, papa."

And so another time the dreadful little snapping pug-dog, next door, made a rush at one of the young princes as he stood on the steps coming home from school, and terrified him out of his wits; and he put his hand through a pane of glass, and bled, bled, bled. When the seventeen other young princes and princesses saw him bleed, bleed, bleed, they were terrified out of their wits too, and screamed themselves black in their seventeen faces all at once. But the Princess Alicia put her hands over all their seventeen mouths, one after another, and persuaded them to be quiet because of the sick queen. And then she put the wounded prince's hand in a basin of fresh cold water, while they stared with their twice seventeen are thirty-four, put down four and carry three, eyes, and then she looked in the hand for bits of glass, and there were fortunately no bits of glass there. And then she said to two chubby-legged princes, who were sturdy though small, "Bring me in the royal rag-bag: I must snip and stitch and cut and contrive." So these two young princes tugged at the royal rag-bag, and lugged it in; and the Princess Alicia sat down on the floor, with a large pair of scissors and a needle and thread, and snipped and stitched and cut and contrived, and made a bandage, and put it on, and it fitted beautifully; and so when it was all done, she saw the king her papa looking on by the door.

"Alicia."

"Yes, papa."

"What have you been doing?"

"Snipping, stitching, cutting, and contriving, papa."

"Where is the magic fish-bone?"

"In my pocket, papa."

"I thought you had lost it?"

"Oh, no, papa!"

"Or forgotten it?"

"No, indeed, papa."

After that, she ran upstairs to the duchess, and told her what had passed, and told her the secret over again; and the duchess shook her flaxen curls, and laughed with her rosy lips.

Well! and so another time the baby fell under the grate. The seventeen young princes and princesses were used to it; for they were almost always falling under the grate or down the stairs; but the baby was not used to it yet, and it gave him a swelled face and a black eye. The way the poor little darling came to tumble was, that he was out of the Princess Alicia's lap just as she was sitting, in a great coarse apron that quite smothered her, in front of the kitchen fire, beginning to peel the turnips for the broth for dinner; and the way she came to be doing that was, that the king's cook had run away that morning with her own true love, who was a very tall but very tipsy soldier. Then the seventeen young princes and princesses, who cried at everything that happened, cried and roared. But the Princess Alicia (who couldn't help crying a little herself) quietly called to them to be still, on account of not throwing back the queen upstairs, who was fast getting well, and said, "Hold your tongues, you wicked little monkeys, every one of you, while I examine the baby." Then she examined baby, and found that he hadn't broken anything; and she held cold iron to his poor dear eye, and smoothed his poor dear face, and he presently fell asleep in her arms. Then she said to the seventeen princes and princesses,

"I am afraid to let him down yet, lest he should wake and feel pain; be good, and you shall all be cooks." They jumped for joy when they heard that, and began making themselves cooks' caps out of old newspapers. So to one she gave the salt-box, and to one she gave the barley, and to one she gave the herbs, and to one she gave the turnips, and to one she gave the carrots, and to one she gave the onions, and to one she gave the spice-box, till they were all cooks, and all running about at work, she sitting in the middle, smothered in the great coarse apron, nursing baby.

By and by the broth was done; and the baby woke up, smiling like an angel, and was trusted to the sedatest princess to hold, while the other princes and princesses were squeezed into a far-off corner to look at the Princess Alicia turning out the sauce-panful of broth, for fear (as they were always getting into trouble) they should get splashed and scalded. When the broth came tumbling out, steaming beautifully, and smelling like a nosegay good to eat, they clapped their hands. That made the baby clap his hands; and that, and his looking as if he had a comic tooth-ache, made all the princes and princesses laugh. So the Princess Alicia said, "Laugh and be good; and after dinner we will make him a nest on the floor in a corner, and he shall sit in his nest and see a dance of eighteen cooks." That delighted the young princes and princesses, and they ate up all the broth, and washed up all the plates and dishes, and cleared away, and pushed the table into a corner; and then they in their cooks' caps, and the Princess Alicia in the smothering coarse apron that belonged to the cook that had run away with her own true love that was the very tall but very tipsy soldier, danced a dance of eighteen cooks before the angelic baby, who forgot his swelled face and his black eye, and crowed with joy.

And so then, once more the Princess Alicia saw King Watkins the First, her father, standing in the doorway looking on, and he said, "What have you been doing, Alicia?"

"Cooking and contriving, papa."

"What else have you been doing, Alicia?"

"Keeping the children light-hearted, papa."

"Where is the magic fish-bone, Alicia?"

"In my pocket, papa."

"I thought you had lost it?"

"Oh, no, papa!"

"Or forgotten it?"

"No, indeed, papa."

The king then sighed so heavily, and seemed so low-spirited, and sat down so miserably, leaning his head upon his hand, and his elbow upon the kitchen table pushed away in the corner, that the seventeen princes and princesses crept softly out of the kitchen, and left him alone with the Princess Alicia and the angelic baby.

"What is the matter, papa?"

"I am dreadfully poor, my child."

"Have you no money at all, papa?"

"None, my child."

"Is there no way of getting any, papa?"

"No way," said the king. "I have tried very hard, and I have tried all ways."

When she heard those last words, the Princess Alicia began to put her hand into the pocket where she kept the magic fish-bone.

"Papa," said she, "when we have tried very hard, and tried all ways, we must have done our very, very best?"

"No doubt, Alicia."

"When we have done our very, very best, papa, and that is not enough, then I think the right time must have come for asking help of others." This was the very secret connected with the magic fish-bone, which she had found out for herself from the good Fairy Grandmarina's words, and which she had so often whispered to her beautiful and fashionable friend, the duchess.

So she took out of her pocket the magic fish-bone, that had been dried and rubbed and polished till it shone like mother-of-pearl; and she gave it one little kiss, and wished it was quarter-day. And immediately it was quarter-day; and the king's quarter's salary came rattling down the chimney, and bounced into the middle of the floor.

But this was not half of what happened—no, not a quarter; for immediately afterwards the good Fairy Grandmarina came riding in, in a carriage and four (peacocks), with Mr. Pickles's boy up behind, dressed in silver and gold, with a cocked hat, powdered hair, pink silk stockings, a jeweled cane, and a nosegay. Down jumped Mr. Pickles's boy, with his cocked hat in his hand, and wonderfully polite (being entirely changed by enchantment), and handed Grandmarina out; and there she stood, in her rich shot-silk smelling of dried lavender, fanning herself with a sparkling fan.

"Alicia, my dear," said this charming old fairy, "how do you do? I hope I see you pretty well? Give me a kiss."

The Princess Alicia embraced her; and then Grandmarina turned to the king, and said rather sharply, "Are you good?"

The king said he hoped so.

"I suppose you know the reason *now*, why my god-daughter here," kissing the princess again, "did not apply to the fish-bone sooner?" said the fairy.

The king made a shy bow.

"Ah! but you didn't *then?*" said the fairy.

The king made a shyer bow.

"Any more reasons to ask for?" said the fairy.

The king said, No, and he was very sorry.

"Be good, then," said the fairy, "and live happy ever afterwards."

Then Grandmarina waved her fan, and the queen came in most splendidly dressed; and the seventeen young princes and princesses, no longer grown out of their clothes, came in, newly fitted out from top to toe, with tucks in everything to admit of its being let out. After that, the fairy tapped the Princess Alicia with her fan; and the smothering coarse apron flew away, and she appeared exquisitely dressed, like a little bride, with a wreath of orange-flowers and a silver veil. After that, the kitchen dresser changed of itself into a wardrobe, made of beautiful woods and gold and looking-glass, which was full of dresses of all sorts, for her and all exactly fitting her. After that, the angelic baby came in running alone, with his face and eye not a bit the worse, but much the better. Then Grandmarina begged to be introduced to the duchess; and, when the duchess was brought down, many compliments passed between them.

A little whispering took place between the fairy and the duchess; and then the fairy said out loud, "Yes, I thought she would have told you." Grandmarina then turned to the king and queen, and said, "We are going in search of Prince Certainpersonio. The pleasure of your company is requested at church in half an hour precisely." So she and the Princess Alicia got into the carriage; and Mr. Pickles's boy handed in the duchess, who sat by herself on the opposite seat; and then Mr. Pickles's boy put up the steps and got up behind, and the peacocks flew away with their tails behind.

Prince Certainpersonio was sitting by himself, eating barley-sugar, and waiting to be ninety. When he saw the peacocks, followed by the carriage, coming in at the window, it immediately occurred to him that something uncommon was going to happen.

"Prince," said Grandmarina, "I bring you your bride."

The moment the fairy said those words, Prince Certainpersonio's face left off being sticky, and his jacket and corduroys changed to peach-bloom velvet, and his hair curled, and a cap and feather flew in like a bird and settled on his head. He got into the carriage by the fairy's invitation; and there he renewed his acquaintance with the duchess, whom he had seen before.

In the church were the prince's relations and friends, and the Princess Alicia's relations and friends, and the seventeen princes and princesses, and the baby, and a crowd of the neighbors. The marriage was beautiful beyond expression. The duchess was bridesmaid, and beheld the ceremony from the pulpit, where she was supported by the cushion of the desk.

Grandmarina gave a magnificent wedding-feast afterwards, in which there was everything and more to eat, and everything and more to drink. The wedding-cake was delicately ornamented with white satin ribbons, frosted silver, and white lilies, and was forty-two yards round.

When Grandmarina had drunk her love to the young couple, and Prince Certainpersonio had made a speech, and everybody had cried, Hip, hip, hip, hurrah! Grandmarina announced to the king and queen that in future there would be eight quarter-days in every year, except in leap year, when there would be ten. She then turned to Certainpersonio and Alicia, and said, "My dears, you will have thirty-five children, and they will all be good and beautiful. Seventeen of your children will be boys, and eighteen will be girls. The hair of the whole of your children will curl naturally. They will never have the measles, and will have recovered from the whooping-cough before being born."

On hearing such good news, everybody cried out "Hip, hip, hip, hurrah!" again.

"It only remains," said Grandmarina in conclusion, "to make an end of the fish-bone."

So she took it from the hand of the Princess Alicia, and it instantly flew down the throat of the dreadful little snapping pugdog, next door, and choked him, and he expired in convulsions.

RUMPELSTILTSKIN

There was once a Miller who was always boasting. "My daughter can spin straw into gold," he told his friends one day. That was so remarkable that one person told it to another, and at last word came to the King. "The Miller's daughter can spin straw into gold," the King was told. That was a very remarkable thing, so the King sent for the Miller.

"Is it true, Miller, that your daughter can spin straw into gold?" the King asked.

"Yes, Your Highness," the Miller replied. But of course it was *not* true.

"Bring your daughter to my palace tomorrow morning," said the King.

"Very well, Your Highness," the Miller replied.

When the Miller's daughter came to the palace, the King led her into a chamber which was full of straw. He gave her a spinning wheel and said, "Now set yourself to work and spin this straw into gold. If you have not done so by tomorrow morning, you shall die." Then he shut the door and left the poor maiden alone.

There she sat all day long, looking at the straw and feeling very, very sad. She knew she could not spin straw into gold, so she would have to die. She cried and cried, when suddenly the door opened and a little man stepped into the room. "Good evening, fair maiden," said he. "Why do you weep?"

"Ah, little man," she replied, "I must spin this straw into gold and I am sure I don't know how."

Then the little Dwarf asked, "What will you give me if I spin it for you?"

"My necklace," said the maiden.

The Dwarf took the necklace and then sat down in front of

the spinning wheel. Whir, whir, whir, he went, whistling and singing:

"Round about, round about,
  Lo and behold.
Reel away, reel away,
  Straw into gold!"

Three times round about the wheel went, and the bobbin was full of gold. Then he put some more straw on the wheel. Whir, whir, whir, three times round again, and a second bobbin was full of gold. So he went all night long, until all the straw was spun into gold.

At sunrise the King came into the chamber and was astonished to see all that glistening gold. "How wonderful!" he said. "You are truly a remarkable maiden. Now let me see if you can do it again."

He led the maiden into a chamber that was even larger than the first and in it was even more straw. "Spin this into gold," said the King, "or tomorrow you die."

The poor maiden, left alone, started to cry. She didn't know how to spin the straw and she didn't want to die. All at once the door opened and the same little man came into the room.

"What will you give me," he asked, "if I spin this straw into gold?"

"The ring on my finger," the maiden replied.

The Dwarf took the ring and started to spin, and whistled and sang:

"Round about, round about,
  Lo and behold.
Reel away, reel away,
  Straw into gold!"

Whir, whir, whir. By morning all the straw was changed into glistening gold. The King was very happy when he saw it, but he was not satisfied. He wanted still more gold. He led the maiden into a room much larger than the others and filled with even more straw.

"This you must spin during the night," he said. "And if you can do it, you shall be my bride."

When the maiden was left alone, the Dwarf appeared for the third time and for the third time he asked, "What will you give me if I spin this straw into gold?"

"Alas, I have nothing left to give," sighed the maiden.

"Then promise me your first-born child," said the Dwarf, and the maiden promised.

In the morning the King found that all the straw had been spun into gold, just as he had ordered. So he married the Miller's daughter and she became the Queen.

About a year after the marriage a little child was born to them. The Queen had long forgotten about the little Dwarf, but one day he suddenly appeared before her.

"You promised me your first-born child," said the Dwarf. "I have come to take him away."

"No, no, no!" the Queen cried. "Please don't do that! I will give you jewels and gold and money. You may have anything you want, but leave me my child."

"I do not care for riches," said the little man. "I want only your child."

The Queen began to groan and weep. She was so unhappy that the Dwarf took pity on her and said: "I will give you three days. If in that time you guess my name, the child is yours. If you cannot guess my name, the child is mine."

All night long the Queen lay awake trying to think of all the names she knew. When the Dwarf came to see her the following morning, she said:

"Is your name Caspar?"

"That is not my name!" the Dwarf replied.

"Is your name Balthassar?" asked the Queen.

"That is not my name!" the Dwarf replied.

"Is your name Goliath?" asked the Queen.

"That is not my name!" the Dwarf replied.

So the Queen sent messengers throughout the country to collect any new names they could find. The second morning, when the Dwarf appeared, she said, "Is your name Ribs-of-Beef?"

"That is not my name!" the Dwarf replied.

"Is your name Sheepshank?" asked the Queen.

"That is not my name!" the Dwarf replied.

"Is your name Whalebone?" asked the Queen.

"That is not my name!" the Dwarf replied.

The Queen was very, very unhappy. There were so many names in the world and how was she to know which one belonged to the little man? But the third morning a messenger came to her palace and said, "I have not found a single new name, Your Highness, but as I came to a high mountain near the edge of the forest I saw a little house. In front of the house a fire was burning, and round this fire a curious little man was dancing on one leg and shouting,

"Tomorrow I brew, today I bake,
And then the child away I'll take
For little deems my royal dame
That Rumpelstiltskin is my name!"

The Queen was very glad when she heard that, and just then in came the little Dwarf.

"Now, my lady Queen, what is my name?" said the Dwarf.

"Are you called Conrad?" asked the Queen.

"That is not my name!" the Dwarf replied.

"Are you called Hal?" asked the Queen.

"That is not my name!" the Dwarf replied.

"Are you called Rumpelstiltskin?" asked the Queen.

"A witch has told you!" shrieked the little man. "A witch has told you!" Rumpelstiltskin became so angry that he stamped his foot on the ground. He stamped it so hard that it sank into the ground up to his waist and, though he pulled and pulled and pulled with all his might, he could never pull it out again.

THE STEADFAST TIN SOLDIER

Adapted from Hans Christian Andersen

There were once twenty-five tin soldiers who all lived together in a little wooden box. One day the lid of the box was opened and the first thing they heard in the world was a little boy's voice saying, "Tin soldiers!"

It was a very happy voice because he was a very happy little boy. This was his birthday, and the box of tin soldiers was his favorite birthday present. He took them all out of the box and stood them on the playroom table.

Each soldier was exactly like every other soldier. Each one had a splendid red-and-blue uniform. Each one shouldered his musket and looked directly before him. Each one stood straight and tall on the table.

There hadn't been quite enough tin to finish them all, however, so one of the little soldiers had only one leg. He stood just as firmly on his one leg as the others stood on their two legs. And it is to this little tin soldier that all the sad but remarkable adventures came.

He looked around the playroom table at all the other toys. There was a magnificent castle made out of cardboard. In front of the castle was a little looking glass that was supposed to be a lake. Around the lake there were lovely green trees made of paper, and on the lake were white swans made of wax. It was all very pretty, but the prettiest thing by far was a little lady who stood in the doorway of the castle. She was made of paper, too, but she wore a dress of pale blue gauze. The dress had a blue ribbon around the neck and in the middle of the ribbon was a shining tinsel rose as big as the lady's face.

This lady was a dancer, so she stood up on one toe and kicked her other foot high in the air. There she held it, straight up in the air, and it looked to the little tin soldier as if she had only one leg.

"Just like me," he said to himself. "She and I should marry, for she would be a lovely wife."

That is what he said to himself, but he was very shy. He didn't know how to become friends with the lovely lady, so he just stood on the playroom table all day and looked at her.

When nighttime came the little boy and all the people in the house went to sleep. That was the time when the toys started to play. They visited one another; they had grand balls; and they played at war. Only the lovely dancing lady and the little tin soldier stayed where they were, standing on one leg and staring at each other.

Suddenly, at midnight, the snuffbox flew open. But there was no snuff in it—only a little black Goblin. You see, it was a trick.

"Tin Soldier," said the Goblin, "don't stare at people whom you don't know!"

The tin soldier pretended not to hear him, and that made the black Goblin very angry.

"Just you wait till tomorrow!" he said. "Something dreadful will happen to you."

And the next morning, when the little boy was playing with his soldiers on the window sill, the window flew open and the little tin soldier fell out. He fell head over heels, down three flights, and landed on the sidewalk. All he could think as he fell was, "This is the Goblin's fault!"

The little boy ran downstairs and out into the street to look for him. But, though the soldier lay on his back and stared right up at the little boy, he couldn't find him.

Soon it began to rain. It rained very hard, and the tin soldier got wet and the sidewalk got wet and, in the gutter by the sidewalk, there was a real stream. When the rain stopped, two boys came along and saw the tin soldier.

"Look," said one of them; "a one-legged tin soldier!"

"Yes," cried the other; "let's make a boat and give him a ride."

They made a boat out of a piece of newspaper and put the soldier in it. They sailed it down the gutter and ran along beside it. But soon the water was running so fast that they couldn't keep up with it and the little paper boat with the little tin soldier in it went sailing down the gutter alone.

After a while the gutter ran into the sewer and the little tin soldier found himself in a dark, dark tunnel.

"It's all the Goblin's fault!" he said to himself. And he wished that the little dancing lady were there beside him, for then he wouldn't care how dark it was.

Suddenly a huge water rat who lived in the sewer came along

and said, "Where is your passport? You must have a passport!"

But the little tin soldier stared straight ahead and pretended not to hear and held on tightly to his musket. The rat was very angry, but the boat sailed on past him and finally it came out of the tunnel to a great canal.

The little tin soldier was glad to see daylight again, but now he noticed that the waves in the canal were so strong that they were tearing the little paper boat. Soon the boat fell to pieces, and the little tin soldier started to sink. Just at that moment he was snapped up by a huge fish and found himself in darkness again.

There he remained, and he didn't know what was happening

to the fish, but what *did* happen was this. The fish was caught and sold to a fish market where it was bought by a cook. The cook took it home with her and cut it open before cooking it for dinner.

Now the cook happened to live in the same house where the tin soldier had lived before. So when she opened up the fish and saw him lying there, as straight and stiff as ever, she was very pleased and excited. She took him up to the little boy's playroom and he was pleased and excited, too.

"My little tin soldier!" he cried.

It was a very happy moment. The boy was happy to have his toy safely home again and the soldier was happy to see the dancing lady, still standing on one foot, still staring at him from the doorway of the castle. But the Goblin's mischief was still at work. A naughty little boy was visiting in the playroom that afternoon and he took the tin soldier and threw him into the fire.

Even in the hot flames he stared at his little dancing lady and loved her. Just then the window flew open again and a breeze blew the dancing lady into the fire with the little tin soldier.

When the little boy looked among the ashes in the fireplace the next day, all he found was the little tin heart of the soldier and the tinsel rose of the dancing lady.

THE EMPEROR'S NEW CLOTHES

Adapted from Hans Christian Andersen

There was once an emperor who was very fond of beautiful clothes. He had dozens and dozens of suits hanging in his wardrobe, one just as elegant and costly as the other.

Other kings and emperors spent hours with their councilors and advisers, deciding important matters of state and discussing how best to rule their countries. But this ruler did not care about his people or his soldiers. Every day he would call the best artists and weavers and tailors of the land into his council chamber and have them design new clothes for him to wear.

Two rogues from a distant country heard about this emperor and they decided to play a trick on him and, at the same time, make a great deal of money for themselves. They sent word that they could make for the emperor a very remarkable suit of clothes. It would be made of the most exquisite material imaginable, which they themselves would weave. They would use only the finest silk, threads of pure gold, and precious jewels.

But this was the most remarkable thing about it: the material would be invisible to those people who were simple in the head and to those who were unworthy of the offices they held.

"Ah," thought the emperor when he received this message, "here is an opportunity for me to have the most magnificent suit of clothes ever worn by a monarch. And at the same time I can find out which of my ministers and councilors are simple in the head and which ones are worthy of the offices they hold."

So he ordered these tailors, who were really impostors, to come to his court. They were given a fine apartment in the palace and were told that no expense would be spared in the making of the emperor's new clothes.

Two large looms were built on which to weave the magic material. Silks and jewels and threads of gold were ordered from all over the world. These the two rogues put in a large sack they had brought with them. And then they pretended to weave the material on the two large looms. All day and far into the night they pretended to weave the precious threads back and forth, but there was really nothing on the loom and nothing in their hands as they worked.

The emperor was eager to know how the work was coming along, but he was afraid to go himself to inspect it. He knew, of course, that he was not simple in the head. And he knew that he alone was fit to be emperor of the land. But, for the first inspection, he thought it would be safest to send someone else. So his most trusted old minister was sent to the tailors' apartment to inspect the remarkable cloth.

He saw the two large looms standing in the center of the workroom, but it seemed to him that they were empty. He put on his spectacles and peered more closely, but still he could see nothing.

"Can it be possible," thought the old minister, "that I am simple in the head or not worthy of my high office? If that be the case," he added quickly, "no one must know."

"Ah, this is lovely cloth," he said out loud. "Truly magnificent. I will tell the emperor."

"Look more closely," said the rogues. "See the glorious colors. Feel the fine texture. Notice the threads of pure gold. Observe how it is studded with costly jewels."

"Beautiful," the old minister sighed. "Exquisite. The emperor will be most pleased."

The emperor was so pleased by the minister's report that the next day he decided he could wait no longer to inspect the remarkable cloth. He went himself to the tailors' apartment. He saw the two large looms standing in the center of the workroom, but it seemed to him that they were empty. He put on his spectacles and peered more closely.

"Can it be possible," he thought, "that I am more simple in the head than my own minister? Am I not fit to be emperor of my own land? If that be the case," he added quickly, "no one must know."

"Ah, that is indeed lovely cloth," he said out loud. "Truly magnificent. The most exquisite colors, the finest texture, the most lustrous jewels."

"Thank you, Your Highness," said the two impostors. "We want only to please Your Majesty."

"I am pleased. Greatly pleased," said His Highness, and he went back to his council chamber.

He told his councilors and advisers that the following week there would be a grand procession. The emperor would wear his new suit of clothes for the first time and every man, woman, and child must be there to see him.

The great day finally arrived. The two rogues came to the emperor's dressing chamber, pretending to carry the precious new suit and pretending to hold it up for the emperor to see.

All the courtiers were standing about, and none of them could see a thing. Each of them was afraid, however, that he would be called simple in the head or unworthy of his office.

So all of them exclaimed loudly, "Ah, what a beautiful suit. Truly magnificent. Worthy of our noble emperor. A great work of art."

The emperor was greatly pleased. He took off the suit he was wearing and pretended to put on the new suit of the magic material. Then, followed by all his courtiers, he started the grand procession.

They went out the front gate of the palace and down the main street of the city. On both sides of the street were crowds and crowds of people, for every man, woman, and child had come to see the emperor's new clothes.

"Oh, how beautiful!" exclaimed some.

"Exquisite! Magnificent!" cried others.

Each person praised the suit as loudly as he could. For each person was afraid to be thought a simpleton if it was known that he saw nothing at all.

Finally a little child saw the emperor coming down the street and he called out loudly, "But the emperor has no clothes on!"

A hush fell on the crowd. And then the child's father said, "Listen to the voice of innocence. The emperor has no clothes on."

"The emperor has no clothes on!" shouted the crowd.

And the emperor knew that it was true. But he was ashamed that the impostors had fooled him, so he pretended that the people were wrong. And he kept on marching down the street, acting as if he were wearing the wonderful suit.

THE APPLE OF CONTENTMENT

by Howard Pyle

There was a woman once, and she had three daughters. The first daughter squinted with both eyes, yet the woman loved her as she loved salt, for she herself squinted with both eyes.

The second daughter had one shoulder higher than the other, and eyebrows as black as soot in the chimney, yet the woman loved her as well as she loved the other, for she herself had black eyebrows and one shoulder higher than the other.

The youngest daughter was as pretty as a ripe apple, and had hair as fine as silk and the color of pure gold, but the woman loved her not at all, for, as I have said, she herself was neither pretty nor had she hair of the color of pure gold. Why all this was so, even Hans Pfifendrummel cannot tell, though he has read many books and one over.

The first sister and the second sister dressed in their Sunday clothes every day, and sat in the sun doing nothing, just as though they had been born ladies, both of them.

As for Christine—that was the name of the youngest girl—as for Christine, she dressed in nothing but rags, and had to drive the geese to the hills in the morning and home again in the evening, so that they might feed on the young grass all day and grow fat.

The first sister and the second sister had white bread (and butter besides) and as much fresh milk as they could drink; but Christine had to eat cheese parings and bread crusts, and had hardly enough of them to keep Goodman Hunger from whispering in her ear.

This was how the churn clacked in that house!

One morning Christine started off to the hills with her flock of geese, and in her hands she carried her knitting, at which she worked to save time. So she went along the dusty road until, by-and-by, she came to a place where a bridge crossed the brook, and what should she see there but a little red cap, with a silver bell at the point of it, hanging from the alder branch. It was such a nice, pretty little red cap that Christine thought she would take it home with her, for she had never seen the like of it before.

So she put it in her pocket, and then off she went with her geese again. But she had hardly gone a step when she heard a voice calling her, "Christine! Christine!"

She looked, and what should she see but a queer little gray man, with a great head as big as a cabbage and little legs as thin as young radishes.

"What do you want?" said Christine, when the little man had come to where she was.

Oh, the little man only wanted his cap again, for without it he could not go back home into the hill—that was where he belonged.

But how did the cap come to be hanging from the bush? Yes, Christine would like to know that before she gave it back again.

Well, the little hill-man was fishing by the brook over yonder when a puff of wind blew his cap into the water, and he just hung it up to dry. That was all that there was about it; and now would Christine please give it to him?

Christine did not know how about that; perhaps she would and perhaps she would not. It was a nice, pretty little cap. What would the little underground man give her for it?

Oh, the little man would give her five dollars for it, and gladly.

No; five dollars was not enough for such a pretty little cap—see, there was a silver bell hanging to it too.

Well, the little man did not want to be hard at a bargain; he would give her a hundred dollars for it.

No; Christine did not care for money. What else would he give for this nice, dear little cap?

"See, Christine," said the little man, "I will give you this for the cap." And he showed her something in his hand that looked just like a bean, only it was as black as a lump of coal.

"Yes, but what is that?" said Christine.

"That," said the little man, "is a seed from the apple of contentment. Plant it, and from it will grow a tree, and from the tree an apple. Everybody in the world that sees the apple will long for it, but nobody in the world can pluck it but you. It will always be meat and drink to you when you are hungry, and warm clothes to your back when you are cold. Moreover, as soon as you pluck it from the tree, another as good will grow in its place. Now, will you give me my hat?"

Oh yes; Christine would give the little man his cap for such a seed as that, and gladly enough. So the little man gave Christine the seed, and Christine gave the little man his cap again. He put the cap on his head, and—puff!—away he was gone, as suddenly as the light of a candle when you blow it out.

So Christine took the seed home with her, and planted it before the window of her room. The next morning when she looked
out of the window she beheld a beautiful tree, and on the tree
hung an apple that shone in the sun as though it were pure gold.
She went to the tree and plucked the apple as easily as though it
were a gooseberry, and as soon as she had plucked it another as
good grew in its place. Being hungry she ate it, and thought that
she had never eaten anything as good, for it tasted like pancake
with honey and milk.

By-and-by the oldest sister came out of the house and looked
around, but when she saw the beautiful tree with the golden
apple hanging from it you can guess how she stared.

Presently she began to long and long for the apple as she had
never longed for anything in her life. "I will just pluck it," said
she, "and no one will be the wiser for it." But that was easier
said than done. She reached and reached, but she might as well
have reached for the moon. She climbed and climbed, but she
might as well have climbed for the sun—for either one would
have been as easy to get as that which she wanted. At last she
had to give up trying for it, and her temper was none the sweeter
for that, you may be sure.

After a while came the second sister, and when she saw the
golden apple she wanted it just as much as the first had done.
But to want and to get are very different things, as she soon
found, for she was no more able to get it than the other had been.

Last of all came the mother, and she also tried to pluck the
apple. But it was no use. She had no more luck of her trying than
her daughters. All that the three could do was to stand under the
tree and look at the apple, and wish for it and wish for it.

They are not the only ones who have done the like, with the
apple of contentment hanging just above them.

As for Christine, she had nothing to do but to pluck an apple
whenever she wanted it. Was she hungry? There was the apple
hanging in the tree for her. Was she thirsty? There was the apple.
Cold? there was the apple. So you see, she was the happiest girl

betwixt all the seven hills that stand at the ends of the earth; for nobody in the world can have more than contentment, and that was what the apple brought her.

One day a King came riding along the road, and all of his people with him. He looked up and saw the apple hanging in the tree, and a great desire came upon him to have a taste of it. So he called one of the servants to him, and told him to go and ask whether it could be bought for a potful of gold.

So the servant went to the house, and knocked on the door— *rap! tap! tap!*

"What do you want?" asked the mother of the three sisters, coming to the door.

Oh, nothing much; only a King was out there in the road, and wanted to know if she would sell the apple yonder for a potful of gold.

Yes, the woman would do that. Just pay her the pot of gold and he might go and pluck it and welcome.

So the servant gave her the pot of gold, and then he tried to pluck the apple. First he reached for it, and then he climbed for it, and then he shook the limb.

But it was no use for him to try; he could no more get it—well —than I could if I had been in his place.

At last the servant had to go back to the King. The apple was there, he said, and the woman had sold it, but try and try as he would he could no more get it than he could get the little stars in the sky.

Then the King told the steward to go and get it for him; but the steward, though he was a tall man and a strong man, could no more pluck the apple than the servant.

So he had to go back to the King with an empty fist. No; he could not gather it, either.

Then the King himself went. He knew that he could pluck it— of course he could! Well, he tried and tried; but nothing came of his trying, and he had to ride away at last without having had so much as a smell of the apple.

After the King came home, he talked and dreamed and thought of nothing but the apple; for the more he could not get it the more he wanted it—that is the way we are made in this world. At last he grew melancholy and sick for want of that which he could not get. Then he sent for one who was so wise that he had more in his head than ten men together. This wise man told him that the only one who could pluck the fruit of contentment for him was the one to whom the tree belonged. This was one of the daughters of the woman who had sold the apple to him for the pot of gold.

When the King heard this he was very glad. He had his horse saddled, and he and his court rode away, and so came at last to the cottage where Christine lived. There they found the mother and the elder sisters, for Christine was away on the hills with her geese.

The King took off his hat and made a fine bow.

The wise man at home had told him this and that. Now to which one of her daughters did the apple-tree belong? asked the King.

"Oh, it is my oldest daughter who owns the tree," said the woman.

So, good! Then if the oldest daughter would pluck the apple for him he would take her home and marry her and make a queen of her. Only let her get it for him without delay.

Prut! that would never do. What! was the girl to climb the apple-tree before the King and all of the court? No! no! Let the King go home, and she would bring the apple to him all in good time; that was what the woman told him.

Well, the King would do that, only let her make haste, for he wanted it very much indeed.

As soon as the King had gone, the woman and her daughters sent to the hills for the goose-girl. They told her that the King wanted the apple yonder, and that she must pluck it for her sister to take to him. If she did not do as they said they would throw her into the well. So Christine had to pluck the fruit; and as soon as she had done so the oldest sister wrapped it up in a napkin and set off with it to the King's house, as pleased as pleased could be. *Rap! tap! tap!* she knocked at the door. Had she brought the apple for the King?

Oh yes, she had brought it. Here it was, all wrapped up in a fine napkin.

After that they did not let her stand outside the door till her toes were cold, I can tell you. As soon as she had come to the King she opened her napkin. Believe me or not as you please, there was nothing in the napkin but a hard round stone!

When the King saw only a stone he was so angry that he stamped like a rabbit and told them to put the girl out of the house. So they did, and she went home with a flea in her ear, I can tell you.

Then the King sent his steward to the house where Christine and her sisters lived.

He told the woman that he had come to find whether she had any other daughters.

Yes; the woman had another daughter, and, to tell the truth, it was she who owned the tree. Just let the steward go home again and the girl would fetch the apple in a little while.

As soon as the steward had gone, they sent to the hills for Christine again. Look! she must pluck the apple for the second sister to take to the King. If she did not do that they would throw her into the well.

So Christine had to pluck the apple and give it to the second sister, who wrapped it up in a napkin and set off for the King's house. But she fared no better than the other, for when she opened the napkin, there was nothing in it but a lump of mud. So they packed her home again with her apron to her eyes.

After a while the King's steward came to the house again. Had the woman no other daughter than these two?

Well, yes, there was one, but she was a poor ragged thing, of no account, and fit for nothing in the world but to tend the geese.

Where was she?

Oh, she was up on the hills now tending her flock.

But could the steward see her?

Yes, he might see her, but she was nothing but a poor simpleton.

That was all very good, but the steward would like to see her, for that was what the King had sent him there for.

So there was nothing to do but to send to the hills for Christine.

After a while she came, and the steward asked her if she could pluck the apple yonder for the King.

Yes; Christine could do that easily enough. So she reached and picked it as though it had been nothing but a gooseberry on the bush. Then the steward took off his hat and made her a low bow in spite of her ragged dress, for he saw that she was the one for whom they had been looking all this time.

So Christine slipped the golden apple into her pocket, and then she and the steward set off to the King's house together.

When they had come there everybody began to titter and laugh behind the palms of their hands to see what a poor ragged goose-girl the steward had brought home with him.

"Have you brought the apple?" said the King, as soon as Christine had come before him.

Yes; here it was. And Christine thrust her hand into her pocket and brought it forth. Then the King took a great bite of it, and as soon as he had done so he looked at Christine and thought that he had never seen such a pretty girl. As for her rags, he minded them no more than one minds the spots on a cherry; that was because he had eaten of the apple of contentment.

And were they married? Of course they were! and a grand wedding it was, I can tell you. It is a pity that you were not there; but though you were not, Christine's mother and sisters were, and, what is more, they danced with the others, though I believe they would rather have danced upon pins and needles.

"Never mind," said they. "We still have the apple of contentment at home, though we cannot taste of it." But no; they had nothing of the kind. The next morning it stood before the young Queen Christine's window, just as it had at her old home, for it belonged to her and to no one else in all the world. That was lucky for the King, for he needed a taste of it now and then as much as anybody else, and no one could pluck it for him but Christine.

Now, that is all of this story. What does it mean?
Can you not see?
Prut! Rub your spectacles and look again!

Folk Tales from Many Lands

In every country in the world there are stories that have been told for so many years that nobody knows who first made them up. Each person who hears one of these stories tells it to another. And probably each person who tells it changes it a little or adds some things to it. These stories are called "folk tales" because they belong to the "folk"—to all the people of a country.

They might also be called "folk tales" for another reason. They all tell you something about what folks—or people —are like. One story tells you that people often wish for so many things that they don't know what they really want to do with them when they have a chance to get the things they ask for. Another story tells you about people who brag and pretend that they are better or stronger than everyone else. Still another tells you that men and women and boys and girls can be very brave when there is something important for them to do.

These stories come from all over the world. I think each one will tell you something about its own land—what the country looks like, how the people live, and something about their customs. But I think you will find that deep down inside people are very much the same whether they live in Holland or Russia, India or America.

WHY THE BABY SAYS "GOO"

A TALE OF THE PENOBSCOT INDIANS

by Gilbert L. Wilson

In a village near the mountains lived an Indian chief. He was a brave man and had fought in many battles. No one in the tribe had slain more enemies than he.

Strange folk were then in the land. Fierce ice giants came out of the North and carried away women and children. Wicked witches dwelt in caves, and in the mountains lived the MIK-UMWESS, or magic little people.

But the chief feared none of them. He fought the ice giants and made them go back to their home in the North. Some of the witches he killed; others he drove from the land.

Everybody loved the chief. He was so brave and good that the villagers thought there was no one like him anywhere.

But when he had driven out all the giants the chief grew vain. He began to think himself the greatest warrior in the world.

"I can conquer anyone," he boasted.

Now it happened that a wise old woman lived in the village. When she heard what the great chief boasted, she smiled.

"Our chief *is* wonderful; but there is one who is mightier than he," she said.

The villagers told the chief what the wise woman had said. He came and visited her in her wigwam.

"Grandmother, who is this wonderful one?" he asked.

"His name is Wasis," answered the wise woman.

"And where is he, Grandmother?" asked the chief.

"He is there," said the wise woman; and she pointed to a place in the wigwam.

The chief looked—and who do you think Wasis was? He was

a plump little Indian Baby. In the middle of the floor he sat, crowing to himself and sucking a piece of maple sugar. He looked very sweet and contented.

Now the chief had no wife, and knew nothing about babies; but he thought, like all vain people, that he knew everything. He thought, of course, that the little Baby would obey him; so he smiled and said to little Wasis:

"Baby, come to me!"

But the Baby smiled and went on sucking his maple sugar.

The chief was surprised. The villagers always did whatever he bade them. He could not understand why the little Baby did not obey him; but he smiled and said again to little Wasis:

"*Baby, come to me!*"

The little Baby smiled back and sucked his maple sugar as before.

The chief was astonished. No one had ever dared disobey him before. He grew angry. He frowned at little Wasis and roared out:

"BABY, COME TO ME!"

But little Wasis opened his mouth and burst out crying and screaming. The chief had never heard such awful sounds. Even the ice giants did not scream so terribly.

The chief was more and more astonished. He could not think why such a little Baby would not obey him.

"Wonderful!" he said. "All other men fear me; but this little Baby shouts back war cries. Perhaps I can overcome him with my magic."

He took out his medicine bag and shook it at the little Baby. He danced magic dances. He sang wonderful songs.

Little Wasis smiled and watched the chief with big round eyes. He thought it all very funny. And all the time he sucked his maple sugar.

The chief danced until he was tired out; sweat ran down his face; red paint oozed over his cheeks and neck; the feathers in his scalp lock had fallen down.

At last he sat down. He was too tired to dance any longer.

"Did I not tell you that Wasis is mightier than you?" said the wise old woman. "No one is mightier than the Baby. He always rules the wigwam. Everybody loves him and obeys him."

"It is even so," sighed the chief, as he went out of the wigwam.

But as he went he could hear little Wasis talking to himself on the floor.

"Goo, goo, goo!" he crowed, as he sucked his maple sugar.

Now, when you hear the Baby saying "Goo, goo, goo," you will know what it means. It is his war cry. He is happy because he remembers the time when he frightened the chief in the wigwam of the wise old woman.

THE WONDERFUL TAR-BABY STORY

After Joel Chandler Harris

The Little Boy asked Uncle Remus, "Didn't Brother Fox ever catch Brother Rabbit?" And Uncle Remus told him:

One day Brother Fox got some tar and mixed it with turpentine and rigged up a contraption that he called a Tar-Baby. Then he stuck this here Tar-Baby in the middle of the big road and hid in the bushes to see what would happen. And he didn't have to wait long, neither. For byenby here comes Brother Rabbit, apacing down the road—lippity-clippity, clippity-lippity—just as saucy as a jay-bird. Brother Fox, he just lay low. Brother Rabbit comes prancing along till he spied the Tar-Baby. Then he fetched up on his hind legs very much astonished. The Tar-Baby just sat there, and Brother Fox, he lay low.

"'Morning!" says Brother Rabbit. "Nice weather this morning," says he.

Tar-Baby says nothing. And Brother Fox, he lay low.

"How do your symptoms seem to exhibit this morning?" asks Brother Rabbit.

Brother Fox, he winks his eye slowly and lays low; and Tar-Baby she says nothing at all.

"How you comin', then? Are you deaf?" says Brother Rabbit. "Because if you are, I can holler louder," says he.

Tar-Baby stays still and Brother Fox just lay low.

"You're stuck up, that's what you are," says Brother Rabbit. "And I'm going to ignore you, that's what I'm going to do," says he.

Brother Fox, he sort of chuckled in his stomach, but Tar-Baby said nothing.

"I'm going to teach you how to talk to respectable folks, if it's the last thing I do," says Brother Rabbit. "If you don't take off your hat and tell me Howdy, I'm going to bust you wide open," says he.

Tar-Baby stays still and Brother Fox, he lays low.

Brother Rabbit keeps on asking Tar-Baby, and Tar-Baby keeps on saying nothing until presently Brother Rabbit draws back with his fist, and Blip! he took her on the side of her head. That's where Brother Rabbit broke his molasses jug! His fist just got stuck and he couldn't pull it loose. The tar just held him tight. But the Tar-Baby stays still and Brother Fox, he lays low.

"If you don't let me loose," says Brother Rabbit, "I'll knock you again," says he. And with that he fetched her a wipe with the other hand, and *that* stuck. Tar-Baby, she ain't saying nothing, and Brother Fox, he lays low.

"Turn me loose," Brother Rabbit says, "before I kick the natural stuffing out of you!" says he. But the Tar-Baby ain't saying nothing. She just held on, and then Brother Rabbit loses the use of his feet in the same way.

Then Brother Rabbit squealed out that if Tar-Baby didn't turn him loose he would butt her flat in the chest. And then he butted and his head got stuck.

Then Brother Fox sauntered out of his hiding, looking just as innocent as one of your mother's mocking-birds.

"Howdy, Brother Rabbit," says he. "You look sort of stuck up this morning," says he. And then he rolled on the ground and laughed and laughed till he couldn't laugh any more. "I expect you'll take dinner with me this time, Brother Rabbit. I laid in some sweet calamus root that you like so much, and I shan't take any excuse," says Brother Fox.

Here Uncle Remus drew a large yam root out of the ashes.

"Did the fox eat the rabbit?" asked the Little Boy.

"That's as far as the story goes," replied Uncle Remus. "He

might have, and then again he mightn't. Some say that Judge Bear came along just then and loosed them. But some say he didn't."

THE COYOTE AND THE FOX
A TALE OF THE NORTH AMERICAN INDIANS

by Elizabeth Willis DeHuff

O-way-way-ham-by-yoh, which means long time ago, a fox felt very hungry, so he went down into prairie-dog town and caught a fine fat prairie dog. Then he built a fire of dry rabbit brush. When the brush had all burned up and left a pile of coals, Mr. Fox took his prairie dog and covered him all up with the hot ashes. That was the way he always roasted meat for his dinner. It required some time for the prairie dog to roast, so Mr. Fox lay down and went to sleep.

Very soon Mr. Coyote came along. Sniff! Sniff! he could smell meat roasting and it smelt very delicious. He saw Mr. Fox fast asleep; so he slipped quietly over to the pile of ashes, stuck his paw in and pulled out the prairie dog. He ran behind a bush and ate all of the meat off, but he left the bones. Then he took a bone and greased the fox's mouth all around with a greasy end of it. After that he put the bones back under the hot ashes and ran away.

When Mr. Fox awoke, he could smell prairie dog grease. He licked his tongue out and tasted grease all around his mouth. "Surely I have not eaten the prairie dog while I was asleep. No, I feel too hungry; but where did this grease come from on my mouth, if I did not eat him?" Mr. Fox was very much puzzled. He went over to the ashes and caught hold of a prairie dog foot and pulled. Out came a long leg bone without any meat on it. "This is funny," thought he.

Just then he spied some tracks in the sand. "Oho!" said he. "Now I understand it all. Coyote-man has played a trick on me and eaten my prairie dog. I'll catch him and kill him for this."

So Mr. Fox trotted off following the coyote tracks. He found the coyote by a high cliff. Mr. Coyote saw Mr. Fox coming and he knew he was angry. He did not have time to run away, so he just leaned against the cliff and called, "Oh, Fox-man, come here quick and help me! Look up there, this cliff is falling! It will kill us both!" Mr. Fox looked up. The clouds were passing over the cliff and made the cliff look as if it were really falling. Mr. Fox jumped quickly over by Mr. Coyote and leaned against the cliff just as hard as he could to hold it up. As soon as Mr. Fox leaned on the cliff, Mr. Coyote jumped away. He made a big jump, just as if the cliff might really fall on him.

"Hold the cliff up, Fox-man, while I go to get a stick to prop it with."

Then Mr. Coyote ran away and left Mr. Fox leaning hard against the cliff.

Mr. Fox stayed there all day waiting for Mr. Coyote to come with the stick. Late that evening he looked up and there were no clouds passing, so he could see that the cliff was not falling. He knew that the coyote had played another trick on him, so he was angrier than ever.

Again he followed the coyote tracks and found the coyote down by the river.

When Mr. Coyote saw Mr. Fox coming, he called:

"Oh, Fox-man, come quick and see what I have for you. I found a cheese and I saved half of it for you; but it has fallen into the river. Look!"

And Mr. Fox looked down into the water. There was the reflection of the half-moon in the water. It looked just like the half of a round cheese and Mr. Fox's mouth began to water for a taste of it. He was very hungry.

"I wonder how I can get that cheese!" he said.

"I'll tell you how. Let me tie the end of this rope"—for Mr. Coyote had a rope all ready—"around your tail and tie the other end to this big stone. Then you can jump into the river and get the cheese. When you have got hold of it, call me and I will pull you out."

Mr. Fox thought that was a good scheme, so he let Mr. Coyote tie the rope around his tail and around the stone. Then Mr. Fox jumped into the river with a big splash.

As soon as he did, Mr. Coyote threw the stone in after him, and if the rope had not slipped off of Mr. Fox's tail when it got wet, that would have been the end of poor old Mr. Fox.

THE FOOLISH, TIMID LITTLE HARE
AN EAST INDIAN TALE

There was once a foolish, timid little Hare who was afraid of everything. She was sure that someday something terrible would happen to her. Then one day, when she was sleeping under a palm tree, some Monkeys who were playing in the tree above her dropped a coconut onto the ground. The coconut made a loud noise as it fell and woke the little Hare up.

"Oh, dear me!" cried the Hare as she heard the noise. "The earth is cracking and it will swallow me up!"

Without looking behind her, she started running away as fast as she possibly could. Presently she met another Hare, who said to her, "Where are you running? And what is your hurry?"

"The earth is cracking," replied the foolish, timid little Hare. "I am running away so it can't swallow me up."

"Oh, dear me!" cried the other Hare. "I must run away, too!" And off they ran together as fast as they possibly could.

Soon they met another Hare. They told him that the earth was cracking and off they ran together. They met another Hare and still another until, at last, there were a hundred thousand Hares all running away as fast as they possibly could.

By and by the hundred thousand Hares met a Deer.

"Where are you running?" asked the Deer. "And what is your hurry?"

"The earth is cracking!" replied the Hares. "We are running away so it can't swallow us up."

"Oh, dear me!" cried the Deer. "I must run away, too!" And she ran off beside the Hares as fast as she possibly could.

Presently they met a Tiger.

"Where are you running?" asked the Tiger. "And what is your hurry?"

"The earth is cracking!" they called to him. "We are running away so it can't swallow us up."

"Oh, dear me!" growled the Tiger. "I must run away, too!" And off he ran, beside the others, as fast as he possibly could.

After a while they met an Elephant.

"Where are you running?" asked the Elephant. "And what is your hurry?"

"The earth is cracking!" the animals answered. "We are running away so it can't swallow us up."

"Oh, dear me!" the Elephant bellowed. "I must run away, too!" And off he ran beside the others, as fast as he possibly could.

At last the Lion, the King of the Animals, saw them all running through the woods. He stood in front of them and ordered them to stop.

"Where are you running?" asked the Lion. "And what is your hurry?"

"Oh, King, the earth is cracking!" answered the animals. "We are running away so it can't swallow us up."

"The earth is cracking?" asked the Lion. "Who saw it crack?"

"Not I!" said the Elephant. "Ask the Tiger, for he told me."

"Did you see the earth crack?" the Lion asked the Tiger.

"Not I!" said the Tiger. "Ask the Deer, for she told me."

"Did you see the earth crack?" the Lion asked the Deer.

"Not I!" said the Deer. "Ask the Hares, for they told me."

"Did you see the earth crack?" the Lion asked the Hares.

"Not I! Not I!" cried the hundred thousand Hares. And they pointed to the one foolish, timid little Hare. "Ask her, for she told us."

"Did you see the earth crack, little Hare?" asked the Lion.

"Yes," said the little Hare. "I was sleeping under the palm tree and a loud cracking noise woke me up. So, of course, I knew that the earth was cracking and that it wanted to swallow me up. So I ran away as fast as I could."

"Well," said the Lion, "let us go to the palm tree where you were sleeping. Let us see what made the noise."

"Oh no, no!" cried the foolish, timid little Hare. "The earth is cracking and I am afraid. I will not go there!"

"I will carry you on my back," said the Lion. "And I will take care of you. Nothing can hurt you."

So finally the little Hare got up on the Lion's back and together they went to the palm tree. Just as they got there, the Monkeys threw down another coconut and there was another loud cracking noise.

This time the Hare saw that the earth was not cracking, that it was only the noise of the coconut falling on the ground.

So the Lion and the Hare went back to all the other animals and the Hare said to them, "The earth is not cracking! And we don't have to run away! There is nothing to be afraid of at all!"

THE THREE WISHES
A SWEDISH TALE

There was once a very poor man who lived with his wife in a humble little cottage. Every day he went into the forest to chop wood. One day when he was in the forest he said to himself: "Oh, dear, I am so unhappy! I am poor, and I have to work so hard all day long. My wife is hungry and I am hungry, too. Oh, I am very unhappy indeed!"

At that moment a beautiful fairy appeared before him. She said to him, "My poor man, I heard everything that you just said. I am very sorry for you and would like to help you. Ask whatever you like, and your first three wishes shall be granted."

Then just as suddenly as she had come the fairy disappeared.

The poor man felt very happy now, and he said, "I shall go home and I shall tell my wife how the fairy has granted me three wishes."

He ran back to his cottage and called to his wife:

"Wife, Wife, I am very fortunate. I saw a fairy in the forest, and she said I could have three wishes. 'Ask for anything you like,' the fairy said, 'and your wish shall be granted!' Oh, Wife, I am so happy."

"I am happy, too," said the woman. "Come, let us go into the house, my dear, and let us decide what our wishes shall be."

The man went into the little cottage and sat down at the table. "I am hungry, Wife," he said. "I would like some dinner. While we eat we can talk about the fairy and the three wishes."

The poor man and his wife sat down at the table and started to eat their dinner, and to talk about the good fairy's promise.

"We can ask for great riches if we want to," said the man.

"Yes," the wife agreed, "we can ask for a beautiful house."

"We can even ask for a whole empire if we want to," said the man.

And his wife replied: "Oh yes, we can ask for pearls and diamonds by the hundred."

"We can ask for a big family," the man added; "five boys and five girls."

"Oh, I would prefer six boys and four girls," insisted the wife.

The man and the woman went on talking like that, but they couldn't decide what three wishes would be the most sensible of all.

The man ate his soup in silence and looked at the dry bread on his plate. "Oh, I wish I had a great big sausage for dinner!" he said.

At that very instant a great big sausage fell onto the table. Naturally, the man was very surprised to see the sausage and so was his wife.

"Oh, Husband," the wife said, "you have been very foolish. You asked for a silly old sausage and so one of the wishes has been granted. Now there are only two wishes left."

"Yes," said the man, "I have been very foolish. But we still have two wishes. We can ask for great riches and an empire."

"Yes," his wife agreed, "we can still ask for riches and an empire, but we can't ask for ten children. And it's your fault for being so foolish. It's your fault for demanding a sausage. You would rather have a sausage than a big family."

The poor woman went on talking like that, complaining, and saying over and over again, "It's all your fault for being so foolish!"

Finally the man lost his patience and said: "I am tired of your complaining! I wish that the sausage were hanging from the end of your nose!"

The next second the sausage was hanging from the end of his wife's nose. Naturally, the poor woman was greatly surprised, and so was her husband.

The woman started to complain again, more loudly than before. "Oh, my husband," she said, "you have been very, very foolish! First you asked for a sausage and then you wished that the sausage were hanging from the end of my nose. That makes two wishes. Two foolish wishes! And we only have one left!"

"Yes," the man agreed; "but we can still ask for great riches."

"What good are riches," the woman complained, "if I have a sausage hanging from the end of my nose? Why, I look ridiculous! And it's all your fault!"

The poor woman started to cry, and the poor man said: "Oh, I wish that sausage weren't here at all!"

Instantly the sausage disappeared, and the man and the woman were right back where they started, as poor as ever. They both complained, but it didn't do them any good, for they had used up their wishes.

The three wishes had been granted and still they had no riches, no empire, no pearls and diamonds, no little boys and no little girls.

And they didn't even have any sausage for dinner!

THE WHITE HARE OF INABI
A TALE OF JAPAN

by Frances Jenkins Olcott

Once upon a time there were eighty-one brothers who were Princes. Eighty of the brothers were jealous of one another, and were always quarreling. But the youngest was good and gentle and did not like their bad ways.

Now each of the quarrelsome brothers wished to marry the Princess of Yakami in Inabi. So they decided to visit her, and persuade her to choose one of them for a husband.

After quarreling very hard, they set out, taking their youngest brother to carry their bag. The eighty brothers went on ahead, for the youngest could not travel fast because the bag was so heavy.

By and by the eighty brothers came to the seashore, and on the sand they saw a little white Hare with most of its fur torn off. The brothers laughed very hard at the poor little thing.

"If you wish your fur to grow again," they cried, "go bathe in the sea; and after you have done so, run to and fro on the top of yonder high hill and let the hot Wind blow on you!" And they laughed again and went on.

The little Hare limped down to the sea, and jumped into the water and bathed. Then it limped up the hill and lay down to let the hot Wind blow on it. The hot Wind blew and blew, and the poor Hare's skin, all wet with salt water, dried, cracked, and split open. And there the little creature lay, moaning with pain, when the gentle youngest brother drew near.

"Where is your fur? Why are you suffering so?" asked the youngest brother.

"Please wait a minute, and I'll tell you," said the Hare, weeping. "I was in the Island of Oki, and wished to cross to this place, so I said to the Crocodiles: 'I want to know how many Crocodiles are in the sea. Arrange yourselves in a row, and let me count you.'

"Then the Crocodiles formed a long line with their horny bodies from the Island of Oki to this beach. I hastened across, leaping from back to back; and when I reached the last Crocodile, I cried out: 'You silly beasts! As if I cared how many Crocodiles are in the sea! I only wished to use you for a bridge!' And immediately that last Crocodile raised its head, and tore off my fur with its sharp teeth."

"Well! Well!" said the youngest brother. "It served you right, for you lied to them. But is this all of your story?"

"No," said the Hare. "Your eighty brothers passed by, and laughed. They told me to bathe in the sea, and to let the hot Wind blow upon me, and I did. My skin dried, and cracked, and split open."

"Ah, my poor little Hare!" said the youngest brother pityingly. "Bathe in fresh water, and roll in the pollen of the sedges, and your fur will come again."

So the little Hare limped down to the river, and bathed in fresh water. Then it rolled in the pollen of the sedges; and immediately its skin was healed, and its fur came again, white and handsome.

Then the grateful Hare ran after the youngest brother, crying: "Your eighty quarreling, wicked brothers shall never get the Princess. It is you she will choose, and you will reign over Inabi."

And so it was. For the eighty brothers quarreled so hard that the Princess turned them out of her kingdom. But she chose the gentle youngest brother; and they were married and ruled happily over Inabi.

THE GIRL WHO COULD THINK

A CHINESE TALE

Lotus-Blossom and Moon-Flower were two young girls who lived long ago in the country of China. Now Lotus-Blossom and Moon-Flower were very good friends and they loved to go to parties.

Sometimes their parents would worry about them. "Oh, dear," the mother of Lotus-Blossom would say, "our daughters never think of anything but parties and merrymaking and pretty clothes."

"I know," the mother of Moon-Flower would agree; "but some day they will get married and settle down and think of more important things."

When Lotus-Blossom and Moon-Flower grew up they married two brothers who lived in a village some distance away. After the wedding celebrations were over, the two young men brought their wives home to live with their mother.

Lotus-Blossom and Moon-Flower were very happy in their new home. They loved their young husbands and they loved their old mother-in-law and they were glad that they could live together in the same house.

But every little while they wanted to go back to their old village and go to parties and make merry with their old friends. They were forever coming to their mother-in-law and saying: "Honored lady, we pray you, let us go and pay a visit to the village of our childhood."

Now their mother-in-law was very fond of Lotus-Blossom and Moon-Flower. Her two daughters-in-law were good and kind and obedient. They would bring her tea whenever she asked them to, and three times a day they would serve her rice on little red lacquer tables. But she didn't like their going away every little while just for some parties and merrymaking. She thought they should stay and take care of their husbands and think of more important things.

So one day she said to herself, "I will put a stop to this once and for all." The very next time that Lotus-Blossom and Moon-Flower asked to go home, the mother-in-law replied: "Yes, my daughters, go. Go and enjoy yourselves. Go as soon as you like. But remember this. You must bring me two gifts when you return, the only two things that I want, or else you shall not return to your husbands and your home."

"We will bring you anything you like!" the two daughters-in-law replied. "Tell us what presents you want and we shall bring them."

"Very well," said the mother-in-law, "listen carefully. You, Lotus-Blossom, must bring me some fire wrapped in paper. And you, Moon-Flower, must bring me the wind in a paper."

The two girls were so anxious to be gone that they did not listen carefully. Without thinking they replied, "Oh yes, honored lady, we will do just as you say! We will bring you anything you want!"

They said good-by to their mother-in-law and they said good-by to their husbands. Then off they went down the road toward the village of their childhood, chatting merrily all the way.

All of a sudden Lotus-Blossom remembered what her mother-in-law had asked her to bring: some fire wrapped in paper. Surely that was impossible! And if she did not bring this present to her mother-in-law, Lotus-Blossom could never see her husband again. She sat down by the roadside and started to cry as if her heart would break.

Then it came over Moon-Flower, too, that she would never see her husband again. For surely it was impossible to bring the wind in a paper! So she sat beside her sister-in-law by the roadside, and the two girls cried and cried as if their hearts would break.

Just then a young girl working in a near-by rice field saw them. She came over to Lotus-Blossom and Moon-Flower and said to them, "Crying will not make things better. Tell me your trouble and perhaps I can help you."

They told her as best they could of all that had happened and the girl said to them, "Surely you have been foolish, but perhaps we can still find a way out. Let us think."

Now Lotus-Blossom and Moon-Flower had never even dreamed of thinking. All their lives they had let other people think for them. But if this girl could think, they said to themselves, why, so could they! So they went off with her, across the fields, to her father's house.

The three sat down on the front porch and tried to think. But the more they thought, the sadder Lotus-Blossom and Moon-Flower became, for they could not think of any way to carry fire or wind in a paper.

Suddenly their new friend sprang to her feet and ran into her father's house. In a few moments she came back carrying a lantern in her hand. It was made entirely of paper and inside the lantern a candle was burning brightly.

"Look!" she said. "Here is fire wrapped in paper."

"Oh, how wonderful!" Lotus-Blossom exclaimed. "Just the present for me to bring back to my mother-in-law."

But poor Moon-Flower was as unhappy as ever. It still seemed impossible that a way could be found to bring back the wind in a paper. All of a sudden their new friend sprang to her feet again and ran into her father's house. This time she brought back a paper fan. She waved it back and forth in front of Moon-Flower and Moon-Flower felt the wind in her face.

"See!" the girl said. "Wind in a paper!"

"Oh, how wonderful!" Moon-Flower exclaimed. "Just the present for my mother-in-law. Now I can return home, too!"

The two girls thanked their new friend again and again and then started back up the road toward home. When their mother-in-law saw the two girls coming up the road she went to the door to meet them.

"What is this?" she asked sternly. "Are these two girls who do not obey their mother-in-law?"

"No indeed, honored lady!" the two girls cried. "We have brought you the presents for which you asked."

Lotus-Blossom held up the lantern for her mother-in-law to see and Moon-Flower waved the fan back and forth, sending the wind against her face.

"Ah," the honored lady cried. "I see someone has done some thinking. Welcome home, my daughters. Let us have a cup of tea, with the lantern lighting the table and the paper fan to cool us."

TOO HEAVY
A TALE FROM PERSIA

by Alice Greer Kelsey

Once the Mullah rode his little donkey to the vegetable bazaar. His own garden did not grow every kind of vegetable that
Fatima wanted for her stew. The market was colorful with its
piles of purple eggplant, green cabbages, and yellow melons. It
was fun bargaining with the farmers who were his good friends.
Before he knew it, the Mullah had bought more than Fatima had
ordered. The vegetables stretched the bag he had brought. He
loaded the heavy beets and melons in the bottom, the medium-
weight eggplant and cabbage in the middle, and the tender herbs
on top. He stooped under the weight of the bag as he dragged it
toward his sleepy donkey. For a minute he stood beside the donkey, looking at her and thinking.

She braced her small feet, expecting him to load the saddlebags
as usual. Instead he whispered into her long twitching ears, "How
tiny you are!" Then he climbed on the donkey's back, holding
the bag of vegetables out at arm's length. He sat, as he often did,
facing backward to be polite to the friends he was leaving behind
in the bazaar. He clucked to the donkey and started jogging
through the village streets toward home. His legs swung loosely at
the donkey's side. He held the vegetables stiffly at arm's length,
first with one hand, then with the other, and then with both. He
rode so awkwardly that women peered at him from behind their
chuddars and boys laughed heartily.

His pupil Shoja the baker's son stared at him. "Why are you
carrying your bag that way?" he asked. "Why don't you put your
vegetables in the donkey's saddlebags where they belong?"

"Oh no!" the Mullah hurried to reply. "These vegetables are

heavy and my donkey is small. It would be too much of a load for the donkey to carry the bag and me too. So I carry the vegetables, and the donkey carries me."

Shoja stood scratching his head, trying to understand, while the Mullah rode on toward home, holding his bag of vegetables out at arm's length, and feeling very happy that he could save his good donkey the extra burden.

TALK
A TALE FROM AFRICA

by Harold Courlander and George Herzog

Once, not far from the city of Accra on the Gulf of Guinea, a country man went out to his garden to dig up some yams to take to market. While he was digging, one of the yams said to him:

"Well, at last you're here. You never weeded me, but now you come around with your digging stick. Go away and leave me alone!"

The farmer turned around and looked at his cow in amazement. The cow was chewing her cud and looking at him.

"Did you say something?" he asked.

The cow kept on chewing and said nothing, but the man's dog spoke up.

"It wasn't the cow who spoke to you," the dog said. "It was the yam. The yam says leave him alone."

The man became angry, because his dog had never talked before, and he didn't like his tone besides. So he took his knife and cut a branch from a palm tree to whip his dog. Just then the palm tree said:

"Put that branch down!"

The man was getting very upset about the way things were going, and he started to throw the palm branch away, but the palm branch said:

"Man, put me down softly!"

He put the branch down gently on a stone, and the stone said:

"Hey, take that thing off me!"

This was enough, and the frightened farmer started to run for his village. On the way he met a fisherman going the other way with a fish trap on his head.

"What's the hurry?" the fisherman asked.

"My yam said, 'Leave me alone!' Then the dog said, 'Listen to what the yam says!' When I went to whip the dog with a palm branch the tree said, 'Put that branch down!' Then the palm branch said, 'Do it softly!' Then the stone said, 'Take that thing off me!'"

"Is that all?" the man with the fish trap asked. "Is that so frightening?"

"Well," the man's fish trap said, "did he take it off the stone?"

"Wah!" the fisherman shouted. He threw the fish trap on the ground and began to run with the farmer, and on the trail they met a weaver with a bundle of cloth on his head.

"Where are you going in such a rush?" he asked them.

"My yam said, 'Leave me alone!'" the farmer said. "The dog said, 'Listen to what the yam says!' The tree said, 'Put that branch down!' The branch said, 'Do it softly!' And the stone said, 'Take that thing off me!'"

"And then," the fisherman continued, "the fish trap said, 'Did he take it off?'"

"That's nothing to get excited about," the weaver said, "no reason at all."

"Oh yes it is," his bundle of cloth said. "If it happened to you you'd run too!"

"Wah!" the weaver shouted. He threw his bundle on the trail and started running with the other men.

They came panting to the ford in the river and found a man bathing.

"Are you chasing a gazelle?" he asked them.

The first man said breathlessly:

"My yam talked at me, and it said, 'Leave me alone!' And my dog said, 'Listen to your yam!' And when I cut myself a branch the tree said, 'Put that branch down!' And the branch said, 'Do it softly!' And the stone said, 'Take that thing off me!'"

The fisherman panted:

"And my trap said, 'Did he?'"

The weaver wheezed:

"And my bundle of cloth said, 'You'd run too!'"

"Is that why you're running?" the man in the river asked.

"Well, wouldn't you run if you were in their position?" the river said.

The man jumped out of the water and began to run with the others. They ran down the main street of the village to the house of the chief. The chief's servants brought his stool out, and he came and sat on it to listen to their complaints. The men began to recite their troubles.

"I went out to my garden to dig yams," the farmer said, waving his arms. "Then everything began to talk! My yam said, 'Leave me alone!' My dog said, 'Pay attention to your yam!' The tree said, 'Put that branch down!' The branch said, 'Do it softly!' And the stone said, 'Take it off me!'"

"And my fish trap said, 'Well, did he take it off?'" the fisherman said.

"And my cloth said, 'You'd run too!'" the weaver said.

"And the river said the same," the bather said hoarsely, his eyes bulging.

The chief listened to them patiently, but he couldn't refrain from scowling.

"Now this is really a wild story," he said at last. "You'd better all go back to your work before I punish you for disturbing the peace."

So the men went away, and the chief shook his head and mumbled to himself, "Nonsense like that upsets the community."

"Fantastic, isn't it?" his stool said. "Imagine, a talking yam!"

THE WISDOM OF SOLOMON
A TALE FROM OLD ISRAEL

Retold by Elizabeth Coatsworth

Now in the days of Solomon's might and glory, the Queen of Sheba heard of his fame and came from her kingdom beyond Egypt to put questions to him.

Their meeting was like the meeting of the sun and the moon; she was as beautiful as he was handsome. All about him stood youths chosen for their comeliness, and about her were gathered maidens like stars shining in a cloudless sky. His crown blinded the eyes, and hers bewildered the mind. When the king arose from his throne to greet her, the attendants stood still with admiration, and when the queen mounted the steps to sit beside him, her grace was such that a sigh of wonder rose from the throng.

Then before the eyes of the wise Solomon the queen had displayed the treasures of her kingdom. Partly by art and partly by magic, her workmen had made things such as had never been seen before—a golden bird which could fly and speak, and animals so real that the mind could not believe that they were made by human hands.

Then, as the wise King Solomon gazed upon these things with admiration, the queen ordered her attendants to bring in two vases of flowers and to stand them at the foot of the throne.

"O Solomon, wisest of living men," said the queen, "I am but a woman and ruler of a weak little kingdom, unworthy of the thought of one so great as thou. So, only to amuse thee, and to make thee smile, I have ordered these playthings to be made for thee. Here, now, are two bouquets: one bouquet is made from living flowers and one is but a copy, which my craftsmen have fashioned of enamels and jewels. Stretch forth thy hand of wisdom, O Solomon the Wise, and say which is which."

Then the Queen of Sheba looked meekly at Solomon, but he knew well enough that this was no sport, but a test of his wisdom and that if he failed, the world would ring with laughter and his glory would be lost to him.

But he smiled courteously at the queen and thanked her for her gifts. Then he turned his eyes upon the flowers. No words can tell you of the beauty of those blossoms. There were the lilies which he loved, and roses, and sweet-smelling jasmine, all with their leaves. At first he looked for perfections, but lo, dew seemed to tremble upon the petals of both bouquets and he could not choose between them.

Then Solomon, the great king and wisest of men, searched for imperfections, and at last he saw one wilted leaf, and he raised his head and was about to stretch forth his hand, when his eye, glancing at the other flowers, saw among them also one wilted leaf.

Then, having found no aid in perfections or in imperfections, the king sat in silence, and the queen's silence was equal to his, and to all their attendants'. And it was a day of late spring, and beyond the curtains drawn between the pillars of his courtyard Solomon, the great king, heard the bees in his gardens, and suddenly he smiled.

"Draw open the curtains there," he said to one of his attendants.

And when the curtains were drawn open, he waited and the queen and all the court waited with him.

And after a while, a bee entered and flew toward the throne and the flowers before it. And Solomon, the great king, smiled in his beard, for the bee had no hesitation. The bee was not deceived by beautiful workmanship, by jewels, or by enamels. Straight as an arrow, the creature flew to its flower, and Solomon turned to the queen and raised his hand to point to the true bouquet.

Now if you think that the Queen of Sheba respected Solomon, the wise king, less because he had been forced to call in a bee to instruct him, you are wrong. She, too, was wise and she saw that the great king understood the universe and knew to whom to go for instruction, if only to a bee. And this time she bowed her head before him, not in mockery, and gave him the treasure which she had brought with her.

A WEEK OF SUNDAYS
AN IRISH TALE

by Margaret Baker

Once upon a time there was a man called Dennis O'Shea, and he had no fondness for work—at least none worth mentioning.

"Shure there's only one day that's any good at all, and that day's Sunday," said he; "but the trouble of it is that it's no sooner Sunday than the week starts all over again."

"For shame on you, the idle creature!" cried his wife Mollie; "a fine example you're setting the children."

One night when the wind was whistling round the chimney, and the rain was slapping against the window, Dennis and Mollie and the children were sitting round the fire watching the potatoes boil for supper, who should come tapping at the door but a fairy? Of course she did not look like a fairy—she looked just like an old beggar-woman.

"Never a bite has passed my lips this day," whined she, "and 'tis a night not fit to turn a pig out!"

Now whatever faults Dennis might have—and to be sure he had several—it was never meanness you could blame on him, and he brought the old woman in and sat her on his own stool, and Mollie bade her help herself to potatoes. The old woman must have had a terrible hunger on her, for she helped herself and helped herself till there was scarcely a mouthful left for anyone else, but never a word said Dennis, nor Mollie neither; and the children just sat and stared with their eyes as round as pennies— 'tis my belief they saw the glint of the golden dress of her through the tears in her old cloak.

Well, the end of it was that the old woman suddenly hopped to her feet, twisted round three times, and turned into a fairy so beautiful it made them blink to look at her.

" 'Tis kind and hospitable creatures you are," said she, "and by way of returning the kindness I'll be granting the next wish that's wished aloud in the houseen." And before they could get their breath again she had vanished up the chimney.

The children wanted to wish for lollipops and dolls and a wooden horse; Mollie was for asking for a hundred pounds, no less; and Dennis found his head so full of wishes that for the life of him he couldn't tell which came first.

" 'Tis Sunday the morn," said Mollie; "we'll be having time then to think what will be the best."

Dennis stretched his lazy legs and yawned fit to crack the top off his head. "Shure, and I wish it was a week of Sundays!" said he before he thought what he was saying.

"That's the end of it!" cried Mollie. "If I'd known you'd be wasting the wish on something as daft-like as that I'd have wished you had a little sense, that I would!"

"Whist now, whist now, Mollie darlint!" said Dennis. "Shure and I never meant to say it—it just popped out of itself. And a week of Sundays will be a fine treat—'tis not such a bad wish at all, at all."

"If it cures the idle bones of you it will be worth something," snapped Mollie, and never another word would she say.

The more he thought about his wish, the more Dennis liked it. It was an elegant feeling entirely to wake up next morning and hear the bells ringing and know there were to be six more Sundays, one after the other, before he need do a stroke of work. Mollie and the children went to church, but Dennis never set foot out of bed till the smell of dinner reminded him he was hungry.

Mollie had a grand piece of roast pork in the oven, and when he had eaten all he wanted, he put on his best coat and sat in the sunshine outside the door, taking life as comfortably as if he were the king himself.

"I couldn't have thought of a better wish if I'd been trying a year, shure and I couldn't," said he.

Next day he lay in bed again till dinnertime, but the dinner was only the picking of the pork bones, and the next day there was nothing to eat but bacon and potatoes, just as though it was Monday and all.

"Indade, Mollie darlint, but you've been forgetting what day it is," said he; "taties and bacon is never a dinner for Sunday, and that's the truth."

"Where can I be buying another roast of pork and all the shops with their shutters up for seven days on end?" asked Mollie. "If you *will* be having a week of Sundays, shure and you'll have to take the consequences!"

"Begorrah!" said Dennis, and rubbed his head, "I never thought of that!"

Next day it was worse than ever, for there was next to nothing for dinner but a cheese and a loaf of bread—and both as stale as a stone.

"I'll be digging some taties from the garden," said Dennis, and I'll not deny he was beginning to think it would be the grand feeling to have a spade in his hands again.

But Mollie would not hear of it. "Digging taties, is it?" cried she; "and what would the neighbors be thinking to see you doing the likes of that on a Sunday? You'll have to be living on bits and scraps till we get a Monday again, and that's all there is to say about it!"

Well, on the fifth Sunday when the church bells began to ring, there was Dennis tossing and turning as though the blankets had been made of nettles; for now he could lie in bed as long as he liked every morning, wasn't he beginning to wish he had to be getting up early again? And even when he'd got the lazy bones of him dressed, things were not any better, for there was nothing to do at all, at all, and the children were pulling at his coat tails and quarreling and whimpering every minute of the time.

"And no blame to them, the darlints!" cried Mollie; "it's five days, no less, that they've had to be wearing their best clothes and not a game can they play for fear of spoiling them. And aren't they likely to get tired of holidays when there's not so much as a day's schooling in between?"

Truth to tell, Dennis was getting tired of holidays himself. He went to church next day to give himself something to do, but it's little comfort he got out of it. "Here's the man!" cried the parson; "here's the mischievous creature that's nearly driven me to my grave with hard work! Don't I have to preach twice every Sunday? And when there's a week of Sundays, isn't it fourteen sermons I have to be giving one after the other, with never a bit of time to turn over me thoughts?"

It was black looks he got from the congregation, too, when the service was over.

"Will you be thinking of the washing there'll be when we get a Monday again?" cried the women.

"And how's the harvest to be got in an' all when there's never a weekday coming round?" asked the men.

Oh! Dennis was beginning to rue his wish, and that's a fact.

There was only one more Sunday left, but, if you'll believe me, every hour of it seemed as long as all the other six days put together. Dennis stood up and sat down again, and wandered round and round the house till the legs of him ached more than if he had been plowing.

"Will the sun never be setting?" said he.

"What for should you be wanting it to set so early?" asked Mollie, innocent-like. "Is it yourself has forgotten it's Monday the morn?"

"Never a bit!" cried Dennis. "Never a bit! It's more than pleased I'll be to see Monday again, though I never thought to say it!"

"Then you'd not be asking for another week of Sundays again?" asked Mollie, pretending, the sly creature, that she didn't know.

"That I would not!" exclaimed Dennis; "shure and there's no enjoying a Sunday unless you've worked six days to earn it. It's the grand lesson I've been learning, and that's the truth."

"It is and all!" said Mollie; "but the next time you want a lesson I'm hoping you'll not be wasting a fairy wish on it."

THE DUTCH BOY AND THE DIKE
A TALE OF HOLLAND

A boy called Hans lived a long time ago in the country of Holland. He lived with his mother and father and sister in a little white cottage that stood on the edge of a tulip field.

Hans loved to wake up in the morning and look out of the window and see tulips of every different color growing in the field. He loved to look around at the old windmills turning slowly—sometimes this way, sometimes that. And he loved to look beyond the bright flowers and beyond the old windmills to the sea in the distance.

Strangely enough, the sea in Holland is on a level with the roofs of the houses and the windmills. This is because Holland lies below the level of the ocean. The land is kept dry and safe by high, strong walls called dikes, which keep the water out.

One day Hans went to visit a friend of his who lived five miles away by the seaside. As he started for home, he noticed that the sun was setting and the sky was growing dark.

"Oh dear, I must hurry," said Hans, "or I shall be late for supper."

"Take the short cut," his friend suggested. "There's a road along the top of the dike."

"I will," said Hans. "Good-by."

"Good-by," his friend replied.

Hans climbed up to the road that went along the top of the dike. As he was hurrying along, he noticed that the water was much higher than usual. It had rained for many days and the sea was swollen.

"It's really very lucky," Hans thought to himself, "that in Holland the dikes are high and strong. Otherwise the whole land would be flooded and our houses and windmills and every living thing would be washed away."

Just then he heard a soft gurgling noise, as though a little stream of water were flowing through a hole. He stopped and bent down, trying to see what made the noise even though he felt sure there could be no hole in the large, strong dike. But as he looked, he saw a tiny leak and water flowing through it.

A leak in the dike! Without even stopping to think, Hans slid down to the bottom of the dike and put his finger in the little hole to keep the water from coming through. Then he looked around for someone to help him, someone to bring word of the leak to the men in the village. But the road was deserted and no one was in sight. He shouted loudly, hoping that someone in a near-by field would hear his calls and come to help him. But only his own echo answered.

It was lonely there. Hans was hungry and tired. His fingers

grew stiff as, one after the other, they kept the hole in the dike plugged up. Hans thought of his mother and father and sister waiting for him in the little cottage on the edge of the tulip field. He thought of his supper waiting for him and of his nice soft bed.

But Hans also thought of what would happen if he deserted his post, if he let the water leak through the hole in the dike. He knew that the water would wash the earth and rock away, making the hole larger and larger, until at last a strong stream of water would flow through and flood the fields and the houses and the windmills.

He looked around for something to plug up the leak so that he could go to the village for help. He put a stone in the hole and then a stick, but each in turn was washed out by the force of the water. No, Hans had to stay there himself and use all his strength if the water were to be kept out.

Every little while he called for help, hoping that someone might be passing near by and hear him. But always his own echo answered and nothing more. All night long Hans stayed at his post. His fingers grew cold and numb and his whole body longed to sleep, but he knew that he had to be strong and patient, that he couldn't give up.

Not till early in the morning did Hans hear the welcome sound that told him someone was coming along the road, that help was near at last. It was the sound of the milk cart rumbling along the road. When it got quite near he shouted at the man driving the cart.

The man was startled, of course, to hear a voice so early in the morning in that deserted place. He stopped his horse and looked around, as if he couldn't believe his ears. Hans shouted again. "Help, help!" he called. "There's a leak in the dike. Here I am at the bottom of the dike. Help, help!"

The man saw Hans this time and hurried down to him. But he still couldn't believe that there was a leak in one of the high, strong dikes which had protected Holland from the sea for so many years. Hans had to show him the leak and the stream of water trickling through it before he could understand what the boy was doing there.

"So you see," Hans said, "I need help and need it quickly. Go to the village and tell the people. Have them send out men to repair the damage as soon as they possibly can."

The milkman did as the boy told him and, though he hurried as fast as he could, Hans had to stay at his post for an hour more. When at last the people of the village arrived, some of them set to work to repair the leak. But the rest, men and women and children alike, lifted their voices in praise of Hans and in praise of the noble deed he had performed that night.

Some of the men carried the boy on their shoulders and bore him into the village, shouting, "Make way for the Hero of Holland! The brave boy who saved our land!"

But even then Hans did not think of himself as a hero. He had done only what he thought was right, and he was glad that he could do so small a thing for the country he loved so much.

THE SNOW MAIDEN
A RUSSIAN TALE

A long time ago, in the land of Russia, there lived near the forest a peasant named Ivan with his wife Marie. These two good people, though they loved each other dearly and had many friendly neighbors, were unhappy, for they had no children. They used to look out of the window and watch the children of their neighbors playing and laughing together and they wished with all their hearts that they, too, had a little child of their own.

One winter day, as they stood at the window of their little

hut, they saw the neighbors' children playing in the snow. The children were having a good time romping, throwing snowballs at each other, and making a big snow man.

Ivan turned to his wife and said: "Look, Wife, the children are having a good time making a man out of snow. Let us go into the garden and make a snow man."

"That is a fine idea," said the wife, and the two good people went out into the garden.

Then Marie turned to her husband. "I've been thinking, Husband," she said. "Since we have no children of our own, let us make a little snow girl instead of a snow man."

"That is a fine idea," said Ivan, and they started to make a little girl out of snow. For so many years they had dreamed of having a little girl of their own that now they fashioned one with love and care—the prettiest maiden ever seen.

They rolled the snow together, and Ivan made a little body with dainty little hands and feet. Marie fashioned a beautiful head with eyes and nose and mouth and hair—all of snow. Then, very carefully, they placed the head on the shoulders of the little statue and looked at their little snow girl. Never had they seen anything so lovely and never had they wished more fervently for a real little girl of their own.

"Little snow maiden," Ivan said, "speak to me!"

"Yes, my darling," said Marie. "Come to life so you can play and romp and laugh like other children!"

Just then they noticed that the snow maiden's eyes began to quiver. A faint rosy color was creeping into her cheeks. At first they thought they were dreaming, but then they saw a real little girl with blue eyes and golden hair and rosy cheeks standing before them, where a moment before the snow figure had stood.

At first they were too astonished to speak and just gazed at the little girl. Then Ivan said: "Where did you come from? And who are you?"

"I came from the land of cold and snow," the child replied. "And I am your daughter, your own little girl."

She ran to Marie and Ivan and kissed them, and all three of them wept for joy. But soon they were talking and smiling again, for this was the happiest moment of their lives. They called to their neighbors in the huts near by, who came over to see what was going on. Word soon got around of the couple's good fortune, and all the little girls of the village came to see the lovely little girl, the daughter of Ivan and Marie. Everybody stayed in the hut till late that night, laughing and singing and dancing to celebrate the glad occasion.

All that winter she played with the other boys and girls while Ivan and Marie would stand in the window of their little hut watching her. Now they were happy, for one of the children playing in the snow was their own child and, it seemed to them, she was the loveliest child of all.

"No child could be prettier than our little girl," Ivan would say.

"Nowhere in the world is there a better child than she is," Marie would add.

And Ivan would agree with her. "She is the best child of all," he would say; "always good, always happy, always sweet."

And indeed it was true. Everyone loved the little snow maiden. Everyone loved to hear her laughing and singing all day long, and they loved to watch her running and dancing with the other children. But when the first signs of spring appeared, when the air became warmer and the snows started to melt, the little girl didn't seem as gay as before. She always seemed tired now and unhappy.

One day she came to Ivan and Marie and sang a sad little song:

"The time has come for me to go
Away up North to the land of snow."

These were the words she sang and, as she sang them, her eyes filled with tears. Her mother and father began to weep when they heard this song and Marie cried out, "Stay with us, my darling! Do not go away!"

Ivan jumped up and barred the door so she could not get out, and Marie put her arms around the little girl and held her tight. But even as she held her, the snow maiden started to melt away, and soon there was nothing left but her white fur cap and her white fur coat and her high white boots in a puddle on the floor.

Ivan and Marie wept bitter tears, and Marie folded away the little clothes, saying, "Maybe she will come back to us some day."

All that summer they were sad and lonely, thinking of the dear little girl who had gone away. And then one night, when winter came, they heard a merry laugh outside their hut and they heard a happy voice singing,

"Mother! Father! Open the door!
The snow has brought me back once more!"

Ivan threw open the door and the snow maiden ran to the arms of her father and mother. All that winter she stayed with them and played with the other children of the village. But in the spring she had to go back North to the land of cold and snow. Ivan and Marie did not mind her going this time, however, for they knew that every winter, when it got cold and the snow began to fall, the little snow maiden would come back to Russia again and live with them until spring.

THE LITTLE ROOSTER
AND THE TURKISH SULTAN
A HUNGARIAN TALE

by Kate Seredy

Somewhere, some place, beyond the Seven Seas, there lived a poor old woman. The poor old woman had a Little Rooster. One day the Little Rooster walked out of the yard to look for strange bugs and worms. All the bugs and worms in the yard were his friends—he was hungry, but he could not eat his friends! So he walked out to the road. He scratched and he scratched. He scratched out a Diamond Button. Of all things, a Diamond Button! The Button twinkled at him. "Pick me up, Little Rooster, and take me to your old mistress. She likes Diamond Buttons."

"Cock-a-doodle-doo. I'll pick you up and take you to my poor old mistress!"

So he picked up the Button. Just then the Turkish Sultan walked by. The Turkish Sultan was very, very fat. Three fat servants walked behind him, carrying the wide, wide bag of the Turkish Sultan's trousers. He saw the Little Rooster with the Diamond Button.

"Little Rooster, give me your Diamond Button."

"No, indeed, I won't. I am going to give it to my poor old mistress. She likes Diamond Buttons."

But the Turkish Sultan liked Diamond Buttons, too. Besides, he could not take "no" for an answer. He turned to his three fat servants.

"Catch the Little Rooster and take the Diamond Button from him."

The three fat servants dropped the wide, wide bag of the Turkish Sultan's trousers, caught the Little Rooster, and took the Diamond Button away from him. The Turkish Sultan took the Diamond Button home with him and put it in his treasure chamber.

The Little Rooster was very angry. He went to the palace of the Turkish Sultan, perched on the window, and cried:

"Cock-a-doodle-doo! Turkish Sultan, give me back my Diamond Button."

The Turkish Sultan did not like this, so he walked into another room.

The Little Rooster perched on the window of another room and cried: "Cock-a-doodle-doo! Turkish Sultan, give me back my Diamond Button."

The Turkish Sultan was mad. He called his three fat servants. "Catch the Little Rooster. Throw him into the well, let him drown!"

The three fat servants caught the Little Rooster and threw him into the well. But the Little Rooster cried: "Come, my empty stomach, come, my empty stomach, drink up all the water."

His empty stomach drank up all the water.

Little Rooster flew back to the window and cried: "Cock-a-doodle-doo! Turkish Sultan, give me back my Diamond Button."

The Turkish Sultan was madder than before. He called his three fat servants.

"Catch the Little Rooster and throw him into the fire. Let him burn!"

The three fat servants caught the Little Rooster and threw him into the fire.

But the Little Rooster cried: "Come, my full stomach, let out all the water to put out all the fire."

His full stomach let out all the water. It put out all the fire.

He flew back to the window again and cried: "Cock-a-doodle-doo! Turkish Sultan, give me back my Diamond Button."

The Turkish Sultan was madder than ever. He called his three fat servants.

"Catch the Little Rooster, throw him into a beehive, and let the bees sting him."

The three fat servants caught the Little Rooster and threw him into a beehive. But the Little Rooster cried: "Come, my empty stomach, come, my empty stomach, eat up all the bees."

His empty stomach ate up all the bees.

He flew back to the window again and cried: "Cock-a-doodle-doo! Turkish Sultan, give me back my Diamond Button."

The Turkish Sultan was so mad he didn't know what to do. He called his three fat servants.

"What shall I do with the Little Rooster?"

The first fat servant said: "Hang him on the flagpole!"

The second fat servant said: "Cut his head off!"

The third fat servant said: "*Sit on him!*"

The Turkish Sultan cried: "That's it! I'll sit on him! Catch the Little Rooster and bring him to me!"

The three fat servants caught the Little Rooster and brought him to the Turkish Sultan. The Turkish Sultan opened the wide, wide bag of his trousers and put the Little Rooster in. Then he sat on him.

But the Little Rooster cried: "Come, my full stomach, let out all the bees to sting the Turkish Sultan."

His full stomach let out all the bees.

And did they sting the Turkish Sultan?

THEY DID!!

The Turkish Sultan jumped up in the air.

"Ouch! Ouch! Ow! Ow!" he cried. "Take this Little Rooster to my treasure chamber and let him find his confounded Diamond Button!"

The three fat servants took the Little Rooster to the treasure chamber.

"Find your confounded Diamond Button!" they said and left him.

But the Little Rooster cried: "Come, my empty stomach, come, my empty stomach, eat up all the money."

His empty stomach ate up all the money in the Turkish Sultan's treasure chamber.

Then the Little Rooster waddled home as fast as he could and gave all the money to his poor old mistress. Then he went out into the yard to tell his friends, the bugs and worms, about the Turkish Sultan and the Diamond Button.

THE BOY WHO DREW CATS
A TALE OF JAPAN

by Lafcadio Hearn

A long, long time ago, in a small country village in Japan, there lived a poor farmer and his wife, who were very good people. They had a number of children, and found it very hard to feed them all. The elder son was strong enough when only fourteen years old to help his father; and the little girls learned to help their mother almost as soon as they could walk.

But the youngest child, a little boy, did not seem to be fit for hard work. He was very clever—cleverer than all his brothers and sisters; but he was quite weak and small, and people said he could never grow very big. So his parents thought it would be better for him to become a priest than to become a farmer. They took him with them to the village temple one day, and asked the good old priest who lived there, if he would have their little boy for his acolyte, and teach him all that a priest ought to know.

The old man spoke kindly to the lad, and asked him some hard questions. So clever were the answers that the priest agreed to take the little fellow into the temple as an acolyte, and to educate him for the priesthood.

The boy learned quickly what the old priest taught him, and was very obedient in most things. But he had one fault. He liked to draw cats during study hours, and to draw cats even where cats ought not to have been drawn at all.

Whenever he found himself alone, he drew cats. He drew them on the margins of the priest's books, and on all the screens of the temple, and on the walls, and on the pillars. Several times the priest told him this was not right; but he did not stop drawing cats. He drew them because he could not really help it. He had what is called "the genius of an *artist*," and just for that reason he was not quite fit to be an acolyte; a good acolyte should study books.

One day after he had drawn some very clever pictures of cats upon a paper screen, the old priest said to him severely: "My boy, you must go away from this temple at once. You will never make a good priest, put perhaps you will become a great artist. Now let me give you a last piece of advice, and be sure you never forget it. *Avoid large places at night; keep to small!*"

The boy did not know what the priest meant by saying, "*Avoid large places; keep to small.*" He thought and thought, while he was tying up his little bundle of clothes to go away; but he could not understand those words, and he was afraid to speak to the priest any more, except to say good-by.

He left the temple very sorrowfully, and began to wonder what he should do. If he went straight home he felt sure his father would punish him for having been disobedient to the priest: so he was afraid to go home. All at once he remembered that at the next village, twelve miles away, there was a very big temple. He had heard there were several priests at that temple; and he made up his mind to go to them and ask them to take him for their acolyte.

Now that big temple was closed up but the boy did not know this fact. The reason it had been closed up was that a goblin had frightened the priests away, and had taken possession of the place. Some brave warriors had afterward gone to the temple at night to kill the goblin; but they had never been seen alive again. Nobody had ever told these things to the boy—so he walked all the way to the village hoping to be kindly treated by the priests.

When he got to the village it was already dark, and all the people were in bed; but he saw the big temple on a hill at the other end of the principal street, and he saw there was a light in the temple. People who tell the story say the goblin used to make that light, in order to tempt lonely travelers to ask for shelter. The boy went at once to the temple, and knocked. There was no sound inside. He knocked and knocked again; but still nobody came. At last he pushed gently at the door, and was quite glad to find that it had not been fastened. So he went in, and saw a lamp burning—but no priest.

He thought some priest would be sure to come very soon, and he sat down and waited. Then he noticed that everything in the temple was gray with dust, and thickly spun over with cobwebs. So he thought to himself that the priests would certainly like to have an acolyte, to keep the place clean. He wondered why they had allowed everything to get so dusty. What most pleased him, however, were some big white screens, good to paint cats upon.

Though he was tired, he looked at once for a writing-box, and found one, and ground some ink, and began to paint cats.

He painted a great many cats upon the screens; and then he began to feel very, very sleepy. He was just on the point of lying down to sleep beside one of the screens, when he suddenly remembered the words, "Avoid large places; keep to small!"

The temple was very large; he was all alone; and as he thought of these words—though he could not quite understand them—be began to feel for the first time a little afraid; and he resolved to look for a small place in which to sleep. He found a little cabinet, with a sliding door, and went into it, and shut himself up. Then he lay down and fell fast asleep.

Very late in the night he was awakened by a most terrible noise—a noise of fighting and screaming. It was so dreadful that he was afraid even to look through a chink of the little cabinet: he lay very still, holding his breath for fright. The light that had been in the temple went out; but the awful sounds continued, and became more awful, and all the temple shook. After a long time silence came; but the boy was still afraid to move. He did not move until the light of the morning sun shone into the cabinet through the chinks of the little door.

Then he got out of his hiding-place very cautiously, and looked about. The first thing he saw was that all the floor of the temple was covered with blood. And then he saw, lying dead, in the middle of it, an enormous, monstrous rat—a goblin-rat—bigger than a cow!

But who or what could have killed it? There was no man or other creature to be seen. Suddenly the boy observed that the mouths of all the cats he had drawn the night before were red and wet with blood. Then he knew that the goblin had been killed by the cats which he had drawn. And then also, for the first time, he understood why the wise old priest had said to him, "Avoid large places at night; keep to small."

Afterward that boy became a very famous artist. Some of the cats which he drew are still shown to travelers in Japan.

THE VEGETABLE TREE
A MAYAN TALE

by Dorothy Rhoads

I had the tale from my mother, who heard it from her mother. And she, no doubt, had heard the tale from her own mother, and so back through the centuries.

It was the very beginning of the world. . . . There were no coconut trees and no mango trees or orange trees or bananas as there are today. And there were no bean plants or squash or chili or cassava. All the vegetables and all the fruits in the world (except corn) grew on one enormous tree which stood in the exact center of the world. And every day the animals came to the tree and ate from it. But man did not know the tree existed.

Who the first man was who found the tree, no one knows. Long ago his name was forgotten. But the man came to the tree, and he saw the vegetables and fruits that drooped heavily from the branches. And he decided to chop down the tree and plant the seed.

All day the man chopped and cut at the tree trunk with his machete. And at the end of the day he was weary, and he went to sleep. And in the morning he awoke. And there was no trace in the tree of the work he had done the day before.

All the second day the man chopped at the tree, and he cut into the trunk a few inches. And when the sun went down he was weary, and he went to sleep. And on the next day when he arose, there was no trace in the tree trunk where the man had worked the day before.

And the man brought one of his friends. And the two men cut and chopped at the base of the tree with their machetes. And they cut away several inches. And when the darkness fell they were weary, and then went to sleep. But when they awoke in the morning, there was no mark or cut in the trunk of the tree.

And the two men called other men. And they chopped and cut at the tree, and by the end of the day the men had cut half-way through the tree trunk. And they were weary, and they went to sleep. And in the morning there was no trace of their work of the day before.

And the whole village set to work to chop down the tree, and they cut and chopped all the day. And when darkness fell, only a small piece of the tree trunk remained to be cut. And the men were weary from their work. And they lay down and went to sleep. And in the morning there was no trace of the cutting and chopping of the day before.

Then one of the men suggested, wisely:

"Let us chop again at the tree. And if it happens that we do not cut through the trunk, let us remain awake and see what takes place during the night."

And all day the men cut and chopped at the tree. And when darkness fell they were weary. And they remained awake.

And in the darkness of the night the animals of the bush gathered about the tree. The jaguar was there, and the deer; and the fox and wild pig and ocelot and serpent and tepizcuintle and the armadillo. Every animal and every bird and every crawling thing of the bush gathered about the tree. And the animals began to work. They took up from around the base of the tree the chips that the men had cut out the day before, and they replaced the chips in the trunk of the tree. They worked all night, each animal and crawling thing and bird, replacing the chips. And before the light returned they had replaced all the chips, and the tree was whole.

All the next day the men worked chopping and cutting at the tree. And when the evening came there was only a small bit of tree trunk that remained to be cut. And the men were weary, but they did not stop. They cut and chopped at the tree in the dark-ness, and the tree trunk was cut through. And the tree fell. And the men gathered the fruit and hurried away to plant the seed.

Today there are coconut trees and mango trees and orange trees and bananas. And there are beans and squash and chili and cassava. Each fruit and each vegetable grows on its own plant and on its own tree.

I heard the tale from my mother, who had it from her mother. And her mother had had it from her own mother back and back through the centuries.

It was in the very beginning of the world. . . .

THE TERRIBLE OLLI
A TALE OF FINLAND

by Parker Fillmore

There was once a wicked rich old Troll who lived on a Mountain that sloped down to a Bay. A decent Finn, a farmer, lived on the opposite side of the Bay. The farmer had three sons. When the boys had reached manhood he said to them one day:

"I should think it would shame you three strong youths that that wicked old Troll over there should live on year after year and no one trouble him. We work hard like honest Finns and are as poor at the end of the year as at the beginning. That old Troll with all his wickedness grows richer and richer. I tell you, if you boys had any real spirit you'd take his riches from him and drive him away!"

His youngest son, whose name was Olli, at once cried out:

"Very well, Father, I will!"

But the two older sons, offended at Olli's promptness, declared:

"You'll do no such thing! Don't forget your place in the family! You're the youngest and we're not going to let you push us aside. Now, Father, we two will go across the Bay and rout out that old Troll. Olli may come with us if he likes and watch us while we do it."

Olli laughed and said: "All right!" for he was used to his brothers treating him like a baby.

So in a few days the three brothers walked around the Bay and up the Mountain and presented themselves at the Troll's house. The Troll and his old wife were both at home. They received the brothers with great civility.

"You're the sons of the Finn who lives across the Bay, aren't you?" the Troll said. "I've watched you boys grow up. I am certainly glad to see you for I have three daughters who need husbands. Marry my daughters and you'll inherit my riches."

The old Troll made this offer in order to get the young men into his power.

"Be careful!" Olli whispered.

But the brothers were too delighted at the prospect of inheriting the Troll's riches so easily to pay any heed to Olli's warning. Instead they accepted the Troll's offer at once.

Well, the old Troll's wife made them a fine supper and after supper the Troll sent them to bed with his three daughters. But first he put red caps on the three youths and white caps on the three Troll girls. He made a joke about the caps.

"A red cap and a white cap in each bed!" he said.

The older brothers suspected nothing and soon fell asleep. Olli, too, pretended to fall asleep and when he was sure that none of the Troll girls were still awake he got up and quietly changed the caps. He put the white caps on himself and his brothers and the red caps on the Troll girls. Then he crept back to bed and waited.

Presently the old Troll came over to the beds with a long knife in his hand. There was so little light in the room that he couldn't see the faces of the sleepers, but it was easy enough to distinguish the white caps from the red caps. With three swift blows he cut off the heads under the red caps, thinking of course they were the heads of the three Finnish youths. Then he went back to bed with the old Troll wife and Olli could hear them both chuckling and laughing. After a time they went soundly to sleep as Olli could tell from their deep regular breathing and their loud snores.

Olli now roused his brothers and told them what had happened and the three of them slipped quietly out of the Troll house and hurried home to their father on the other side of the Bay.

After that the older brothers no longer talked of despoiling the

Troll. They didn't care to try another encounter with him.

"He might have cut our heads off!" they said, shuddering to think of the awful risk they had run.

Olli laughed at them.

"Come on!" he kept saying to them day after day. "Let's go across the Bay to the Troll's!"

"We'll do no such thing!" they told him. "And you wouldn't suggest it either if you weren't so young and foolish!"

"Well," Olli announced at last, "if you won't come with me I'm going alone. I've heard that the Troll has a horse with hairs of gold and silver. I've decided I want that horse."

"Olli," his father said, "I don't believe you ought to go. You know what your brothers say. That old Troll is an awfully sly one!"

But Olli only laughed.

"Good-by!" he called back as he waved his hand. "When you see me again I'll be riding the Troll's horse!"

The Troll wasn't at home but the old Troll wife was there. When she saw Olli she thought to herself:

"Mercy me, here's that Finnish boy again, the one that changed the caps! What shall I do? I must keep him here on some pretext or other until the Troll comes home!"

So she pretended to be very glad to see him.

"Why, Olli," she said, "is that you? Come right in!"

She talked to him as long as she could and when she could think of nothing more to say she asked him would he take the horse and water it at the Lake.

"That will keep him busy," she thought to herself, "and long before he gets back from the Lake the Troll will be here."

But Olli, instead of leading the horse down to the Lake, jumped on its back and galloped away. By the time the Troll reached home, he was safely on the other side of the Bay.

When the Troll heard from the old Troll wife what had happened, he went down to the shore and hallooed across the Bay:

"Olli! Oh, Olli, are you there?"

Olli made a trumpet of his hands and called back:

"Yes, I'm here! What do you want?"

"Olli, have you got my horse?"

"Yes, I've got your horse but it's my horse now!"

"Olli! Olli!" his father cried. "You mustn't talk that way to the Troll! You'll make him angry!"

And his brothers looking with envy at the horse with gold and silver hairs warned him sourly:

"You better be careful, young man, or the Troll will get you yet!"

A few days later Olli announced:

"I think I'll go over and get the Troll's money-bag."

His father tried to dissuade him.

"Don't be foolhardy, Olli! Your brothers say you had better not go to the Troll's house again."

But Olli only laughed and started gaily off as though he hadn't a fear in the world.

Again he found the old Troll wife alone.

"Mercy me!" she thought to herself as she saw him coming, "here is that terrible Olli again! Whatever shall I do? I mustn't let him off this time before the Troll gets back! I must keep him right here with me in the house."

So when he came in she pretended that she was tired and that her back ached and she asked him would he watch the bread in the oven while she rested a few moments on the bed.

"Certainly I will," Olli said.

So the old Troll wife lay down on the bed and Olli sat quietly in front of the oven. The Troll wife really was tired and before she knew it she fell asleep.

"Ha!" thought Olli, "here's my chance!"

Without disturbing the Troll wife he reached under the bed, pulled out the big money-bag full of silver pieces, threw it over his shoulder, and hurried home.

He was measuring the money when he heard the Troll hallooing across to him:

"Olli! Oh, Olli, are you there?"

"Yes," Olli shouted back, "I'm here! What do you want?"

"Olli, have you got my money-bag?"

"Yes, I've got your money-bag but it's my money-bag now!"

A few days later Olli said:

"Do you know, the Troll has a beautiful coverlet woven of silk and gold. I think I'll go over and get it."

His father as usual protested but Olli laughed at him merrily and went. He took with him an auger and a can of water. He hid until it was dark, then climbed the roof of the Troll's house and bored a hole right over the bed. When the Troll and his wife went to sleep he sprinkled some water on the coverlet and on their faces.

The Troll woke with a start.

"I'm wet!" he said, "and the bed's wet, too!"

The old Troll wife got up to change the covers.

"The roof must be leaking," she said. "It never leaked before. I suppose it was that last wind."

She threw the wet coverlet up over the rafters to dry and put other covers on the bed.

When she and the Troll were again asleep, Olli made the hole a little bigger, reached in his hand, and got the coverlet from the rafters.

The next morning the Troll hallooed across the Bay:

"Olli! Oh, Olli, are you there?"

"Yes," Olli shouted back, "I'm here! What do you want?"

"Have you got my coverlet woven of silk and gold?"

"Yes," Olli told him, "I've got your coverlet but it's my coverlet now!"

A few days later Olli said:

"There's still one thing in the Troll's house that I think I ought to get. It's a golden bell. If I get that golden bell then there will be nothing left that had better belong to an honest Finn."

So he went again to the Troll's house taking with him a saw and an auger. He hid until night and, when the Troll and his wife were asleep, he cut a hole through the side of the house through which he reached in his hand to get the bell. At the touch of his hand the bell tinkled and woke the Troll. The Troll jumped out of bed and grabbed Olli's hand.

"Ha! Ha!" he cried. "I've got you now and this time you won't get away!"

Olli didn't try to get away. He made no resistance while the Troll dragged him into the house.

"We'll eat him—that's what we'll do!" the Troll said to his wife. "Heat the oven at once and we'll roast him!"

So the Troll wife built a roaring fire in the oven.

"He'll make a fine roast!" the Troll said, pinching Olli's arms and legs. "I think we ought to invite the other Troll folk to come and help us eat him up. Suppose I just go over the Mountain and gather them in. You can manage here without me. As soon as the oven is well heated just take Olli and slip him in and close the door and by the time we come he'll be done."

"Very well," the Troll wife said, "but don't be too long! He's young and tender and will roast quickly!"

So the Troll went out to invite to the feast the Troll folk who lived on the other side of the Mountain and Olli was left alone with the Troll wife.

When the oven was well heated she raked out the coals and said to Olli:

"Now then, my boy, sit down in front of the oven with your back to the opening and I'll push you in nicely."

Olli pretended he didn't quite understand. He sat down first one way and then another, spreading himself out so large that he was too big for the oven door.

"Not that way!" the Troll wife kept saying. "Hunch up a little, straight in front of the door!"

"You show me how," Olli begged.

So the old Troll wife sat down before the oven directly in front of the opening, and she hunched herself up very compactly with her chin on her knees and her arms around her legs.

"Oh, that way!" Olli said, "so you can just take hold of me and push me in and shut the door!"

And as he spoke he took hold of her and pushed her in and slammed the door! And that was the end of the old Troll wife!

Olli let her roast in the oven until she was done to a turn. Then he took her out and put her on the table all ready for the feast.

Then he filled a sack with straw and dressed the sack up in some of the old Troll wife's clothes. He threw the dressed up sack on the bed and, just to glance at it, you'd suppose it was the Troll wife asleep.

Then Olli took the golden bell and went home.

Well, presently the Troll and all the Troll folk from over the Mountain came trooping in.

"Yum! Yum! It certainly smells good!" they said as they got the first whiff from the big roast on the table.

"See!" the Troll said, pointing to the bed. "The old woman's asleep! Well, let her sleep! She's tired! We'll just sit down without her!"

So they set to and feasted and feasted.

"Ha! Ha!" said the Troll. "This is the way to serve a trouble-some young Finn!"

Just then his knife struck something hard and he looked down to see what it was.

"Mercy me!" he cried, "if here isn't one of the old woman's

beads! What can that mean? You don't suppose the roast is not Olli after all but the old woman! No! No! It can't be!"

He got up and went over to the bed. Then he came back shaking his head sadly.

"My friends," he said, "we've been eating the old woman! However, we've eaten so much of her that I suppose we might as well finish her!"

So the Troll folk sat all night feasting and drinking.

At dawn the Troll went down to the water and hallooed across: "Olli! Oh, Olli, are you there?"

Olli who was safely home shouted back:

"Yes, I'm here! What do you want?"

"Have you got my golden bell?"

"Yes, I've got your golden bell but it's my golden bell now!"

"One thing more, Olli: did you roast my old woman?"

"Your old woman?" Olli echoed. "Look! Is that she?"

Olli pointed at the rising sun which was coming up behind the Troll.

The Troll turned and looked. He looked straight at the sun and then, of course, he burst!

So that was the end of him!

Well, after that no other Troll ever dared settle on that side of the Mountain. They were all too afraid of the Terrible Olli!

AH TCHA THE SLEEPER
A CHINESE TALE

by Arthur Bowie Chrisman

Years ago, in southern China, lived a boy, Ah Tcha by name.
Ah Tcha was an orphan, but not according to rule. A most peculiar orphan was he. It is usual for orphans to be very, very poor.
That is the world-wide custom. Ah Tcha, on the contrary, was
quite wealthy. He owned seven farms, with seven times seven
horses to draw the plow. He owned seven mills, with plenty of
breezes to spin them. Furthermore, he owned seven thousand
pieces of gold, and a fine white cat. The farms of Ah Tcha were
fertile, were wide. His horses were brisk in the furrow. His mills
never lacked for grain, nor wanted for wind. And his gold was
good sharp gold, with not so much as a trace of copper. Surely,
few orphans have been better provided for than the youth named
Ah Tcha. And what a busy person was this Ah Tcha. His bed was
always cold when the sun arose. Early in the morning he went
from field to field, from mill to mill, urging on the people who
worked for him. The setting sun always found him on his feet,
hastening from here to there, persuading his laborers to more
gainful efforts. And the moon of midnight often discovered him
pushing up and down the little teakwood balls of a counting
board, or else threading cash, placing coins upon a string. Eight
farms, nine farms he owned, and still more stout horses. Ten
mills, eleven, another white cat. It was Ah Tcha's ambition to become the richest person in the world.

They who worked for the wealthy orphan were inclined now
and then to grumble. Their pay was not beggardly, but how they
did toil to earn that pay which was not beggardly. It was go, and
go, and go. Said the ancient woman Nu Wu, who worked with a

rake in the field: "Our master drives us as if he were a fox and we were hares in the open. Round the field and round and round, hurry, always hurry." Said Hu Shu, her husband, who bound the grain into sheaves: "Not hares, but horses. We are driven like the horses of Lung Kuan, who . . . It's a long story."

But Ah Tcha, approaching the murmurers, said, "Pray, be so good as to hurry, most excellent Nu Wu, for the clouds gather blackly, with thunder." And to the scowling husband he said, "Speed your work, I beg you, honorable Hu Shu, for the grain must be under shelter before the smoke of Evening Rice ascends."

When Ah Tcha had eaten his Evening Rice, he took lantern and entered the largest of his mills. A scampering rat drew his attention to the floor. There he beheld no less than a score of rats, some gazing at him as if undecided whether to flee or continue the feast, others gnawing—and who are you, nibbling and caring not? And only a few short whisker-lengths away sat an enormous cat, sleeping the sleep of a mossy stone. The cat was black in color, black as a crow's wing dipped in pitch, upon a night of inky darkness. That describes her coat. Her face was somewhat more black. Ah Tcha had never before seen her. She was not his cat. But his or not, he thought it a trifle unreasonable of her to sleep, while the rats held high carnival. The rats romped between her paws. Still she slept. It angered Ah Tcha. The lantern rays fell upon her eyes. Still she slept. Ah Tcha grew more and more provoked. He decided then and there to teach the cat that his mill was no place for sleepy heads.

Accordingly, he seized an empty grain sack and hurled it with such exact aim that the old cat was sent heels over head. "There, old Crouch-by-the-hole," said Ah Tcha in a tone of wrath. "Remember your paining ear, and be more vigilant." But the cat had no sooner regained her feet than she changed into . . . Nu Wu . . . changed into Nu Wu, the old woman who worked in the fields . . . a witch. What business she had in the mill is a puzzle. However, it is undoubtedly true that mills hold grain, and grain is worth money. And that may be an explanation. Her sleepiness is no puzzle at all. No wonder she was sleepy, after working so hard in the field, the day's length through.

The anger of Nu Wu was fierce and instant. She wagged a crooked finger at Ah Tcha, screeching: "Oh, you cruel money-grubber. Because you fear the rats will eat a pennyworth of grain you must beat me with bludgeons. You make me work like a slave all day—and wish me to work all night. You beat me and disturb my slumber. Very well, since you will not let me sleep, I shall cause you to slumber eleven hours out of every dozen. . . . Close your eyes." She swept her wrinkled hand across Ah Tcha's face. Again taking the form of a cat, she bounded downstairs.

She had scarce reached the third step descending when Ah Tcha felt a compelling desire for sleep. It was as if he had taken gum of the white poppy flower, as if he had tasted honey of the gray moon blossom. Eyes half closed, he stumbled into a grain bin. His knees doubled beneath him. Down he went, curled like a dormouse. Like a dormouse he slumbered.

From that hour began a change in Ah Tcha's fortune. The spell gripped him fast. Nine-tenths of his time was spent in sleep. Unable to watch over his laborers, they worked when they pleased, which was seldom. They idled when so inclined—and that was often and long. Furthermore, they stole in a manner most shameful. Ah Tcha's mills became empty of grain. His fields lost their fertility. His horses disappeared—strayed, so it was said. Worse yet, the unfortunate fellow was summoned to a magistrate's yamen, there to defend himself against a lawsuit. A neighbor declared that Ah Tcha's huge black cat had devoured many chickens. There were witnesses who swore to the deed. They were sure, one and all, that Ah Tcha's black cat was the cat at fault. Ah Tcha was sleeping too soundly to deny that the cat was his. . . . So the magistrate could do no less than make the cat's owner pay damages, with all costs of the lawsuit.

Thereafter, trials at court were a daily occurrence. A second neighbor said that Ah Tcha's black cat had stolen a flock of sheep.

Another complained that the cat had thieved from him a herd of fattened bullocks. Worse and worse grew the charges. And no matter how absurd, Ah Tcha, sleeping in the prisoner's cage, always lost and had to pay damages. His money soon passed into other hands. His mills were taken from him. His farms went to pay for the lawsuits. Of all his wide lands, there remained only one little acre—and it was grown up in worthless bushes. Of all his goodly buildings, there was left one little hut, where the boy spent most of his time, in witch-imposed slumber.

Now, near by in the mountain of Huge Rocks Piled, lived a greatly ferocious *loong*, or, as foreigners would say, a dragon. This immense beast, from tip of forked tongue to the end of his shadow, was far longer than a barn. With the exception of length, he was much the same as any other *loong*. His head was shaped like that of a camel. His horns were deer horns. He had bulging rabbit eyes, a snake neck. Upon his many ponderous feet were tiger claws, and the feet were shaped very like sofa cushions. He had walrus whiskers, and a breath of red-and-blue flame. His voice was like the sound of a hundred brass kettles pounded. Black fish scales covered his body, black feathers grew upon his limbs. Because of his color he was sometimes called *Oo Loong*. From that it would seem that *Oo* means neither white nor pink.

The black *loong* was not regarded with any great esteem. His habit of eating a man—two men if they were little—every day made him rather unpopular. Fortunately, he prowled only at night. Those folk who went to bed decently at nine o'clock had nothing to fear. Those who rambled well along toward midnight, often disappeared with sudden and complete thoroughness.

As everyone knows, cats are much given to night skulking. The witch cat, Nu Wu, was no exception. Midnight often found her miles afield. On such a midnight, when she was roving in the form of a hag, what should approach but the black dragon. Instantly the *loong* scented prey, and instantly he made for the old witch.

There followed such a chase as never was before on land or

sea. Up hill and down dale, by stream and wood and fallow, the cat woman flew and the dragon coursed after. The witch soon failed of breath. She panted. She wheezed. She stumbled on a bramble, and a claw slashed through her garments. Too close for comfort. The harried witch changed shape to a cat, and bounded off afresh, half a li at every leap. The *loong* increased his pace and soon was close behind, gaining. For a most peculiar fact about the *loong* is that the more he runs the easier his breath comes, and the swifter grows his speed. Hence, it is not surprising that his fiery breath was presently singeing the witch cat's back. In a twinkling the cat altered form once more, and as an old hag scuttled across a turnip field. She was merely an ordinarily powerful witch. She possessed only the two forms—cat and hag. Nor did she have a gift of magic to baffle or cripple the hungry black *loong*. Nevertheless, the witch was not despairing. At the edge of the turnip field lay Ah Tcha's miserable patch of thick bushes. So thick were the bushes as to be almost a wall against the hag's passage. As a hag, she could have no hope of entering such a thicket. But as a cat, she could race through without hindrance. And the dragon would be sadly bothered in following. Scheming thus, the witch dashed under the bushes—a cat once more.

Ah Tcha was roused from slumber by the most outrageous noise that had ever assailed his ears. There was such a snapping of bushes, such an awful bellowed screeching that even the dead of a century must have heard. The usually sound-sleeping Ah Tcha was awakened at the outset. He soon realized how matters stood—or ran. Luckily, he had learned of the only reliable method for frightening off the dragon. He opened his door and hurled a red, a green, and a yellow firecracker in the monster's path.

In through his barely opened door the witch cat dragged her exhausted self. "I don't see why you couldn't open the door sooner," she scolded, changing to a hag. "I circled the hut three times before you had the gumption to let me in."

"I am very sorry, good mother. I was asleep."

"Well don't be so sleepy again," scowled the witch, "or I'll make you suffer. Get me food and drink."

"Again, honored lady, I am sorry. So poor am I that I have only water for drink. My food is the leaves and roots of bushes."

"No matter. Get what you have—and quickly."

Ah Tcha reached outside the door and stripped a handful of leaves from a bush. He plunged the leaves into a kettle of hot water and signified that the meal was prepared. Then he lay down to doze, for he had been awake full half a dozen minutes and the desire to sleep was returning stronger every moment.

The witch soon supped and departed, without leaving so much as half a "Thank you." When Ah Tcha awoke again, his visitor was gone. The poor boy flung another handful of leaves into his kettle and drank quickly. He had good reason for haste. Several times he had fallen asleep with the cup at his lips—a most unpleasant situation, and scalding. Having taken several sips, Ah Tcha stretched him out for a resumption of his slumbers. Five minutes passed . . . ten minutes . . . fifteen. . . . Still his eyes failed to close. He took a few more sips from the cup and felt more awake than ever.

"I do believe," said Ah Tcha, "that she has thanked me by bewitching my bushes. She has charmed the leaves to drive away my sleepiness."

And so she had. Whenever Ah Tcha felt tired and sleepy—and at first that was often—he had only to drink the bewitched leaves. At once his drowsiness departed. His neighbors soon learned of the bushes that banished sleep. They came to drink of the magic brew. There grew such a demand that Ah Tcha decided to set a price on the leaves. Still the demand continued. More bushes were planted. Money came.

Throughout the province people called for "the drink of Ah Tcha." In time they shortened it by asking for "Ah Tcha's drink," then for "Tcha's drink," and finally for "Tcha."

And that is its name at present, "Tcha," or "Tay," or "Tea," as some call it. And one kind of Tea is still called "Oo Loong"— "Black Dragon."

THE LAZY FARMER
A TALE OF INDIA

by Jane Prescott

Many years ago in India, there lived a farmer who was very lazy. He was also very stupid, as you will see.

One day the lazy farmer thought to himself, "If I could grow my corn already cooked, I would be saved the trouble of cooking it later."

No sooner said than attempted, so he fried up a batch of corn and planted it in his field.

Now I don't need to tell you that nothing came up. But the farmer was so stupid that he thought someone must have been stealing from him. So one night he hid in a tree to watch for the thief.

In those days all this part of the country was the playground for the Celestial Elephant. This was the elephant that belonged to Indra, a great god of India. It was at least three times the size of an ordinary elephant—probably more—and had enormous wings.

The very night the farmer was on watch, the Celestial Elephant flew down to his field and frolicked about.

"Aha!" the silly farmer thought to himself. "This is the thief!" And he tried to catch the elephant by seizing its tail.

Away flew the elephant, with the farmer still clinging to its tail. Back to the kingdom of Indra it flew, and the great god Indra, as you can imagine, was much surprised to see what his elephant had brought.

When the farmer had told his story, Indra was so much amused that he gave the farmer a handful of magic corn to replace the crop he had lost. The elephant carried the silly farmer home, and he planted the magic corn before the sun was up.

Before the sun went down that night, the corn was full grown. All his neighbors were astonished and asked him what he had done.

When they heard his story, naturally all the neighbors wanted some of the magic corn for themselves, and the farmer offered to help them get some.

Every night for many weeks, they all kept watch in the farmer's field. And at last the Celestial Elephant came there again to play.

At once the farmer caught him by the tail, and as he rose into the air, all the neighbors caught hold of the farmer and each other, until they were strung out across the sky in a line like the tail of a kite.

Seeing the ground disappear below, some of the neighbors began to lose heart. "How tall does this magic corn grow?" they asked.

"Oh, this tall," said the farmer, stretching his hands wide. Of course he had to let go of the elephant's tail, and the whole string of people went tumbling to earth.

Indra, who had been watching with great amusement, set each one down safely in his own field. And I can assure you that from that time on, no harder-working people could be found in all of India.

THE TIGER'S TAIL
AN INDONESIAN TALE

by Harold Courlander

A farmer was coming home from his rice field one evening. His mind wandered gently over thoughts of eating, sleeping, and playing his flute. As he walked along the trail he came to a pile of rocks. Protruding through a crack he saw a tail switching back and forth. It was a tiger's tail. It was very large.

The farmer was overcome with panic. He thought of running to the village. But then he realized that the tiger was waiting for him to appear around the turn of the trail. So he dropped his sickle and seized the tiger's tail.

There was a struggle. The tiger tried to free himself. He pulled. The farmer pulled. They tugged back and forth. The tiger snarled and clawed. The farmer gasped and perspired, but he clung furiously to the tail.

While the struggle was going on a monk came walking along the trail.

"Oh! Allah has sent you!" the farmer cried. "Take my sickle from the ground and kill this fierce tiger while I hold him!"

The holy man looked at him calmly and said:

"Ah, I cannot. It is against my principles to kill."

"How can you say such a thing?" the farmer said. "If I let go this tail, which sooner or later I must do, the angry animal will turn on me and kill me!"

"I am sorry, brother," the monk said. "But my religion won't permit me to kill any living creature."

"How can you argue this way?" the farmer cried. "If you don't help me you will be the cause of my death. Isn't the life of a man worth as much as the life of a tiger?"

The monk listened thoughtfully and said calmly:

"All around us the things of the jungle kill each other, and for these things I am not responsible. I cannot take a life, it is written so."

The farmer felt his strength leaving him. The tiger's tail was slipping from his tired hands. At last he said:

"Oh, my holy, kindhearted friend, if it is so written, it is so written. Hold this tiger's tail so that I may kill him!"

The monk looked into the sky and thought.

"Very well, there is nothing written that says I may not hold a tiger's tail."

So he came forward and took hold of the tail.

"Do you have it?" the farmer asked.

"Yes, I have it," the monk replied.

"Do you have it firmly?"

"Yes, I have it firmly."

The farmer released his hold. He wiped the sweat from his face with his head cloth. He picked up his sickle from the ground where he had dropped it. He straightened his clothes and brushed the dust from his hands. Then he started toward the village.

The tiger renewed the tug of war with great energy. The monk clung frantically to the tail. They pulled back and forth desperately.

"Kill him! Kill him quickly!" the monk shouted.

The farmer continued toward the village.

"Where are you going? I can't hold out much longer!" the monk cried in alarm. "Kill him with your sickle!"

The farmer turned around placidly. His face was very peaceful.

"Oh, holy and venerable man," he said. "It was good to listen to your sacred words and to hear what is written. I have been moved by your feeling for living things. You have converted me. I now believe as you do. And as it is written. I may not kill any living creature. If you hold on with patience, other men who do not have such high ideals as we do may soon come this way and destroy the tiger for you."

And the farmer bowed and continued his way to the village.

DAVY CROCKETT
A TALE OF THE U.S.A.

by Michael Gorham

The best way to get acquainted with Davy Crockett is to listen to what he said about himself.

"I'm a screamer," Davy said. By that he meant that he could outshout and outtalk anybody on the whole Kentucky frontier, and there were plenty of screamers there—take my word for it.

"My father can lick any man in Kentucky," Davy said, "and I can lick my father. I can run faster, dive deeper, stay under longer, and come out drier than any man this side of the Mississippi. I can carry a steamboat on my back and wrassle a lion. I can walk like an ox, run like a fox, swim like an eel, yell like an Indian, fight like a devil, and swallow a congressman if you butter his head and pin his ears back."

Now Davy was being modest when he said all this. He could do everything in the list and a lot more, too, as you shall see.

In the days when Davy lived on the frontier in Kentucky and Tennessee, along about 1825, a man had to be a hunter if he wanted to eat. Davy was such a good shot that he never missed, and so he always had plenty of bear and deer and raccoon. But round lead bullets and powder for his muzzle-loading rifle were scarce. So Davy invented a way of getting raccoons without shooting them.

One day Davy had a raccoon up a tree. It looked so solemn that Davy couldn't help laughing. He just stood there on the ground and grinned. And the first thing he knew, he'd grinned that raccoon right out of the tree. He had it without firing a shot.

Well, after that Davy never lacked for meat. On a moony night he just went out and grinned raccoons. He even got so good that he could grin a panther out of a tree.

Then one day Davy met another hunter in the woods. This fellow was taking aim at something in a black gum tree.

"Wait a minute," Davy said. "Don't waste your powder. I'll grin that raccoon down for you."

Davy braced himself against a log, so his own grin wouldn't knock him over backward, and went to work. But nothing happened.

Now the other hunter was tickled pink. The great Davy Crockett couldn't do what he'd bragged about.

After a while Davy said, "I never saw such a spunktiliferous animal in all my days." And he climbed the tree to look into the matter. When he got up there, he found he'd been grinning at a knot that *looked* like a raccoon. But he didn't feel too bad about it. He'd grinned every bit of bark off that tree.

About the time Davy was really famous in the woods he had a queer experience. That was the day his dog Rattler treed a raccoon and Davy got himself all set and braced and ready. But before he could let fly with his grin, the raccoon lifted a paw to catch Davy's attention and said politely:

"Is your name Crockett?"

"You are right for once," Davy answered. "My name is Davy Crockett."

"In that case, don't trouble yourself," the raccoon said. "I know I might just as well come down without any argument." And down he came.

Davy watched the critter, who had considered himself dead, and he felt kind of flattered.

"I've never had such a compliment in my life," he said, patting the raccoon on the head. "I hope I may be shot before I hurt a hair of your hide."

"Thank you," said the raccoon. "Seeing as you feel that way, I'll just take a little walk. Not that I doubt your word—but in case you change your mind."

One morning Davy Crockett ate a rousing good breakfast of sausages made from bear meat and crocodile liver. He felt as warm inside as the weather was cold outside, so he made up his mind to take the day off from his hunting work and pay a visit to his next-door neighbor, Luke Twig. Luke lived only fifteen miles away.

As Davy walked along, he got colder and colder, until at last he thought he'd better make a fire. Now, he'd forgotten to bring along the flint and steel he generally used to start a fire, but he found he could strike his fist against a rock and make sparks. The only trouble was, the weather had turned so cold the sparks froze. So Davy decided he'd do like the animals—he'd crawl inside a hollow tree to get warm.

Inside the tree he thrashed around and swung his arms up and down. Davy made considerable noise, but the racket all froze in the cold, so a wolf coming along didn't notice that Davy had first dibs on that hollow tree. The wolf tried to get in, but then he saw Davy and decided he didn't like the man's looks. He turned away to hunt for another hollow tree. As he turned, his tail poked through a knothole.

Davy hadn't meant to go hunting that day, but he felt kind of mischievous. He grabbed that wolf's tail and pulled it through the knothole. Then he tied a figure-eight knot in it so it couldn't slip back out.

About that time, the weather thawed a little. Davy climbed out of the tree and walked on toward Luke Twig's place, and all the way there he could hear the wolf letting out some mighty unprintable howls.

One of the things Davy liked best in the world was a good thunderstorm. He said:

"A regular, round-roaring, savage peal of thunder is the greatest treat in all creation. It sets everything but a coward shouting in his very heart and soul, till he swells so eternally big with natural glorification that he feels as if he could swallow the entire creation at one gulp."

Well, one day Davy was out in a storm, feeling full of thunder glory, and he just stood stock-still with his mouth open. Right then a teetotal thunderbolt came along, and he swallowed it. That streak of lightning was so powerful it blew off his hip pockets, and it heated up his insides something remarkable. For a month after that, Davy ate raw food, and the leftover lightning cooked it as it went down.

Now Kill-Devil was the name of Davy's favorite gun. And Davy was a mighty fine shot. But one particular day he hadn't seen anything to shoot at. Instead of going home empty-handed, he decided to sleep out on a hillside and try for better luck tomorrow. He leaned Kill-Devil up against a tree and hung his powder horn on a branch.

Next morning he shouldered Kill-Devil, but there was no powder horn in sight. Davy looked around everywhere for it. He looked all day. He was still looking when night came and the new moon started skimming toward him through the sky above the hill. There, on one sharp point of the moon, hung Davy's powder horn. The new moon had come by the night before while Davy was asleep and just accidentally hooked the powder horn off the tree above him. Naturally Davy grabbed the horn, and after that he shot three bears, two catamounts, and a rabbit. But from that day to this he never hung his powder horn on a tree again.

Davy was mighty proud of Kill-Devil and what he could do with it. He'd never been beaten in a shooting contest until one day he ran across Mike Fink. And even then it wasn't poor aim that made Davy lose.

Mike Fink was a river boatman. But when he wasn't working—which was when he didn't want to—Mike had to shoot his own groceries out of the woods.

Davy spent the night in Mike's cabin, and the next morning Mike showed he was a screamer, just the way Davy was.

"I've got the handsomest wife," said Mike, "and the fastest horse and the sharpest shootin' iron in all Kentuck."

This put Davy's dander up. "I've got nothing to say against your wife, Mike," said he. "For it can't be denied she's a shocking handsome woman. And Mrs. Crockett's in Tennessee, and I've got no horses."

Davy didn't exactly like to call Mike a liar about what he could do with a rifle, but he did raise his voice a little when he said he had his doubts. And then he added to Mike:

"See that cat sitting on the top rail of your fence about two hundred yards off? He'll have to start today growing a new set of whiskers."

Then Davy took one shot and shaved the whiskers off one side of that cat's face, as clean as if he'd used a razor. The cat looked up, a little surprised like, as if something had tickled it, and while its head was turned, Davy shaved the other side with a second shot.

"Talk about your rifle after that, Mike," Davy boasted.

Mike wasn't worried one bit. "See that sow and her pigs off at the farthest end of that far pasture?" he said to Davy. Then he raised his gun. Off went the sow's tail. Then, one after another, Mike shot off the little pigs' tails.

"Now, let's see you shoot them back on again," said Mike, feeling pretty proud of himself.

"That's on-possible, Mike," Davy said, "and you know it. But you left one of those pigs about an inch of tail to steer by. If I'd been doing it, I'd never have made that mistake."

Then Davy took aim and snipped off the inch of tail.

This made Mike kind of wrothy. He turned around and took aim at his wife, who was going to the spring for water. His bullet knocked half the comb off her head without stirring a hair. Then he called out to her to stand still so Davy could shoot at the other half of the comb.

Mike's wife was used to such tricks from long practice.

"No, Mike," said Dave Crockett, "my hand would be sure to shake if this shooting iron pointed within a hundred miles of a woman, and I give up."

That was the only time Davy Crockett ever was beaten at anything.

Myths and Fables

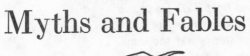

Long and long ago people found it very hard to explain how the world came to be and what makes things happen as they do. What makes night and day, or storms? Where did the first people come from? Or the stars? Perhaps you have wondered about such things yourself. Well, when people don't know the answers to questions, they sometimes make up the best guess they can think of, and the stories of these guesses are sometimes called myths. People in different parts of the world made up different myths and told about their giants and gods and devils over and over again, until some came to believe that these are the really truly stories of what happened. Of course they do not all agree, but many of them are very interesting stories just the same.

Other stories that people tell in all parts of the world are about the ways men and women and boys and girls deal with one another—especially about the ways of thoughtless or foolish people. These stories are called fables, and most of them pretend to tell about animals. You know, of course, that animals do not really talk to each other and to people the way the fables tell about them. Yet they are made to say and do things much as people say and do them. In this way they may help us understand people better. And they sometimes help us to understand ourselves better, too.

Like many of the make-believe folk tales and myths, fables are sometimes truer than true stories.

THE WIND AND THE SUN

An Aesop Fable

One summer afternoon the Wind and the Sun were having a conversation. Each one was boasting about the great things he had done. The Sun was telling how he had once pushed all the water out of a tremendous lake. The Wind was telling how he had once pulled all the trees of a great forest up by the roots. Each one was trying to make himself out to be the more powerful.

Presently the Wind said, "Let us have a test to see which of us is really the stronger." The Sun agreed, but asked, "How shall we test our strength?"

The Wind sniffed around and pretty soon came upon a traveler walking along the highway as if he didn't have a care in the world. Then the Wind said to the Sun, "Let us see which of us is strong enough to pull that traveler's cloak off."

"Very well," said the Sun; "you make the first trial."

Then the Wind began to blow. It got very cold. The air blew more and more furiously around the man. But the colder it got, and the harder the Wind blew, the more tightly did he pull the cloak around himself. And although the Wind blew as hard as he could, the traveler held on to his cloak throughout the storm.

Then the Sun began. Gradually the sky cleared; the clouds drifted away. It became warmer and warmer. The Sun beat his rays down on the man's back. The traveler unbuttoned his cloak. But it was getting warmer. He took off his cloak and carried it on his arm. The air was getting still warmer. He took off his coat and walked in his shirt sleeves. Finally he sat down in the shadow of a hay cock, as it was too hot to go farther.

So the gentle rays of the Sun succeeded where the blustering Wind was unable to do what he tried.

THE FOX AND THE GRAPES

An Aesop Fable

A hungry fox who had been unable to find anything to eat for a long time saw some ripe grapes hanging along the top of a tall wall. The sight of them made his mouth water. But when he

reached up to get some grapes, they were away above his head. He jumped up, but could not get at them. He climbed and he jumped again and again, but without being able to get a single grape.

Some birds in a tree close by were chirping away, greatly amused by the fox's poor luck. Now he was not only annoyed by his hunger and his failure, but also by the jeering of the birds.

He stopped jumping for the grapes and turned away. Looking up at the birds, he said, "Those are very sour grapes. I really don't want any. I wouldn't eat them if they were right before me on the ground." And so he walked off.

But the birds understood why he said that the grapes were sour.

THE COUNTRY MAID
AND HER MILK PAIL

An Aesop Fable

A country maid was walking along the road carrying a pail of milk on her head. She was walking slowly and daydreaming as she went.

"I shall sell this milk when I get to the village," she thought. "And with the money I get for it I shall buy three hundred eggs. Of course, some of the eggs may be bad, so only two hundred and fifty of them will hatch into little chicks. The chicks will be grown by Christmas time and then I will take them into the market and sell them. Poultry always gets a high price at Christmas time, so I shall make a lot of money. With the money I shall buy me a new gown. I think it will be green. Or perhaps it should be blue. No, I am prettier in green. I shall buy a new green gown and I shall wear it to the fair on May Day. Naturally, all the young fellows will want to dance with me, but not one of them shall be my partner. I shall refuse them all," she thought.

By this time her daydream was so real to her that she tossed her head proudly and over went the milk pail. All the milk spilled on the ground and there was no money, no eggs, no chickens, and no new green dress.

The moral of this tale is: Don't count your chickens before they are hatched.

KING MIDAS AND THE GOLDEN TOUCH

Midas was the son of a poor farmer who later became king of a certain ancient city. Having been poor in his youth, he came to feel that he would like to have great riches and to have power over people, as he had seen men using power over others with gold. So by the time he became king he thought that getting gold is the most important thing in the world. And he did indeed gather great stores of gold.

One day as he was feasting with some friends an old man stumbled in and the servants started to put him out. But Midas recognized the old man as a teacher of Bacchus, the god of wine, and let him remain several days until he was ready to leave.

For this, Bacchus was very grateful and offered to grant Midas one wish. Midas did not take long to think but said, "I wish I could change anything into gold by just touching it."

"My son," Bacchus said kindly, "that is not a very wise wish; but I shall keep my promise, if that is what you want."

"Yes, that is what I want," said Midas; and Bacchus walked away.

Then Midas wondered whether he really had the magic power. He touched a stick and it at once turned into gold. He plucked a fruit from a tree; it too turned to gold. Midas was greatly excited. He began to think of all the gold he would have. "How wonderful!" he thought.

The king came back to the palace so happy that he ordered his servants to prepare a feast. All his friends were invited to eat and drink and rejoice with the king.

Midas sat down and reached for a cup of wine. He did not notice that the cup turned to gold, but when the wine touched his lips it froze into solid gold!

Then he took hold of a piece of bread. That also turned to gold. Now he began to fear that he would not be able to eat. He tried different kinds of food, but each turned to gold. Then he realized that he would not be able to eat or drink.

He wondered whether he was really so lucky to have this wonderful gift. He went into the garden and there was his little girl, whom he loved more than riches. She ran toward him and he raised her up to kiss her and the child suddenly turned into gold.

Then Midas realized with a shock how foolish he had been. He was indeed very miserable. He went into the grove and prayed to Bacchus to take back his gift. "I do not want so much gold," he cried. "I do not want so much power. I want to be able to eat and drink like other people. I want to be able to love my children."

Bacchus said that he would take back the golden touch, but Midas pleaded, "Can I get my child back? That is worth more than all the gold in the world!"

Bacchus said to Midas, "Follow this stream up into the mountains, to its very beginning, and take with you a large pitcher. When you get there, dip your whole body into the water. That will wash away the golden magic. Before you go ashore, fill the urn with water from the source and bring it back to wash the gold out of your daughter's body."

Midas did as he was told. He climbed the mountains to the very beginning of the stream. When he dipped himself into the water, the sands around him turned to gold. And when he came out he was no longer able to turn things into gold by touching them.

He carried the heavy load of precious water from the source of the stream back to the palace. The golden image of his daughter was standing in the garden and he eagerly poured the water over the head and body. The yellow color disappeared. The cheeks turned pink. The eyes of the child opened. Her arms reached out toward her father. He grasped the living child in his arms, tears rolling down his cheeks.

Later, whenever he remembered the agony of this time, he thought to himself, "That was a terrible dream! Why does anyone want so much gold? Why does anyone want so much power?"

PROMETHEUS

Before there were any animals or people on the earth, according to old Greek legends, great Titans, or Giants, inhabited the world. The gods asked one of these giants, called Prometheus, to make some animals for the world. This he did, using earth stuck together with sea water. From the seeds mixed in with the earth and water, these shapes became alive.

And to each animal Prometheus gave what it would need to keep alive. To the birds, he gave beaks and wings; to the fish he gave scales and fins. To some animals he gave fur; to others, hard shells or tough hide. He made some animals swift to move about and others so that they could hide from enemies. Some received sharp eyes, others keen scent or hearing.

Then Prometheus thought to make something superior to the animals and he kneaded some mud into the form of the gods themselves. But then he had given so much to the other animals that he had hardly anything for his favorite, man. So this first man could not run as fast as the rabbit, nor could he fly like an insect or a bird. He had no fur or feathers or scales to protect his thin skin. His nails were not strong like those of the lion or bear. And he could not see as far as the eagle or smell as did the dog or the deer.

But Prometheus did give man a clever hand and a speaking voice and a superior brain. And Athene, the goddess of wisdom, who admired what Prometheus had done, promised to breathe the spirit of life into the first man.

Yet Prometheus was not satisfied. He flew up into the sky, and as Apollo was passing by in his chariot he caught some fire from the sun with a bundle of reeds. This he brought down to earth and gave to man, showing him how to use it.

"With fire," Prometheus said, "you can make up for what all the other animals have. Even if your teeth are weak, you can cook your food and be able to eat it. Even if your nails are weak, you can make spears and knives from metal and overcome any animal. Your skin is thin and bare, but fire will help you to use the fur of other animals and make shelters and keep warm wherever you may roam. You will be able to make tools and force the earth to yield more food."

By giving man fire, Prometheus started him off to get ahead of all the other animals, and of many evil spirits too. With fire man learned to do all kinds of things and to make everything he might want.

For stealing the heavenly fire and giving it to man, however, Prometheus drew the anger of the gods upon himself. They feared that with fire man might become too powerful or too much like themselves. Zeus was especially displeased and resolved to punish Prometheus severely. He had Prometheus chained to the rocky top of high Mount Caucasus. There he suffered the heat of the sun all day and the freezing cold all night. In addition, Zeus sent a vulture to tear at his organs and destroy his liver—which grew again each night and renewed the torture.

Prometheus knew a secret about something that would befall Zeus, but he would not give it to Zeus and continued to suffer for a very long time, until he was actually released by Hercules.

PANDORA'S BOX

According to an old Greek story, the gods in Olympus continued to feel angry toward Prometheus for having stolen the heavenly fire and giving it to man, although he was already severely punished for that. They thought to harm his favorite creation, man.

They wanted something that would attract him, yet always plague him. So the craftiest gods made up a woman out of earthy clay; and in heaven all the gods and goddesses gave her special gifts. Venus gave her beauty; Athene gave her wisdom, Apollo gave music. Some gave her all the graces and charms. They called her Pandora, which means "all the gifts," although not all the gifts were meant to be helpful.

Mercury, the messenger of the gods, was ordered to take Pandora down to earth for the first man. Zeus gave her a golden box containing all the gifts. He warned Pandora, however, never to open the box and to give it to her husband. When Mercury left her, Pandora was very curious about what the box contained. She remembered what Zeus had told her, but she could not restrain herself. She thought it could do no harm to open the box just a teeny bit and peek in. So she opened it carefully just a teeny bit. But all at once all the gifts, good and bad, rushed out in all directions, like a cloud. There were pain and sickness, but also dance and song; grief and anxiety and friendship and humor. Hatred and strife came out and also laughter and joy. There were jealousy and envy and kindness and helpfulness.

The gifts came out so fast and were blown away with the wind that Pandora quickly shut the lid down. But it was too late, for everything had already gone out.

Everything, that is, except one gift, the last, at the bottom of the box, which man could always keep.

That was Hope.

ANDROCLES AND THE LION

Androcles was a brave soldier and one of the emperor's favorites. But once he displeased the emperor by shooting a deer or a boar that the emperor had missed. So the man was sold to be a slave and sent far from his home.

After being a slave for some time, Androcles managed to escape, and wandered off in the hills and deserts, trying to find his way back to his own land. One very hot day he crawled into a cave to get out of the sun. He was very hungry, but hoped he could find something to eat later in the day. While he was resting from his wanderings, he heard a strange sound. He knew that an animal was coming into the cave. But he could not tell what it was. The steps did not sound like the steps of any animal that he knew. But he was frightened, and he held his breath so as to make no sound by which the animal could find him.

As he waited there, holding his breath, the animal came nearer. It was a lion. But he did not look fierce. He did not walk as if he were the King of Beasts. In fact, he was limping on three legs, holding one of his front paws in the air. He looked very unhappy indeed for a lion.

Androcles felt so sorry for the lion that he forgot to be afraid. The lion walked up to him and stopped right there in front of him. He held up his paw and made a soft miaow, like a sad and hungry kitten, only louder. Then Androcles saw that the poor lion had a thorn in his paw. That was why the lion was so mild and so unhappy. He could not put his foot down as firmly as a lion should.

Androcles bent over and gently pulled the thorn out of the lion's foot. It must have hurt, for the lion squeaked a little. But it probably did not hurt as much as walking on the thorn did. The lion purred and shook his head gently at Androcles, then turned around and walked out of the cave.

Androcles wandered about for days and weeks, living as best he could on roots and berries and nuts. At last he came to a camp made up of many tents. He was very glad, because he thought that now he could get food and be safe from wild animals. But when he came to the camp he saw that it was filled with the emperor's soldiers, and the captain recognized Androcles. They made a prisoner of him and after a while brought him back to Rome.

The emperor disliked Androcles even more now, because he had run away from his master. So the emperor decided on a very cruel punishment. He ordered Androcles put into the arena, where a hungry lion should destroy him. There Androcles was, and the gate to the lion's cage was opened.

The lion came out growling and sniffing. He walked about as if he were looking for something to eat. Pretty soon he came to where Androcles was lying on the ground, expecting to be devoured the very next minute. But when the lion stood over Androcles, instead of springing on him he began to lick him gently with his tongue.

Everybody was amazed, and they soon brought word to the emperor that Androcles must be a strange magician, for the lion would not eat him, as lions had always eaten other prisoners. The emperor ordered Androcles brought before him and asked him to explain what his power was that protected him from the lion.

Then Androcles told the story of the lion in the desert, from whose foot he had removed the thorn. The emperor forgave him and took him back into his favor.

THE SHEPHERD BOY AND THE WOLF

An Aesop Fable

A shepherd boy thought it was very dull to watch the sheep all day, but that was his task and that's what he did. He wondered why nothing ever happened to make his work exciting. He wondered what could possibly happen.

One day he thought he would play a trick on his neighbors. It was a dull, warm summer day. The sheep were quietly eating grass. The bees were buzzing the same tune they had always been buzzing. It was very dull, and the boy wished something would happen.

Suddenly he called out, at the very top of his voice, "Wolf! Wolf!"

When the sound of his voice reached the village in the valley, all the boys who heard him stopped whatever they were doing and started to run up to the meadows. And all the men stopped whatever they were doing. They dropped their tools and reached out for the nearest club, or stick, or pitchfork. And they started to run toward the fields to get after the wolf who, they thought, would be robbing the flock.

While they were still some distance away, they could see the sheep quietly eating grass. But when they came quite close, the shepherd boy burst out laughing. "Ha, ha!" he shouted. "I fooled you that time. There was no wolf."

The men were very angry. Some of them scolded him for being so foolish and unkind. Some of them muttered unfriendly words for making them lose time from their work and for making them run on such a hot day. Not even the boys who came for the excitement thought it was funny.

A few days later the shepherd boy was again feeling rather dull. He wondered what might happen to make things more interesting. But he could not think up a new trick. So he suddenly called out at the very top of his voice, only louder this time, "Wolf! Wolf! Wolf!"

Again the boys dropped their play. Again the men dropped their work. Again all came tearing up the hills as fast as they could run, with any clubs or sticks or pitchforks they could grab.

And when they came to the field, the sheep were again eating grass quietly, as though nothing could disturb them. And again the boy burst out laughing, "Ha, ha! Ha, ha!"

And this time the men were very angry indeed, and some of them wanted to beat the boy. But the others thought it better to go off and have nothing more to do with the shepherd.

The shepherd boy, however, was pleased with himself. He thought that was a good trick he had thought up. It had worked twice. Some day, he thought, he would try it again.

Not many days later, while the sheep were quietly eating grass, and the boy was half asleep in the shadow of a tree, a pack of wolves quietly stole up toward the flock. Some of the sheep began to bleat, "Baa, baa!" and woke the boy up.

He saw at once that the wolves had come. And he shouted the loudest he could ever shout, "Wolf! Wolf! Wolf!" And he was scared and excited.

And he shouted again, "Wolf! Wolf! Wolf!" And he kept on shouting, while the wolves were attacking the sheep and killing the best of them.

But nobody came to help him.

WHY THE SEA IS SALT

Adapted from George Webbe Dasent

Once upon a time, but it was a long, long time ago, there were two brothers. One of the brothers was very rich and the other was very poor. When Christmas Eve came around the poor one didn't even have a crust of bread to eat, so he went to see his rich brother.

"My wife and I haven't even got a crust of bread for our Christmas feast," he said. "Surely you will give us something."

"I will give you a whole flitch of bacon," his brother replied, "if you will do what I ask you."

"Why, of course," the poor man said. "I will do anything you say."

"Here is the flitch of bacon then," said the rich one. "And now go straight to the land of Nowhere."

The poor brother always kept his word, so he took the bacon and started off, trying to find the road to Nowhere. He walked and walked and at last, in the evening, he came to a place where he saw a very bright light shining through a house made entirely of glass.

"Maybe this is the place," he said to himself.

So he stopped and looked around, and he saw an old, old man with a long white beard chopping wood.

"Good evening," he said to the wood chopper.

"The same to you," the wood chopper replied. "Where are you going so late on Christmas Eve?"

"Oh, I am going to the land of Nowhere," the poor man told him. "But I don't know the way."

"You are very lucky then," said the wood chopper. "For that is Nowhere right there behind the glass walls. When you get inside, everyone will want to buy your bacon, for meat is very scarce there. But be sure you don't sell it unless they give you the little quern which stands behind the door. It can grind out anything in the wide world you want. That is, if you know how to work it. And when you come out again, I will teach you how."

So the poor man thanked the wood chopper for his good advice and then he knocked on the big glass door of the glass house. When he got inside, it was just as the old wood chopper had said. There were hundreds of little gnomes about, all working busily, but when they saw the flitch of bacon they stopped working and wanted to buy it.

"I want this bacon so that my wife and I can celebrate Christmas," the poor man said; "but I will give it to you if you give me that little hand mill that stands behind the door."

At first the gnomes would hear of no such bargain, but the bacon looked so good to them that they finally gave the poor man their hand mill. Off he went with it, and the old wood chopper showed him how to work it. He thanked him kindly and then went home as fast as his legs would carry him.

When he got to his own door, he called out, "Come here, Wife, and you shall see what you shall see."

His wife came to greet him, and he put the quern on the table. Then he started it working and made it grind out a tablecloth and meat and ale and cakes and every good thing he could think of to eat for Christmas dinner.

Husband and wife had a fine feast, and so it went every day, all through the holiday season. On New Year's Day they decided to have a specially fine feast and to invite all their friends.

All the neighbors came, and everyone enjoyed the party except the rich brother. When he saw all the wonderful food on the table and all the food in the kitchen, he became very jealous. Of course he had plenty of food in his own house, but he didn't want his brother to have any.

"Where did all this wealth come from?" he asked angrily.

And his brother showed him the remarkable little hand quern

which could grind out anything in the wide world.

"I must have that quern!" the rich brother said to himself, and he begged and coaxed until finally it was his—for the price of three hundred dollars.

He was so afraid that his brother would change his mind that he paid the three hundred dollars and took the mill home as fast as he could. He went so fast, in fact, that he forgot to find out how it worked.

The next day, at dinnertime, he said to his wife, "Now you go into the parlor and sit down while I get dinner ready."

He took the hand quern into the kitchen and bade it grind out herrings and broth. It was very easy to get the quern to work, but it wasn't so easy to get it to stop. So herrings and broth started pouring out of it, first filling up the bowls on the table,

then flowing over onto the table itself, and then onto the floor. Herrings and broth, herrings and broth poured out of the mill till at last the kitchen was filled to the ceiling. Then herrings and broth started to pour into the parlor and into every room in the house.

The man did everything he could to stop it, but it would not stop. So he took it back to his brother's house, running as fast as he could while herrings and broth kept pouring out all over the road.

"Here, take this thing away from me," he shouted when he got to the door. "Take it and make it stop or else the whole countryside will be flooded with herrings and broth."

The brother took it, but only after he had received three hundred dollars more.

Now he had the money and the quern besides. He lived comfortably with his wife for many years, and every time they wanted something the little quern would grind it out for them.

Naturally everyone was curious about this remarkable mill, and people came from far and wide to see it. It became famous all over the country. All over the world, in fact.

One day a sea captain came to see the quern, and the first thing he asked was whether it could grind salt. When he heard that it could, he said that he must have it no matter how much it cost.

"For then," he thought, "I won't have to take those long sea voyages to distant lands just to bring back salt."

At first the man wouldn't dream of parting with his precious quern, but the sea captain begged and coaxed so hard and offered so much money that he finally consented.

The captain was afraid that the man would change his mind, so he paid the money and went away with the little mill as fast as he could. He went away so fast, in fact, that he didn't find out how to work it.

He got on his boat and, after he had sailed far out to sea, he bade the mill grind salt. Now it was very easy to start the quern working but very hard to make it stop. So it started grinding salt, and it ground and it ground till the whole deck was covered. Still it kept on grinding, till the boat was filled with salt and, try as he would, the captain couldn't make it stop.

So, of course, the boat being filled with salt, it was heavier than you can possibly imagine and it sank to the bottom of the ocean. There it lies to this very day while the quern keeps right on grinding. And that is why the sea is salt.

Bible Stories

These are some of the stories that have been told and retold for centuries by the people of two great religions, the Christians and the Jews. The book from which these stories are taken is called the Bible. The first four are from the Old Testament. The next seven are from the life of Jesus in the New Testament.

I have used as nearly as possible the same words that were used when the Bible was first translated into English. The Bible stories have been told so many times and for so many years that they have come to be a part of our everyday language and our everyday thinking.

THE FLOOD AND NOAH'S ARK

There came a time when the people were wicked before God, unfair and dishonest. And the earth was filled with violence for men were fighting and killing. But Noah was a just man and perfect in his time and he walked in the way of God. And Noah had three sons, Shem, Ham, and Japheth.

And God said unto Noah, All life displeases me; for there is too much evil in the earth, and, behold, I would destroy these evil ones. Make thee then an ark of gopher wood with many rooms. Make thou the ark and pitch it within and without with pitch. And in this fashion shalt thou make it: The length of it shall be three hundred cubits, the breadth of it fifty cubits, and the height of it thirty cubits. Make thou also a window to the ark, and set the door of the ark in the side thereof. And make it with lower, second, and third stories.

And, behold, I shall bring a flood of waters upon the earth, to destroy all flesh, wherein is the breath of life, from under heaven; and every thing that is in the earth shall die. But with thee will I establish a promise; and thou shalt come into the ark, thou, and thy sons, and thy wife, and thy son's wives with thee. And of every living thing of all flesh, bring into the ark two of every sort to keep them alive with thee; they shall be male and female.

Thus did Noah; according to all that God commanded him, so did he.

And the Lord said unto Noah, Come thou and all thy house, into the ark; for I have seen thee, that thou art righteous before me in this generation.

Then Noah, and Noah's wife, and Shem, and Ham, and

Japheth, the three sons of Noah, and the three wives of his sons with them, all entered into the ark; they and every beast after his kind, and all the kinds of cattle, and every creeping thing that creepeth upon the earth, and every fowl, every bird of every sort. And they went in unto Noah into the ark, two and two of every kind.

In the selfsame day all the fountains of the great sea were broken up, and the windows of heaven were opened. And the rain came upon the earth forty days and forty nights.

And the flood was forty days upon the earth. And the waters increased, and lifted up the ark. And the waters covered every thing, and lifted the ark up above the earth. The waters increased greatly upon the earth; and the ark went upon the face of the waters. And the waters rose up exceedingly upon the earth; and all the high hills under the whole heaven were covered. Fifteen cubits upward did the waters rise; and the mountains were covered.

And all beings died that moved upon the earth, both of fowl, and of cattle, and of beast, and of every creeping thing that creepeth upon the earth, and every man. All in whose nostrils was the breath of life, all that lived in the dry land, died. And every living substance was destroyed from the earth. Noah only remained alive, Noah and they that were with him in the ark.

And the waters ruled over the earth an hundred and fifty days.

But God remembered Noah, and made a wind to pass over the earth, and the waters went down; and he stopped also the fountains of the deep sea and the rain from heaven. And the waters went back from off the earth, and the ark rested in the seventh month, on the seventeenth day of the month upon the mountains of Ararat. And the waters decreased continually until the tenth month: and then were the tops of the mountains seen.

And it came to pass at the end of forty days, Noah opened the window of the ark which he had made: and he sent forth a raven, which came not back to the ark, but went to and fro over the waters until they were dried up from off the earth.

Then Noah sent forth a dove from him, to see if the waters were abated from off the face of the ground. But the dove found no rest for the sole of her foot, and she returned unto the ark, for the waters were still on the face of the whole earth. Then Noah put forth his hand, and pulled her into the ark.

And he waited yet other seven days; and again he sent forth the dove out of the ark, and in the evening, the dove came in to him, and, lo, in her mouth was an olive leaf plucked off. Then Noah knew that the waters were abated from off the earth.

And Noah waited yet other seven days, and sent forth the dove; which returned not again any more, for now the waters were dried up from off the earth. Then he removed the covering of the ark and looked, and, behold the face of the ground was dry.

And God spake unto Noah, saying, Go forth from the ark, thou and thy wife, and thy sons, and thy sons' wives with thee. Bring forth with thee every living thing that is with thee, of all flesh, the fowl, and cattle, and every creeping thing that creepeth upon the earth; that they may breed abundantly in the earth, and be fruitful, and multiply upon the earth.

And Noah went forth and his wife, and his sons, and his sons' wives with him: every living thing, all after their kinds, went forth out of the ark, two by two.

And Noah prayed and gave thanks unto the Lord.

And the Lord was pleased with Noah and blessed him and his sons. And God set the rainbow in the sky as a sign of his promise to Noah. And the Lord said I will not again smite any more every thing living, as I have done. While the earth remaineth, seedtime and harvest, and cold and heat, and summer and winter, and day and night shall not cease.

JOSEPH AND HIS BRETHREN

Jacob had twelve sons, but he loved Joseph the youngest more than all his children, because he was the son of his old age. And he made Joseph a coat of many colours. But when his brethren saw that the father loved him more than all his brethren, they hated him, and could not speak peaceably unto him.

Once Joseph had a dream, which he told unto his brethren. In his dream he saw his sheaf of grain stand upright, but the sheaves of his brethren bowed down to his sheaf. And they hated him the more for his dream.

And Joseph had yet another dream, and he told it unto his father and unto his brethren. In the dream the sun and the moon and eleven stars made obeisance unto Joseph. And his brethren hated him the more for his dream.

Now it came to pass that his brethren went to the hills to feed their father's flocks. And Israel, the father, said unto Joseph, Thy brethren are feeding the flocks in the hill, come, and I will send thee unto them.

And Joseph said to him, Here am I.

And the father said, Go, I pray thee, see whether it be well with thy brethren, and well with the flocks; and bring me word again.

So Joseph went after his brethren, where they were with the flocks. And when they saw him afar off, even before he came near, they plotted against him to slay him.

And they said one to another, Behold, this dreamer cometh. Come now, and let us slay him, and cast him into some pit. And we will say, Some evil beast hath devoured him: and we shall see what will become of his dreams.

Reuben the eldest heard it, and he would save Joseph out of their hands; and he said unto his brethren, Let us not kill him. Shed no blood, but cast him into this pit that is in the wilderness.

Reuben thought he might thus get Joseph out of their hands, to deliver him to his father again.

And it came to pass, when Joseph was come to his brethren, that they stript him of his coat, his coat of many colours that was on him. And they took him, and cast him into a pit: and the pit was empty, there was no water in it.

Then they sat down to eat bread. And as they lifted up their eyes and looked, behold, a company of Ishmaelites came from Gilead with their camels bearing spicery and balm and myrrh, going to carry it down to Egypt. And Judah, one of the brethren, said unto his brethren, What profit is it if we slay our brother, and conceal his blood? Come, and let us sell him to the Ishmaelites, and let not our hand be upon him; for he is our brother and our flesh. And his brethren agreed.

Then there passed by another company of merchantmen. And the brethren lifted Joseph out of the pit, and sold him to the Ishmaelites for twenty pieces of silver. And the merchantmen brought Joseph into Egypt.

Later Reuben returned unto the pit, thinking to take Joseph out: and, behold, Joseph was not in the pit. And Reuben rent his clothes and cried out. And he returned unto his brethren, and said, The child is not and I am sore distressed. What now shall

I say unto our father? And I, whither shall I go?

Then the brethren thought to deceive Israel, their father. And they took Joseph's coat, and killed a kid of the goats, and dipped the coat in the blood. Then they sent the coat of many colours to their father; and said, This have we found. Know now whether it be thy son's coat or not.

And Israel knew it, and said, It is my son's coat; an evil beast hath devoured him; Joseph is without doubt rent in pieces. And the father Jacob rent his clothes, and put sackcloth upon his loins, and mourned for his son many days.

And all his sons and all his daughters rose up to comfort him. But he refused to be comforted. And he said, For I will go down into the grave mourning my son. Thus his father wept for him.

But the Ishmaelites who had bought Joseph from his brethren brought him down to Egypt. And there the Ishmaelites sold Joseph again, unto an Egyptian, Potiphar by name. Now Potiphar was an officer of the King Pharaoh and captain of the guard.

And the Lord was with Joseph, and made him to prosper. And Joseph was in the house of his master the Egyptian.

And his master Potiphar saw that the Lord was with Joseph,

and that the Lord made all that he did to prosper in his hand. And Joseph found grace in the sight of Potiphar and he served him. Potiphar made Joseph overseer over his house and his lands; and all that he had he put into his hand, trusting Joseph.

MOSES IN THE BULRUSHES

At one time there arose up a new king Pharaoh over Egypt, which knew not Joseph, and his works.

And in the time of Pharaoh the children of Israel increased abundantly, and multiplied. They grew exceeding mighty; and the land was filled with them. And the king said unto his people, Behold, the people of the children of Israel are more and mightier than we. It may come to pass, if there come to be any war, that they join unto our enemies, and fight against us. Come then, let us deal wisely with them; lest they multiply and become too great.

Therefore did the king and his people set taskmasters over the Hebrews to oppress them with their tasks. But the more they drove them, the more they multiplied and grew. And the Egyptians were grieved because of the children of Israel.

Then Pharaoh thought to overcome the Israelites still further. He charged therefore all his people, saying, Every son that is born to the Israelites ye shall cast into the river, and every daughter ye shall save alive.

And there was a man of the house of Levi, of the children of Israel and his wife. To them was born a son. The mother saw that he was a good child, and she loved him, and would not that

he be cast into the river, as the king had commanded, so she hid
him for three months.

And when she could no longer hide him, she made for him an
ark of bulrushes from the river, and daubed the ark with mud
and with pitch, and put the child therein. And she laid it in
among the rushes by the river's brink. And she bade the child's
sister to stand afar off, to watch what would be done to the babe.

And it came to pass in a short time that the daughter of
Pharaoh came down to wash herself at the river; and her maidens
walked along by the river's side. When she saw the ark among
the rushes she sent her maid to fetch it. And when she had
opened it, she saw the child: and, behold, the babe wept.

Then Pharaoh's daughter felt pity on the child and said, This
is one of the Hebrews' children. But she took the babe in her
arms, and she thought to save the child from the river.

Then the sister of the child, who had been watching by the
river, said to Pharaoh's daughter, Shall I go and call to thee a
nurse of the Hebrew women, that she may nurse the child for
thee?

And Pharaoh's daughter said to her, Go.

And the sister went and called the child's own mother.

And when the mother was come, Pharaoh's daughter said unto
her, Take this child away, and nurse it for me, and I will give
thee thy wages.

And the Hebrew woman took her own child and nursed it. And when he was too grown for her to nurse she brought him unto Pharaoh's daughter. And she kept him to be as her own son. And Pharaoh's daughter called his name Moses, because, she said, I took him out of the water.

DAVID AND GOLIATH

Now the Philistines gathered together their armies to battle. And Saul and the men of Israel were gathered together and set the battle in array against the Philistines. And the Philistines stood on a mountain on the other side: and there was a valley between them.

And there went out a champion out of the camp of the Philistines, named Goliath, of Gath, whose height was six cubits and a span. And he had an helmet of brass upon his head, and he was armed with a coat of mail; and the weight of the coat was five thousand shekels of brass. And he had greaves of brass upon his legs, and a target of brass between his shoulders. And the staff of his spear was like a weaver's beam; and his spear's head weighed six hundred shekels of iron: and one bearing a shield went before him.

And he stood and cried unto the armies of Israel, and said unto them, Why are ye come out to set your battle in array? Am not I a Philistine, and ye servants to Saul? Choose you a man for you, and let him come down to me. If he be able to fight with me, and to kill me, then will we be your servants: but if I prevail against him, and kill him, then shall ye be our servants, and serve us. And the Philistine said, I defy the armies of Israel this day; give me a man, that we may fight together.

When Saul and all Israel heard those words of the Philistine, they were dismayed, and greatly afraid. And the three eldest sons of Jesse went and followed Saul to the battle: and the names of his three sons that went to the battle were Eliab the firstborn, and next unto him Abinadab, and the third Shammah.

And David was the youngest son of Jesse. And David went to and fro from Saul to feed his father's sheep at Bethlehem. And the Philistine drew nigh morning and evening, and challenged the Israelites forty days.

And Jesse said unto David his son, Take now for thy brethren an ephah of this parched corn, and these ten loaves, and run to the camp to thy brethren. And carry these ten cheeses unto the captain of their thousand, and look how thy brethren fare, and take their message.

And David rose up early in the morning, and left the sheep with a keeper, and took, and went as Jesse had commanded him. And he came to the trench, as the host was going forth to the fight, and shouted for the battle. For Israel and the Philistines had put the battle in array, army against army.

And David left his carriage in the hand of the keeper of the carriage, and ran into the army, and came and saluted his brethren. And as he talked with them behold, there came up the champion, the Philistine of Gath, Goliath by name, out of the armies of the Philistines, and spake according to the same words: and David heard them.

And all the men of Israel, when they saw the man, fled from him, and were sore afraid. And the men of Israel said, Have ye seen this man that is come up? Surely to defy Israel is he come up. And it shall be, that the man who killed him, the king will enrich him with great riches, and will give him his daughter, and make his father's house free in Israel.

And David spake to the men that stood by him, saying, What

shall be done to the man that killeth this Philistine, and taketh away the reproach from Israel? For who is this heathen Philistine, that he should defy the armies of the living God?

And the people answered him after this manner, saying, So shall it be done to the man that killeth him.

And Eliab his eldest brother heard when he spake unto the men; and Eliab's anger was kindled against David, and he said, Why camest thou down hither? And with whom hast thou left those few sheep in the wilderness? I know thy pride, and the haughtiness of thine heart. For thou art come down that thou mightest see the battle.

And David said, What have I now done? Is there not a cause?

And he turned from him toward another, and spake after the same manner; and the people answered him again after the former manner.

And when the words were heard which David spake, they rehearsed them before Saul: and he sent for him.

And David said to Saul, Let no man's heart fail because of him; thy servant will go and fight with this Philistine.

And Saul said unto David, Thou art not able to go against this Philistine to fight with him: for thou art but a youth, and he a man of war from his youth.

And David said unto Saul, Thy servant kept his father's sheep, and there came a lion, and a bear, and took a lamb out of the flock. And I went out after him, and smote him, and delivered it out of his mouth: and when he arose against me, I caught him by his beard, and smote him, and slew him. Thy servant slew both the lion and the bear: and this vile Philistine shall be as one of the beasts, since he hath defied the armies of the living God.

David said moreover: The Lord that delivered me out of the paw of the lion, and out of the paw of the bear, He will deliver me also out of the hand of this Philistine.

And Saul said unto David, Go, and the Lord be with thee.

And Saul armed David with his armour, and he put an helmet

of brass upon his head; also he armed him with a coat of mail. And David girded his sword upon his armour, and he tried to go; for he had not tested it.

And David said unto Saul, I cannot go with these; for I have not proved them. And David put them off him.

And he took his staff in his hand, and chose him five smooth stones out of the brook, and put them in a shepherd's bag which he had, a scrip; and his sling was in his hand. And he drew near to the Philistine.

And the Philistine came on and drew near unto David: and the man that bare the shield went before him. And when the Philistine looked about, and saw David, he disdained him: for he was but a youth, and ruddy, and of a fair countenance.

And the Philistine said to David, Am I a dog, that thou comest to me with staves?

And the Philistine cursed David by his gods. And the Philistine said to David, Come to me, and I will give thy flesh unto the fowls of the air, and to the beasts of the field.

Then said David to the Philistine, Thou comest to me with a sword, and with a spear, and with a shield: but I come to thee in the name of the Lord of hosts, the God of the armies of Israel, whom thou hast defied. This day will the Lord deliver thee into mine hand; and I will smite thee, and take thine head from thee. And I will give the bodies of the Philistines this day unto the fowls of the air, and to the wild beasts of the earth; that all the earth may know that there is a God in Israel.

And it came to pass, when the Philistine arose, and came and drew nigh to meet David, that David hasted, and ran toward the army to meet the Philistine.

And David put his hand in his scrip and took thence a stone, and slang it, and smote the Philistine in his forehead; and he fell upon his face to the earth.

So David prevailed over the Philistine with a sling and with a stone, and smote the Philistine, and slew him; but there was no sword in the hand of David.

Therefore David ran, and stood upon the Philistine, and took his sword, and drew it out of the sheath thereof, and slew him and cut off his head therewith.

And when the Philistines saw their champion was dead, they fled.

THE NATIVITY

Now in the sixth month the angel Gabriel was sent from God unto a city named Nazareth, in Galilee. He came to a virgin whose name was Mary. Mary was betrothed to Joseph, of the house of David.

And he came unto her, and said, Hail, Mary, thou that art highly favored; for the Lord is with thee.

Mary wondered greatly at the saying of the angel, knowing not what his greeting might mean.

And the angel said unto her, Fear not, Mary: for thou hast found favor with God. And behold, thou shalt bring forth a son, and he shall be great. Thou shalt call his name Jesus, and he shall be called the Son of the Most High. The Lord God will give unto him the throne of his father David: And he shall reign over the house of Jacob forever; and there shall be no end of his kingdom.

And Mary said unto the angel, How can this be? For she could not understand.

And the angel answered and said unto her, The Holy Spirit shall come upon thee; and the Son which thou wilt bear shall be called the Son of God.

And Mary said, Behold, I am the servant of the Lord; Let it be unto me according to thy word. And the angel departed from her.

Now it came to pass in those days, that the emperor Caesar Augustus sent out a decree, and ordered that all the people of the world should be recorded.

And all went, every one to his own city, for all had to have their names written in the rolls.

And Joseph also went up out of the city of Nazareth in Galilee. For he was of the house and family of David and had to go to Bethlehem, the city of David. So he went to enroll himself with Mary, who was betrothed to him, and was expecting her child.

And it came to pass, while they were there, the time had come that Mary should be delivered of her child. Now there was no room for them in the inn and the only place they could find was a stable.

And there Mary brought forth her first-born son; and she wrapped him in swaddling clothes, and laid him in a manger.

At that time there were shepherds in the same country near Bethlehem abiding in the field, and keeping watch by night over their flock.

And an angel of the Lord stood by them, and the glory of the Lord shone round about the shepherds and they were sore afraid.

And the angel said unto them, Be not afraid; for behold, I bring you good tidings. There shall be great joy to all the people: for there is born to you this day in the city of David a Saviour, who is Christ the Lord. And this is the sign to show unto you the truth of this saying: Ye shall find a babe wrapped in swaddling clothes, and lying in a manger.

And as the angel spoke, there suddenly appeared a host of heavenly angels praising God, and saying,

Glory to God in the highest, and on earth peace
Among men in whom the Lord is pleased.

And when the angels had gone away from them the shepherds said one to another, Let us now go even unto Bethlehem, and see this thing that is come to pass, which the Lord hath made known unto us.

And they came with haste, and found both Mary and Joseph in the cow shed, and the babe was lying in the manger.

And when they saw it, they told of all that the angels had spoken to them about this child.

And all the people that heard them wondered at the things which the shepherds were saying.

But Mary pondered all these sayings, and cherished them in her heart.

And the shepherds returned, glorifying and praising God for all the things that they had heard and seen, even as the angels had spoken unto them.

And when eight days were fulfilled, the babe was named Jesus.

JESUS IN THE TEMPLE

And Jesus' parents went every year to Jerusalem at the feast of the passover. And when Jesus was twelve years old, they took him with them to the feast.

And when they had fulfilled the days, and were returning, the boy Jesus tarried behind in Jerusalem; but his parents knew it not. They supposed him to be in the company of travelers. After a day's journey, they sought for him among their kinsfolk and acquaintance. And when they found him not, they returned to Jerusalem, seeking for him.

And it came to pass, after three days his parents found him in the temple, sitting in the midst of the teachers, both hearing them, and asking them questions.

And all that heard him were amazed at his understanding and his answers.

And when the parents saw him, they were astonished; and his mother said unto him, Son, why hast thou thus dealt with us? Behold, thy father and I sought thee sorrowing.

And he said unto them, How is it that ye sought me? Knew ye not that I must be in my Father's house?

But they understood not the saying which he spake unto them.

And Jesus went down with them, and came to Nazareth; and he abided dutifully with his parents.

And his mother kept all *these* sayings in her heart; albeit she understood them not.

And they who were with Jesus came unto Bethsaida.

And they brought to Jesus a blind man. And they said, We beseech thee to touch him.

And Jesus took hold of the blind man by the hand, and brought him out of the village; and then he spat on his eyes, and laid his hands upon him. And he asked him, Seest thou aught?

And the man looked up, and said, I see men; for I behold them as trees, walking.

Then again Jesus laid his hands upon his eyes; and he looked steadily and was restored; and then he saw all things clearly.

And Jesus sent him away to his home, saying, Do not even enter into the village.

And they came to Jericho: and as Jesus went out from Jericho,

with his disciples and a great multitude, the son of Timaeus, Bartimaeus, a blind beggar, was sitting by the wayside.

And when he heard that it was Jesus the Nazarene, he began to cry out and say, Jesus, thou son of David, have mercy on me.

And many rebuked him that he should be quiet and hold his peace. But he cried out the more a great deal, Thou son of David, have mercy on me.

And Jesus heard and stood still. And he said, Call ye him unto me.

And they called the blind man, saying unto him, Be of good cheer: rise, he calleth thee.

And Bartimaeus casting away his garment, sprang up, and came to Jesus.

And Jesus answered him, and said, What wilt thou that I should do unto thee?

And the blind man said unto him, Rabbi, that I may receive my sight.

And Jesus said unto him, Go thy way; thy faith has healed thee and made thee whole.

And straightway the blind man received his sight, and followed Jesus on the road.

THE LOAVES AND FISHES

And Jesus came forth and saw a great multitude, and he had compassion for them, because they were as sheep not having a shepherd and not knowing their way. And he began to teach them many things.

And when it was late in the day his disciples came unto him, and said, This place is desert, and the day is now far spent; send these people away, that they may go into the towns and villages round about, and buy themselves somewhat to eat.

But Jesus answered and said unto them, Give ye them to eat.

And they say unto him, Shall we go and buy two hundred shillings' worth of bread, and give them to eat?

And he saith unto them, How many loaves have ye? go and see.

And when they looked, they said, Five loaves of bread and two fishes.

And he commanded them that all should sit down by companies upon the green grass.

And they sat down in ranks, by hundreds, and by fifties.

And he took the five loaves and the two fishes, and looking up to heaven, he blessed, and brake the loaves. Then he gave to the disciples the five loaves to set before all the people and the two fishes divided he among them all.

And they all ate, and were filled.

And they took up broken pieces, twelve basketfuls, and also of the fishes.

And they that ate the loaves were five thousand men.

And straightway he asked his disciples to enter into the boat, and to go before him unto the other side of Bethsaida, while he himself sendeth the multitude away. And after he had taken leave of them, he went up into the mountain to pray.

And when even was come, the boat was in the midst of the sea, and Jesus alone was on the land.

And looking to the sea, Jesus beheld his disciples distressed in rowing, for the wind was against them. And he cometh out to them, walking on the sea.

And he would have passed by them: But they, when they saw him walking on the sea, were troubled. For they supposed that it was a ghost, and they cried out.

But he straightway spake with them, and saith unto them, Be of good cheer: it is I; be not afraid.

And he went up unto them into the boat; and the wind ceased: and they were sore amazed in themselves; for they understood not concerning the loaves; neither understood they his walking on the sea. And when they had crossed over, they moored to the shore.

And when they came out of the boat, straightway the people knew that it was Jesus. And they ran round about that whole region, and began to carry about on their beds those that were sick to bring them where Jesus was.

And wheresoever he entered, into villages, or into cities, or into the country, they laid the sick in the marketplaces, and besought Jesus that they might touch if only the border of his garment. And all who so touched him were made whole.

THREE PARABLES OF JESUS

THE LOST SHEEP

Now all the publicans and sinners were drawing near unto Jesus to hear him.

And both the Pharisees and the scribes murmured, saying, This man receiveth sinners, and eateth with them.

And Jesus spake unto them this parable, saying, If any man of you, having a hundred sheep, and loseth one of them, doth he not leave the ninety and nine in the wilderness, and go after that which is lost, until he find it?

And when the shepherd hath found the lost sheep, he layeth it on his shoulders, rejoicing.

And when he cometh home, he calleth together his friends and his neighbors, saying unto them, Rejoice with me, for I have found my sheep which was lost.

I say unto you, that even so there shall be joy in heaven over one sinner that repenteth, more than over ninety and nine righteous persons, who need no repentance.

THE GOOD SAMARITAN

A certain lawyer stood up and said, Teacher, what shall I do to inherit eternal life? And Jesus said unto him, What is written in the law? how readest thou? And the lawyer answering said, Thou shalt love the Lord thy God with all thy heart, and with all thy soul, and with all thy strength, and with all thy mind; and thy neighbor as thyself. And the lawyer said unto Jesus, And who is my neighbor?

Jesus made answer and said, A certain man was going down from Jerusalem to Jericho; and he fell among robbers, who both stripped him and beat him, and departed, leaving him half dead.

And by chance a certain priest was going down that way: and when he saw him, he passed by on the other side. And in like manner a Levite also, when he came to the place, and saw him, passed by on the other side.

But a certain Samaritan, as he journeyed, came where he was: and when he saw him, he was moved with compassion, and came to him, and bound up his wounds, pouring on them oil and wine; and he set him on his own beast, and brought him to an inn, and took care of him.

And on the morrow he took out two pence, and gave them to the host, and said, Take care of him; and whatsoever thou spendest more, I, when I come back again, will repay thee.

Which now of these three, thinkest thou, proved neighbor

unto him that fell among the robbers? And the lawyer said, He that showed mercy on him.

And Jesus said unto him, Go, and do thou likewise.

THE PRODIGAL SON

A certain man had two sons: and the younger of them said to his father, Father, give me the portion of thy wealth that shall be my share. And the father divided unto his sons all that was to be theirs.

And not many days after, the younger son gathered all that was his and took his journey into a far country. And there he lived with wild companions and in riotous living.

And when he had spent all he had there arose a mighty famine in that country; and soon he was in want.

And he went to one of the citizens of that country for work to earn his wage. But all he was given to do was to feed the swine in the fields.

And he was so hungry, he would have eaten the husks that the swine did eat: and no man gave anything unto him.

But when he thought things over to himself, he said, So many hired servants of my father's have bread enough and to spare, while I perish here with hunger! I will arise and go to my father, and will say unto him, Father, I have sinned against heaven. I have done wrong in thy sight: I am no more worthy to be called thy son. Make me as one of thy hired servants.

And he arose, and went to return to his father. But while he was yet afar off, his father saw him. And in his love he was moved with compassion for his son. And he ran, and fell on his son's neck, and kissed him.

And the son said unto him, Father, I have sinned against heaven, and in thy sight: I am no more worthy to be called thy son.

But the father said to his servants, Bring forth quickly the best robe, and put it on him; and put a ring on his hand, and shoes on his feet; and bring the fatted calf, and kill it, and let us eat, and make merry, for this is my son who was dead, and now is alive again. He was lost, and now he is found.

And they began to be merry.

Now the elder son was in the field: and as he came and drew nigh to the house, he heard music and dancing.

And he called to him one of the servants, and inquired what these rejoicings might be.

And he said unto him, Thy brother is come; and thy father hath killed the fatted calf, because he hath received him safe and sound.

But the elder son was angry, and would not go in: and his father came out, and entreated him.

But he answered and said to his father, Lo, these many years do I serve thee, and I never disobeyed a commandment of thine; and yet thou never gavest me a kid, that I might make merry with my friends: but when this other son came, who hath devoured thy substance and wasted all in foolish living, and with wild companions, thou killedst for him the fatted calf.

And the father said unto him, Son, thou art ever with me, and all that is mine is thine. But it was right for us to make merry and be glad: for this thy brother was dead, and he is alive again; he was lost to us, and now is found.

Tales of Laughter

We like to read some stories because they are like the things that happen to us every day. We like to read some stories because they tell us how people live in faraway lands or how they used to live a long time ago. Reading others is like pretending that anything—that anything in the wide world—might really happen.

But there are some stories we like to read just because they make us laugh. Some of these stories and poems are full of funny ideas and funny rhymes and some of them are just nonsense. But all of them will make you laugh.

POOH GOES VISITING
AND GETS INTO A TIGHT PLACE

by A. A. Milne

Edward Bear, known to his friends as Winnie-the-Pooh, or Pooh for short, was walking through the forest one day, humming proudly to himself. He had made up a little hum that very morning, as he was doing his Stoutness Exercises in front of the glass: *Tra-la-la, tra-la-la,* as he stretched up as high as he could go, and then *Tra-la-la, tra-la—oh, help!—la,* as he tried to reach his toes. After breakfast he had said it over and over to himself until he had learnt it off by heart, and now he was humming it right through, properly. It went like this:

Tra-la-la, tra-la-la,
Tra-la-la, tra-la-la,
Rum-tum-tiddle-um-tum.
Tiddle-iddle, tiddle-iddle,
Tiddle-iddle, tiddle-iddle,
Rum-tum-tum-tiddle-um.

Well, he was humming this hum to himself, and walking along gaily, wondering what everybody else was doing, and what it felt like, being somebody else, when suddenly he came to a sandy bank, and in the bank was a large hole.

"Aha!" said Pooh. (*Rum-tum-tiddle-um-tum.*) "If I know anything about anything, that hole means Rabbit," he said, "and Rabbit means Company," he said, "and Company means Food and Listening-to-Me-Humming and such like. *Rum-tum-tum-tiddle-um.*"

So he bent down, put his head into the hole, and called out, "Is anybody at home?"

There was a sudden scuffling noise from inside the hole, and then silence.

"What I said was, 'Is anybody at home?'" called out Pooh very loudly.

"No!" said a voice; and then added, "You needn't shout so loud. I heard you quite well the first time."

"Bother!" said Pooh. "Isn't there anybody here at all?"

"Nobody."

Winnie-the-Pooh took his head out of the hole, and thought for a little, and he thought to himself, "There must be somebody there, because somebody must have *said* 'Nobody.'" So he put his head back in the hole, and said:

"Hallo, Rabbit, isn't that you?"

"No," said Rabbit, in a different sort of voice this time.

"But isn't that Rabbit's voice?"

"I don't *think* so," said Rabbit. "It isn't *meant* to be."

"Oh!" said Pooh.

He took his head out of the hole, and had another think, and then he put it back, and said, "Well, could you very kindly tell me where Rabbit is?"

"He has gone to see his friend Pooh Bear, who is a great friend of his."

"But this *is* Me!" said Bear; very much surprised.

"What sort of Me?"

"Pooh Bear."

"Are you sure?" said Rabbit, still more surprised.

"Quite, quite sure," said Pooh.

"Oh, well, then, come in."

So Pooh pushed and pushed and pushed his way through the hole, and at last he got in.

"You were quite right," said Rabbit, looking at him all over. "It *is* you. Glad to see you."

"Who did you think it was?"

"Well, I wasn't sure. You know how it is in the Forest. One

can't have anybody coming into one's house. One has to be careful. What about a mouthful of something?"

Pooh always liked a little something at eleven o'clock in the morning, and he was very glad to see Rabbit getting out the plates and mugs; and when Rabbit said, "Honey or condensed milk with your bread?" he was so excited that he said, "Both," and then, so as not to seem greedy, he added, "But don't bother about the bread, please." And for a long time after that he said nothing . . . until at last, humming to himself in a rather sticky voice, he got up, shook Rabbit lovingly by the paw, and said that he must be going on.

"Must you?" said Rabbit politely.

"Well," said Pooh, "I could stay a little longer if it—if you——" and he tried very hard to look in the direction of the larder.

"As a matter of fact," said Rabbit, "I was going out myself directly."

"Oh, well, then, I'll be going on. Good-by."

"Well, good-by, if you're sure you won't have any more."

"*Is* there any more?" asked Pooh quickly.

Rabbit took the covers off the dishes, and said, "No, there wasn't."

"I thought not," said Pooh, nodding to himself. "Well, good-by. I must be going on."

So he started to climb out of the hole. He pulled with his front paws, and pushed with his back paws, and in a little while his nose was out in the open again . . . and then his ears . . . and then his front paws . . . and then his shoulders . . . and then——

"Oh, help!" said Pooh. "I'd better go back."

"Oh, bother!" said Pooh. "I shall have to go on."

"I can't do either!" said Pooh. "Oh, help *and* bother!"

Now by this time Rabbit wanted to go for a walk too, and finding the front door full, he went out by the back door, and came round to Pooh, and looked at him.

"Hallo, are you stuck?" he asked.

"N-no," said Pooh carelessly. "Just resting and thinking and humming to myself."

"Here, give us a paw."

Pooh Bear stretched out a paw, and Rabbit pulled and pulled and pulled. . . .

"Ow!" cried Pooh. "You're hurting!"

"The fact is," said Rabbit, "you're stuck."

"It all comes," said Pooh crossly, "of not having front doors big enough."

"It all comes," said Rabbit sternly, "of eating too much. I thought at the time," said Rabbit, "only I don't like to say anything," said Rabbit, "that one of us was eating too much," said Rabbit, "and I knew it wasn't *me*," he said. "Well, well, I shall go and fetch Christopher Robin."

Christopher Robin lived at the other end of the Forest, and when he came back with Rabbit, and saw the front half of Pooh, he said, "Silly old Bear," in such a loving voice that everybody felt quite hopeful again.

"I was just beginning to think," said Bear, sniffing slightly, "that Rabbit might never be able to use his front door again. And I should *hate* that," he said.

"So should I," said Rabbit.

"Use his front door again?" said Christopher Robin. "Of course he'll use his front door again."

"Good," said Rabbit.

"If we can't pull you out, Pooh, we might push you back."

Rabbit scratched his whiskers thoughtfully, and pointed out that, when once Pooh was pushed back, he was back, and of course nobody was more glad to see Pooh than *he* was, still there it was, some lived in trees and some lived underground, and——

"You mean I'd *never* get out?" said Pooh.

"I mean," said Rabbit, "that having got so far, it seems a pity to waste it."

Christopher Robin nodded. "Then there's only one thing to be done," he said.

"We shall have to wait for you to get thin again."

"How long does getting thin take?" asked Pooh anxiously.

"About a week, I should think."

"But I can't stay here for a *week!*"

"You can *stay* here all right, silly old Bear. It's getting you out which is so difficult."

"We'll read to you," said Rabbit cheerfully. "And I hope it won't snow," he added. "And I say, old fellow, you're taking up a good deal of room in my house—*do* you mind if I use your back legs as a towel-horse? Because, I mean, there they are—doing nothing—and it would be very convenient just to hang the towels on them."

"A week!" said Pooh gloomily. "*What about meals?*"

"I'm afraid no meals," said Christopher Robin, "because of getting thin quicker. But we *will* read to you."

Bear began to sigh, and then found he couldn't because he was so tightly stuck; and a tear rolled down his eye, as he said, "Then would you read a Sustaining Book, such as would help and comfort a Wedged Bear in Great Tightness?"

So for a week Christopher Robin read that sort of book at the North end of Pooh, and Rabbit hung his washing on the South end . . . and in between Bear felt himself getting slenderer and slenderer. And at the end of the week Christopher Robin said, "*Now!*"

So he took hold of Pooh's front paws and Rabbit took hold of Christopher Robin, and all Rabbit's friends and relations took hold of Rabbit, and they all pulled together. . . .

And for a long time Pooh only said "*Ow!*" . . . And "*Oh!*" . . .

And then, all of a sudden, he said "*Pop!*" just as if a cork were coming out of a bottle.

And Christopher Robin and Rabbit and all Rabbit's friends and relations went head-over-heels backwards . . . and on the top of them came Winnie-the-Pooh—free!

So, with a nod of thanks to his friends, he went on with his walk through the forest, humming proudly to himself. But Christopher Robin looked after him lovingly and said to himself, "Silly old Bear!"

THE ELEPHANT'S CHILD

by Rudyard Kipling

In the High and Far-Off Times the Elephant, O Best Beloved, had no trunk. He had only a blackish, bulgy nose, as big as a boot, that he could wriggle about from side to side; but he couldn't pick up things with it. But there was one Elephant—a new Elephant— an Elephant's Child—who was full of 'satiable curtiosity, and that means he asked ever so many questions. And he lived in Africa, and he filled all Africa with his 'satiable curtiosities. He asked his tall aunt, the Ostrich, why her tail-feathers grew just so, and his tall aunt the Ostrich spanked him with her hard, hard claw. He asked his tall uncle, the Giraffe, what made his skin spotty, and his tall uncle, the Giraffe, spanked him with his hard, hard hoof. And still he was full of 'satiable curtiosity! He asked his broad aunt, the Hippopotamus, why her eyes were red, and his broad aunt, the Hippopotamus, spanked him with her broad, broad hoof; and he asked his hairy uncle, the Baboon, why melons tasted just so, and his hairy uncle, the Baboon, spanked him with his hairy, hairy paw. And *still* he was full of 'satiable curtiosity! He asked questions about everything that he saw, or heard, or felt, or smelt, or touched, and all his uncles and his aunts spanked him. And still he was full of 'satiable curtiosity!

One fine morning in the middle of the Precession of the Equinoxes this 'satiable Elephant's Child asked a new fine question that he had never asked before. He asked, 'What does the Crocodile have for dinner?' Then everybody said, 'H U S H !' in a loud and dretful tone, and they spanked him immediately and directly, without stopping, for a long time.

By and by, when that was finished, he came upon Kolokolo Bird sitting in the middle of a wait-a-bit thorn-bush, and he said, 'My father has spanked me, and my mother has spanked me; all my aunts and uncles have spanked me for my 'satiable curtiosity; and *still* I want to know what the Crocodile has for dinner!'

Then Kolokolo Bird said, with a mournful cry, 'Go to the banks of the great grey-green, greasy Limpopo River, all set about with fever-trees, and find out.'

That very next morning, when there was nothing left of the Equinoxes, because the Precession had preceded according to precedent, this 'satiable Elephant's Child took a hundred pounds of bananas (the little short red kind), and a hundred pounds of sugar-cane (the long purple kind), and seventeen melons (the greeny-crackly kind), and said to all his dear families, 'Good-bye. I am going to the great grey-green, greasy Limpopo River, all set about with fever-trees, to find out what the Crocodile has for dinner.' And they all spanked him once more for luck, though he asked them most politely to stop.

Then he went away, a little warm, but not at all astonished, eating melons, and throwing the rind about, because he could not pick it up.

He went from Graham's Town to Kimberley, and from Kimberley to Khama's Country, and from Khama's Country he went east by north, eating melons all the time, till at last he came to the banks of the great grey-green, greasy Limpopo River, all set about with fever-trees, precisely as Kolokolo Bird had said.

Now you must know and understand, O Best Beloved, that till that very week, and day, and hour, and minute, this 'satiable Elephant's Child had never seen a Crocodile, and did not know what one was like. It was all his 'satiable curtiosity.

The first thing that he found was a Bi-Coloured-Python-Rock-Snake curled round a rock.

' 'Scuse me,' said the Elephant's Child most politely, 'but have you seen such a thing as a Crocodile in these promiscuous parts?'

'Have I seen a Crocodile?' said the Bi-Coloured-Python-Rock-Snake, in a voice of dretful scorn. 'What will you ask me next?'

' 'Scuse me,' said the Elephant's Child, 'but could you kindly tell me what he has for dinner?'

Then the Bi-Coloured-Python-Rock-Snake uncoiled himself

very quickly from the rock, and spanked the Elephant's Child with his scalesome, flailsome tail.

'That is odd,' said the Elephant's Child, 'because my father and my mother, and my uncle and my aunt, not to mention my other aunt, the Hippopotamus, and my other uncle, the Baboon, have all spanked me for my 'satiable curtiosity—and I suppose this is the same thing.'

So he said good-bye very politely to the Bi-Coloured-Python-Rock-Snake, and helped to coil him up on the rock again, and went on, a little warm, but not at all astonished, eating melons, and throwing the rind about, because he could not pick it up, till he trod on what he thought was a log of wood at the very edge of the great grey-green, greasy Limpopo River, all set about with fever-trees.

But it was really the Crocodile, O Best Beloved, and the Crocodile winked one eye—like this!

' 'Scuse me,' said the Elephant's Child most politely, 'but do you happen to have seen a Crocodile in these promiscuous parts?'

Then the Crocodile winked the other eye, and lifted half his tail out of the mud; and the Elephant's Child stepped back most politely, because he did not wish to be spanked again.

'Come hither, Little One,' said the Crocodile. 'Why do you ask such things?'

' 'Scuse me,' said the Elephant's Child most politely, 'but my father has spanked me, my mother has spanked me, not to mention my tall aunt, the Ostrich, and my tall uncle, the Giraffe, who can kick ever so hard, as well as my broad aunt, the Hippopotamus, and my hairy uncle, the Baboon, and including the Bi-Coloured-Python-Rock-Snake, with the scalesome, flailsome tail, just up the bank, who spanks harder than any of them; and so, if it's quite all the same to you, I don't want to be spanked any more.'

'Come hither, Little One,' said the Crocodile, 'for I am the Crocodile,' and he wept crocodile-tears to show it was quite true.

Then the Elephant's Child grew all breathless, and panted, and kneeled down on the bank and said, 'You are the very person

I have been looking for all these long days. Will you please tell me what you have for dinner?'

'Come hither, Little One,' said the Crocodile, 'and I'll whisper.'

Then the Elephant's Child put his head down close to the Crocodile's musky, tusky mouth, and the Crocodile caught him by his little nose, which up to that very week, day, hour, and minute, had been no bigger than a boot, though much more useful.

'I think,' said the Crocodile—and he said it between his teeth, like this—'I think to-day I will begin with Elephant's Child!'

At this, O Best Beloved, the Elephant's Child was much annoyed, and he said, speaking through his nose, like this, 'Led go! You are hurtig be!'

Then the Bi-Coloured-Python-Rock-Snake scuffled down from the bank and said, 'My young friend, if you do not now, immediately and instantly, pull as hard as ever you can, it is my opinion that your acquaintance in the large-pattern leather ulster' (and by this he meant the Crocodile) 'will jerk you into yonder limpid stream before you can say Jack Robinson.'

This is the way Bi-Coloured-Python-Rock-Snakes always talk.

Then the Elephant's Child sat back on his little haunches, and pulled, and pulled, and pulled, and his nose began to stretch. And the Crocodile floundered into the water, making it all creamy with great sweeps of his tail, and *he* pulled, and pulled, and pulled.

And the Elephant's Child's nose kept on stretching; and the Elephant's Child spread all his little four legs and pulled, and pulled, and pulled, and his nose kept on stretching; and the Crocodile threshed his tail like an oar, and *he* pulled, and pulled, and pulled, and at each pull the Elephant's Child's nose grew longer and longer—and it hurt him hijjus!

Then the Elephant's Child felt his legs slipping, and he said through his nose, which was now nearly five feet long, 'This is too butch for be!'

Then the Bi-Coloured-Python-Rock-Snake came down from

the bank, and knotted himself in a double-clove-hitch round the Elephant's Child's hind legs, and said, 'Rash and inexperienced traveller, we will now seriously devote ourselves to a little high tension, because if we do not, it is my impression that yonder self-propelling man-of-war with the armour-plated upper deck' (and by this, O Best Beloved, he meant the Crocodile), 'will permanently vitiate your future career.'

That is the way all Bi-Coloured-Python-Rock-Snakes always talk.

So he pulled, and the Elephant's Child pulled, and the Crocodile pulled; but the Elephant's Child and the Bi-Coloured-Python-Rock-Snake pulled hardest; and at last the Crocodile let go of the Elephant's Child's nose with a plop that you could hear all up and down the Limpopo.

Then the Elephant's Child sat down most hard and sudden; but first he was careful to say 'Thank you' to the Bi-Coloured-Python-Rock-Snake; and next he was kind to his poor pulled nose, and wrapped it all up in cool banana leaves, and hung it in the great grey-green, greasy Limpopo to cool.

'What are you doing that for?' said the Bi-Coloured-Python-Rock-Snake.

' 'Scuse me,' said the Elephant's Child, 'but my nose is badly out of shape, and I am waiting for it to shrink.'

'Then you will have to wait a long time,' said the Bi-Coloured-Python-Rock-Snake. 'Some people do not know what is good for them.'

The Elephant's Child sat there for three days waiting for his nose to shrink. But it never grew any shorter, and, besides, it made him squint. For, O Best Beloved, you will see and understand that the Crocodile had pulled it out into a really truly trunk same as all Elephants have to-day.

At the end of the third day a fly came and stung him on the shoulder, and before he knew what he was doing he lifted up his trunk and hit that fly dead with the end of it.

' 'Vantage number one!' said the Bi-Coloured-Python-Rock-

Snake. 'You couldn't have done that with a mere-smear nose. Try and eat a little now.'

Before he thought what he was doing the Elephant's Child put out his trunk and plucked a large bundle of grass, dusted it clean against his fore-legs, and stuffed it into his own mouth.

''Vantage number two!' said the Bi-Coloured-Python-Rock-Snake. 'You couldn't have done that with a mere-smear nose. Don't you think the sun is very hot here?'

'It is,' said the Elephant's Child, and before he thought what he was doing he schlooped up a schloop of mud from the banks of the great grey-green, greasy Limpopo, and slapped it on his head, where it made a cool schloopy-sloshy mud-cap all trickly behind his ears.

''Vantage number three!' said the Bi-Coloured-Python-Rock-Snake. 'You couldn't have done that with a mere-smear nose. Now how do you feel about being spanked again?'

''Scuse me,' said the Elephant's Child, 'but I should not like it at all.'

'How would you like to spank somebody?' said the Bi-Coloured-Python-Rock-Snake.

'I should like it very much indeed,' said the Elephant's Child.

'Well,' said the Bi-Coloured-Python-Snake, 'you will find that new nose of yours very useful to spank people with.'

'Thank you,' said the Elephant's Child, 'I'll remember that; and now I think I'll go home to all my dear families and try.'

So the Elephant's Child went home across Africa frisking and whisking his trunk. When he wanted fruit to eat he pulled fruit down from a tree, instead of waiting for it to fall as he used to do. When he wanted grass he plucked grass up from the ground, instead of going on his knees as he used to do. When the flies bit him he broke off the branch of a tree and used it as a fly-whisk; and he made himself a new, cool, slushy-squshy mud-cap whenever the sun was hot. When he felt lonely walking through Africa he sang to himself down his trunk, and the noise was louder than several brass bands. He went especially out of his way to find a broad Hippopotamus (she was no relation of his), and he spanked her very hard, to make sure that the Bi-Coloured-Python-Rock-Snake had spoken the truth about his new trunk. The rest of the time he picked up the melon rinds that he had dropped on his way to the Limpopo—for he was a Tidy Pachyderm.

One dark evening he came back to all his dear families, and he coiled up his trunk and said, 'How do you do?' They were very glad to see him, and immediately said, 'Come here and be spanked for your 'satiable curtiosity.'

'Pooh,' said the Elephant's Child. 'I don't think you peoples know anything about spanking; but *I* do, and I'll show you.'

Then he uncurled his trunk and knocked two of his dear brothers head over heels.

'O Bananas!' said they. 'Where did you learn that trick, and what have you done to your nose?'

'I got a new one from the Crocodile on the banks of the great grey-green, greasy Limpopo River,' said the Elephant's Child. 'I asked him what he had for dinner, and he gave me this to keep.'

'It looks very ugly,' said his hairy uncle, the Baboon.

'It does,' said the Elephant's Child. 'But it's very useful,' and he picked up his hoary uncle, the Baboon, by one hairy leg, and hove him into a hornet's nest.

Then that bad Elephant's Child spanked all his dear families for a long time, till they were very warm and greatly astonished. He pulled out his tall Ostrich aunt's tail-feathers; and he caught his tall uncle, the Giraffe, by the hind-leg, and dragged him through a thorn-bush; and he shouted at his broad aunt, the Hippopotamus, and blew bubbles into her ear when she was sleeping in the water after meals; but he never let any one touch Kolokolo Bird.

At last things grew so exciting that his dear families went off one by one in a hurry to the banks of the great grey-green, greasy Limpopo River, all set about with fever-trees, to borrow new noses from the Crocodile. When they came back nobody spanked anybody any more; and ever since that day, O Best Beloved, all the Elephants you will ever see, besides all those that you won't, have trunks precisely like the trunk of the 'satiable Elephant's Child.

ASK MR. BEAR

by Marjorie Flack

Once there was a boy named Danny. One day Danny's mother had a birthday.

Danny said to himself, "What shall I give my mother for her birthday?"

So Danny started out to see what he could find.

He walked along, and he met a Hen.

"Good morning, Mrs. Hen," said Danny. "Can you give me something for my mother's birthday?"

"Cluck, cluck," said the Hen. "I can give you a nice fresh egg for your mother's birthday."

"Thank you," said Danny, "but she has an egg."

"Let's see what we can find then," said the Hen.

So Danny and the Hen skipped along until they met a Goose.

"Good morning, Mrs. Goose," said Danny. "Can you give me something for my mother's birthday?"

"Honk, honk," said the Goose. "I can give you some nice feathers to make a fine pillow for your mother's birthday."

"Thank you," said Danny, "but she has a pillow."

"Let's see what we can find then," said the Goose.

So Danny and the Hen and the Goose all hopped along until they met a Goat.

"Good morning, Mrs. Goat," said Danny. "Can you give me something for my mother's birthday?"

"Maa, maa," said the Goat. "I can give you milk for making cheese."

"Thank you," said Danny, "but she has some cheese."

"Let's see what we can find then," said the Goat.

So Danny and the Hen and the Goose and the Goat all galloped along until they met a Sheep.

"Good morning, Mrs. Sheep," said Danny. "Can you give me something for my mother's birthday?"

"Baa, baa," said the Sheep. "I can give you some wool to make a warm blanket for your mother's birthday."

"Thank you," said Danny, "but she has a blanket."

"Let's see what we can find then," said the Sheep.

So Danny and the Hen and the Goose and the Goat and the Sheep all trotted along until they met a Cow.

"Good morning, Mrs. Cow," said Danny. "Can you give me something for my mother's birthday?"

"Moo, moo," said the Cow. "I can give you some milk and cream."

"Thank you," said Danny, "but she has some milk and cream."

"Then ask Mr. Bear," said the Cow. "He lives in the woods over the hill."

"All right," said Danny. "Let's go ask Mr. Bear."

"No," said the Hen.

"No," said the Goose.

"No," said the Goat.

"No," said the Sheep.

"No-no," said the Cow.

So Danny went alone to find Mr. Bear.

He ran and he ran until he came to a hill, and he walked and he walked until he came to the woods and there he met—Mr. Bear.

"Good morning, Mr. Bear," said Danny. "Can you give me something for my mother's birthday?"

"Hum, hum," said the Bear. "I have nothing to give you for your mother's birthday, but I can tell you something you can give her."

So Mr. Bear whispered a secret in Danny's ear.

"Oh," said Danny. "Thank you, Mr. Bear!"

Then he ran through the woods and he skipped down the hill and he came to his house.

"Guess what I have for your birthday!" Danny said to his mother.

So his mother tried to guess.

"Is it an egg?"

"No, it isn't an egg," said Danny.

"Is it a pillow?"

"No, it isn't a pillow," said Danny.

"Is it a cheese?"

"No, it isn't a cheese," said Danny.

"Is it a blanket?"

"No, it isn't a blanket," said Danny.

"Is it milk or cream?"

"No, it isn't milk or cream," said Danny.

His mother could not guess at all. So—Danny gave his mother
a Big Birthday
      Bear Hug.

THE MERRY-GO-ROUND
AND THE GRIGGSES

by Caroline D. Emerson

The merry-go-round whirled round and round and the music
played. The horses and the ponies and the zebras rose and fell on
their shiny poles as they dashed past. The Griggses watched the
merry-go-round and the merry-go-round watched the Griggses.
Every last Griggs was there and never had the merry-go-round
seen them look so happy and triumphant, and he had seen them
every day since he had come to town.

But *today was different from any other day.* There was joy
and excitement in the heart of every Griggs; in the heart of Mary
Griggs, aged eleven; in the heart of Tommy Griggs, aged nine;
likewise in Betty Griggs, aged seven, and in Billy Griggs, aged
five. The same feelings were equally alive in Jennie and Jimmie,
the twins, aged four. For today each Griggs held five cents
gripped in his right hand. *They were going to ride on the merry-
go-round!*

"I'm glad that they got the money together in time," thought
the merry-go-round. "It's my last day here. I suppose those bigger
two had to earn it for the whole crew. Five, ten, fifteen, twenty,
twenty-five, thirty," he counted as he whirled by, "they had to get

thirty cents just for one ride. That *is* a lot!"

The merry-go-round felt himself go slowly and more slowly. It was time for him to stop. The people who were riding the horses and the ponies climbed down and the boy jumped off the zebra.

"He seemed to think he could make me go faster by kicking me," complained the zebra. "I'm glad his money is all used up."

"You shouldn't mind things so much," said the merry-go-round comfortingly. "He hasn't hurt your paint any."

Then came the Griggses. They swarmed over the merry-go-round like a drove of monkeys. They tried every horse and they tried every seat before they were satisfied. Mary and Tommy lifted the twins into one of the coaches and told them to sit very still, which they did not do. They hung over the edge and shouted. Tommy mounted a gallant black charger and Mary chose a milk-white steed. Betty climbed onto the complaining zebra and Billy upon a brown pony. But Billy very soon fell off and they put him into the coach with the twins.

"All aboard!" whistled the merry-go-round. "Hang on tight. I'm starting!"

The merry-go-round man shut the gates so that no one else could enter. The music began to play. The engine started and away they went.

At first the Griggses sat very still. They hung on as tight as they could and did not say a word. Things felt a little strange and queer to the Griggses. The merry-go-round was disappointed.

"Aren't they going to like me?" A fear crept into the valves of the merry-go-round. "Have they waited a whole week and earned thirty whole cents and then aren't they going to like me? Oh dearie me!" sighed the merry-go-round.

But a few turns more and his doubts vanished. The Griggses were becoming accustomed to the new motion and they began to shout to each other. You could hear them even above the music. Round and round they spun. Up and down went the horses. The Griggses became more and more exhilarated.

"I can change horses," shouted Tommy. "Watch me!"

He swung over to the next mount. The others cheered.

"I can ride without holding on," screamed Betty.

"Not for long," said the zebra as she promptly fell off and had to be picked up and put back on again by the merry-go-round man.

The merry-go-round was quite satisfied. Carrying Griggses was a pleasure to him.

But the best of things must end. The merry-go-round had gone as far as he ever went for a five cent fare. The music stopped. The merry-go-round ran slowly and more slowly. The ride was over. The Griggses had no more five cents. They would have to get off!

They climbed down quietly, every last Griggs of them. Even the twins at four knew that "no more" meant no more with the Griggses. They did not even cry.

Then a strange thing happened.

"I have been doing just what that merry-go-round man has told me to do ever since I was a child," said the merry-go-round. "To-day for once I'm going to do what I want to do. I don't care if I have given them a five cent ride. I'm not going to stop! *I'm going to keep right on going!*"

So instead of stopping the merry-go-round went faster and faster until he was whirling around as before with the music playing and the flags flying.

"Stop!" shouted the merry-go-round man as he ran round and round after the merry-go-round; but no good did shouting do him.

"*Stop!*" shouted all the people who were waiting to get on, and they ran round and round the merry-go-round; but no good did shouting do them.

"*Keep on going!*" shouted all the Griggses and that is just what the merry-go-round did do.

The children climbed back to their places. The horses rose higher than they had ever risen before. The music played louder than ever. Never in the days of merry-go-rounds was there such a ride!

When the merry-go-round could run no longer for want of steam and the music could play no longer for want of breath, they both had to stop. Off tumbled the Griggses. They had had five times as much ride as they had expected. The merry-go-round man was very cross but there was nothing to do about that.

The Griggses jumped to the ground, but—they were so dizzy that they could scarcely stand. Indeed they did not stand long. The twins laughed and sat down heavily. Mary fell over them, while Betty and Billy hung on to the turnstile. The trees and the houses spun round and round. All that the children could do was to sit on the ground and laugh.

The merry-go-round man was worried. Whatever was he going to do with them? He picked them up carefully and put them on their feet and started them off towards home.

"Good-by," they shouted back to the merry-go-round, "and thank you!"

"Don't mention it," chuckled the merry-go-round as he started off with his new load of passengers.

He watched them out of sight. The twins sat down twice and had to be picked up and put on their feet again. And this is the way their tracks looked all the way down the street.

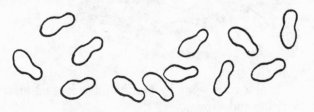

THE STORY OF FERDINAND

by Munro Leaf

Once upon a time in Spain there was a little bull and his name was Ferdinand.

All the other little bulls he lived with would run and jump and butt their heads together, but not Ferdinand.

He liked to sit just quietly and smell the flowers.

He had a favorite spot out in the pasture under a cork tree.

It was his favorite tree and he would sit in its shade all day and smell the flowers.

Sometimes his mother, who was a cow, would worry about him. She was afraid he would be lonesome all by himself.

"Why don't you run and play with the other little bulls and skip and butt your head?" she would say.

But Ferdinand would shake his head. "I like it better here where I can sit just quietly and smell the flowers."

His mother saw that he was not lonesome, and because she was an understanding mother, even though she was a cow, she let him just sit there and be happy.

As the years went by Ferdinand grew and grew until he was very big and strong.

All the other bulls who had grown up with him in the same pasture would fight each other all day. They would butt each other and stick each other with their horns. What they wanted most of all was to be picked to fight at the bull fights in Madrid.

But not Ferdinand—he still liked to sit just quietly under the cork tree and smell the flowers.

One day five men came in very funny hats to pick the biggest, fastest, roughest bull to fight in the bull fights in Madrid.

All the other bulls ran around snorting and butting, leaping and jumping so the men would think that they were very very strong and fierce and pick them.

Ferdinand knew that they wouldn't pick him and he didn't care. So he went out to his favorite cork tree to sit down.

He didn't look where he was sitting and instead of sitting on the nice cool grass in the shade he sat on a bumblebee.

Well, if you were a bumblebee and a bull sat on you what would you do? You would sting him. And that is just what this bee did to Ferdinand.

Wow! Did it hurt! Ferdinand jumped up with a snort. He ran around puffing and snorting, butting and pawing the ground as if he were crazy.

The five men saw him and they all shouted with joy. Here was the largest and fiercest bull of all. Just the one for the bull fights in Madrid!

So they took him away for the bull fight day in a cart.

What a day it was! Flags were flying, bands were playing . . . and all the lovely ladies had flowers in their hair.

They had a parade into the bull ring.

First came the Banderilleros with long sharp pins with ribbons on them to stick in the bull and make him mad.

Next came the Picadores who rode skinny horses and they had long spears to stick in the bull and make him madder.

Then came the Matador, the proudest of all—he thought he was very handsome, and bowed to the ladies. He had a red cape and a sword and was supposed to stick the bull last of all.

Then came the bull, and you know who that was, don't you? —F e r d i n a n d.

They called him Ferdinand the Fierce and all the Banderilleros were afraid of him and the Picadores were afraid of him and the Matador was scared stiff.

Ferdinand ran to the middle of the ring and everyone shouted and clapped because they thought he was going to fight fiercely and butt and snort and stick his horns around.

But not Ferdinand. When he got to the middle of the ring he saw the flowers in all the lovely ladies' hair and he just sat down quietly and smelled.

He wouldn't fight and be fierce no matter what they did. He just sat and smelled. And the Banderilleros were mad and the Picadores were madder and the Matador was so mad he cried because he couldn't show off with his cape and sword.

So they had to take Ferdinand home.

And for all I know he is sitting there still, under his favorite cork tree, smelling the flowers just quietly.

He is very happy.

THE MONKEY AND THE CROCODILE

by Ellen C. Babbitt

A monkey lived in a great tree on a river bank.

In the river there were many Crocodiles. A Crocodile watched the Monkeys for a long time, and one day she said to her son: "My son, get one of those Monkeys for me. I want the heart of a Monkey to eat."

"How am I to catch a Monkey?" asked the little Crocodile. "I do not travel on land, and the Monkey does not go in the water."

"Put your wits to work, and you'll find a way," said the mother.

And the little Crocodile thought and thought.

At last he said to himself: "I know what I'll do. I'll get the Monkey that lives in a big tree on the river bank. He wishes to go across the river to the island where the fruit is so ripe."

So the Crocodile swam to the tree where the Monkey lived. But he was a stupid Crocodile.

"Oh, Monkey," he called, "come with me over to the island where the fruit is so ripe."

"How can I go with you?" asked the Monkey. "I do not swim."

"No—but I do. I will take you over on my back," said the Crocodile.

The Monkey was greedy, and wanted the ripe fruit, so he jumped down on the Crocodile's back.

"Off we go!" said the Crocodile.

"This is a fine ride you are giving me!" said the Monkey.

"Do you think so? Well, how do you like this?" asked the Crocodile, diving.

"Oh, don't!" cried the Monkey, as he went under the water. He was afraid to let go, and did not know what to do under the water.

When the Crocodile came up, the Monkey sputtered and choked. "Why did you take me under water, Crocodile?" he asked.

"I am going to kill you by keeping you under water," answered the Crocodile. "My mother wants Monkey-heart to eat, and I'm going to take yours to her."

"I wish you had told me you wanted my heart," said the Monkey, "then I might have brought it with me."

"How queer!" said the stupid Crocodile. "Do you mean to say that you left your heart back there in the tree?"

"That is what I mean," said the Monkey. "If you want my heart, we must go back to the tree and get it. But we are so near the island where the ripe fruit is, please take me there first."

"No, Monkey," said the Crocodile, "I'll take you straight back to your tree. Never mind the ripe fruit. Get your heart and bring it to me at once. Then we'll see about going to the island."

"Very well," said the Monkey.

But no sooner had he jumped onto the bank of the river than —whisk! up he ran into the tree.

From the topmost branches he called down to the Crocodile in the water below:

"My heart is way up here! If you want it, come for it, come for it!"

THE PRINCESS
WHOM NOBODY COULD SILENCE

by Veronica Hutchinson

There was once upon a time a king, and he had a daughter who would always have the last word; she was so cross and contrary in her speech that no one could silence her. So the king therefore promised that whoever could outwit her should have the princess in marriage and half the kingdom besides. There were plenty of those who wanted to try, I can assure you; for it isn't every day that a princess and half a kingdom are to be had.

The gate to the palace hardly ever stood still. The suitors came in great flocks from east and west, both riding and walking. But there was no one who could silence the princess. At last the king announced that those who tried and did not succeed should be branded on both ears with a large iron; he would not have all this running about the palace for nothing.

Now there were three brothers who had heard about the princess, and as they were rather badly off at home, they thought they would try their luck and see if they could win the princess and half the kingdom. They were good friends and so they agreed to set out together.

When they had gone a bit on their way, Boots found a dead magpie.

"I have found something, I have found something!" cried he.

"What have you found?" asked the brothers.

"I have found a magpie," said he.

"Oh, throw it away; what can you do with that?" said the other two, who always believed they were the wisest.

"Oh, I've nothing else to carry; I can easily put it in my pocket," said Boots.

When they had gone on a bit farther, Boots found an old willow twig, which he picked up.

"I have found something! I have found something!" he cried.

"What have you found now?" cried the brothers.

"I have found a willow twig," said he.

"Oh, what are you going to do with that? Throw it away," said the two.

"Oh, I have nothing else to carry; I can easily put it in my pocket," said Boots.

When they had gone still farther he found a broken saucer, which he also picked up.

"Here, lads, I have found something! I have found something!" said he.

"Well, what have you found now?" asked the brothers.

"A broken saucer," said he.

"Pshaw! Is it worth while dragging that along with you too? Throw it away!" said the brothers.

"Oh, I've nothing else to carry; I can easily take it with me," said Boots.

When they had gone a little bit farther he found a crooked goat-horn and soon after he found the mate to it.

"I have found something! I have found something, lads!" said he.

"What have you found now?" said the others.

"Two goat-horns," said Boots.

In a little while he found a wedge.

"I say, lads, I have found something! I have found something!" he cried.

"You are everlastingly finding something! What have you found now?" asked the two eldest.

"I have found a wedge," he answered.

"Oh, throw it away! What are you going to do with it?" said they.

"Oh, I have nothing else to do; I can easily carry it with me," said Boots.

As he went across the king's fields, which had been freshly

plowed, he stooped down and took up an old boot sole.

"Hello, lads! I have found something! I have found something!" said he.

"Heaven grant you may find a little sense before you get to the palace!" said the two. "What is it you have found now?"

"An old boot sole," said he.

"Is that anything worth picking up? Throw it away! What are you going to do with it?" said the brothers.

"Oh, I have nothing else to do; I can easily carry it with me, and—who knows—it may help me to win the princess and half the kingdom," said Boots.

"Yes, you look a likely one, don't you?" said the two.

At length they went in to the princess, the eldest first.

"Good day!" said he.

"Good day to you!" answered she, with a shrug.

"It's terribly hot here," said he.

"It's hotter in the fire," said the princess. The branding iron was lying waiting in the fire.

When he saw this he was struck speechless; and so it was all over with him.

The second brother fared no better.

"Good day!" said he.

"Good day to you," said she with a wriggle.

"It's terribly hot here," said he.

"It's hotter in the fire," said she. With that he lost both speech and wits, and so the iron had to be brought out.

Then came Boots' turn.

"Good day!" said he.

"Good day to you!" said she, with a shrug and a wriggle.

"It's very nice and warm here!" said Boots.

"It's warmer in the fire," she answered. She was in no better humor, now that she saw the third suitor.

"Then there's a chance for me to roast my magpie on it," said he, bringing it out.

"I'm afraid it will sputter," said the princess.

"No fear of that! I'll tie this willow twig round it," said the lad.

"You can't tie it tightly enough," said she.

"Then I'll drive in a wedge," said Boots, and brought out the wedge.

"The fat will be running off it," said the princess.

"Then I'll hold this under it," said the lad, and showed her the broken saucer.

"You are very crooked in your speech," said the princess.

"No, I am not crooked," answered the lad; "but here is something that's crooked"; and he brought out one of the goat-horns.

"Well, I've never seen the like!" cried the princess.

"Well, here is the mate," said he.

"Have you come here to wear out my soul?" asked she.

"No, I have not come to wear out your soul, for I have one here which is already worn out," answered the lad, and brought out the boot sole.

The princess was so dumfounded at this that she was completely silenced.

"Now you are mine!" said Boots.

And so he got her and half the kingdom into the bargain.

RHYMING INK

by Margaret Baker

Once upon a time there was a good man called Simon Smug;
his wife was called Sarah and they kept a shop.

Every morning at eight o'clock precisely Simon unbolted the
shop-door and took down the shutters; then he stood behind the
counter and weighed out sugar and currants and wrapped up
parcels and made out bills and said, "What next can I get for
you, ma'am?" and "Dreadful weather for the time of year!" to all
the customers. And every evening as the clock struck seven,
Simon put up the shutters again and fastened the door. "Now
I'm going to enjoy myself!" he would say, rubbing his hands with
satisfaction.

Sometimes he enjoyed himself by sitting with his feet in the
fender reading the paper to Sarah; sometimes he enjoyed himself
pottering about the back-yard and painting the water-butt or
sowing Virginian Stock seed in the rockery; and sometimes he
enjoyed himself by just falling asleep in his chair.

And then one day he decided to become a poet.

"You'd be surprised at the thoughts that come into my head,
Sarah," said he; "I'm going to put them into poetry and become
famous."

He got a very large sheet of paper and a very large pen and a
very large bottle of ink and sat down at the kitchen table. Sarah
looked at him proudly. "Just fancy me a poet's wife!" she
thought, and held her head two inches higher than usual.

Simon began to write as fast as he could. "Just listen to this and
tell me if you ever heard so fine a beginning to a poem," cried he.

"Some poets praise the hairy lion;
I praise the hippopotamus . . ."

and look after the shop as you used to do. I've had more than enough poetry and that's the end of it!"

To tell the truth, Simon had had more than enough poetry, too, and was quite glad to be back behind the counter; but Sarah was wrong when she thought that emptying the bottle out of the window was the end of the matter. The Virginian Stocks began to behave in a most extraordinary way; instead of being miserable and straggling, they grew and budded and blossomed as though ink was their favorite fertilizer.

"What a charming back-yard you have," exclaimed all Simon's visitors, "your rockery is as pretty as a poem!"

Which just shows what rhyming ink can do—at least the kind at ten shillings a bottle.

SAMSON

by Peggy du Laney

Samson was a lion.
He was big.
He had a long mane.
He thought he was a very fine lion!

"Aaaaarrrooah!"
When Samson would go
"Aaaaarrrooah!" all the other
animals would stand still and say, "What a GREAT LION Samson is!"

Now, Samson was in a circus, and the circus was moving to a new town to give a show. Samson sat in his cage and thought, "Everyone will come to see me—for I can roar louder than any other lion in the world!"

And just to prove it, he did:

"Aaaaaarrrrrrrroooah!"

He sat there smiling, very much pleased.

"I have a mighty good voice today," said Samson to himself.

So he spent the night roaring louder and louder—and louder still, so that he would be the loudest roaring lion in the world.

It started to rain. First it drizzled, and then it poured, and then it rained puddles and ponds and lakes and rivers and oceans, almost.

The circus train puffed on through the night, and all the animals curled up in their beds and slept snug and warm out of the rain.

That is, all the animals except Samson. Samson stood in the rain that came into his cage and practiced:

"Aaaarrrrooooah!"

So pleased was Samson at the sound of his voice that he kept it up all night.

The next morning, the train reached the circus grounds. All the animals were put into their cages in a big tent so that the boys and girls and grown people could see them.

Samson waited very proudly in his cage. Soon the people came through the tent to see and hear the

LOUDEST ROARING LION IN THE WORLD

This was the moment Samson had been waiting for. Samson stood up. He looked around at the smiling faces.

He bowed.

And he took a deep, deep, deep breath!

Then he roared. But it wasn't a roar. It was only a strange, weak little sound that came out!

Samson tried again:

"aaa . . ."

But again that strange, weak little sound came out.

"Oh," thought Samson, "where is my wonderful roar?"

He tried again.

He took a deep, deep, DEEP BREATH!

. . . And out came a very queer little sound:

"arraa . . ."

How the little girls laughed!

Why, even the grownups laughed!

"Is this the LOUDEST ROARING LION IN THE WORLD?" they asked the lion tamer. "This lion just whispers. Ha, ha, ha! Hee, hee! Ho, Ho! Ha, Ha!"

How they all laughed!

The lion tamer looked angry.

Samson no longer thought himself very fine. He felt very, very foolish.

"Oh, why, why," he thought, "can't I make my wonderful roar?"

The circus men were very unhappy, too. They wondered what could be wrong with Samson. Was Samson hungry?

The lion tamer brought him a huge juicy steak. But Samson didn't eat it. He was too sad.

A nice lady gave Samson a raspberry lollipop. If there was anything Samson liked, it was raspberry lollipops. But he didn't even smile! He was very, very sad.

The ice-cream man gave Samson a plate of chocolate ice cream. Samson loved ice cream too. But he didn't even look at it. He sat there, unhappy.

Then a funny little man, with a brown bag, came into the cage. "I'm the doctor," he said, and he took out his watch.

He felt Samson's pulse. He felt down Samson's throat. He listened to Samson's heart.

Very importantly he said to Samson, "You have a cold."

"What?" whispered Samson.

"You have a cold," said the doctor a tiny bit louder.

"A what?" asked Samson.

"YOU HAVE A COLD IN YOUR HEAD!" shouted the doctor.

"Oh, my, so that's why I can't roar," said Samson. "Will you help me get my wonderful roar back? All these people want to hear me roar. I simply have to roar. I'm the LOUDEST ROARING LION IN THE WORLD!"

The doctor shook his head. He was thinking very hard. He took off his glasses and wiped them and put them back on his nose. And then he said:

"I can give you a pill."

Samson opened his mouth and took the pill. It was a bad-tasting pill. Samson made a funny face.

"Try now," said the doctor. Samson took a deep . . . deep breath. But alas, he could only whisper "arra——"

"I can give you another pill," said the doctor helpfully.

Samson took another pill—and made a funnier face. Then he took a deep . . . deep breath—and while Samson's mouth was open the doctor sprayed his throat with some medicine from a spray gun.

"aaaarr——" Samson whispered, and looked more and more unhappy.

"I can give you another pill," the doctor said to Samson.

Samson opened his mouth again. This time the doctor, instead of giving him just one pill—GAVE HIM THE WHOLE BOTTLE!

Samson jumped up.

He shook his tail.

He shook himself all over.

He spun around in a circle.

He took a deep breath—and made a funny face. Then he took a deep, deep, deep, DEEP BREATH—and

"Aaaaaarrrrooooooah!"

went Samson.

The tent poles shook! The bars on his cage shook! The cage itself jumped two feet off the ground! The doctor fell flat in the sawdust! The people all ran away.

The lion tamer laughed and laughed.

"Come one, come all!" he shouted.

"THE LOUDEST ROARING LION IN THE WORLD!"

OL' PAUL AND HIS CAMP

by Glen Rounds

For many years there have come drifting out of the timber country strange tales of a giant logger and inventor, Paul Bunyan by name. He is said to have been the inventor of logging. At night, around the pot-bellied bunkhouse stoves in the lumber camps, around campfires of road construction crews, and even in the hobo jungles, I have heard the stories of his great strength and wonderful inventions told and retold.

But most of these stories are based on hearsay alone, so of course can't be depended on to give the true facts. Such as the story that he kept his great beard in a buckskin bag made from the skins of seventy-seven deer, and took it out only on odd Sundays and legal holidays to comb it. The truth of the matter is that the bag was made of the skins of one hundred and sixteen elk, and he wore it only at night to keep catamounts and such from bedding down in his whiskers.

So I feel it is my duty to write down the *true* story of Paul Bunyan.

Some of these stories you may find a mite hard to believe, but you must remember that folks who do things that are easy to believe don't often have stories told about them, anyway.

Not much is known of Ol' Paul's childhood. He never spoke about it to me, and having been raised in a country where it was considered bad form, not to say downright unhealthy, to be too curious about a man's past, I never asked.

But from chance remarks he dropped from time to time and from old Indian legends, I think it is safe to suppose that he was born of French-Canadian parents somewhere near the headwaters of the St. Lawrence River. He seems to have been a mighty husky shaver from the first. There is a story that when but two weeks old he caught and strangled with his bare hands a full-grown grizzly bear. And one day, while playing by the river, he fell in. When fished out by the neighbors, there were found caught in his long beard, which he is said to have had from birth, some sixteen or seventeen beaver. This pleased his father more than somewhat, the pelts bringing him a mighty nice sum.

At the age of three months he had outgrown his parents' cabin, and the neighbors were complaining about the damage he was doing to fences and timber as he played among the little farms. So he packed his clothes in a warbag and, telling his folks good-by, went back in the hills to a great cave he knew of. Here he spent his time growing up and inventing hunting and fishing.

When next heard of, he was a man grown, had already invented logging, and somewhere had found Babe, the Mighty Blue Ox, who was his constant companion. As for the size of the Ox, it is said that one hundred and seventy-one ax handles, three small cans of tomatoes, and a plug of chewing tobacco laid end to end would exactly equal the distance between his eyes. So you can figure just how big he must have been.

At first Ol' Paul carried on his logging in a small way, felling the trees himself, and having Babe skid them to the river. But as time went on he invented newer and better ways of doing things, and his fame began to spread. Soon others took advantage of his having invented logging and went into the business themselves, thereby inventing competition. But as the stories of his almost unbelievable doings spread, men fell over themselves to work for him. To be able to say you'd once worked for Ol' Paul marked you as a real he-coon among loggers, and before long he had a picked crew, the like of which has never been seen since.

There was Ole, the Big Swede, probably the best blacksmith the woods have ever seen, who could shoe six horses at one time, holding them in his lap like puppies the while.

And Shot Gunderson, the woods boss, who could swing a double-bitted ax in each hand and fell four trees at a time. He was quite a hand to chew snuff, and I once saw him knock a wildcat out of the top of a bull pine with one squirt of tobacco juice.

Sourdough Sam, the camp cook, invented sourdough flapjacks, which became the favorite breakfast in Paul's camps, although they set a trifle heavy on any but the most rugged stomachs.

Hot Biscuit Slim, Sourdough's assistant, did all the rest of the cooking, not being a breakfast specialist. He was a mournful looking duck, who never spoke except on cloudy Thursdays.

And in later years there was Johnny Inkslinger, who did the bookkeeping, and figured so fast that it took a bucket brigade of thirty men to keep his inkwell filled.

When I first saw Ol' Paul's camp, it was so big that the Indians who came to pick over the leavings back of the cookshack often got lost and had to have search parties sent out for them.

Sam's cookshack itself was over two miles long. One whole side was taken up by the great griddle, on which he fried the sourdough flapjacks for which he was famous. It kept a whole bunkhouse full of cookees busy hauling wood for it. The batter was mixed in a big reservoir Paul had dug on a hill back of camp. The mixing was done with an old river steamboat, which was kept busy steaming back and forth across the lake of sourdough. When the breakfast whistle blew, the floodgates were opened and the batter poured through a flume to a sprinkler system that squirted the cakes on the griddle.

Flunkies with sides of bacon strapped to their boots skated over the smoking surface, greasing it and turning the flapjacks with scoop shovels. As fast as they were done they were stacked on wagons drawn by four horses, which galloped to the mess hall, up a ramp, and down the middle of the great table, while men with cant hooks rolled the cakes off onto the plates. Another four-horse outfit, hitched to a sprinkler wagon, followed close behind with the syrup. The tables were so long that by the time

a wagon reached the end it was nearly noon, so they loaded up
with salt and pepper and on the return trip filled the shakers for
supper, getting back to the cookshack at ten minutes to six.

Naturally, with a crew of that size using ordinary bunkhouses,
the camp would have spread out so that Paul would never have
been able to keep track of it. So he built the bunkhouses in inter-
locking sections, like beehives, and set them in stacks, one on
top of the other. After supper he would take the sections down
and let the men in, then pile them up again. In warm weather
he left them outside, but when it got cold he stacked them up in
his office.

These men, I'm right proud to say, were friends of mine, and
of all the oddments in my warbag, I think the thing I set most
store by is the letter of recommendation Ol' Paul gave me when
I left, informing whoever it concerned that I was probably the
biggest liar he'd ever had in camp.